Safar e Mehram

Jannath ki Raahguzar

Safiya Abdul

notionpress.com

INDIA • SINGAPORE • MALAYSIA

ISBN
Paperback 979-8-89588-772-1
Hardcase 979-8-89588-810-0

What is the purpose of a heart that yearns, if all desires end in emptiness……!!!

Contents

Note and Disclaimer

Before you begin reading this story, there are a few things I wish to share with you…

This is the tale of a person who became entangled in the web of the world, a stubborn, peculiar, self-centered individual who believed that he controlled his own life. It is his journey that compelled me to pick up the pen.

His path touched my heart so deeply that I couldn't hold myself back from bringing his story to the world—I never saw myself as a writer, nor did I ever imagine I would complete an entire book, but his story pushed me to write.

His determination and transformation inspired me to narrate his journey in words, and now I want this story to reach everyone.

It is the story of a person who believed that success was measured only by worldly achievements, unaware that the Creator of the universe holds the reins of his life.

A person who thought that sustenance came from his own hands and not from above, and who felt superior by looking down on others.

This is the story of a man who, in his obsessive pursuit of goals, found himself in a darkness so deep that there was no trace of light. He became trapped in an 'Endless Time Loop' from which he could not escape.

They say time is loyal to no one; you never know when or how it will change someone's life. And as for who controls the wheel of time, I don't need to tell you that—you already know, don't you?

When he returned, he was no longer the man I had been talking about until now.

This is the story of a person who found a light in that darkness, one that led him to his 'Journey of Enlightenment' and taught him to walk the path toward Paradise.

The characters, locations, and some scenes in this story are fictional and unreal.

If the name of any character or business resembles real names, consider it purely coincidental, as I do not intend to harm anyone.

My story will test your patience, and I hope that those who read it will stay with it until the end. Every test of patience brings a sweet reward, and as the author of this tale, I wish for the sweetest reward to be in the basket of my dear readers.

Thank you to all who considered my story worth reading. I won't bore you further with my words; you are free to move ahead and dive into the story…

Remember me in your prayers.

Assalamualaikum,

Safiya Abdul.

EPISODE -1

(I Will Not Spare Her...........!!!)

Some boys and I, all around the same age, were playing together in the playground when suddenly, a man stormed in angrily, muttering to himself. He grabbed one of the boys by the collar and started beating him mercilessly. The man had a simple appearance – a light beard, a mustache, and a cap on his head – but his rage was in stark contrast to his modest looks.

"Ufff,"

I let out a deep breath when I saw the man holding a long, thin belt in his hand, using it to hit the boy...

The man's anger showed no signs of subsiding, and mustering my courage, I tried to stop him from beating the child. "Why are you hitting him, uncle...? He might die...!!"

The man's eyes were bloodshot, as if burning lava was flowing within them, and taking a deep breath, he looked at me and said in a harsh tone,

"He's, my son; I can hit him, break him, do whatever I want. What's it to you...? Get out of here...!!!" *-There's no goodness left in this world... But I couldn't bear to watch the boy being beaten like that.*

"According to the Indian constitution, the juvenile justice [care and protection of children] Act, 2015. Under section 75 – Whoever, having the actual charge of, or control over a child, assaults, abandons, abuses, exposes or willfully neglects the child or causes or procures the child unnecessary mental or physical suffering, shall be punishable with imprisonment for a term which may extend to three years one with fine of one lakh rupees or with both. According to this law we have the right to be protected by the government."

I blurted out everything in a single breath, and suddenly, an eerie silence fell over the playground. Everyone's eyes were wide open in shock.

The man, breaking the silence, spoke,

"So, do you think children have the right to trouble their parents?"

He tightened his grip on the boy's shirt collar and took a step toward me.

I shook my head in denial and, in a soft tone, replied, "I didn't mean it that way, you're misunderstanding," but his response came as another harsh strike to the boy's head.

"Then ask him where he disappeared for three days without telling anyone! Why didn't he come home? Wandering around like a vagabond. We were so worried… His mother nearly lost her mind with fear."

Tears welled up in his eyes as he expressed his sorrow.

'Alright, better not get involved here… "So, why stop, uncle? Go ahead, keep hitting him, and throw in a few from my side too," I said with a slight smirk before walking away.

I'm not interested in such dramas.

I have a habit of stirring the pot. Instead of saving the boy, I left him in trouble and walked off.

A short while later, that same boy started following me. I took out my bicycle and began riding.

"Hey… what's your name?" he asked.

"Ilham," I replied, my eyes on the road as I picked up speed on my bicycle.

"My name's Fateen, Fateen Razzaq," he responded, matching my pace on his bicycle.

"Where do you live?" he asked another question, and I thought to myself, *'Why does he need to know where I live?'*

I glanced away from him, fixing my gaze ahead, and replied, "Just nearby."

"Come on, let's go to your place," he said, and I quickly realized that this clingy kid wanted to be friends.

I gave a faint smile and said, "I'm not going home right now," then sped up, leaving him behind. But he followed me, saying,

"Fine, wherever you're going, let's go there." He let out a deep breath.

"Why are you following me?" I raised an eyebrow.

"Because from today, you and I are officially friends."

We spent quite some time racing through every street and corner of the city, enjoying each other's company...!!

I usually prefer being alone, but this clingy guy turned out to be good company. Our friendship lasted a long time. He never stopped following me, and our bond began when we were just five years old.

* * *

"Fateen...???"

"Fateen...???"

Uncle Razzaq called out as he reached my house, looking for Fateen.

"Hey, get up! Your dad is here."

I said this to Fateen, who had been staying at our place since last night. I don't know why, but this kid seems to prefer other people's homes over his own. Now, he has taken to living at my house instead of other's.

"Man, my dad is something else," Fateen said, a hint of annoyance in his voice.

"Why don't you stay at your own house? Why are you here with me?" I finally asked the question I had been pondering, and immediately regretted it.

"I enjoy being with you, that's why," Fateen replied, chuckling in his playful manner.

"Get lost, you creep…" I nudged him, and we both burst into laughter as we peeked through the upper window to listen to our dads talking outside.

"Assalamualaikum, I heard Fateen is here. Could you please call him? I'm his father," Fateen's dad said gently to my father.

"Walaikumassalam. Yes, who are you…? And who is this, Fateen?" my dad asked, extending his hand for a handshake.

"I am Fateen's father, Razzaq Mustafa. I live in the alley behind here, and I've a to take him home after hearing from his friends that he's been staying here," Fateen's father said with a slight smile. It was fortunate that my dad didn't know the neighbors too well.

"Who are these friends of yours who are informing your father about everything?" I asked Fateen, who was scratching his head upon seeing his dad.

"I don't know, man…" Fateen replied with a hint of annoyance.

"I am Osman Ahmed Khaan… I'm Ilham's father. Nice to meet you," my dad continued the conversation with Uncle Razzaq.

"Who doesn't know you, Mr. Osman? And Ilham? Oh, so you're Ilham's father… Masha Allah! You are quite fortunate to have such a clever child," Uncle Razzaq remarked with a slight smile, or rather, his face was beaming.

"I'm sorry, I didn't quite understand…" my dad responded.

"Now, I am gone…" I said with a deep breath.

"Hey, you don't know? Your son, Masha Allah, is quite bright. He has a good understanding of the Indian Constitution and speaks English as if he were a native, not a desi…" Uncle Razzaq elaborated.

"They're giving best praise, but to the wrong person…" I thought to myself.

"I don't know what your dad finds so impressive about my brief compliment, but since then, he hasn't stopped praising me," I told Fateen.

"Because of you, he doesn't say anything to me either... I just mention your name and walks away," Fateen replied with a laugh.

"You're such a horrible man," I said to Fateen, who was smiling uncontrollably.

"Yeah, that's true." Fateen admitted.

"Okay, you should come inside. I'll call Fateen. It seems they both might be sleeping in their rooms... There's a boy in Ilham's room with him."

My dad glanced toward the window, and I stepped back, watching him as he looked at Uncle Razzaq.

"If he's with Ilham, then I have no problem. If he's in good company, he'll do well," Uncle Razzaq said. Fateen and I exchanged glances and laughed at Uncle Razzaq's words. He waved goodbye and walked away.

I already knew what was about to happen. As I made my way towards the hall, Fateen followed me down.

"Ah, come, come, O Prince," my father said to me, and don't for a second think he was calling me "Prince" out of affection—no, not at all.

"Yes, I'm here. What is it?" I replied in the same tone he usually spoke to me.

"Reshma...?" My father's habit of calling my mother into the conversation like this never sits well with me. Seriously, just talk to me yourself, why drag her in as if she's some sort of transmitter? Huh...

"Yes? What's going on?" my mother responded, looking at both of us, just as she always does.

"Do you have any idea what your 'Prince' has been up to all over the neighborhood?" my father started his melodrama.

How would my poor mother know? She's busy with household matters from morning till night and, the rest of the time, she's caught up in listening to my father's endless complaints. The neighborhood gossip? That's always delivered by my father in the royal court of our home. What would my mother know about it?

"What has he done this time?" My mother responded, exhausted, looking at me as if to ask. I motioned back to her—*I haven't done anything.*

"He's studying law now, and he's been going around lecturing everyone about it," my father complained, turning to my mother. Frustrated, my mother let out a deep sigh and looked over at me, while I stood there, doing absolutely nothing wrong.

"I'm not going around giving everyone a lecture. I was only saying what needed to be said in that moment," I replied, as my father stepped right in front of me.

Some parents see their child being sharp and proactive at this age and feel a surge of pride. But no, not my family. Instead, they try to oppress me—*seriously?*

"Yes, but why are you getting involved in all this? This is not your goal, Ilham, do you understand? Stop studying all this. You are *not* going to become a lawyer—absolutely not," my father said sternly. But why would I care? Like always, I listened with one ear and let it pass out the other.

"And you're not even at the age to be focusing on these things. Kids your age are out wandering around, acting like fools. You should be focusing on your studies or sports," he added, clearly hinting at Fateen, which made it impossible for me to hold back my laughter. Fateen was trying to avoid eye contact, looking around the room uncomfortably.

"Did you hear what I'm saying?" My father raised his voice, while my mother, as usual, looked weary from our constant back-and-forth.

"Oh, Baba, please, don't start in the morning. I'm already getting a headache," I responded dismissively, picking up the TV remote and turning it on.

"And now Baba's words are getting under his skin. Who knows what he'll end up doing as he grows older? Are you watching him?" my father asked my mother, continuing his melodramatic rant. Why does he make such a big deal out of everything? Ugh.

"She's been watching me ever since I was born, how much longer do you want her to keep watching me?" I joked.

"Mumma, you're not getting bored watching me, right?" I asked my mother in a playful tone. She just shook her head, telling me to be quiet.

"What did you say...?" My father was starting to get angry.

-It was definitely time to stop here, or else I'd end up spending the night outside again. Ever since Nano passed away, I've had to stay on the streets whenever things got out of hand.

"Nothing, just moving my lips," I replied, turning on the TV and starting to play some music.

"You've been moving your lips a lot these days! Stop reading these books, and focus on the goal I've set for you... That's all I want you to concentrate on. I won't hear anything else, Ilham!" My father said, leaving the room finally. Not that I ever took his words seriously, nor did I intend to.

As soon as he was gone, Fateen and I started dancing to the music, having fun as the loud music echoed through the hall. If anyone with a delicate or faint heart walked in, they might have just died from the shock. I had set up speakers all around the hall, just like in my room—blaring music in every corner.

We danced and sang along to every word of the song:

Kaisa junoon khwaabon ki anjuman mein tha

(What a passion was there in the gathering of dreams)

Fateen and I were shouting the lyrics in sync with the loud music, completely lost in the rhythm.

Kya mein kahoon kya mere baagpan mein tha

(What should I say, what was in my innocence?)

Ranish Ka Chala Tha -Fateen jumped in, completing the next lines as we vibed and danced along to the song: **Fhobwara**

Phoota jo khwaab ka goobbara

(When the balloon of dreams burst)

Abb phirta hoon mein

(Now I roam around)

London, Paris, New York, San Francisco

Dil mein mere hai, Dard-e-Disco

(In my heart is the pain of disco)

Dard-e-Disco…

Dard-e-Disco…

* * *

"Mumma—will it be a sister or a brother?" I asked my mother while feeding her fruits, as she stroked my hair with love.

"Who do you want?" she asked, smiling at me and then looking down at her large tummy.

I'm eleven years old, and after all these years, I'm finally getting a sibling. *I'm excited.*

"I don't care if it's a brother or sister—they're both the same to me," I replied.

"That's fine, Ilham, but you need to stop arguing so much with your father. If you're going to have a little brother or sister, they'll look up to you. Children learn from their elders," she said softly. I stopped feeding her and lay my head in her lap.

"Mumma—I don't argue. It's your husband who always starts it," I replied.

"Then you should stay quiet," she said, running her fingers through my hair.

"And why did you beat up that boy yesterday? Do you know how scared your father was when he saw you in court? If it weren't for his connections with the CM, you'd be in juvenile detention right now. You broke that boy's bones; he's not even able to walk," she said gently. I listened patiently, but that patience only lasts until my mom becomes *Mrs. Osman.*

"Mumma—he started the fight. I won't explain why I hit him, but you know how my anger works, right? I'll repay one punch with a thousand," I said, laughing.

"Why don't you behave like Sarem Uncle's daughter? She's exactly how your father likes—she prays, respects her elders, how patient she is, and is so well-mannered. She's such a lovely girl," my mom said.

"Mumma—please. If I say anything in anger, you'll end up crying. And don't ever bring her up in front of me again. I *hate* her. I've been humiliated so many times because of her. If Baba thinks of her as his daughter, he should go to her house and be her father there. Why does he need to put up her flags of praise here?" I snapped, irritated.

My mom just smiled at me, pulling me back into her lap.

"I hope one day you'll understand what I'm trying to say. Your father and I worry about you, Ilham. You're our only son, and our lives revolve around you. What will we do if something happens to you in one of these fights?" she said. I didn't deny it, but Baba's love for me? *That's doubtful—so, so doubtful.*

"And that girl—Sarem Uncle's daughter—I swear, one day I'll put her in her place. Just pray she never crosses my path.

I just hate her—

I don't even know what she's like, who she really is—I have no interest in meeting her. That's how much I despise her. And why shouldn't I, when my Mumma and Baba always praise her, always tell me I should be more like her?

Like, me, Ilham, become like her? What even is she…?

"Ilham, you scored really well, beta," Mumma said, kissing my forehead.

"Ilham and good grades—they go hand in hand, Mumma," I replied, feeling at peace for a moment.

"May Allah grant you even more success, and may you make a name for yourself in the future," Mumma prayed for me, like she always does. It feels like every prayer in this world is reserved just for me. Mumma never stops praying for me.

"Mumma, when I become a successful lawyer, we'll move to Canada. I'll show you the whole world. Let's leave Baba behind." I said to her, and she softly laughed.

"No, I won't go without my husband," Mumma refused.

"Why not? You two are always so lovey-dovey. Does that mean I don't matter to you?" I asked.

"You do matter, but if I had to choose between you and your father, I'd choose him. Wives belong with their husbands, and your Baba can't live without me, and I can't live without him. He's my *mehram* on this journey, and I can't just leave him and go with you. A husband's loyalty is tested from youth to old age—how devoted her husband has been to her. Since the moment your Baba and I got married, he has been completely faithful to me. And a wife's test comes when age starts catching up—how loyal she remains to her husband, how well she takes care of him, and how she stands by his side at every step," Mumma said gently. She had a point—she's never even gone to Nano's place for vacations because she can't spend even a day without Baba.

My dad is obsessed with his wife. And I stopped visiting Nano's place after her death. She was the only one who truly understood me, who always agreed with me in every matter.

But even after all that talk, my mind is stuck on one thing. Mumma's words keep echoing in my head—*She's so respectful, so graceful in her prayers, such a lovely girl, with so much patience and manners.*

"Who the hell are you?" I muttered under my breath. I'm so irritated by that girl.

"Alright, go pray. The call to prayer is sounding," Mumma said.

"One mother's love couldn't convince you to come with me—so what can the love of seventy mothers would do? And anyway, I don't need to pray, because I am not in any need." I said, exhaling deeply.

"Ilham, how many times have I told you not to say such things?" Mumma was upset now. She rarely ever gets upset with me.

"Damn it—" I got up and left, not to pray, but to retreat to my room and sleep in peace.

"Ilham—come here…!"

* * *

"Alright, Sarem, you're right about that…"

Baba was deep in conversation with his best friend. I was lying face down on the couch, eating an apple from the fruit basket.

After a while, he started talking to his precious little darling. Why is she always so clingy with my Mumma and Baba? Doesn't she have her own parents? Like—

"Lie properly! What kind of way is this?" Baba snapped in irritation. I then realized that he wasn't just on a call; it was a video call. But I didn't bother looking at the screen because—I—just—hate—her.

If it had been any other girl, I probably would've glanced at the screen a thousand times, but her? Look at her?

"No way," I muttered to myself, and as usual, Baba felt peaceful after finishing his chat with his beloved daughter.

Mumma came in from the kitchen with tea for Baba.

"Ilham, should I bring you some too?" she asked me gently. I shook my head to decline, and at that moment, my two-year-old sister started crying.

"Ilham, can you go check on your sister? I'm busy," Mumma said. I only listen to my Mumma up to a certain point, so I got up and went to Suzy.

I picked her up. "I'll hit you if you make another sound," I said to her. She looked at me with tear-filled eyes, then swatted my cheek with her tiny hands and started laughing.

"Don't touch me," I told her, but her face was glowing with happiness.

A small smile spread across my face. Suzy is adorable. Of course she is, after all, she's, my sister.

"Why do you always have to cry?" I asked her, and she smiled while gripping my finger with her little fist. I took her to the balcony and paced back and forth with her. After a little while, Suzy was peacefully asleep.

"Asleep?" I asked. She really had drifted into a deep sleep. I laid her down on her Montessori bed, but as usual, she refused to let go of my hand, which she had been holding tightly.

That Montessori bed was big enough for me to sleep in too, and since it was already quite late, I lay down next to Suzy, resting her on my chest, and fell asleep.

It was around 1 a.m. when I got a call from Fateen. I pressed the side button and put my phone on silent.

Ilham: Yeah, speak...

Fateen: Not speak—come outside. Let's go for a drive.

Ilham: No, I can't. I can't leave Suzy alone.

Fateen: You're with Suzy?

Ilham: Yeah.

Fateen: Alright, we'll go another time. I'm heading to your room now.

Ilham: Okay, hang up and let me sleep.

Fateen: But—

I ended the call and went back to sleep peacefully.

* * *

"Bhaa—iii—,"

Suzy, sitting in Mumma's lap, was calling out to me. Her little mouth could only say my name. I glanced at her and smiled.

"She didn't say Mumma or Baba, whose donkey's name did she just say?" Baba commented, sitting next to Mumma, trying to get Suzy to say "Baba," even if just once.

"If I respond to that, it's going to turn into an argument..." I said, continuing to lie down in the same position. Phuphi and Phupha had come over.

"Suzy looks so adorable, she's completely taken after Osman," Phuphi said.

"Correction, she's Ilham's sister, so she's like Ilham," I replied.

"I'm her father... and yours too," Baba said.

"Oh, really? Then why did you just call me donkey? You know what it means....???" I responded sarcastically.

"Shut up with your nonsense," Baba shot back. I gave him a mischievous smile and noticed Phuphi glaring at me, clearly annoyed that I hadn't bothered to greet her properly with a bow—whatever, that's how Phuphi always is…!

My phone rang; it was Fateen calling, and it was around midnight.

Ilham: Yeah, speak…

Fateen: Let's go grab some tea at Charminar, our special Irani chai.

Ilham: I don't drink tea.

Fateen: I'll be outside your house in five minutes, just come out.

Dealing with Fateen is better than being stuck here. I got up, went to my room, changed my clothes, and headed downstairs.

"Where are you going?" Phuphi asked.

"Off to be a professional wanderer… want to come? It'll be fun!" I replied.

"Can't you talk respectfully?"

"Ilham has never had, does not have, and will never have any acquaintance with manners, because you are not someone who could ever associate with such a concept." I said with a laugh, walking out of the house, where Baba was sitting in the lounge, fuming. He gives too much importance to his relatives.

I left with Fateen, and after some driving, we arrived at Charminar—yes, you might be wondering why I said "driving." Here, we don't drive based on age but on the passion in our hearts.

Fateen and I stood in front of the famous Charminar, its grand arches glowing softly in the night, bathed in warm golden light under the sky. The four towering minarets stood tall and proud, reflecting the rich cultural heritage of Hyderabad. The intricate designs, a blend of Islamic and Indo-Persian architecture, spoke of centuries-old stories, while the bustling bazaar around it was full of life and energy.

As Fateen sipped on his hot Irani tea, the fresh aroma filled the air, blending with the gentle breeze. The night scene of Charminar was mesmerizing, the moonlight reflecting off the pale stone of the monument, casting a serene glow. The vibrant hustle and bustle below contrasted with the timeless beauty of the historic landmark, giving me a rare moment of peace amidst the fast pace of city life.

The bright minarets seemed to rise into the sky like beams of light, while the vivid colors of nearby shops and stalls added a modern touch to the ancient scene. The calm of the night allowed me to soak in the grandeur of Charminar, as if it were whispering secrets of Hyderabad's royal past.

"Mom, no, I don't need anything. If you must, just get me some books…" A girl's voice reached my ears.

"No, your cousin's wedding is coming up. You should shop for it. Look, your dad won't take us shopping again and we won't find these things there, so it's better you buy now," her mother replied. They were sitting nearby, sipping tea, both of them veiled.

"Mom, exactly! It's my cousin's wedding, not mine, so why should I spend so much? When it's my turn to be a bride, then I'll shop for the most expensive red dress, and everyone will be stunned, by God…" she said with a soft laugh. A smile crept onto my face at her words.

Girls' dreams and desires seem to revolve more around their wedding outfits than the groom himself.

"Quiet, you silly girl… Finish your tea quickly before your dad comes. I don't know when you'll get rid of this tea addiction…" her mother remarked.

"The world might end, but my tea addiction will never go away," the girl replied, and they both got up to leave. I realized that her voice had compelled me to eavesdrop.

And then they disappeared into the busy marketplace.

"Is your tea finished yet?" I asked Fateen.

"Yeah, it's done," Fateen replied. He was chatting with me while sipping his tea, but today, I wasn't paying attention to his words. My mind was lost in the sound of that girl's voice.

* * *

"Did you see, Osman, how well my child scored again this time? He came first in the whole school!" Mumma praised me while speaking to Baba.

"Now let's see how their darling daughter competes with me," I thought, sitting on the sofa, using my phone.

"There's no use, Reshma… Do you remember how last week he beat up Farooq? Every time, his fights end up getting him into either jail or court. He will never be like Sarem's daughter. The issue has never been about his grades but…"

If parents don't know how to give compliments, they shouldn't say anything at all. It's why my hatred for that girl grows stronger every day.

I was about to leave when Baba stopped me.

"Wait, where are you going?"

"To the club… want to come? It'll be fun!" I replied carelessly.

"Ilham…" Mumma emphasized with a stern tone.

"Don't be disrespectful, Ilham," Baba said seriously.

"Let's go pray… it might give you wisdom, and you'll straighten up," Baba added.

"Take your darling daughter with you… I'm fine being the bad one," I replied and walked out of the lounge, heading to the lawn. I put on my headphones and started listening to music while walking.

My mind is constantly occupied with her existence. I've never felt so much hatred for anyone as I do for Sarem Uncle's daughter.

She's two years younger than me, but her status is somehow higher than mine?

"Shit, man...

Every time, this girl ruins my mood!

I will not spare her......!!!!!

* * *

EPISODE – 2

(Only Three Words & I was Calm....!!!!)

"Ilham...???"

A girl's voice echoed. I blinked. I was in a deep sleep, and even in my sleep, this girl's voice wouldn't let me rest.

I don't know who this girl is or where she's from, but her voice seems to have permanently settled behind my closed eyelids. If I want to hear her, I have to fall asleep.

It was around 5 AM when my dad knocked on my door. I pulled the blanket over myself and pretended to sleep.

"Ilham...? Get up and pray if you're awake...?" Baba knocked on the door and spoke softly.

"I'm not awake," I replied and turned over to sleep again.

"Ya Allah, guide him... Ameen," Baba said and finally left. He asks me this every day, and I give him the same reply, and he prays the same thing to God. It's on repeat. Why does one need to pray anyway...?

When Allah Himself is the Master, the Supreme Being of this universe, why would He need prayers from people like us?

"Whatever..."

I shook my head, took a deep breath, and fell back into a peaceful sleep.

I'm in 10th grade, taking my first step towards my destination. I was getting ready for school and made my way to the breakfast table.

With my headphones on, whistling and dancing, I reached the table.

As usual, my dad, my little sister Susaina, and Mumma were sitting there. I put down my bag, and before sitting for breakfast, I started messing with Susaina's hair.

I love her hair—they're silky, straight, and brown. Her eyes are just like mine—*brown*—and her beauty comes from Mumma.

"Ammi..." Susaina looked towards Mumma to complain, but Mumma gestured for both of us to stay quiet by putting her finger on her lips.

I don't usually eat breakfast because I'm not in the habit, and that habit is, thanks to my dear father.

I had just started eating when my dad began talking, so I turned up the volume in my headphones. But I could still understand what he was saying.

"Your school will end next month, so just remember, I'm sending you to your elder uncle in Canada, Ontario. You'll take a business management course there and then do an MBA. After that, you'll come back to India and run your own business...!! Got it...?!" My dad left no room for choice, but Ilham doesn't need options—his decision is enough. I didn't respond because I didn't think it was necessary. I just kept eating. This argument between us had become a daily thing.

"Are you even listening to what I'm saying...?" Baba said sternly, trying to remove my headphones.

"What's there to hear when I'm not going to do what you want? I've already decided what I'm going to do, so keep your suggestion to yourself...!" I replied and continued eating. Neither the food tasted good nor did this conversation. I mean, what's their problem with me becoming a lawyer?

"You, see? This... this is why I don't like him becoming a lawyer! Lawyers' earnings are often haram (forbidden)!" Baba lost his temper, as usual.

"Oh, for God's sake, Baba, don't start again! And as for halal or haram... whatever, I have my own principles, and I won't take on cases built on lies.

So, please don't bring this up in front of me again! I'm sick of your halal and haram debates! And lastly, I will go to Canada, but not to stay with Mamu… I'll get my own apartment, live alone, and be free!" Saying this, I left my breakfast unfinished, as usual, after yet another argument, and headed outside.

If anyone knows how to ruin your mood early in the morning, it's my Baba.

"Ilham…, at least have some breakfast, dear. Don't show your displeasure over food; come back after eating," Mumma said in a soft tone. She always finds herself stuck between me and Baba.

"Feed your husband; I'll eat somewhere outside… I won't starve to death," I replied sarcastically and left the house, heading toward school.

My dad believes that every lawyer earns haram (forbidden) income, just like my uncle—my younger uncle Anwar Ateeq do.

But I don't care about halal or haram; I just know that I won't get involved in any false case because proving the truth to be a lie is child's play, while proving the truth to be the truth is the real adventure.

And that's what I need in my life… I, Ilham, don't like easy paths; if there aren't any interesting things on the journey, life becomes boring. And Ilham is allergic to boredom…!!

* * *

"He's been drinking again today. Astaghfirullah—look at him, Reshma…, and go ahead, put him on a pedestal above your head, look at his eyes…, he looks like the devil…" Baba shouted, commenting on my appearance.

He was complimenting me, I suppose. I didn't look that bad, though—after all, I was wearing a branded black shirt and pants today, which had impressed quite a few girls.

"Get out of my way, I need to go to my room," I said to Baba, trying to go upstairs, but he grabbed me from behind and shoved me outside the house.

"You're not coming back inside tonight."

"Ya Allah, where will he go in this cold weather—look how freezing it is, Osman," my mother said worriedly, stroking Suzy, who was asleep in her shoulder.

"Let him wander, I don't care. And Reshma, you have no idea from where I had brought him back today—if I told you, you wouldn't believe it," Baba said, locking the door behind him. Where I gone? The red-light district, of course, what's a big deal...?? I gave a slight smile and started walking away, my feet carrying me through the empty streets.

As I walked, I ended up near a large house with an open field nearby. That's when I heard the sound of a cat. Looking around, I saw it near my feet, rubbing itself against my legs. I pushed it away gently with my foot and then took off my leather jacket, sitting down on a nearby rock.

The cat came back to me, rubbing its head against my legs.

"Don't have a home either, do you? Neither do I, tonight." I picked the cat up as I spoke. It was a golden-colored cat, trembling from the cold and meowing non-stop. She answered me with a soft "meow" when I spoke, and I sat her down in my lap.

"Did you eat anything?" I asked, running my hand over her head.

She let out another soft "meow."

It was clear from her condition that she hadn't eaten—she must've been starving.

"Well, don't expect much from me. I've only got cigarettes and drugs on me—nothing useful." I told her, and she gave a faint, soft meow, resting her head on my thigh, finally at peace.

“I could’ve taken you home, but tonight I’m homeless myself—Hitler over there threw me out of the house. He always does this. Sure, I drank, but I’m not so drunk that I’ve lost my senses—see, you’re just a little kitty. Your paw’s hurt, the wound is fresh, but your hunger pains are worse, gnawing at you from the inside. Three vehicles have already passed by—a Bullet, a Jupiter, and a Suzuki car. There are five dogs around here, waiting for a chance to attack you. But don’t worry—I won’t let that happen. And people say I’m not in my senses? If I weren’t, how could I notice all this so clearly?” I said, lying down on the rock. The cold was biting, but it didn’t feel as bad with the cat beside me.

The cat was still shivering from the cold, and the cat curled up against my neck, where I had left the top two buttons of my shirt open. I took off my leather jacket and covered her with it, lying back down on the stone.

“Are you a girl?” I asked, chuckling softly.

She answered with a long meow as if to agree, rubbing her face against mine. And suddenly, I felt completely at peace.

“That’s why you’re getting so close to me—if you were actually a girl, you wouldn’t have come this close. I guess you’re lucky,” I said with a light laugh, petting her as I drifted off to sleep.

The cat and I fell asleep in the cold, and once again that voice echoed in my mind—*Ilham…!!!*

I wanted to open my eyes, but I couldn’t when I felt the light of a mobile torch on my face. The air smelled so sweet that it could intoxicate anyone who breathed it in. Suddenly, I felt warmth, as if someone had turned on a heater or covered me with a warm blanket. With that sense of comfort, I passed out completely.

* * *

Hyderabad Blue Sky Academics:

"Everyone, write this down in your notes, and I'll be giving you a similar question as homework. Make sure to complete it!" the teacher instructed.

"I'm taking attendance now, so everyone be quiet for a moment," the lecturer said in a soft tone as she began taking roll call. She was our new teacher, recently hired to replace Miss Martin.

As usual, I started staring out the window. I always read up on laws. Whatever I study, it sticks in my mind after just one read. Pretty interesting, right?

But today, I was lost in my own thoughts. A question constantly lingered in my mind:

"What is the purpose of a heart that yearns, if all desires end in emptiness?"

Why is it that whenever I do something I think will bring me peace or pleasure, instead of feeling satisfaction, I'm left with this emptiness? Why?

Why do I feel this hollowness, when this is exactly what I thought I wanted? Then why does the heart yearn like this? Why do I always feel like something is missing—but what? The answer to that question——————

Just then, Fateen nudged me and said, "Ilham, the teacher is calling you."

I raised my hand in response to the lecturer but drifted back into my thoughts, gazing outside.

Across the school entrance, there was an open field with a large fountain, the water shooting upwards and flowing gracefully.

"Where were you lost…? And don't you think it's necessary to respond?" The lecturer's raised voice broke through my thoughts, but I couldn't stand her tone.

She was new, which is why I hadn't responded. I stayed silent. Repeating 10th grade is so annoying—

Yes, I'm repeating. Why…? That's a story for another time.

"I asked, where was your presence of mind…? Stand up and write on the blackboard what I just taught, come on," the lecturer said angrily, stepping toward my desk. I slammed my hand on the table in frustration, and the entire class fell silent.

Everyone knew what happens to people who talk to me like that.

"If I write exactly what you taught, will it be acceptable? Are you sure you won't say it's wrong…?" I asked the teacher.

"Why would I say it's wrong if you write it correctly…?" she replied, forcing a smile.

Without saying another word, I walked toward the board and wrote down the complex math problem exactly as she had explained it, highlighting the parts I wanted her to pay attention to.

"This is wrong," the teacher declared, and everyone began checking their notes.

But a girl from the back spoke up, "But ma'am, Ilham wrote it correctly. Look, it's exactly what we copied from board to in our notes."

The teacher looked at her notes and couldn't utter a word. It was as if her voice had been silenced.

I gave a devilish grin and started erasing the board, preparing to write the correct answer. The whole class erupted in applause, starting with Fateen.

"This is the correct answer. My mind was present the entire time—it was your explanation that made it seem absent, ma'am," I said, tossing the chalk into the air and heading toward the door.

"You're so rude. Give me your father's number, I'll speak to him," the teacher said angrily, but I just laughed.

"Oh, sure, write it down. He's probably sitting idle, go ahead, file as many complaints as you want. You teachers and your obsession with PTMs—I'm sick of it," I said, and she stared at me, stunned. I've had more complaints sent to my house than any student's report cards.

"What do you mean by 'idle'? Doesn't your father work...?" she asked, curious.

"Yes, he does. He's probably at work right now," I replied.

"Then how is he 'idle'? What does your father do...?" she asked, irritated.

"Why don't you go see for yourself? Just go straight from here, and at the first block on the ground floor, you'll find a large, luxurious office. You can see for yourself," I pointed out.

"What do you mean? That's the Dean's office, the owner of this school, so, you mean you are the Dean's child...??" she said, shocked. This wasn't the first time a teacher was stunned by this revelation.

"Should I show DNA report...???" I said, knocking the wind out of her. Her breath seemed to catch in her throat. Being the Dean's son isn't a small thing, but when I'm with him, he makes me feel like it is—*just a dad being a dad.*

"Alright, fine, go back to your seat..." she said. I smiled sarcastically, then started heading toward the door.

"Where do you think you're going...? Class isn't over yet," the teacher said, this time addressing me with respect. *Ugh, this self-serving society.*

"Miss..., it's break time. Class is over, and I have no interest in attending your extra lesson, especially since all you do is teach the wrong things anyway," I said. She lowered her gaze, humiliated in front of everyone.

"Well..., I just joined recently, so I'm not that familiar with the class timings," she said, glancing at the students.

"No problem. You'll get used to it, and over time, you'll get used to my attitude as well," I said, saluting her mockingly with my right hand before walking out into the corridor with a mischievous smile.

I headed toward the ground when suddenly a girl called out to me,

"Ilham…?"

It was Rebecca from Section B. I looked at her but didn't respond, casually chewing my gum.

I glanced her over from head toe.

Her long, dyed golden hair contrasted with her fair skin. Her makeup looked perfectly applied—*Who wears makeup to school…?*

After a moment, I lost interest in looking at her.

"Ilham, can we go to the club tonight if you're free?" she invited me to the club.

"Sure,"

I quickly agreed, though I was surprised that a girl was inviting me to the club, and especially *me*.

It's not like it was the first time I had received such an invitation, but this was the first time it had come from someone younger than me.

Usually, I hang out with older girls or guys at parties and clubs because being around underage girls is just a headache.

"But how will you come?" I asked, curious. "I mean, it's illegal for you to go to a club—just so you know. We guys could go, but you—" I left the sentence unfinished when Rebecca started laughing.

"Don't worry, it's my dad's club. We can go easily," she explained, revealing that her father owned the club.

Wow, this girl has it easy—she has her own club? I thought to myself.

"Okay, done. Fateen and I will come," I agreed, leaning against the wall.

Now, you must be thinking how quickly I said yes to the club invitation, even before the wind could change direction.

Well, I love going to parties, clubs, and pubs. You have to enjoy life sometimes, and if you don't, what's the point of living?

As I started walking towards the ground, Rebecca grabbed my hand.

"Wait, where are you going?" she asked, trying to come closer. I hate girls who try to get close to me for no reason—*it's not me; it's my heart that feels suffocated in moments like these.*

"Washroom. Do you want to join me?" I asked with a faint smile. Her smile vanished, and she quickly let go of my hand.

"No, no. See you tonight," she said and left.

Bitch— I muttered under my breath as she walked away.

Just then, Fateen, teasing as always, placed his hand on my shoulder and said, "What's this? Holding hands now? Are you interested in her?"

Fateen knew well that I had no interest in girls, especially not someone like Rebecca. I see relationships as distractions, and distractions have no place in Ilham's life—not until I reach my goals or find *her*.

"Interest? In Rebecca?" I started laughing at Fateen's question.

"She's pretty, and she's giving you hints. So, what's the problem?" Fateen raised his eyebrows. He has a habit of asking every detail about things.

I shook my head. "Yeah, she might be pretty, but not to me." I started walking towards the ground again. "And as for the hints and all, I'm not interested in relationships right now. To me, relationships are like prisons, and I'm preparing to lock people up, not to be locked up myself. They're distractions, I'm already distracted by someone. This is all temporary pleasure, and as quickly as it comes, it ends even worse. I'm not going to waste my life on these trivial pursuits."

I started playing basketball with Fateen, who still looked amused. "Forget all that, she invited us to the club. Let's go—it's been ages since we hit a club." I smirked, trying to dodge the ball Fateen was attempting to steal from me.

It's not easy living with parents and still going to clubs, pubs, or parties. You've already seen what happened to me last time.

"Alright, let's go. But tell me, why were you so rude to that new lecturer? You know she's new to the school. How are we going to survive your Hitler this time? We might end up repeating 10th grade again," Fateen said, laughing. He had also suffered with me which made to repeat 10th grade.

"Just drop it, bro," I said, exhaling deeply. We continued playing our game.

"Okay, I'll drop it. But if you keep acting this rude, you're never going to get anywhere. We'll be stuck here forever," Fateen said with a playful jab, clearly worried about us failing exams again. Last time, my dad didn't sign our hall tickets, and we got suspended—*Want to know why? I'll tell you later.*

"I don't care, Fateen. This time, I'm going straight to Canada after this," I said, stealing the ball from him, just as he had done to me earlier.

"You should care, bro. Your behavior marks are in their hands," Fateen tried to reason with me and becomes my father.

"Ilham doesn't chase marks. Marks should chase Ilham," I said confidently. "And goal!" I exclaimed as I scored, flashing a grin at Fateen.

On a chilly winter afternoon, with the cold winds blowing, Fateen and I were playing basketball during our break. I don't know why, but I felt someone's gaze on me—like a warm presence in the cold air. I looked around but didn't see anyone.

We focused back on our game when Fateen said, "By the way, you're not the only topper anymore. A new student has matched your percentage in the entrance exam. And thanks to your dad's influence, she's been admitted even though she joined late."

I missed my shot. *Another topper? I can't accept that.*

"Who is she?" I asked Fateen.

"She's a junior, don't worry. She's not in our class," Fateen replied calmly, but I wasn't satisfied. Fateen glanced toward the junior block, smiling.

"Who is she? I need to know. Who dared to make me her competition? Doesn't she know that beating Ilham's percentage is no easy task?" I said, looking at him with intensity. My gaze made it clear that I was feeling jealous. Why wouldn't I? I'm obsessed with my percentage, and now someone is trying to match it? ~~I want to prove to my dad that I'm better than her.~~

"Ilham, you can't be the only topper in the world. Get over it," Fateen sighed, sounding exasperated.

"Maybe not in the world, but in this school, Ilham's record will stand, and I won't let anyone reach it. Now tell me who is she?" I asked, now more serious.

Sensing my seriousness, Fateen said, "You and your obsession with percentage is out of my thinking. Alright, fine. I'll tell you. She's probably in the library right now."

He motioned with a smirk as he made one last shot at the goal and turned toward me.

Fateen is like the school's CCTV camera, always knowing everyone's business. I wasn't surprised that he knew all about this girl. I followed him to the library, matching his steps.

When we entered the library, I scanned the room carefully—*it was my first time there.*

"There, at the third table, that's her," Fateen pointed.

She was the first girl I'd ever seen wearing a hijab. I couldn't see her face because she had it hidden behind a book—and not just any book, but one she was carefully guarding as if it were a treasure.

I walked toward her table and sat down across from her, trying to remain calm. She was silent, absorbed in whatever she was reading, but I couldn't see her face. And I wanted to.

Ilham, what are you doing? You're acting weird. A voice inside me questioned my behavior, but I couldn't shake the urge to see her face.

She seemed like a quiet, lonely girl. She wasn't talking to anyone, and I wasn't surprised. She was a new student, and being admitted on my father's recommendation probably didn't make her popular. No doubt, the other students had given her a hard time, calling it "ragging."

Just then, some of my classmates arrived and started teasing me.

"Hey, Ilham, is the end of the world near or something?" Rehan joked, seeing me in the library.

"The end will come when you finally learn something from these books," I shot back, not holding back in my response. When I looked back at the girl, she was already gone.

"Okay, but what are *you* doing here?" Rehan asked curiously, now in a softer tone.

"Relax, I didn't come here to check in on Instagram or show off like you," I replied, now scanning the room for Fateen.

And, of course, that rat was surrounded by girls as usual. He's like a beehive, and those girls are the buzzing bees.

"Fateen…" I called out, motioning for him to come over. He waved goodbye to the girls with a smile and walked towards me.

"Yeah, what's up?" Fateen asked calmly, hands in his pockets, chewing gum, and glancing at another junior girl.

"I want to know everything about that girl," I said calmly, but I wasn't calm at all. My heart felt something weird—I don't want to express it, though.

"Everything? What do I look like to you?" Fateen smirked, asking playfully as he glanced back at the junior girls with a grin.

"Everything means everything. Every detail," I said, sighing deeply as I playfully smacked him on the head to get him to focus, not on those buzzing bees.

"And about what do I look like? You look like a strange two-legged creature to me," I teased him.

Fateen grabbed me by the neck, playfully choking me as we both laughed and walked out of the library.

"Sometimes you should try talking to me like a normal person," Fateen joked, knowing full well how I am.

"Stop dreaming, Fateen. A father never talks to his son in a normal tone," I replied, laughing as we both left the library, I only laugh when I'm with Fateen; his antics are always so amusing that he never fails to make me smile.

A sudden obsession to know everything about that girl had taken over me.

I didn't know why, but I wanted to learn everything. Even after school was over, I stayed behind for a while, waiting for her, but she didn't appear.

"How long will you keep hiding? One day or another, I will find you."

* * *

I was studying the basics of my law course because I wanted to learn about the Canadian Constitution as well just as I read everything about Indian Constitution.

Immersed in my studies and taking mock tests, I glanced at the clock after finishing my last test. The hands showed 9 PM.

I closed my books and laptop, stretched, and took a deep breath. The mosque near my house broadcasted the call to prayer loudly, making me feel a strange restlessness.

Shaking off the feeling, I began getting ready. After all, tonight, Fateen and I were heading to the club.

I pulled on my black shirt and jeans and, as usual, grabbed my leather jacket.

This time, I chose the brown one. I styled my hair neatly, though, to be honest, no matter how much I tried, my hair always ended up looking messy. I liked it that way; the unruly look suited me. Finally, I sprayed on my favorite perfume: *Nette - The Vanille Eau de Parfum.* I'm a bit of a perfume enthusiast, and *Chanel* and *Dior* are among my favorites.

My uncle, who lives in Canada, sends me perfumes every time. For my recent birthday, he sent me a bunch of *Versace* ones, though I haven't used them yet.

I started working out back in 8th grade, so I've had a decent height and physique since then. Maybe that's why all the girls seem to hover around me.

Grabbing my bike keys, I walked out of my room. "Mumma, I'm heading out. I'll eat outside," I informed her before stepping out of the house, only to run into my dad.

"Where are you going?" he asked.

"Just out with friends. I'll be back," I replied curtly, starting my bike. And yes, you might want to know what kind of bike I have—it's a *BMW S1000RR.*

This is my third one, though, as the first two were lost to accidents.

"Fine," my dad said sternly, loosening his tie, "but remember, if you drink or get involved in any nonsense, I won't let you back in this house. You'll be wandering the streets of Hyderabad like a stray. You've been warned."

He had just returned from work, clearly exhausted.

"Chill," I muttered under my breath, shaking my head slightly in irritation. I took a deep breath and rode out of the driveway. A little while later, my phone rang.

I stopped my bike and saw it was Rebecca calling. I hoped she wasn't canceling the plan. After all, it had been a while since I had a chance to hit the club. I answered the call.

Rebecca: "Hello, Ilham, you're coming, right?"

Ilham: "On my way!"

I hung up. Don't take my dad's words too seriously. He believes I went to the red-light district drunk out of my mind, but honestly, nothing like that happened. I went there fully sober.

Yes, I did go to the red-light district once, with my clubmates, the ones I race bikes and do car drifts with.

They're a bit older than me, so it's easy to go along with them. But when I got there, I was stunned to see women of all ages standing there like showpieces. There was even a girl my age, though she had made herself look so different that I thought she was older than me.

In the heart of Hyderabad lies Koti, an area known for its two contrasting faces. By day, it's a bustling market, alive with the vibrant energy of the city. Vendors sell their goods, and people navigate the narrow streets, a constant hum of life.

But as soon as the sun sets, the atmosphere changes entirely. Koti transforms into a shadowy, mysterious world, one of the oldest and most infamous parts of Hyderabad.

The daytime sparkle fades into the darkness, and the area becomes a hub of clandestine and illegal activities. The stark contrast between day and night gives Koti its unique character, a place where the city's heartbeat never stops.

When all my friends disappeared with a woman—each of them off to their own— I was left confused about what to do next. Fateen wasn't there, and even if he had been, he wouldn't have come.

I tried to do what my friends did, but when the girl grabbed my hand, I felt suffocated. It was as if I was being dragged into quicksand, a feeling I get every time a girl comes near me.

It's the voice that keeps me from getting close to anyone. Her touch didn't feel right. I pulled my hand back and walked out of there, finally able to breathe.

And that's when I ran into my father, who had been searching for me and brought Fateen along, holding him by the ear.

I hadn't even done anything, yet my father believes I'm a regular customer at the red-light district. But, if I'm going to be there, it should be for something worth my money.

But what I saw was a place where people go just for a moment's pleasure—nothing more.

For me, though, pleasure is meaningless if it doesn't fill the emptiness inside. And besides, the kind of pleasure, peace, and passion I'm searching for can't be found there—*it just can't.* If it could, I'd feel excitement, not suffocation.

I only went to see if the hype around that place was justified, but in the world of those selling their bodies, I found no pleasure, no peace, no passion—nothing.

I reached Fateen's house to pick him up. I stopped my bike and looked towards his house, where I saw him scaling the wall to sneak out. His father, Razzaq Uncle, never lets him go out this late.

I've named him "the animal on two legs" for a reason. He proves it every time.

While I was waiting, I glanced up at the roof and saw a girl dressed in black dress, watching me. As soon as I noticed her, I quickly looked away.

"Come on, come on, come on!" Fateen jumped on the bike, urging me to hurry before his dad spotted us. I revved the engine, and we sped off towards the club. Nightclubs have a certain charm to them—the music, the dancing, the atmosphere—it fills me up, even if just for a while.

"Why were you so late?" Fateen asked.

"I was studying and lost track of time,"

I replied, turning slightly to face him.

At that moment, a girl suddenly appeared in front of the bike. Thankfully, I hit the brakes just in time and swerved to avoid her.

"Are you blind—You," I shouted at her, clenching my teeth in anger. We had barely avoided an accident.

"I'm so sorry," she whispered softly, her three words——————————-Just 'Three Words' and instantly my rage goes calm……………………………..

Her voice had an undeniable calm to it, and her eyes—dark and deep—were mesmerizing.

She had lined her eyes with kohl, making them a weapon that could strike straight to anyone's heart. Her innocence was apparent in her gaze, and I realized she had stepped in front of the bike to save a cat.

"If I hadn't come, the cat would've died. Next time, drive more carefully," she said gently and walked away, cradling the cat in her arms.

I watched her walk off, a smile spreading across my face. She was dressed in a black abaya and niqab, her steps taking her further away, but her sight was getting closer as she kept looking back at me.

She watched me, and I watched her.

Fateen gave me a nudge. “Ilham…? Come on, man, we’re getting late.”

I started the bike, and we sped off. Within 15 minutes, we reached the club at full speed.

There isn’t a single light in this world that hasn’t shone on me. Yet, what is this light I’m searching for, the one that eludes me?

Why can’t I find it?

What is the purpose of a heart that yearns if all desires end in emptiness?

* * *

EPISODE – 3

(The Gun....!!!)

The club atmosphere was electric and alive with energy, just like every other time.

The air was thick with intoxicating smoke, glittering lights, and loud music that made my heart race in the moment.

When Fateen and I arrived, Rebecca immediately approached us. Like all the other girls there, she wore a short knee-length bodycon dress, her legs bare from the knees down.

Her golden, thick, straight hair had silky wine-red streaks that shimmered under the club lights, and of course, her face was caked with 50 layers of makeup.

I quickly averted my gaze and asked her,

"So, what's the plan?"

A few of my other classmates were also present in the club. We all gathered around a leather couch, and Rebecca sat next to me.

We talked for a while, catching up, and of course, took turns grabbing beers from the cans we had brought.

Meanwhile, Fateen had disappeared, as usual.

He always had a thing for the girls here, while I started playing games with a few of my classmates.

"Alright, let's spin and play truth or dare."

I wasn't exactly excited about the idea—this game never thrilled me—but since I was here, I decided to go along with it.

Rebecca spun the bottle first, and it landed on Aswad.

"Truth or dare?" she asked.

"Dare," he replied without hesitation.

"Okay, expose your feelings by kissing your crush," Rebecca teased, jumping straight into the childish games.

If I had been given a chance, I would've suggested something far more dangerous, like, *"Shoot yourself by keeping one bullet in your gun."*

Aswad belonged to a political family, and guns and knives were an open secret for him.

I would've enjoyed seeing if the one who carries a gun is worthy of holding it- *Call me a psychopath if you want, but this is who I am.*

Aswad laughed, shaking his head. "She's not here," he said, and everyone sighed in disappointment.

"Ohhh..." they groaned.

But really, is it worth letting someone else into your arms just because your crush isn't around? Ugh. These boys always pick girls at clubs for fun, but when it comes to love or marriage, they want someone pure and untouched-*I'm sick of this hypocritical society.*

Rebecca spun the bottle again.

The dim lights flickered around the club, casting strange shadows on everyone's faces as they bounced off the shiny neon lights.

The faint smell of alcohol lingered in the air as the bottle slowed down and came to a stop, pointing towards Aswad again and, fatefully, me.

Perhaps death had decided to play a game with me tonight.

I leaned back on the couch, casting a devilish grin towards Aswad.

The game of truth or dare had been going on for a while, but things got serious when I made my move.

"Shoot yourself with your revolver, keeping one bullet in it," I said. The room fell into an immediate, tense silence.

Aswad's hands trembled as he glanced between the revolver on the table and me, sitting casually with an unnatural calmness.

Regret was written all over his face for choosing "dare," while I felt superior for his poor choice.

"You're joking, right? This is just a game," Ranjaish Khurana muttered under his breath, trying to lighten the atmosphere that I wasn't about to let soften.

I laughed, my voice filling the silence of the club.

"Yeah, just a game. But Aswad chose dare, and now he has to either do it or admit he's a coward." Everyone turned to Aswad, waiting for his decision.

The mood had turned deadly serious, and after a moment, Aswad nodded slowly. His voice wavered.

"I'm not doing this, Ilham. This is madness." My laughter rang out again, clear and cold, because I didn't care.

I never cared about anyone.

"Scared? I thought you were braver than this. I'm disappointed. You're not even worthy of holding that gun, let alone firing it. If I were in your place, I wouldn't back down, even if it meant dying. I wouldn't prove myself to be a coward like you."

I took another sip from my beer, unfazed by the growing tension in the room as I continued to provoke him.

The bottle was spun again, and this time, it pointed straight at me. Seizing the opportunity, Aswad smirked and said,

"Fine, Ilham, it's your turn. Do what you told me to do." And Aswad, who was terrified just a moment ago, took advantage of the opportunity and said…

Laughter bubbled up in me again, this time with even more amusement.

"That's it…? This is all you could come up with…? You could have thought of something better… It's a shame that you lack both courage and intellect." Without a second thought, I reached for the revolver as if it were a mere toy, not a weapon that could end my life in an instant.

I calmly spun the cylinder, the metallic click echoing ominously in the hushed club. Then, without hesitation, I lifted the revolver to my temple.

Rebecca, who was sitting next to me, couldn't take it anymore.

She grabbed my arm, her voice pleading.

"Ilham, don't do it. Please." I shrugged her hand off, giving her a devilish smile.

"Relax…" Before anyone could stop me, I pulled the trigger.

Click.

The hole was empty. I'd already calculated with instincts where the bullet would have landed when I spun the cylinder.

But even if I had miscalculated, it wouldn't have mattered.

I wouldn't have backed down, even in the face of death.

After all, even death fears Ilham.

A collective sigh of relief washed over the room, though the intensity of the moment left everyone shaken. I placed the revolver back on the table with a smile.

"If you'd done it first, maybe you would've won, Aswad. Maybe the bullet would've hit me instead. But you chose to be a coward."

I chuckled softly, while everyone around me stared in disbelief, unsettled by my madness.

They were nervous, anxious, and most of all, scared. I think they were realizing what kind of a person they were really sitting with.

It would've been more fun if they had joined me in my insanity. But none of them were on my level.

None of them had the guts to challenge death the way I did.

Ugh… boring people……!!

The bottle spun again, this time by a girl who was one of Rebecca's friends. She wasn't from our school, but we'd run into each other at clubs before.

The bottle pointed towards Rebecca, and I downed more beer than I should have.

"So, truth or dare?" her friend asked, and as they exchanged secretive glances, I knew it was my cue to leave. I

knew Rebecca too well—she had an unhealthy interest in me, but her interest only went skin-deep, and that didn't sit well with me. "Excuse me, I'm out," I muttered, standing up and walking away just as Rebecca's friend began asking her questions.

I headed towards Fateen, who was dancing with a group of girls. They were all hanging on him like bees around honey, and I couldn't help but smirk at the sight.

A few girls started walking toward me, but I held myself back from letting anyone get too close.

~~Even if I wanted to, it wouldn't be possible. The one who's inside me won't allow it~~—She is damn possessive about me.

After some time dancing, Rebecca joined us on the floor.

The music was so energetic that everyone was caught up in the rhythm. Rebecca was a great dance partner—she knew every move, and her sense of rhythm was perfect, enough to keep up with the vibe, at least in my eyes.

While we're dancing, how about an introduction? Let's begin…

My name is Ilham Osman Khan, and the stories begins with me. My father, Osman Ahmed Khan, thinks I'm the heir to the Qasr-e-Shahi Khan legacy—the torchbearer. What thinks? Of course I *am*—

Naturally, he wants me involved in the family business, but honestly? I'm not interested.

I mean, come on, there are far more exciting things to do in life. Business? Especially a ready-made one?

Nah. *Tssk*... Not my thing.

I want that kick, that craze, that passion, that adventure, that thrill... in my life. I've decided that I'm going to be an attorney. There's a unique thrill in arguing in court, especially when the other party is lying, and you get to expose their lies in front of everyone.

Just imagine the embarrassment they'd feel-*Now, don't think I'm crazy just because I like that sort of thing. It's just who I am.*

And I'm obsessed with my grades, my academic track record. I can't stand seeing anyone surpass me—not that anyone is even capable of it, really- ~~*My obsession, I think, stems from her.*~~

My father doesn't have a problem with my education or anything else, but he has a real issue with my decision to become a lawyer.

And his disapproval? It's gotten under my skin to the point where I've practically stopped speaking to him directly ~~Seeing his fondness for that girl, I stopped speaking to him directly~~. *I mean, he can't force me into his business.*

This is the problem with Indian parents. They'll either force you or emotionally blackmail you. But Ilham isn't someone you can pressure or blackmail. *I'm Ilham, after all.*

I've made a promise to myself: I will carve my career with the same golden words I've written on my wall. Because I am...

"Ilham Osman Khan. What I think, I do. And what I do, everyone witnesses."

Am I boring you with my introduction?

I'm the kind of person who's obsessed with chasing the colors of life. Adventure and thrill are the fuel for my soul. Whatever gives me pleasure, I pursue without hesitation.

~~I might seem self-obsessed~~, though I'd never admit it.

My self-admiration is a facet of my personality I've carefully hidden.

But deep down, I truly believe no one's better than me—because there's *no one.*

In my mind, I'm always *ahead*, always the *best*, always *superior.*

My style, my thoughts, my vision—they're all unmatched.

I'm someone the world has never seen before.

My thoughts soar high, and my approach to life is nothing short of a daring adventure.

After dancing for a while, the DJ switched to softer songs for the couples. I was about to leave when Rebecca stopped me.

"One dance…?" she asked, pulling me closer.

"Not interested," I said, trying to free my hand, but she didn't let go.

"Come on, Ilham. Just one dance as a thank you," she insisted. I agreed, not because I couldn't refuse, but because… *well, I'll let you guess.*

We started dancing together, though I didn't place my hands on her waist or hold hers.

I kept both my hands behind me.

From behind, Fateen nudged me, causing Rebecca and me to get even closer.

She placed one hand on my chest and the other on my shoulder as we matched steps.

Rebecca began getting too close for my comfort.

Her touch was starting to disgust me.

I wouldn't have minded if she hadn't tried to touch me like that.

"Rebecca, stop,"

I warned her, though she assumed I was too drunk to know what I was saying. I was drunk, sure, but not enough to lose control.

"Let it be, Ilham…" she whispered softly.

Her hands crept up to my neck, and she was about to kiss me when her voice echoed in my mind—her voice.

"Ilham…….."

"Just move……….."

I shoved Rebecca away instantly, and she fell to the dance floor.

"Don't you ever dare to do that again,"

I hissed through gritted teeth.

It's because of this girl's voice that I can't let anyone else get close to me. Why…?

Fateen came over and began to pull me away.

"You bitch!" I spat at Rebecca.

Why was I so angry?

Was it because that girl kept haunting my thoughts, or because she had gotten so close that I couldn't bear the touch of any other girl?

"Not a bitch, a dog—he's calling me a dog,"

Fateen joked, trying to diffuse the tension as he guided me out of the club.

He started the bike, and with his help, I managed to get on the seat behind him.

We rode to a nearby lake, a quiet spot where we often came to escape the world.

This wasn't the first time something like this had happened, and Fateen always handled the situation.

We sat by the lake, a few cans of beer beside us.

The view was peaceful, the cold breeze brushing against our faces, and the stillness around us was calming.

Isn't it funny how the world gets so serene when everyone else is asleep?

"What's wrong with you, man? She was just trying to kiss you. You should've let her. It's not like she was asking you to marry her,"

Fateen said calmly, offering me a beer.

"Shameless. Just shut up," I muttered, giving him a light shove.

We cracked open our cans—*Tsss*—and took a few sips.

"Tell me the truth, though. She was so close. You didn't feel anything? Not even a bit of temptation? Or... are you saving yourself for someone? Maybe you're in love?"

Fateen teased, mischief in his voice. I never understood why he asked me such questions.

"Temptation? Seeing her that close, I felt disgusted by every breath she took. And me, in love? If I ever fall in love, it'll be a sign of the apocalypse," I said, taking another swig from my can.

"What's your problem, man? You've never been interested in any girl, and you've never let anyone get close to you. What do you want?"

Fateen asked, tossing his empty can into the lake and watching me intently.

"I don't know. I've never met a girl who impressed me. And honestly, even if someone tried, they'd never succeed. I'm too hard to impress, and besides, impressing me is something even her future seven generations won't be able to achieve."

I replied. I never usually shared my innermost thoughts, but the alcohol had loosened me up.

Maybe, deep down, I did want to share things with Fateen—tonight just gave me the chance.

"So, what kind of girl are you looking for? She wasn't asking for a marriage proposal, man. You could've thought of it as something temporary,"

Fateen exhaled deeply.

Yeah, like everyone else, I could think of things as temporary.

But no girl has ever appealed to me. ~~Or perhaps, I haven't yet met the girl whose voice has truly impressed me.~~

The one whose voice haunts my dreams—the one I've never seen.

Her face? I have no idea.

Who is she?

Where is she?

I don't know, but I know her voice, and the way she says my name—*Ilham*—with such tenderness.

Whenever I hear my name from her lips, a strange peace spreads through me.

"She's someone who should ignite the same madness, passion, obsession, and addiction that I seek in everything. There can't be anything missing there. And as for temporary? Sure, I can understand that. But I don't crave fleeting lust or confuse brief pleasure with real peace,"

I said, cracking open another beer. *Tsss.*

"And do you really think you'll find someone like you?"

Fateen laughed, though his laughter grated on my nerves.

"I haven't searched for… nor do I need to,"

I replied, though deep down, ~~I was searching. I just hadn't found her.~~

"And if you do find someone like you, will you accept her? Have you ever seen your own reflection?"

Fateen's question hit me like a blow, striking at every sensitive nerve.

I didn't respond, instead downing the rest of my beer.

"If we find someone like us, may Allah forgive us," Fateen said with a laugh, turning it into a joke, but it wasn't a joke to me.

What does that mean?

If I find someone like me, I'll need God's forgiveness?

"What do you mean by that?"

I asked, without holding back my curiosity.

"Look, Ilham, when it comes to marriage, every man wants a pious, virtuous woman to take care of his home. And I'm no different. I don't want a woman like me," Fateen admitted.

I found his words unbearable.

This isn't something to be dismissed with *'may Allah forgive.'* This is the mindset of men like Fateen and Aswad.

"Then you should work on being a virtuous man yourself. It doesn't make sense to demand a virtuous woman while being her complete opposite," I shot back, my tone sharp with truth.

Fateen smiled, letting the conversation die as he turned his gaze to the lake's gentle waves.

"Yeah, but it's the truth that to run a household, you need a homely woman. Not someone like us," Fateen said softly.

"And it's also true that a woman needs a 'Man' besides her. Not someone like you," I retorted sarcastically, aiming straight at his pride.

Fateen, still smiling, let it slide and changed the topic.

"I've got my eye on someone, Ilham," Fateen confessed suddenly.

He'd never talked to me about a girl before, so this meant she was special to him.

"Who?" I asked. Even if I hadn't, he would've made me ask eventually.

"A junior,"

He said, his voice calm as he looked up at the sky.

The moonlight illuminated his face and dark eyes, and my mind immediately went to the girl I suspected he was talking about—*the class topper.*

"Which junior? The new girl in the hijab?" I asked, my tone serious.

~~*Was it only seriousness? Or was it… something more?*~~

"I'll tell you when something happens,"

Fateen cut off the conversation, but the unfinished business gnawed at me. I tossed my empty can into the lake.

"Hmm,"

I muttered, letting the conversation end, though my mind was stuck on the thought of Fateen liking that girl.

But why was I thinking so much about the hijab-wearing girl? *Whatever.*

Fateen and I spent the rest of the night by the lake, sitting on the cold, iron bench, talking until, at some point, I must have dozed off.

I never know how she senses it, but the moment my eyes close, she comes. She comes to complete the unfinished feelings and remind me of her absence in my existence.

آنکھ بند ہوئی نہیں، تیرا دیدار ہوا

دیدار بھی ایسا، کچھ ادھورا سا احساس لگا

مل کر بھی نہ ملے، ایسا ادھورا سا احساس ہوا

بس ایک تیری آواز جو احساس خاص لگا

-My eyes had not yet closed, yet *You* appeared to me,

But even *Your* sight felt like a half-felt plea.

We met, yet it felt like *we* were worlds apart,

It was only *Your* voice stirred something deep in my heart.

Ilham.....................................

There was a smile on my face, and I was at peace, I find complete calm just by hearing her voice.

* * *

EPISODE – 4

(I'm Not Eves Dropping….!!)

The sunlight streaming through the leaves on my eyes, the hum of cars, and people on their morning jogs—these were the things that woke me up.

When I opened my eyes, I saw Fateen clinging to me like a girl, and not just sleeping—he was smiling, the filthy idiot.

I shoved him off, sending him tumbling to the floor, waking him up.

"Morning's here, get up," I said, while Fateen stretched and tried to hug me again.

"I swear, I'll drown you in this lake if you don't stop your filthy antics," I told him, running a hand through my hair and slipping on my jacket.

"Oh baby, why are you getting upset?" Fateen teased, making me laugh despite myself.

Fateen always had a playful, carefree nature, the kind of guy whose cheerful no matter what, and only he could make me laugh like that.

"Come on, or else your dad's going to be the one upsetting you,"

I said, and we got on the bike to head back home.

We still had to go to school, and just like Fateen had jumped over the wall to sneak out, he did the same on our return.

Watching him, I decided I'd do the same today—climb the wall to get inside the house.

I slept for a while after, just to look normal, because I never get up before 8 a.m. anyway.

8: 30 AM -

I got dressed in my school uniform, grabbed my bag, and whistled my way downstairs like I do every day.

As usual, Dad, Suzy, and Mom were already at the dining table for breakfast. I tossed my bag to the side and, before sitting down, messed up Suzy's hair.

"Bhai, where were you yesterday?" Suzy asked, and I felt the urge to give my sweet little witch of a sister a good punch.

Like really, is this the time or place to bring that up, especially in front of Baba?

I didn't let the awkwardness show on my face though.

Maintaining my calm, I smoothly lied,

"I was home, in my room," I replied, and started eating. As soon as I took a bite, I could feel Dad's gaze on me.

"Don't look at me like that; you'll fall in love with me," I teased, clapping my hands together with Suzy.

"Should I take notes? Might come in handy later," Suzy laughed, playing along.

Even though she's only seven, my little sister has inherited all the mischievousness from her big brother.

"Shut up!" Dad scolded, serious now, and I fell silent.

"Where did you go? And where were you all night? And why on earth were you jumping over walls so early in the morning? I saw you!"

Dad fired off questions one after the other.

I don't know how, but Dad always finds out about everything I do.

It's like he has a sixth sense.

But then again, he *is* Osman Ahmed Khan, my father.

"If you already saw, why bother asking, Mr. Osman?" I joked again, challenging Dad, and turned to high-five Suzy as we laughed together.

"Should I note that down too?" Suzy asked, pretending to type it into her little tablet, and I couldn't help but smile.

Dad slammed his hand on the dining table in anger, and I thought, *okay, it's better to stop now.*

"I was at Fateen's place. It got late, so I stayed over. Now, chill. I wasn't in the mood to hear your nonsense first thing in the morning, that's why I came in that way,"

I answered, standing up, leaving my breakfast unfinished as usual.

"Ilham! My child, don't leave your breakfast like that, come back," Mom called out to me.

"I'm not hungry! I'm not going to die if I skip a meal for a day," I snapped back and walked out of the house.

They won't let me eat in peace and then expect me to have breakfast while they nag me.

I started my bike, put on my sunglasses, and sped off to school at full throttle.

I reached school, and while I used to look forward to school all these years, now I only wait for the break.

I have to see *her*. Why? I'm not sure. I just want to.

It's become a stubborn urge of mine—or maybe I just want to see who dares to think she can beat my percentage.

Finally, after what felt like ages, the break arrived.

I was heading towards the library when I spotted her, not in the library, but sitting in the corridor with Maryam.

I approached them, leaning against the wall, and casually took a book from another girl's hand with a playful smile before sitting down behind them. The girl was thrilled that I took her book.

I sat there, listening to their conversation—*I'm not eves dropping.*

"What do you keep reading all the time? It's neither academic books nor anything for self-improvement," Maryam asked.

We all knew Maryam—she's good at painting and has won several awards and medals. She's also the daughter of one of my father's business colleagues.

She had chosen her company well, after all. "Oh, stop shouting, quiet down. And why should I tell you?" the girl snapped at Maryam, and I found that intriguing.

~~I've heard that voice somewhere before…~~

"Why won't you tell me? I'm your friend…" Maryam pressed. Maryam was the kind of girl who was always friendly and well-liked, and she didn't easily take a liking to just anyone.

"No, I don't have any friends… You're just clinging to me," the girl replied curtly, and for some reason, I liked her sharp tone.

"Oh, so I'm not your friend?" Maryam responded, pretending to be hurt, while the girl next to her suddenly said,

"Maryam, girl give me back my book." She sounded either irritated or anxious.

"Not until you tell me! You're always so quiet, you never talk or make friends. I must be the only fool who keeps chasing after you," Maryam said. She had a point; this girl did seem to keep to herself a lot.

"I don't know how to make friends, or maybe people just don't think I'm worth befriending," the girl replied. There was a depth to her words that piqued my curiosity about her past.

"Why would they think that?" Maryam asked gently.

"It's a long story, Maryam… Now, can you please give me back my book?" she insisted softly, almost pleading.

"Alright, alright. But we've got plenty of time today, so why not tell me? This way, I'll get to know you better… and you'll get to know me too. Plus, we've got free periods for the rest of the day," Maryam coaxed with a soft smile. Maryam's voice was so soothing, I knew the girl wouldn't refuse her.

"You're not going to let this go, are you?" The girl sighed deeply.

"Nope… I really like you," Maryam said, laughing lightly.

"Fine, I'll tell you. It's not a big deal. My mom used to be a teacher at my old school, and everyone thought I was this spoiled, pampered kid who got special treatment because of it. My grades were really good, and everyone hated me for it. That's why I never made any friends, and I don't know what it's like to have one. Now I've grown used to being alone, and I'm happy that way… I feel safe," she explained.

"Because every face wears a mask, and when everyone's hiding behind one, staying alone is the smartest move. It keeps you safe," she added.

I could hear the loneliness in her voice. *How long has she been this alone?* Why do you even care, Ilham? Why you are taking such an interest?

"Well, it seems like you've figured things out. But look, I don't even wear a niqab," Maryam joked, referring to the fact that she didn't wear a hijab or niqab.

"I'm not talking about that kind of mask or niqab, silly. I mean the invisible one's people wear on their faces," the girl corrected her.

"If you never try, how will you ever make friends?" Maryam asked, her tone becoming serious.

"I've gotten used to being alone. I don't want to make friends anymore. The very idea of friendship scares me now," she said calmly, as if she had made peace with it.

"Alright, don't try. I'll try for you. Just give me a chance to be your friend," Maryam offered with a gentle smile.

"I'll think about it… Now, give me my book," the girl said, reaching for it. *Why is she so nervous about that book?*

"Why are you so anxious about this book?" Maryam asked, echoing my thoughts.

"You're not going to let this go, are you?" the girl asked again.

"Nope," Maryam replied, giggling softly.

"Alright, fine, I'll tell you. I read novels—romance novels," the girl confessed in a quiet voice. I hadn't expected that.

"What? Novels? That too ROMANCE novels?" Maryam's voice rang out loud.

"Oh Allah, keep your voice down, Maryam!"

The girl clamped Maryam's mouth shut, glancing around nervously.

I scanned the area too, checking if anyone else had overheard them.

Walls have ears, and doors have tongues after all.

"You know we're not allowed to bring novels to school, especially romance ones. It's against the rules," Maryam warned.

"I didn't know you were hiding romance novels under those book covers. I mean, you… reading those kinds of books?" Maryam began, but the girl cut her off.

"They're not *those* kinds of novels. I mostly read decent novels, and there are some that match my taste too. So, chill out," she said, relaxing again.

"Alright, but if anyone finds out, it could be trouble. You know how many tattletales there are around here," Maryam cautioned.

She was right.

If she got caught, that Hitler wouldn't let her off lightly. Suspension would be the least of it; he'd drag her reputation through the mud in front of her parents too.

"Who's going to tell? Only you know, and I don't talk to anyone else. You're going to be my friend now, right?" The girl smiled slyly at Maryam; her tone smooth.

For some reason, I found her voice captivating, and a smile crept onto my face.

"Alright, alright. I won't tell anyone. But be careful, sweetheart," Maryam said gently.

"As you say, my love," the girl replied.

I couldn't help but chuckle to myself.

Do girls really talk to each other like this? Interesting.

"Okay, enough about those books. Now tell me about yourself. I want to know more about you," Maryam said, echoing my own curiosity.

I was just as eager to learn more about this girl.

"You want an introduction about me?" she asked, her voice tinged with a slight softness.

"Yeah, something like that," Maryam laughed softly.

"Okay. So, I'm Zieba Ansari, the only daughter of Ansari family. My blood in my veins is from Mumbai, but my tongue is pure Hyderabadi,"

Zieba introduced herself in detail. *Zieba—beautiful...*

She continued as if reciting from her personal Wikipedia.

"In a world where people have two faces, I have two different worlds. And I'm happier in my world of fantasies than in reality. My stories and I, we're very happy together," Zieba said, sounding almost delusional.

"Wow, Zieba, your introduction is as fascinating as those novels you read. You really love this delusional world of yours, don't you?" Maryam asked, her curiosity mirroring my own.

We were both growing more intrigued by Zieba.

"Yes, I love it a lot. I find peace in using my escape button," Zieba replied. Her words held a depth that would require a keen mind to fully understand.

"Wow, you're really something," Maryam said with a deep breath.

"You could be interesting too if you started reading. Want to give it a try?" Zieba asked, and I already knew what Maryam's answer would be.

"No thanks. I enjoy the shocks of reality far too much. I'm not interested in falling for these fictional, non-existent creatures," Maryam said, and Zieba responded with a soft laugh.

"You should try it once. This particular character is my favorite, and he's shown me the truth about life in so many ways," Zieba said.

She seemed far more mature than her age, and it was clear that her novels had shaped her perspective.

"So that means you've come to know the world without ever really seeing it, Zieba?" Maryam asked.

"Yeah, that's the beauty of novels; they weave reality through fiction," Zieba's words struck a chord with me.

"Girl, you're making me want to read now," Maryam said, half-seriously.

"What did you think I was doing this whole time? Wasting my precious words on you for nothing? I've been talking to you all this while just to manipulate you into reading! So, tell me, will you read now? Will you walk with me through my world of stories?" Zieba asked playfully, like a child pestering for a treat. I couldn't help but smile at her antics.

"Alright, alright! Since we're friends now, I guess I'll have to play along. I'll walk with you, right by your side. Just finish that book and pass it on to me," Maryam agreed.

"Yes! And then we'll both obsess over the MMC [Main Male Character] together," Zieba said with a laugh, and I had to stifle mine.

This girl was certainly interesting.

"Oh, absolutely!" Maryam giggled.

They were engrossed in their conversation for a while, and I was completely drawn into their conversation.

Then, a third voice cut through the air, harsh and demanding.

"New girl! Didn't I tell you to collect everyone's notes during the break and hand them over to the teacher? Why haven't you done it?" It was a girl addressing Zieba in a tone that rubbed me the wrong way. ~~How dare she speak to Zieba like that?~~ I was just about to step in when Zieba beat to it before me.

"You are talking to Zieba Ansari. You should watch your words and your tone. Because when Zieba decides to speak, things can get really messy," she shot back, her voice cool and calm but with an underlying edge. ~~I couldn't help but feel a surge of pride.~~

"Girl, you—"

"Zieba. Zieba Ansari. That's my name, and just because I've been quiet doesn't mean your tongue should start wagging. Get that straight," Zieba retorted, leaving the girl completely speechless.

"You talk too much. I'm the class representative," the girl spat, trying to regain her composure.

"You made me talk. I've been watching you, waiting for the right moment to give you the response you deserve. So now, you'll listen, and in the future, don't try to pick a fight with me. You're not even worth Zieba's time or words," Zieba declared, shutting her down completely.

There was no way this girl would ever dare mess with her again, and ~~if she did, I'd make sure to handle it myself.~~

"Yeah, Sahila, you're talking too much. Why are you bothering her?" Maryam interjected. "Just because she's new doesn't mean you get to act like this. If you're so eager to cause trouble, check yourself first where you stand when you are in front of her because Zieba has connections with the Dean of the school, while you only have sway with one class teacher." Maryam added.

Connections with the Dean? What's her link with the school's Dean?

And how does Hitler fit into this?

The girl must have left because after a long silence, Zieba and Maryam burst into laughter.

"You know, for someone who rarely talks, when you do, you really lay it on thick. But I'm sorry, Zieba, you're new here, and people are already treating you this way. It's embarrassing," Maryam said apologetically.

"I'm used to dealing with people like her. This isn't the first time something like this has happened to me. I don't care what others think, it's not Zieba's style, and you don't need to be sorry for this. I'm perfectly fine on my own," Zieba replied, showing just how tough she was. I had to admit, she's pretty savage.

"What's up, girls?" A voice rang out just as the girl walked away.

I didn't even need a second.

That irritating drawl belonged to none other than Farooq.

And there he was—standing like he owned the world, his flock of equally obnoxious friends lingering behind like background noise.

A flicker of annoyance sparked in me. *Of course, it's him.*

Like... Ewwww.

With no hesitation, I pulled the book down from my face, popped my gum with deliberate drama, and shot them a glare.

My eyes locked on them, jaw tight, head tilted. Just one look—and like scared pigeons, his friends scattered.

All except Farooq.

He didn't notice me.

"Nothing," Maryam replied curtly, clearly uninterested.

Zieba didn't say a word. Her silence was louder than anything she could've spoken.

Farooq, of course, had zero sense of boundaries.

"Don't worry about that girl, Zieba, hmm? I already finished your work."

That was it.

My blood boiled. My fists curled.

I was about to get up and rearrange his face—

But Zieba beat me to it. Calm. Collected. Savage.

"Why?" she asked, her tone ice cold. "Why would you do that?"

"Well…" Farooq shrugged with that smug grin, "I aim to impress, I guess."

I nearly laughed. *Seriously? This clown thinks he's Romeo.*

Then Zieba delivered the final blow—clean and classy.

"Impressing me isn't all that difficult," she said, casually insulting him. "Just don't make the mistake of stepping out of your limits."

Boom. That was it. My girl didn't even blink.

Ilham you called her 'My girl..!'

Did I?

Of course you did.

Well then shut up!

I sat back, a slow, proud smirk tugging at my lips. *Now that's what I call class.* Zieba was pure fire, and I was officially a fan.

"Wow, you really are one tough cookie," Maryam said with a laugh.

"Thanks to the 'bade sahab,' by God." Zieba said addressing someone.

"Who's this bade sahab?" Maryam asked.

"That… that…" Zieba hesitated, clearly unsure how to answer.

"Your father?" Maryam guessed, though I was certain that wasn't who she was talking about.

"Yeah…" Zieba eventually nodded.

A little while later, they both got up to leave. I quickly hid behind my book again, but just as they were about to pass by, Zieba glanced at me.

"Do people read books upside down here? Interesting," she remarked, her voice dripping with playful sarcasm.

And just like that, I was hit with a wave of embarrassment. Damn…

I said to myself as they both walked away. I took a deep breath, closed my eyes, and let the sound of her voice wash over me… Her voice was so calming.

Wait a minute…!!

That's the same girl I met yesterday, just before going to the club. I remember wanting to skip the club and follow her instead, and yeah, it's her the word 'by God' girl from past years ago at Charminar.

Yes…!!! She's the one!

-Now before you jump to conclusions, let me clarify—I'm not interested in her like that. I just wanted to see what she looks like... *Or perhaps, I'm just really good at making excuses...*

You believe me, right?

I reached the playground where I was meeting my friends to play football.

Every week, we had a match between juniors and seniors, and today was game day. Ilham had never lost a game, and Ilham will not lose today either.

The game started, and, as usual, a bunch of girls were cheering for our team, even some of the juniors.

Obviously, it's because Fateen and I were playing. Now, I'm not bragging—just stating facts—because Fateen and I were the most handsome and charming guys in the entire school.

And between the two of us, I'm the most handsome.

Didn't I tell you ~~I'm a little self-obsessed?~~

After scoring a bunch of points, I wiped the sweat from my forehead. That's when I noticed something in the corridor.

My eyesight is sharp.

It was that same girl, and Farooq was following her, talking to her again... ~~Could it be? Is he after her too?~~

My focus shifted from the game.

Without thinking, I stopped playing and started sprinting toward Block B.

"Ilham...?? The game...??"

Fateen called out, but I knew he could handle it without me.

"I'm out..." I shouted as I ran toward the corridor.

By the time I reached, they had already gone inside a classroom, and *I wasn't allowed in there. I know you're curious, but for now, I'll keep it a suspense.*

"Hey, Ilham?" Maryam called out as I caught my breath, ~~still feeling the burn from running.~~

"Maryam," I replied, panting.

"What are you doing here? Is the game over already? I was planning to come watch it with my friend," she said softly, and for some reason, her words made me feel surprisingly ~~good.~~

"Well then, come on. Where's your friend?" I asked, though my gaze was fixed on the classroom where *she* had gone.

"We'll be there in a bit," Maryam said gently as she walked inside.

I headed back to the field and rejoined the game.

"This is not allowed, Ilham bhai!" The juniors gathered around me, complaining that I'd left mid-game.

I slapped one on the back of the neck playfully and said,

"Don't teach your father." Then I jumped right back into the match, playing ~~as if I were trying to impress her.~~

One eye on the game, the other on the entrance, waiting for her to appear.

After scoring three goals, I noticed Maryam arriving with someone else. But it wasn't the girl in the hijab.

"Damn, ~~disappointed.~~" I muttered under my breath, annoyed.

I continued playing, and as expected, we won.

After the game, Fateen jumped on me in celebration, followed by the rest of the team.

A little later, I walked over to Maryam and asked in a low voice,

"You said you were bringing your friend, didn't you?" My frustration must've been visible in my eyes.

"Yes, I did, and here she is," Maryam said, gesturing to the girl next to her.

"Oh, for God's sake, I didn't mean this friend, I meant the one in the hijab! She's your friend, isn't she?" I lightly tapped Maryam on the forehead.

"Ilham, to her, I'm her only friend. But to me, both she and this one are my friends. And besides, she didn't want to come. Said she doesn't waste her time on pointless things," Maryam said, punching me lightly on the arm.

"Well, if you're her only friend, then she should be your only friend too. Break ties with this one, and be just her friend. And, yeah, she's right—maybe you could learn something from her about not wasting time here. And lastly, never raise your hand to me again, or I'll break it,"

I teased sarcastically, pulling the tape off my hand as I walked back toward the classroom.

After school, I returned home and slumped onto the couch, my thoughts drifting once again to the girl in the hijab.

Why couldn't I stop thinking about her?

"What are you, even human?" My father stormed into the room, his words crashing down on me like a thunderstorm.

"Doesn't seem like you think so, do you?" I replied casually, kicking off my shoes and leaning back, settling into the couch.

"If I thought you were, why would I ask? Do I look like I'm crazy to you?" His voice was thick with anger.

I don't understand why he's always so harsh toward me. It makes me want to be even more defiant. My mother signaled for me to stay quiet, but Ilham doesn't listen to anyone.

"If I thought you were, I'd tell you. Don't worry," I answered, shrugging off his anger as I leaned back further, making myself comfortable.

Just then, my mother came closer and scolded me, "Aren't you ashamed of how you're speaking to your father? Apologize right now, Ilham!"

"You just got back from school. Don't you know how to freshen up and sit properly? And I'm sick of hearing these constant complaints about you from school, Ilham." my father said, unloading the usual barrage of grievances.

"Then stop listening to them—what's it costing you to hear those complaints?" I shot back, my tone cold as I rested my hands behind my head and propped my feet up on the coffee table.

"Don't you have any shame, speaking like that?" he asked, his forehead creasing in frustration.

"Does a conversation require shame now?" I smirked, throwing the comment out like a challenge.

"Don't get smart with me, Ilham. What are you even doing in class that you're always zoned out? And why do you think it's okay to skip your math teacher's classes?!"

My father questioned, sitting down on the sofa across from me as he took off his suit and handed it to my mother.

He ran his hand through his hair—hair as thick as any man could hope for. *He's handsome too, just like me.*

"You know they're all obsessed with me. That's all. Chill out. As for that math teacher, she can't teach to save her life. She's always wrong, and I don't waste my time on people who don't know what they're doing," I said, closing my eyes as if the conversation bored me.

"Listen to me. I'm warning you, Ilham—if I get one more complaint, you won't like what happens next. Just because the dean is your father doesn't mean you get to take advantage of that," my father said sternly.

My mother sat beside him, trying to calm him down, and he took her hand, gently stroking the back of it with his thumb.

They're obsessed with each other.

"Yeah, and no one could be worse than you. There's no peace in this house, not even for a second. I'm sick of it."

My anger surged, and I grabbed my bag and stormed off to my room, leaving my shoes discarded where they were, Asi Aunt will get that to my room back.

"Your disrespect keeps getting worse by the day. Mark my words, Ilham—there'll come a day when you won't be able to face anyone, not even me, because of that attitude of yours," my father spat out, his teeth clenched in frustration.

As always, I let his words go in one ear and out the other.

I don't need to face anyone in this life. I know how to live; I know what I'm going to do. Ilham will be someone people want to emulate. Watch and see...

* * *

EPISODE – 5

(Distraction...!! Obsession...!!!)

I was just as lost in my thoughts during class, neither thinking about law updates nor studying anything related to law. My heart and mind were entirely consumed by thoughts of that girl.

A girl I hadn't met, hadn't even seen her face—yet I was so drawn to her just by the sound of her voice. *Ilham, this is all just a distraction. Stay focused on your goals. You have a name to make for yourself, and you must reach your destination...*

I shook my head, trying to snap out of it. I realized the class had already ended, the lecturer had taken attendance, and it was almost time for the break.

Fateen came over and stood by my desk, hovering over me like a second shadow.

"Where do you keep zoning out every time?"

Fateen asked, leaning on my desk.

There's no way I could tell him I was thinking about that girl.

"I'm not zoning out. I was just thinking about my next course,"

I lied as I stood up from my seat.

"Alright, come on, let's go to the field for a game,"

Fateen said, patting my shoulder.

"You go ahead. I'll catch up," I replied, walking out of the classroom. Without even thinking, my feet led me towards the library.

I never usually even glanced at the library, but this girl had me making countless trips just to catch a glimpse of her face.

I scanned the library, but she wasn't there.

Letting out a deep sigh, I turned and headed for the field, disappointed.

I joined my classmates for a game of football, and that's how the rest of my time passed.

تجھے دیکھنے کی لو اب بھی ہے روشن

پر تو میری اس حالت سے اب بھی ہے انجان-

-The flame to see you burns steady and bright,

Yet you remain unaware of my plight.

* * *

After school, when I arrived home, Baba called me downstairs. I slipped on my t-shirt and made my way to the living room.

"Come, sit here," Baba said softly, gesturing towards a chair. I took my seat and, feeling completely at ease, crossed my legs on the tea table before me.

"I need to talk to you about something important, and I hope you'll listen calmly and understand," Baba spoke gently.

No matter how softly he spoke, he wouldn't be able to convince me.

"Go ahead, I'm listening, but I can't guarantee I'll meet your expectations." I replied while grabbing an apple from the fruit bowl in front of me and taking a bite.

"Listen, Ilham, I want you to take up a course in Business Management and take over my business. Life will be easier; everything is already established." Baba spoke to me gently for the first time, but even with that softness, his request was something I couldn't accept.

"Exactly, Baba! That's what I've been trying to explain to all of you. I don't want to manage an already set-up business. I want to build my own name, to achieve something on my own terms. My only goal is to become a lawyer, and I will pursue that dream no matter what."

I responded, taking another bite of the apple.

"I said you will study Business Management, and that's final!" Baba snapped, slamming his hand down on the table in anger.

"And I said I will only pursue Law!" I retorted, mimicking his gesture by slamming my hand down as well.

Baba thinks I'll become a lawyer like Uncle Anwar, who sells his profession for money. But I won't be that kind of lawyer. Baba needs to understand that.

"Fine, do whatever you want, but on one condition. After this year's annual day, you must do something I ask of you. If you do it, I'll accept your decision, and I'll give in to your stubbornness."

Baba said with a stern look. For some reason, I found the whole situation amusing. Whatever the challenge, it didn't faze me. *After all, I'm Ilham—fear is afraid of my name.*

"Alright, but what do I get out of this?" I asked with a sly smile.

"I already told you, if I lose, you'll get whatever you want," Baba said, frowning at me.

"That's your loss if you lose. We still haven't discussed what I'll gain from winning. You've already laid out your side of the wager, but what about mine?" I maintained my smile as I pressed further.

"What do you mean?" Baba asked, clearly confused.

"I mean, if you lose, you'll forfeit your right—that's your loss. But if I win, what do I gain? I need something as a prize for my victory too." I shrugged nonchalantly, keeping my grin intact.

"What do you want? And if you lose, what will you give up?" Baba asked, narrowing his eyes.

"When I win, I'll ask for it then. And Baba, Ilham never loses," I said confidently, standing up to leave.

"Listen, since you're heading out, take these papers to Sarem, will you?" Baba asked, handing me some documents. Just hearing that name irritated me—*I despise her.*

"I'm not going that way." I made up an excuse and walked out of the house.

"He never helps with a single task,"

Baba grumbled, as usual, using the same old line.

"If you already know that, then what's the point of asking?"

I muttered under my breath as I started the bike.

I drove out, relishing the fresh air outside, when my phone rang.

It was Fateen calling.

Fateen: "Ilham, my brother! Congratulations, once again you've come first in the midterms, just like always."

[As if he's telling me something I don't already know.]

Ilham: "I know. Ilham has always been first."

Fateen: "Yeah, but this time… no one's talking about you. Everyone's praising that girl."

Ilham: "What do you mean?"

Fateen: "She missed beating you by just one percentage point, and now, as the new student, she's the talk of the school. Everyone's singing her praises."

Ilham: "But she's still behind me, right? She didn't surpass me… Anyway, I've got to go."

Fateen: "Alright, but you're coming to the Annual Day tomorrow, right?"

Ilham: "Of course. I have to. Hitler won't spare me otherwise."

I hung up the call and took a deep breath, looking up at the sky. She tried to reach my percentage—shouldn't I be annoyed? ~~Why do I feel proud instead?~~ Just then, I got a call from Maryam.

I answered,

Maryam: Hello…, Ilham?

Ilham: "Yes, speaking."

Maryam: "Ilham, I need your math notes. We've just started our 10th standard syllabus. Will you lend them to me?"

Ilham: "Since when do you care about studying?"

Maryam: "Good question… I don't. My friend needs them. Studying isn't really my thing."

Ilham: "Your friend, the one with the hijab?"

Maryam: "You know, I've noticed something strange. Every time her name comes up, it sounds weird coming from your mouth. Do you… like her?"

Ilham: "You're an idiot. I'm just trying to make sure that the person I'm giving my notes to is actually worthy of keeping them."

Maryam: "Yeah, yeah. It's for her, the friend with the hijab."

Ilham: "Why isn't she asking me directly? Why are you asking on her behalf?"

Maryam: "Well, in the heat of the moment, I told her I already had the notes… which I don't. Help me out, Ilham. Please. I said that to impress her and now I need to deliver."

Ilham: "See? I was right. You're an idiot. Fine, come to my class tomorrow and get the notes."

Maryam: "Oh, stop it already! By the way, are you coming to the Annual Day?"

Ilham: "Yeah, I'm coming. Is your friend coming?"

Maryam: "Again her… No, her father is pretty strict. Actually, he's very weird; he doesn't let her go anywhere. She's already said no. Besides, she doesn't like loud parties or crowded places."

Ilham: "But she's getting an award, isn't she?"

Maryam: "Yeah, I asked her the same thing, but she still refused."

Ilham: "Alright, then convince her father to let her come."

Maryam: "And how am I supposed to do that?"

Ilham: "Maryam, for someone who plays innocent so well, you're not as naïve as you pretend to be. The wise only need a hint. Get her to the Annual Day."

I hung up, but for some reason, I couldn't stop thinking about that girl.

Why am I thinking about her so much?

I mean, I haven't even met her yet, but her voice—it brings me such peace. I could listen to her all day, just her.

~~This is all a distraction… I need to stay away from these thoughts. Ilham, focus!~~

تجھ دیکھنے کی جو لو لگی ہے، پتا نہیں کب بجھے گی.....؟
کب تیرے دیدار پر اس دل کو چین کو راحت ملے گی
بنا دیکھے ہی اس قدر لپیٹ میں لیے رکھا ہے تم نے،
اے ظالما، اگر تیرا دیدار ہو جائے
تو پتا نہیں کس مقام پر پہنچا دے گی

-A flame ignited to see your face;
I wonder when this yearning will cease…
When will this restless heart of mine,
Find solace in your sight, in peace?
Without a glance, you've bound me so,
O heartless one, what fate awaits?
If ever your beauty graces my eyes,
Who knows to what heights you'll elevate!

* * *

EPISODE – 6

(Shu…!! Shu..!!)

Time: 8:00 PM -

Day: Saturday

Date: 24th February.

I was getting ready for the annual function.

I slipped into my Hermes white shirt and beige pants, leaving the first two buttons of my shirt casually undone.

After fixing my hair and spraying on my favorite perfume—a gift from Bade Mamu, Tom Ford's "*The Black Orchid*"—I felt the familiar sense of confidence wash over me.

This wasn't just any perfume; its scent was a statement, a brand in itself, much like Ilham. And that's precisely why it's my favorite—I am a brand too.

Admiring my reflection in the mirror, I couldn't help but flex. Handsome and dashing, that's who I am—there's no doubt about it. Yeah, ~~I know I'm self-obsessed.~~ I told you that already.

Grabbing my bike keys and spinning them around my finger, I headed downstairs.

"Mumma, I'm leaving," I called out. Suzy, lost in her tablet, didn't even glance up, so I gave her a light tap on the head as I passed.

"You…" Suzy grumbled, annoyed.

"Say 'I'll be back,' Ilham, and always say 'Fi Amanillah.' And button up those top buttons," Mumma sighed with concern.

I wondered why all these "Mummas" are always so worried. People leave, and they come back. *As for death—it's inevitable for everyone, so what's the point of being so afraid? It's just death.*

"Okay, okay. See you later," I said, walking out the door. Starting my bike, I sped off toward school, enjoying the ride.

The trip was only ten minutes from my house, but I always made it in five. Sure, I didn't need a bike, but nothing beats the thrill of riding one, especially when it's a chance to show off.

"Hey, Ilham, you made it?" Fateen greeted me with a grin as I arrived.

Fateen looked good too today, decked out in a sleek black Versace shirt and matching formal pants.

He'd styled his hair with gel, unlike my artfully tousled look. He was clean-shaven like me and, like me, had his shirt sleeves rolled up to his elbows.

The veins in our hands were a touch of our shared elegance, and the watches on our wrists only added to our charm.

"Can't you see I'm here?" I smirked as we walked toward the auditorium.

When we entered, my eyes caught Farooq deliberately bumping into someone, spilling his deviled eggs all over a girl's red dress or perhaps something else—at least I think it was a dress.

"Are you blind Farooq, God my scarf…!!"

All I could hear with lot' of noise.

The place was too dim to make out much.

Trying to get a closer look, I couldn't see who she was, so I let it go and sat down beside Fateen.

"Man, these juniors really outdid themselves with the decorations," Fateen commented, admiring the lights and décor in the auditorium.

I had to admit, it was impressive.

The place had never looked this good for any of our previous functions.

"Yeah, you're right," I agreed, glancing around.

"And why wouldn't it be? That new girl was the team lead for the event organization,"

Fateen said with a hint of a smile.

A slight grin spread across my face at the mention of that girl.

She's really something. I*f she plans a farewell like this, how will I even leave…?*

Ilham, don't get ahead of yourself—she didn't do this for you.

Stop overreacting.

Shut up, I know…!!

Suddenly, the lights dimmed, leaving only the stage illuminated.

The event was about to begin, and I had to admit, the planning and organization were top-notch.

As I focused on the stage, two girls sat down in front of me. It was still too dark to see clearly, or maybe I just wasn't paying attention. The opening performance began with some students dancing and giving speeches—the usual boring stuff.

And the worst part? The teachers' speeches. Ugh…!

The event had started, but in the middle of this crowd, my eyes were searching for the girl in the hijab.

It wasn't hard to spot her in this sea of students—after all, she was the only one in our school who wore it.

But today, she was nowhere to be found. It seemed like Maryam hadn't succeeded in convincing her father to let her come.

Soon, it was time for the best student awards to be handed out for academic excellence.

"Ladies and gentlemen, it is my great pleasure to invite to the stage the best student and top achiever of this academic year, a consistent performer throughout his entire academic journey—the one and only Ilham Osman Khaan! Let's give him a big round of applause!" the junior anchor announced.

This was the only reason I had come here—to collect my award. Once that was done, I'd say goodbye to 'Hitler' and get out of here. I've never liked these school functions.

I walked up on stage, received my award from my father, and returned to my seat amidst the cheers and whispers of the girls.

Half of them were smitten with me just because I'm the Dean's son, and the rest, well, I didn't have to do anything—they were infatuated nonetheless.

They call me all sorts of names, but the most common one is "Siz… "—anyway, never mind. You'll think I'm bragging again.

As I sat back down, I turned to Fateen.

"Let's go," I said to him, just as the anchor made another announcement.

"We could never have imagined that a new student would arrive like a breath of fresh air and become the second topper and one of the best students of the year. Excelling not only in academics but also as an all-rounder, she has impressed us all with her exceptional behavior. Please join me in welcoming the remarkable Zieba Ansari. Let's give her a big round of applause!"

Hearing this, I started glancing around, and just then, the girl sitting in front of me stood up and began making her way to the stage—

She hasn't veiled herself today...??

And she's been sitting here all this time...??

How did I, Ilham, not notice...??

My eyes were carelessly scanning the crowd as I tried to make sense of why she hadn't covered herself today, but everything seemed to freeze the moment the lights turned towards the stage entrance.

There she was—*Zieba Ansari*—walking forward to accept her award. The stage lights painted her in golden hues, highlighting every delicate feature of her beauty.

Time: 9:38PM

Exact time where I lost myself.

She stood there in a red saree, radiating elegance and grace, her black, slightly brownish waves cascading freely over her shoulders, framing her fair face in a mesmerizing glow.

But what truly captivated me was her smile—a soft, beautiful smile that deepened the solitary dimple on her left cheek as she smiled.

A small, charming mole on her right cheek gave her face a celestial touch, making her look even more breathtaking than the moon itself. She is the very definition of the word *'beautiful.'*

And her black eyes, sharp and piercing, felt like arrows striking straight through my heart.

With every blink of her eyelids, I could feel my heartbeat stutter. Each step Zieba took back to her seat was slow, graceful, and dignified, yet every single step seemed to pull my heartstrings a little tighter—

Ilham, focus...!!!

But I can't man..........

I was lost, completely engrossed in watching her, my breath caught in my throat, utterly entranced by a beauty and unfamiliarity I had never experienced before.

Zieba's light makeup only accentuated her natural beauty, and her presence—simple yet devastatingly alluring—was simply breathtaking.

As soon as she reached her seat and began showing her award to Maryam, carefully adjusting her saree and hair, a pang of strange pain hit me—a slight sting from seeing her act so effortlessly.

Damn, stop smiling, Zieba…!!!

I instinctively started rubbing my chest—The closer she got, the harder it became to tear my eyes away from her.

"I've never felt like this before—not for someone *two years* younger, dammit." I muttered to myself.

This subtle anxiety, the racing heartbeat, the difficulty in breathing—

what is happening to me…?

For the first time in my life, I, Ilham, who never cared for anyone, felt my heart becoming restless.

And it was Zieba—without even knowing it, she had captured my heart in that very moment.

Her beauty, her smile, her entire being—it all culminated into a moment that left Ilham Osman Khaan utterly breathless.

I couldn't even breathe properly, and my heart was aching for a girl I had either met for the first time today or… ~~maybe I had met her somewhere before…?~~

She sat down, and just then, Fateen said, "Let's go." I took a deep breath, finally feeling a slight relief as her face was no longer directly in front of me, easing my sense of helplessness.

"No, I'm not leaving. I'm starting to like it here."

I refused, still looking at *Zieba. Zieba… Just Zieba…..!!*

I kept repeating her name to myself—her name was just as beautiful as she was—~~what are you even saying Ilham…!!~~

"What do you mean you like it here or—is it someone here you're starting to like?" Fateen teased.

"Shut your nonsense, stop ~~disturbing me— disturb~~ me please, Fateen—" I told him as I continued watching Zieba.

My eyes were fixated on her every move as she talked to Maryam.

I didn't want to blink even for a second, absorbing every tiny little detail of her as if someone might steal her away if I blink even for a second.

"She looks like a princess, doesn't she? Are all the girls from Mumbai this beautiful?" Fateen asked, looking at Zieba. And for some reason, I had the sudden urge to pluck his eyes out with which he dared to look at her.

"Eyes down, you're never going to look at her again. And how do you know she's from Mumbai…??"

I asked Fateen, a useless question because as I've said before, he's like our school's CCTV camera—he's always messing things up for everyone.

"This beautiful piece where she manufactured those companies were originally belonged to Mumbai," Fateen joked, laughing. I punched him in the stomach.

"Talk about her with respect," I warned, still keeping my eyes on Zieba—*I couldn't take my eyes off her…!!!*

She started laughing and chatting with Maryam, and with one swift move, she sent my heart into a whirlpool.

She tossed her flowing hair back, the very strands that had fallen in front of her face.

The scent wafting from her hair made me lose my senses, and the familiar fragrance of jasmine was intoxicating.

I closed my eyes—~~they closed on their own~~—and I imagined running my fingers through her soft, wavy locks, feeling her fragrance fill every vein in my body.

Zieba's hair was wavy, naturally brownish-black, untouched by any dye or treatment; her simplicity was the most beautiful thing about her.

Two free strands of her hair framed her face, giving her a delicate look.

She kept trying to push them back, but they seemed stubborn, repeatedly brushing against her cheeks as if they didn't want to leave her face—

It's not their fault; if I were in their place, I'd probably do the same.

I couldn't stop running my fingers through her hair in my mind… - *Are you just as quiet as your silent waves…?*

I wondered as I imagined caressing her soft locks with my fingers.

تیرے دیدار پہ یہ لو بجھنے کی آس تھی

پر یہ کیسی لو ہے جو بجھنے کے بجائے آتش فشاں بنی جا رہی ....؟

کچھ تو بات ہے تیری خاموشی میں جو مجھے متاثر کر رہی

یا پھر تو بات ہی کچھ ایسی ہے جس کی خاموشی بھی متاثر کر رہی

-I sought your sight, wishing this flame would fade,

Yet how curious—this flame blazes fiercer, a volcano in its wake…

There's a mystery in your silence that draws me in,

Or perhaps it's you—so profound, even your quiet stirs within…

Throughout the event, I couldn't take my eyes off her, gently running my fingers through her hair, admiring her. She's pure, inside and out—I'm sure of it. *After all, Ilham has a knack for reading people.*

When the event ended, everyone headed toward the refreshment area, and Zieba went with Maryam.

~~Naturally, I followed.~~ I needed a drink, ~~but more than that, I needed to stay close to her.~~

I stood a few feet away, watching as she began tying her hair up with a band.

Just then, Maryam playfully tugged Zieba's arm, causing the band to slip from her hand. The two of them started making funny faces and snapping pictures together.

She looks adorable when she pouts.

Maryam was also wearing a black saree, her straight, silky brown hair adding to her allure. It was clear Maryam had helped Zieba get ready.

Maryam doesn't wear pardah, and today, Zieba didn't either.

A joint decision, it seems.

She looked beautiful, though.

~~But I must admit, I prefer her in those modest seven veils.~~

"Well, well, why don't you just go ahead and marry her while you're at it…" Fateen teased, snapping me out of my thoughts.

"Shut up,"

I muttered, brushing off his comment, my eyes still fixed on Zieba.

"You don't build a home by just staring, my friend. You've got to lay the bricks yourself. Come on, let's talk to them," Fateen said, pulling me toward Zieba and Maryam.

"So, what do you think—" Zieba stopped mid-sentence as we approached.

"Hello, ladies! I'm Fateen, and this is Ilham. We're your seniors… or rather, your super-seniors," Fateen introduced us, with his typical flair.

"Fateen and Ilham? I already know who you are," Maryam said, rolling her eyes, as if she didn't know we were really here for Zieba.

"And who told you that? We're addressing the new student," I quipped back, though my gaze never left Zieba, who had her head lowered, nervously rubbing her hands together.

She's an introvert, I realized.

For some reason, I find myself drawn to her…

~~What are you even thinking, Ilham? Get a grip.~~

Oh, shut up…!!

My inner voices are busy in fighting with each other where I found myself staring at her.

She looked even more beautiful in that moment of shyness, but I wanted her to look at me, just once—~~and then forever.~~

"So, Miss Zieba, how does it feel to lose to a senior? I heard you worked pretty hard for that defeat," I teased her, hoping to provoke a reaction.

Just as I expected, she snapped her head up, glaring at me with annoyance.

I flashed a small, satisfied smile—my plan was working. *I was proud of myself.*

There was something special about her dark, deep eyes, a light within them that drew me in, like I was a vast, shadowy ocean, and she, a brilliant light outshining the moon. For a brief moment, our eyes met, and time? Time simply stopped.

Fateen gave me a nudge, breaking the spell.

"Are you here to smooth things over, or make them worse?" he muttered, rubbing his temple in exasperation.

"I don't waste my time on attention seekers like you, who are ready to go to them," Zieba shot back, her sharp tone slicing through the moment. *And I liked it.*

No girl has ever spoken to me like that before. And the one I wanted to speak to *gently* was speaking to me *harshly*.

"You're incredibly rude... Is this what your parents taught you?" I said, offering her a teasing smile.

My eyes lingered on the small, charming mole on her cheek that only added to her beauty.

While Zieba and I were locked in this back-and-forth, Fateen and Maryam seemed lost in their own conversation.

I noticed Fateen's growing interest in Maryam—his expression gave him away.

"Yes, and they also taught me that if the need arises, I shouldn't hesitate to slap someone across the face. And you know what? I'm quite fond of slapping people like you, by God." Zieba retorted sharply, her gaze never wavering from mine. *The intensity of her eye contact was damn captivating.*

"Yeah, but even that won't change the fact that you couldn't—won't—ever beat me," I replied, drawing out my final words as I leaned in slightly, my voice low but clear, just enough to provoke her further.

I was enjoying this sharp-tongued banter of hers more than I should have. As long as her biting words didn't turn into actual violence, we'd be fine.

~~Though, even if she did slap me, I think I could take it.~~

"If I need to, I'll show anyone their true place, but sadly for you, Mr. What-so-ever..., you don't even deserve that. You're not even worth my precious time, so why would I waste it on someone like you? That arrogance of yours might take you to your knees, but maybe again back to the tenth grade—oh, wait, would that be your third time around?"

Damn... She left me speechless. Ilham, she just left you speechless, and you love it.

We were engrossed in our conversation when suddenly a group of boys dashed past us, chasing each other. One of them bumped into me, and I nearly lost my balance, almost colliding with Zieba— *At least don't slap me…!!*

But luckily, I caught myself by leaning against the wall, regaining my composure just in time—

There was barely a five-inch gap between us.

Zieba's eyes widened in shock, her breath hitched, and her hands trembled slightly.

"Are—you—okay, Zieba?" I asked softly.

Hesitantly, she pulled a sharp pin from her hair and without thinking, pressed it firmly against my chest, as if trying to push me away with it.

The pain was real, but even that pain felt precious—*precious* enough that ~~I wished the moment would never end.~~

My gaze lingered on her, searching for myself in her eyes, hoping to catch a glimpse of me in them the way I could see her in mine.

Meanwhile, she was busy on inflicting a small wound on my chest, her trembling pink lips trying to form words.

After a long effort, she managed to say just two.

"Shu shu."

"What…?? Shu?"

I asked softly, stepping back, struggling to suppress my laughter.

What did she just say? *Shu*?

Did she think I was some kind of animal?

What on earth? Oh God, why is she being so impossibly cute? Her behavior—seriously—I love it.

"Move, let the air in,"

She said, flipping her hair back in one swift motion. I closed my eyes and took one last breath of the lingering scent of her hair, watching her walk away.

With that, I bent down, picked up the hair band she had dropped earlier, and slid it onto my wrist.

I glanced around for Fateen, but he and Maryam had disappeared. I assumed Zieba was looking for Maryam, too, as she approached from the other side.

"You're not looking for me, are you?" I teased, unable to resist.

"Your face! Have you even looked in the mirror? Why would on Earth I be looking for you?" she snapped, heading toward the auditorium.

What does she mean by that? As if she hadn't noticed how handsome I am—she must not have taken a good look at me yet. Honestly, what's with all this attitude? She would never find a handsome guy like me in whole Hyderabad.

Just then, Fateen and Maryam emerged from the auditorium, walking side by side. Maryam laughed, her voice light as she teased,

"So, are you two done arguing yet?"

"We were starting to wonder if you'd end up killing each other in the middle of all that banter," she added, continuing to poke fun at us.

"Maryam, shut up," I replied, shaking my head at her.

"Oh, excuse me—talk to my friend with respect," Zieba snapped, glaring at me. A smile crept onto my face at her words.

"Ilham and 'respect' don't really go together, Miss," I shot back.

"Looking at you, I'd say you don't even go together in this world, Mister," Zieba quipped, before turning on her heel and walking away with Maryam. *Honestly, she's the first girl who's ever left me speechless.*

Maryam and Zieba headed toward the exit, chatting animatedly as they went. I figured it was time for us to leave too.

"Let's go drifting," I said to Fateen, my spirits high for reasons *I couldn't fully explain. Zieba… She had made me happy, somehow. And when Ilham is happy, the very air around him feels it.*

Fateen nodded and said,

"I'll go gather the others," before disappearing inside again. My eyes drifted back to Zieba and Maryam. They were laughing and chasing each other, their carefree antics bringing a smile to my face.

"What is it about you that makes it impossible to look at anything else?" I muttered to myself, watching her.

Right before they left, Zieba glanced back at me.

I raised my hand and waved.

Her expression changed, and she quickly averted her gaze, turning back toward Maryam.

"Why do you act like that, girl?" I murmured, watching her walk away.

Fateen returned, and soon we were all headed to a deserted road for some bike drifting.

Despite Hyderabad's strict patrols and controlled areas, we always managed to find a time and place to indulge in a bit of rebellion.

This is my favorite kind of entertainment, and doing it in the dead of night only adds to the thrill.

I am Ilham Osman Khan, the ruler of the midnight hour.

When the city sleeps, my drift mates and I take our bikes and cars out onto the deserted streets.

Drifting cars and bikes aren't just a hobby—it's my obsession.

There's always a sly smile on my face, as if I'm staring death in the eyes at every turn and defeating it.

Challenging death—now that's my favorite pastime.

With the engine roaring and the blare of the bike's horn, I feel invincible.

Every drift, every turn brings with it a fresh sensation, like time itself has frozen.

Someone once said, *"India is not for beginners."* It's a place where illegal activities are done out of sheer passion, turned into habits—and I'm one of those people.

You might say, "You're studying law and doing illegal things?" Yes, I am. Like I said, I'm addicted to thrills and adventures, and nothing feels more thrilling or adventurous than bending the rules.

We've got a group—drifters, party-goers, adrenaline junkies—and yes, I dabble in drugs too. In Hyderabad, it's easier to get a plate of Biryani than it is to find drugs, nearly impossible thanks to our strict government.

But, where there's a will, there's always a way.

We're shameless like that.

The entire night was spent indulging in this thrill, and whenever I've had too much to drink or too many drugs, I never go home.

I avoid fighting with my father at all costs, so I usually crash at Fateen's place.

It was 3 a.m. Darkness had stretched across the city, and Fateen brought me to his house. As soon as we arrived, he called his sister.

A moment later, she quietly opened the door.

She was dressed in a plain, soft-gray outfit, a light dupatta draped over her, barefoot with her nails painted in a subtle shade of gray. Her hands were always adorned with henna—a scent that has always bothered me.

Her dark hair was loosely tied back with a clip, and as she adjusted her dupatta, she stepped forward and took hold of my arm to help me walk.

I gently shook off her hand and pulled away—*Don't touch me. I hate it when girls touch me.*

"Shameen, go, I'll handle him," Fateen told her softly.

"Alright, brother. His shirt's soaked; give him one of yours," she said as she walked away.

"Your sister… she's nice, but… tell her… tell her to stay away…" I was trying to speak, but Fateen quickly clamped his hand over my mouth, silencing me.

Once we were in his room, I took off my shirt, and we both crashed. I take drugs, but Fateen doesn't.

He sticks to drinking.

He used to dabble in drugs, but after that one time, when blood poured from my nose uncontrollably because of them, Fateen panicked more than I did. He swore to himself he'd never touch the stuff again.

People say you lose yourself when you're high, but I say they're lying.

I've yet to find a drug that can make me forget.

While everyone else was waking up the next morning, we were still out cold…

"Ilham…………"

آنکھوں کا بند ہونا ایک قدرتی اصول ہے

پر تیرا ان بند آنکھوں کے پیچھے آنا

یہ کون سا اصول ہے……؟؟

-The closing of eyes, a law of the night,

But your presence behind them…

What rule defies this quiet sight?

I was jolted awake by the sound of a voice—

That voice…??

"Zieba…??"

"Zieba's voice…??"

"Yes—it's Zieba's voice—the same one I heard on the street, the one whose eyes had left an impression on me, whose voice had stirred something within me.

Yes, it's all the same—Zieba.

So, it's you… the one who hid her face behind seven layers of veils."

Just then, the call to Fajr prayer echoed in my ears.

I grabbed the pillow from under Fateen's head and pressed it over my ears.

"The mosque is far from here, so why is the sound so loud…? Man, they don't even let me sleep," I muttered, forcing my eyes shut again as I drifted back into sleep.

* * *

EPISODE – 7

(Well, It's Just a QURAN…!!!)

"Ilham…? Wake up,"

"Ilham…"

I was deep in sleep, her hair lightly tickling my face.

I brushed her hair away with my hand and slowly opened my eyes. Standing before me was none other than Shameen.

"Ilham…? Get up. It's been a while, don't you have to go to school?" she asked, stepping back as she looked at me.

I rubbed my eyes, trying to wake up fully.

Shameen stood there in a pink kameez, her damp hair clinging to her shoulders.

The morning sunlight gently illuminated her face, her nose pin glimmering in the soft rays, and her brown eyes were fixed on me with a quiet intensity.

She tucked her hair behind her ear and gave a slight smile, which only made me sigh with irritation. Seeing Shameen standing there like this, without her dupatta, bothered me. If it had been someone else, I wouldn't have cared, but Shameen…

"You need to change this habit of coming in front of me like this, Shameen. Where's your dupatta?"

I asked, keeping my gaze lowered. Fateen was still asleep, completely unaware of anything around him.

"I'm sorry, it won't happen again. I just saw the time and rushed to wake you up, otherwise your Baba might get up,"

Shameen explained, her voice filled with concern.

She was genuinely worried about me.

I got up from the bed and started putting on my shirt, noticing that her eyes hadn't left me-

I was certain she was staring at the tattoo numbers inked across my skin—a story for another time.

"Shameen..."

"I'm awake now. Go. And for God's sake, wear a dupatta next time. You don't appear in front of strange men like this. I really don't like girls who behave like that."

I said this sharply, knowing that Shameen didn't respond well to a gentle tone. She only understood when spoken to firmly.

I grabbed my phone and was about to leave the room when Shameen caught my hand.

"You always see my mistakes, Ilham, but why can't you see that I trust you? That's why I come to you without hesitation, why I come like this only in front of you. I want you to notice me."

Shameen's voice was soft, but her words hit hard.

If she weren't my friend's sister, I wouldn't have tolerated this.

By now, her face would've been unrecognizable.

"Shameen, get a grip. I'm like a brother to you, and you're like a sister to me—"

"And if I really wanted to see you, Shameen, I'd see you through even in seven veils. You wouldn't need to stand here, uncovered, like this." I tried to explain gently, but Shameen was stubborn. Perhaps a harsher tone was necessary.

"Do you not find me beautiful? Or is there something wrong with me…? Ilham, I truly love you. No lies, no deceit." Shameen's words always felt honest, but the truth was, I didn't love her back.

"Shameen kid, you're a good girl, and there's nothing wrong with you… it's me," I tried to explain, but she cut me off before I could finish.

Tears started rolling down her cheeks—I *just can't stand girls who cry over small things. I really hate it.*

The only reason I was tolerating it was because she's my best friend's sister, which makes her like a sister to me too.

Every time I look at Shameen, I'm reminded of Suzy.

"I'll make up for every flaw you have, Ilham, just give me a chance," Shameen sobbed, clutching my hand as she let each tear fall with every word.

I handed her my handkerchief to wipe her tears.

"Shameen, if you continue like this, you'll ruin your life. And… I… I love someone else. I can't betray her." I used this excuse to pull my hand away gently.

"What? Really? But you said you'd never fall in love. How… now?" She wasn't as naive as I sometimes thought.

"Yes, I didn't tell you about her because I didn't want to hurt you. I'm like your brother, Shameen, and I always will be. Okay?"

I said, trying to reason with her, but honestly, if she wasn't Fateen's sister, I wouldn't have been this patient. I would've snapped long ago.

Sighing deeply, I made my way towards home.

As I entered my house, I could hear Baba talking excitedly to someone on the phone—*Not again…!!*

"It's great that you've moved here, Sarem. My lovely daughter told me about it. Yes, I'll come visit when I get some time. You know, after school I have business meetings to attend…"

"Yes, yes, I'll bring the family… and I'll bring Suzy, my dear daughter."

Baba's tone softened when he mentioned her, as he said his goodbyes.

I tried to sneak past him and head upstairs, but of course, he caught me.

"Ilham… come here." —Damn it, here we go…!!

"Yes?" My head was already throbbing from lack of sleep.

"Where were you after the Annual function?" Baba's voice was loud, demanding an answer.

Why is it that he can talk so calmly to everyone else, but when it comes to me, he yells? —That's why I can't stand her.

With her, he's so sweet, but with me? *I hate you, Sarem's daughter…!! I hate you…!!*

"I was out with friends," I replied, rubbing my hand over my tired face.

"And What's this?" Baba pulled out a video clip, clearly showing the stunts I had pulled last night.

"Can't you see?" I responded nonchalantly, not in the mood for this.

"Cut the nonsense and answer me properly!" Baba snapped, his raised voice making my headache worse.

"Yeah, I was driving with my friends. What's the big deal?" I shrugged, indifferent.

"I made a huge mistake by getting you that bike… How many accidents will it take? How many times will you flirt with death?" Baba's voice was strained with frustration, clearly worried about my reckless behavior.

I could tell an 'honor' lecture was coming.

"Well then, don't make the same mistake again," I replied coolly. "And playing with death? That's my hobby—it's not changing anytime soon."

Leaning casually against the wall, I smiled that mischievous smile I knew would irritate him.

Just then, Suzy, watching the video, chimed in,

"Woahh… Super cool, bro… You're looking hot!" I gave my sister a playful wink, and she winked back at me.

Baba, however, scolded Susaina and sent her inside.

"Do you have any regard for your father's honor at all?" Baba asked me, his voice serious.

The constant reminders of being the son of a respectable man and the never-ending comparisons—*I was sick of it.*

"And what exactly happened to your honor in this? Honestly, your honor seems pretty fragile, Baba. You should probably rein it in because it keeps slipping over every little thing, I do…"

I responded; my tone indifferent. Baba's anger escalated, his eyes reddening with fury.

"I've made a decision. You're not studying Law Management anymore, nor are you going abroad. You're becoming just like Anwar—his shadow—and I will not allow that!" Baba said through gritted teeth.

"Well, I've made my decision too," I replied calmly.

"I'll study Law Management, and I'll go abroad to Canada. Ilham doesn't become anyone's shadow; others will want to be mine. Now this conversation is over." I turned to head upstairs when Baba spoke again.

"You've seen Sarem's daughter—"

"If you ever mention that girl's name to me again, you'll regret it, Baba. I'm tired of hearing about how perfect she is. If you like her so much, crown her and make her the queen of this house, but for heaven's sake, leave me out of it!" My voice rose in frustration.

"Watch your mouth!" Baba shouted.

"Who started it?" I shot back, voice louder.

"Now, leave me alone and let me live my life." I turned away, ready to leave. Baba, red with anger, was trembling.

Mumma held his arm, trying to calm him down.

Honestly, if she weren't there, Baba might've hit me for what I just said about his beloved daughter.

"Fine. Live your life however you want," Baba said coldly, "but before you do, you're going to recite the Quran to me from memory. If you do that, I'll agree to everything you want. But remember, you only have two weeks. No more."

With that, Baba pulled out a chair by the dining table, sat down, and began his breakfast. But my mind was stuck on what he had said.

"The Quran? Why do I need to memorize the Quran? What's that going to prove? Is this even a real challenge?" I muttered to myself, feeling an uneasy restlessness.

Not that Ilham was afraid, but something about it felt different.

"Get ready to lose, Baba," I whispered, making my way upstairs when Mumma's voice stopped me.

"Why do you argue with him like this? You know how angry—" Mumma started, but Baba interrupted her.

"Reshma, you don't understand. He doesn't even pray once a day, and when you try to talk to him, he insults everyone like he's better than them. He thinks he owns his life, that he's in control of everything, and the drinking… May Allah forgive him… And did you know he's doing drugs too? I'm worried about him—he's our only son, Reshma. I want him to understand the value of faith, of time. Life can change in an instant, and I don't want to see him condemned for eternity." Baba's words were the same as always.

Ignoring his speech, I headed to my room, freshened up, and got ready for school. But today, something felt different.

I couldn't shake this uneasy feeling.

Baba's words were ringing in my head, louder than ever before.

Usually, I'd let his words go in one ear and out the other.

So why the restlessness now?

I felt even stranger today because Fateen didn't come to school. Normally, I'm not used to him being around, but I don't know why I kept thinking that if he'd been here, maybe his pointless rambling would've distracted me.

Sitting in the corridor near the garden with my law books in hand, I closed my eyes. The headache just wouldn't go away…

"Well, it's just the Quran. I've read so many thick books, how hard can it be to read that too…?"

Just then, the sweetest, most soothing voice reached my ears—Zieba's.

A faint smile spread across my face as soon as I heard her voice, and the restlessness I'd been feeling slowly began to fade.

The creases on my forehead gradually smoothed out as she started talking.

"You know what happened yesterday, Maryam? Tauqeer almost opened my books to start reading them—just imagine! Thank God I got there just in time. Everyone was sitting in the lounge, by God!"

Her words, just like her, were sweet and innocent.

She was scared that she might get caught actually reading those books—

how cute.

I closed my eyes again and just listened to her melodious voice, as if she were giving me some kind of therapy.

"Wow, you've stared death in the face! Congratulations," Maryam joked. Both of them started laughing. Zieba's laugh, though, was controlled. I could tell she wasn't laughing from her heart.

"Yeah, you're right. Oh, do you know what else—?" Zieba was about to say something, but Maryam, the fool, interrupted her.

"You know something, Zieba… I feel like I'm doing something wrong," Maryam whispered, her voice heavy with guilt. "I feel like… I'm drifting away from my Lord. It's like He's upset with me…"

I didn't know what triggered her to think all this, but her words felt like a confession she had been holding in for too long.

Zieba's voice, calm and composed as always.

"That's not true, Maryam," she replied gently.

"We're human. Being flawed is a part of our nature. There isn't a single soul that Allah created who hasn't been trapped in sin at some point in life. What matters is that when you do fall into error, you gather the courage to accept it. And then… you seek protection—from your own self, from your desires—and turn back to your Lord."

I usually zone out when it comes to religious talks. But for some reason, I was really listening to her… *peacefully.*

"I don't know," Maryam said, eyes lowered.

"It just feels like… maybe He won't forgive me…"

And then—within a heartbeat—Zieba's voice rose softly into the silence. Her tone was pure, soothing… almost like a warm breeze after a storm.

She recited something, and it echoed like a balm to the soul: *my soul:*

"قُلْ يَا عِبَادِيَ الَّذِينَ أَسْرَفُوا عَلَىٰ أَنفُسِهِمْ لَا تَقْنَطُوا مِن رَّحْمَةِ اللَّهِ إِنَّ اللَّهَ يَغْفِرُ الذُّنُوبَ جَمِيعًا إِنَّهُ هُوَ الْغَفُورُ الرَّحِيمُ"

"What does it mean...?" Maryam asked before I could. I was equally curious.

Zieba spoke softly.

"It means: *Say, 'O My servants who have transgressed against themselves [by sinning], do not despair of the mercy of Allah. Indeed, Allah forgives all sins. Indeed, it is He who is the Most Forgiving, the Most Merciful.'* Surah Az-Zumar, verse 53."

"Zieba... you recite the Qur'an so beautifully," Maryam said, a sense of awe in her voice. "Do you really know all the translations by heart?"

Zieba chuckled lightly.

"Not the entire Qur'an, no. But the verses that are closest to my heart—the ones I revisit every day, the ones where I find my peace... those, I remember. The rest... I'm trying to learn, slowly."

Of course, I thought to myself. That's so like her. Honestly, I'm impressed she's read so much already.

"InshaAllah, you'll do it." Maryam said with a hopeful smile.

"InshaAllah, I will," Zieba replied.

"Oh, look at this... isn't he riding like a pro? Isn't he hot? Have you seen Ilham? Did you see him?"

Maryam said, showing something on her phone.

I was pretty sure she was deliberately showing our video from last night.

"Hot? That Mr. Attention Seeker? In that half-buttoned shirt?" Zieba started laughing—*what exactly is so funny? And Mr. Attention Seeker? What kind of name is that?*

Zieba laughed harder. "Not hot. He looks like a total wannabe."—

Wannabe?—

Me?—

This girl takes insults to a whole new level.

I lowered my book from my face and cleared my throat.

"Mm-hm. Hello, Miss J3…" I said to Zieba.

Her dark, wide eyes were frozen in shock, staring at me, her breath caught in embarrassment. I gave a slight smile, raised my hand, and waved a 'Hi' at her.

She quickly gathered her books, picked up her bag, and left.

Zieba left.

Maryam started laughing.

I glared at her.

"Why are you looking at me? I was the one who said you were hot, didn't you hear?" Maryam shrugged.

"Yeah, well, change her opinion of me. You're a friend, do something as a friend!" I said to Maryam, but my eyes were still fixed on Zieba.

"Her friend, or yours?" Maryam asked with a stupid expression.

"Her friend—and from today, mine too," I said. She gave me a faint smile.

"Stop smiling," I said to Maryam as I waved goodbye to Zieba, who, in response, playfully gestured as if she was going to punch me. *She always chooses violence when it comes to me.*

"Why don't you handle it yourself? Winning her over is impossible. And me—do I look like I can do it? Look at this innocent face. She's way too stubborn, rude, and sharp," Maryam said, packing up her books.

"That's exactly why I like her so much," I muttered to myself.

"By the way, why didn't your friend come today?"

Maryam asked, her curiosity piqued about Fateen—Fateen, who clearly had a thing for Maryam, and Maryam, for him. *So, she's the junior…*

Fateen has pretty good taste.

Maryam is the nicest girl around, and we've known each other since childhood.

"Fateen's on a date with some girlfriend of his," I lied to Maryam.

Her eyes flared with anger, and she gritted her teeth while staring at her phone.

"Alright, I'm going to class. Bye." She stormed off, heading towards her classroom, and I started laughing—*yeah, I knew I lied, but I wanted to make fun.*

I kept replaying Zieba's voice in my head as I glanced at the hairband, still wrapped around my wrist.

What are you, Miss J3? You're driving me crazy.

"You will recite the Holy Quran by heart…"

"You will recite the Holy Quran by heart…"

I covered my ears as my father's voice echoed in my head—*Oh, shut up… just shut up…*

* * *

EPISODE – 8

(Mr. Attention Seeker—Miss. J3...!!)

I locked myself in my room for the next two weeks, deciding to memorize the Quran.

I've read countless books, and to this day, I can still recall every word of them by heart. So, I have enough confidence in myself to believe I can do this too. The only time I left my room was to get food.

A week later, Fateen started calling me, but I didn't pick up. Then, around 1 a.m., I received a call from his home's landline. Could it be an emergency?

Ilham: "What's wrong, Fateen?"

A girl's voice answered from the other side.

Shameen: "Ilham, it's me, Shameen. Are you okay?"

Ilham: "Forget that. Why are you calling so late? Is there a problem? Is Fateen alright?"

Shameen: "Yes, yes, Alhamdulillah, everything's fine. I was just worried about you. You haven't been to school in a week, and my brother said you're not answering any calls, so I got concerned."

Ilham: "Shameen, I'm fine. I've just been busy, which is why I haven't been to school. Don't worry, kid, now go to sleep—it's pretty late."

Shameen: "Yeah, I'll sleep, but can't you talk to me for a little while?"

Ilham: "Shameen, have you forgotten what I told you?"

Shameen: "Whatever you said, my heart doesn't accept it. I can't forget you, Ilham. Why don't you understand? How can I make you believe in my love?"

Ilham: "Shameen, I'm hanging up now, and it would be best if you don't talk to me again."

Shameen: "You never talk to me anyway, Ilham. Do you really think that by avoiding me, my love will disappear? I've loved you in your absence, through the distance between us."

Ilham: "Shameen, you're too young for love or these foolish things—especially with me? This isn't possible. You're like my sister. You need to learn to respect relationships."

Shameen: "That's a relationship you created, not Allah. My brother is Fateen, and no one else. Ilham, you are my love, and I'm telling the truth. Haven't you ever felt, even once, that my love for you is real?"

Ilham: "No, I haven't. Because I'm in love with someone else. And I could never betray her, nor Fateen. Now, put these foolish ideas out of your mind and go to sleep."

I hung up the call, certain she was crying, but it's better for her to endure the pain now than to suffer later.

It's better to dry the tears now than to face the flood they may bring later.

It's better to heal the wound now than to live with scars that linger in memories.

I just don't understand why Shameen says these things to me. What am I supposed to do with this girl? I can't even tell Fateen, or else it would be too cruel to Shameen.

And I don't want to be the cause of any problems in her life.

If I had any interest in her, it would've been different.

I put my phone on silent and let myself drift off to sleep. And as soon as I closed my eyes, Zieba's face appeared, wrapped in a long white veil. Around her were beautiful, fragrant, multicolored flowers, blooming just like her. She sat by the edge of a lake, inhaling the scent of the flowers, smiling at me. It was hard to tell if I was dreaming or awake…

"Ilham…"

She said my name………

خواب ہے یا حقیقت، چھو کر دیکھ لوں ایک دفعہ؟
یا تیری جستجو میں، کھو کر دیکھ لوں ایک دفعہ؟
چھوڑو یہ افسانہ، جو ہوا تو کیوں خوامخواہ،
لمحوں کی دھند میں تم، کھو جاؤ گی ایک صفحہ۔
افسانہ ہو جو تم، تو گمان بن کے چھپ جاؤ،
یا خوابوں کے قفس میں، خود کو کھو کر مٹ جاؤ۔
نظروں سے تم ہو چھپتی، جیسے ہو رنگ خواب،
قریب آؤ گی جب تم، پھر ہوں گے سب حساب۔
خواب ہے یا حقیقت، چھو کر دیکھ لوں ایک دفعہ؟
دل کہے یہ فریب، یا ہے کوئی سلسلہ محبت کا؟

-Is it a dream or reality? Should I touch, just once, to, see?

Or in seeking you, should I lose myself in mystery?

Forget the tale—if it's true, why linger in despair?

In moments lost, you'll vanish, like a page in air.

If you're but a story, hide as a fleeting disguise,

Or in the cage of dreams, lose yourself, let the self-untie.

You evade my sight, like a hue in a dream,

But when you come close, the truth will gleam.

Is it a dream or reality? Should I touch, just once, to, see?

Is it but a trick of the heart, or love's sweet decree?

Her voice brings me an indescribable peace, and I just want to listen to her every day, every moment.

"Say something, Zieba—even if it's just my name—"

"Ilham…"

She smiled.

Oh—my heart—she smiled.

She looked at me and she smiled, and I smiled back at her, just as vibrant flowers bloom and brighten under the touch of raindrops.

That's exactly how I felt…

I was dreaming, and as I shifted in my sleep, I heard the call to prayer echoing. I pulled the pillow over my head and drifted back to sleep.

* * *

Two weeks had passed, and like always, Ilham would win again.

I put on my school uniform and headed downstairs to the dining room.

In India, parents don't usually get their children's IQ tested.

If they did, they'd know exactly what kind of a person Ilham is. Baba would never have given me such trivial challenges if he truly knew.

As I came down, I overheard Baba and Mumma talking. I took my seat, gently tugged at Suzy's cheek, and gave her a small smile.

That's when Baba broke the silence and turned to me, saying,

"Your two weeks are up. Have you studied? Did you understand the significance of the Quran? Did you grasp what your father was trying to teach you?" he asked, his tone sharp.

"Yes, I've read it," I replied, starting to eat breakfast.

"Are you saying you memorized the entire Quran? Do you think I'm a fool?" Baba questioned, his brows furrowing in disbelief.

"Test me if you want, Mr. Osman," I said confidently, spreading butter on my toast. Baba was taken aback by my confidence, and after a brief pause, he asked,

"Fine, recite verse 63 of Surah Al-A'raf."

Without missing a beat, I recited in one breath, as if I were reading a simple sentence:

أوعجبتم أن جاءكم ذكر من ربكم على رجل منكم لينذركم ولتتقوا ولعلكم ترحمون»

سورة الأعراف))

Mumma and Baba exchanged astonished glances.

"Do you even know what you just recited means?"

Baba asked, looking at me with disbelief. As a Hafiz of the Quran, he knew the meaning behind every word of the holy book.

"Excuse me, but I think you're forgetting something. You only asked me to memorize it, not to understand its meaning. I completed my challenge, and you lost, Mr. Osman. Ilham wins…!"

I said, leaving my toast half-eaten as I stood up from my seat.

"Simply memorizing the Quran doesn't make you a Hafiz, Ilham. You need to understand the meaning behind every word," Baba said, turning around to look at me.

"Again, excuse me, when did I ever say I wanted to become a Hafiz-e-Quran? Not at all interested, Baba. It was just a challenge, and that's the only reason I read that book. Otherwise, I have absolutely no interest in it. And I've already won this challenge. I'm holding my prize in reserve, and when I want it, you'll have to give it to me. Got it?"

I said, locking eyes with Baba, whose gaze at me now seemed as if he was looking at a stranger, not his son.

"What… what is this, Reshma? What kind of child has Allah given us…? Did I commit some sin to deserve this punishment in the form of such a worthless son…?"

Baba lamented to Mumma, starting his melodrama all over again.

I shook off his words and headed to school, ignoring the commotion behind me.

* * *

As soon as I reached school, Fateen came up from behind, placing his hand on my shoulder and asking,

"What happened to you? Why haven't you been to school for two weeks? I called you so many times, and I even came to your house."

"It's nothing, I just had some things to take care of," I replied, brushing off his concern and chewing gum casually.

"Alright, fine," Fateen responded, knowing that even if he insisted, I wouldn't tell him anything.

Just then, I saw Zieba walking down the corridor. A faint smile appeared on my face—a*ctually, it wasn't faint, it was a pretty big smile. After all, I was seeing her after two weeks.*

I removed my glasses, waved my hand in the air, and said, "Hi," not just waving this time, but also giving a playful wink.

Zieba was startled, glanced at me, and then quickly covered her mouth with her hand, embarrassed, as she walked away.

She's really something. I quite like how flustered she gets.

"She's never going to fall for you," Fateen commented as we walked toward the classroom.

"What do you mean?" I asked, surprised.

"She's not into you, brother. She's into Farooq." Fateen's words ignited an unfamiliar fire in my chest, a burning sensation I had never felt before.

"What do you mean she's into Farooq? And who told you this?" I asked, growing serious.

"I don't know, but the whole school is talking about it. They're saying Farooq proposed to her on Annual Day, and she might have said yes… maybe," Fateen said softly, but those words felt like sharp nails piercing my heart.

Without responding further, I sat down, my mind racing with thoughts about Zieba and Farooq.

No, Miss J3, you can't do this. ~~*I won't let this happen.*~~

I couldn't focus in class. My mind was elsewhere, so I made an excuse and left. Wandering the corridor, the fresh air helped a little, but I couldn't shake the thought that Zieba's standards were so low. *—Farooq… seriously? She doesn't even have the bare minimum standard for herself.*

Still consumed by these thoughts, I ended up in the library.

After some time, it was break, and as always, Zieba entered the library with Maryam.

Just then, Farooq called her, and the two of them were laughing and talking*—she's never smiled like that with me, so why with him? She's never even spoken to me properly, and here she is laughing with him?*

They sat in their usual spot, Zieba opening her books and starting to read. I couldn't take my eyes off her, staring without blinking.

A smirk spread across my face.

After a while, Zieba seemed to feel my gaze on her. She closed her book, rested her elbows on the table, leaned toward me, and said in a low voice,

"People come here to study, Mr. Attention Seeker. The attention you're looking for won't be found here. It would be better if you leave." Zieba's voice was calm but firm, as we were in the library.

"I didn't come here seeking attention, Miss J3," I replied, leaning back in my chair, crossing my arms, and locking eyes with her.

"Then why are you here, and why are you staring at me like that?" she asked, her gaze steady, not blinking for even a second. *Stop looking at me like that, girl…* ~~I'm loving it.~~

"I was just surprised to see that someone who speaks so eloquently and sensibly is also interested in this kind of stuff. I didn't expect that from you, Miss J3," I teased, trying to provoke her for an answer.

"Interested in what? What are you trying to say? And for your information, Zieba is never what you or anyone expects—she's always the unexpected," Zieba responded with energy, her voice sharp.

-Yeah, go ahead, keep giving these dramatic lines while I'm sitting here, burning inside.

"So, you can play the game too, huh? You're even sharper than I thought," I said sarcastically, still feeling uneasy after hearing about Zieba and Farooq.

"Shut up with your nonsense, and if you have something to say, say it straight, or just get lost and stop bothering me," Zieba snapped in irritation.

"Seriously…? Out of all the guys, you chose Farooq…? Do you even know how many girlfriends he's had before you?" I asked, my restlessness spilling over, unable to hold back anymore.

"So what? What do I care about his past? And what's with this 'out of all the guys'—why are you referring to yourself?" Zieba raised her eyebrows, questioning me. But I couldn't get past her casual response—*So what?* Is she for real…?

Agitated by her indifference, I got up from my seat, pushed Maryam aside, and sat next to Zieba.

“Take it easy, you,” Maryam muttered, and I tossed a book in her face. Turning back to Zieba, I pulled her chair closer to me.

“Are you blind or just fed on grass at home? You’re his girlfriend, and you’re saying you don’t care about his past? Can you be real for once?” I leaned in, expressing my frustration.

“What did you just say? Girlfriend? Farooq’s girlfriend? Do you want me to beat you up? You’re the blind one here, and the biggest idiot of all,” Zieba shot back, pointing her finger at me as Maryam burst into laughter. I glared at Maryam, who was trying hard to suppress her giggles.

“It’s not just me, the whole school is saying it…” I said in a calm tone.

“I have no interest in such nonsense, and for the record, I’m not Farooq’s girlfriend, nor anyone else’s,” Zieba declared as she began gathering her books to leave.

“I didn’t tell you to leave yet, sit down,” I said, snatching her books from her.

“And who are you to give me orders? Move, or I’ll slap some sense into you,” Zieba threatened, her eyes filled with a strange mix of anger and annoyance.

“Okay, okay, fine. But why do you smile so much when you talk to him?” I asked softly, trying to smooth things over. She was offended by what I’d said, ~~and I was trying to make it right.~~

“So, if I laugh, it’s love, and if I speak angrily, it’s hate? If I’m annoyed, does that mean I’m going to kill you? Honestly, where were you when common sense was being handed out?” Zieba shot back as she walked out of the library, with me following closely behind like her shadow.

“I’m sure I was following you just like this,” I muttered to myself.

"Why do want to kill me in your love story?" I teased, knowing that with Zieba, you had to provoke her to get a conversation going.

Zieba, clearly exasperated, turned around abruptly, grabbed my collar, and through gritted teeth said,

"Listen, I've already told you I have nothing to do with Farooq. So, it'd be better if you stop with your nonsense… or else…"

She was so close to me, and for the first time, I didn't feel the suffocation I usually felt around other girls. "That was not a smile…, I was not smiling at him…I—I—I was mocking him…!!"

My heart was racing, my breaths were becoming shallow.

Seeing Zieba up close made her even more beautiful.

I hoped I wouldn't die from lack of air.

Zieba, still staring into my eyes, took a deep sigh.

"Fragrance is exotic, right? Do you like it?" I asked in a soft voice.

Zieba kept looking at me, and I smiled as I watched her.

Today, I had used Tom Ford Oud Wood perfume, as I mentioned, I'm a bit of a perfume enthusiast.

The fragrance is a mix of oud, sandalwood, and spices—basically, the best choice for attracting girls.

"Shut up," she snapped, "It'd be better if you stayed out of my way." Zieba released her grip on my collar, ~~much to my disappointment~~—I didn't want to be freed from her hold.

"You pull me so close, then tell me to stay away…?" I whispered.

"What did you say?" Zieba asked sharply. *Why does this girl get so angry?*

"Nothing, Miss J3," I replied, and Zieba began walking toward her class.

"All that aside, just stay away from him, please… it's my personal suggestion. He's not as good as he seems," I advised her gently.

"That sounded more like a request than a suggestion. Fine, I'll stay away from that Farooq kid and from you too,"

Zieba said, nodding slightly.

That's when it hit me—I had just asked her *please.*

Ilham, who never speaks politely to anyone, had just pleaded with this girl.

I started walking alongside her, keeping pace with her steps.

منزل کا کسے ہوش ہے...؟ ساتھ میرے جب تُم ہو، جانا

قدم سے قدم تو مل گئے...، اب دل سے دل کب ملاؤگے، جانا...؟

لفظوں میں ہے شعر و سخن، پر دل کی آرزو کیا ہے جانا...؟

وہ آرزو جو چھپی ہے، اس کا پتا بتا دے جانا

منزل کا کسے ہوش ہے؟ ہمسفر میرا جب تُم ہو، جانا

راہِ حیات گلزار ہے، جب سایہ تیرا ہے،

سایہ بھی تیرا کافی، کیونکہ یہ دل تو بس تیرا ہے، جانا۔

-Who cares for the destination…?

When you're by my side, my love!

Our steps have aligned,

but when will our hearts unite, my love?

My words may weave poetry,

but what does the heart truly desire, my love?

Tell me of that hidden longing,

unveil its secret, my love.

Who cares for the destination?

When you are my companion, my love!

The path of life blossoms like a garden,

as long as your shadow is with me, my love.

Even your shadow is enough,

because this heart belongs to you alone, my love!

"Why will you avoid me…? What did I do wrong…?" I asked, but Zieba remained silent, walking ahead of me. I followed her closely.

"Stop following me…" Zieba said, growing irritated.

"Why shouldn't I…?" I teased her further.

"I don't like it when you follow me like this," she replied, visibly annoyed.

"Well, I enjoy following you…" I responded playfully, continuing to tease her.

"But I don't, and that's what matters," Zieba retorted, her tone firm.

"Maybe you'll start to like it if you give me some attention…" I said, keeping pace with her.

"Mr. Attention Seeker, enough, or I'll punch you…" Zieba warned, and she wasn't wrong—I did seek her attention.

Why? I wasn't sure, but I did.

"I wouldn't mind getting hit by you, Miss J3," I continued teasing her in a softer tone.

Zieba didn't respond. We kept walking side by side down the corridor.

"Is that a letter in your book…?" I asked, noticing something, and Zieba quickly hid her book.

Without replying, Zieba walked away, but before entering the classroom, she glanced back at me.

I gave her a playful wink, and she shook her head in exasperation before disappearing into the room.

I started laughing, and suddenly, all the restlessness in my heart faded away. I felt happy, truly happy.

I glanced down at the hairband I wore on my wrist, thinking back to my conversation with Zieba and how close she had been... That moment stayed with me.

"Stop blushing..."

Maryam said, appearing in front of me out of nowhere.

I cleared my throat, trying to compose myself as I looked at her.

"What do you mean, blushing? I'm not blushing,"

I protested, but I could feel she was right.

"Oh, come on, Ilham. Just admit that you—" Maryam started, but I threw a book at her before she could finish.

"Get lost," I told her.

"Mmm-hmmm,"

she teased me as she walked away, and my smile grew even wider.

After a while, I found myself near the storeroom, and suddenly someone grabbed my hand and pulled me inside, locking the door behind us. She started moving toward me.

"Shameen...? What's going on? Why did you drag me in here like this?"

I asked, my voice serious.

Shameen was definitely crossing the line.

"I just wanted to see you. It's been two weeks since I last saw you," she said, stepping closer to me.

"Shameen, if someone sees us like this, it'll ruin your reputation… and I don't want that to happen, kid," I tried reasoning with her, but she was stubborn.

"You understand everything, Ilham, but why don't you understand my feelings?" she said, suddenly pressing herself against my chest.

"Shameen, back off."

I tried to free myself from her grip, but she wouldn't let go.

"You foolish girl, let go—"

I yelled, pushing her away with all my strength, and slapped her hard across the face.

She started crying.

It was a strong slap—perhaps no one had ever hit her like that before.

"I'm not sorry, Shameen, because this slap will remind you of the huge mistake you've made,"

I said, my tone harsh. I was furious at her ridiculous behaviour.

"I'll endure a thousand slaps from you, Ilham," Shameen said, holding her cheek, her gaze lowered.

She was clearly in pain from the slap, but she deserved it.

Not just one, but many more.

And now I realized she had lost her senses.

I guided her to sit down on a nearby chair, and she obeyed. I handed her my handkerchief and tried to reason with her.

"Look, Shameen, you say you love me, right? Then you should understand what the person I love means to me. If your love is true, it doesn't mean I should betray my own love. I'm loyal to her,"

I explained, trying to keep my tone as gentle as possible.

Shameen looked at me with uncertainty but nodded after a moment.

"Do you really love her…? Am I not as beautiful as she is?" Shameen asked innocently. But this wasn't about beauty.

Even, if it were about beauty, I would never able to like someone ~~except Zieba.~~

"Love may be beautiful, but it's never about beauty, Shameen. Love is a feeling, and a feeling can only be felt," I told her, sitting right in front of her. She nodded at my every word.

"Did you feel that love for her…?"

Shameen asked, wiping her tears with the back of her hand.

I gave a small smile and nodded.

"Yes, I did," I lied. I didn't love anyone. And perhaps I never would. If I ever do, it will only be for one person—the one who may not be destined for me.

"I'll accept what you've said, but I need you to listen to me carefully, too. After today, I will neither speak of my love for you again, nor come near you. I'm ashamed of my actions and I sincerely apologize."

"But you cannot take away my right to love you. I loved you in your absence for so long, and perhaps I will continue to love you for the rest of my life. But I also respect your love. I'll wait for the day, Ilham, when you yourself will say that Shameen loved me so deeply, so selflessly, that she didn't even care for her own life…"

With those words, Shameen respectfully kissed my hands for the last time, placed them against her forehead, opened the door, and left.

"What have I done to make her love me like this?" I began to question myself, running a hand over my face.

As I stepped out of the storeroom, I crossed paths with my cousin, Saniya, my aunt's daughter.

"Ilham, you and—" She glanced at Shameen as she walked away, her question hanging in the air.

"Mind your own business," I replied sharply, heading toward my class.

"Where were you?"

Fateen asked in a low voice, just as our last class was about to begin.

"I was just wandering around,"

I replied, flipping through my books.

"You skipped all the other classes today. This is the only one left,"

Fateen said, handing me his notes while keeping an eye on the blackboard. I wondered why he didn't come looking for me, spending his time instead taking notes for me.

I smiled faintly as I took the notes, but that smile faded when I looked closely at what he had written. My head started spinning.

"Seriously, man, it would've been better if you hadn't taken notes at all," I said, laughing.

"Kindness is a thankless job," Fateen muttered, taking his book back.

"No one wants that kind of kindness, least of all me," I teased him.

We spent the rest of the class just like that, joking and laughing with each other. By the time school was over, we set off for home.

"Do you even know what that verse means?... Not again..."

I shook my head in frustration and took a deep breath, but I couldn't shake off what Baba had said.

I pulled a small packet of white powder from my pocket, inhaling it through my nose, and suddenly, everything became quiet. Baba's whispers faded, the world around me dimmed, and for a moment, time itself seemed to stop. The entire world was silent, and I felt a strange sense of relief coursing through my veins.

But then the same question arose once more—

What is the purpose of a heart that yearns, if all desires end in emptiness?

* * *

EPISODE – 9

(The Slap....!!)

We all gathered near the dining table for dinner.

It was a tradition in the Khaan family that everyone ate together.

Suzy was engrossed in her phone.

"Put your phone down and eat, Suzy,"

Baba said firmly. Susaina set her phone aside and started eating.

"Ilham, listen to me. Alright, I'm fine with whatever you want to do with your life, but just reassure me of one thing—that you won't get involved in anything forbidden. No drugs, no intoxication, and… I fear you might start taking an interest in women there as well,"

Baba said as he served me food.

"Baba, I can take care of myself. Relax," I said as I began eating.

"Yes, you might be able to take care of yourself, but that's not the point I'm making. Do you understand what I'm trying to say?" Baba gently held my hand, his tone softer now.

"Don't worry, Mr. Osman Ahmed Khaan, I won't disappoint you," I replied, focusing on my food.

"A father's concerns will only make sense to you once you become a father yourself," Baba said gently. I laughed.

"I don't even want kids, nor do I intend to get married. I just want to enjoy life—"

"Oh, so you want to live in sinful relationships with women?" Baba said, turning serious.

"I'm not that kind of person," I snapped angrily, taking another bite.

"Then what kind of person are you?"

"I'm not interested in women!" I exclaimed.

"So, are you interested in men…?" Baba's voice faltered in shock. "Oh Allah, Reshma—-"

"Oh, Mr. Osman, stop overreacting. It's nothing like that," I cut him off.

"Then why did you go there if you weren't interested in women?" Baba demanded, his face flushed with anger, mirroring mine.

He wore the same black T-shirt as me.

"I just wanted to see what all the hype was about," I replied.

"That's it? You went just out of curiosity? And you expect me to believe such foolishness?" Baba said, exasperated, taking a deep breath.

"I never asked you to believe me. I don't care what you think, Mr. Osman," I responded coldly, taking another bite.

"You think I don't know what youth is like? I've lived it, Ilham. No one will believe that you're innocent after these actions. I certainly won't," Baba said, his tone biting. Mumma was gently holding his hand, trying to calm him.

"If you ever cared to pay attention to your own son, you might understand him, instead of obsessing over Mr. Sarem's daughter." I retorted in anger.

"How dare you! If you say one more word about my daughter, Ilham, I swear, my hand won't stop at just words. Don't take advantage of my love for you," Baba warned, his anger ruining my mood even more. I pushed my plate away and stood up.

For that girl, you'd raise your hand against me?

The thought made me furious, filled with resentment and anger toward her. I hate Sarem's daughter.

"Finish your food, Ilham. Don't disrespect it. One day, you might find yourself starving for a mere morsel, and food won't be within your reach," Baba warned sternly.

"Oh please..." I was saying he didn't let me finish it.

"Never take Allah's mercy for granted. Be grateful for every morsel you eat, you have, you get — for you never know, tomorrow even a single grain of food might not have your name written on it. It could be right in front of you, yet you wouldn't be able to eat it, because it was never destined for you."

His anger wasn't about me not eating but about what I had said regarding his beloved daughter.

"The world is a big place, Baba. I'll find something to eat. I don't believe in relying on anyone. I have faith in my abilities because Ilham's fate is controlled by Ilham, and no one else," I declared, walking away toward my room.

-They don't let me eat in peace and then say food will elude me. Do they not understand that the world has everything?

Money can buy anything, and I have the capability to earn my own living-

In my room, I sat by my study table, staring at the hairband wrapped around my wrist.

My anger, resentment, and frustration gradually melted away into calm, tenderness, and an odd sense of relief. Deep in thought, Zieba once again crossed my mind.

I couldn't understand why I was so drawn to her, even though she spoke to me so rudely.

Yet, there was something about her words that I liked.

Even her harsh words felt like a sweet punishment to Ilham.

Just looking at her face brought me a strange sense of peace—a peace I couldn't find anywhere else.

Who are you, Miss J3…?

* * *

"Bhai…?? Look at this—bring me these chocolates, please…"

Suzy, sitting on my back, showed me some foreign chocolates on my tablet as I was doing one-arm push ups.

"I'll get them for you when I go abroad," I replied.

"Fifty—" I had completed fifty-one-arm push ups with that little troublemaker perched on my back.

"And you expect me to wait for you to go abroad? No way." Suzy retorted, messing with my hair.

"Yeah…" I answered and continued my push ups.

"Why don't you ask Baba? He can bring them from here…" Suzy was quite fond of chocolates.

Baba always brought them for her, but she had already finished all of them yet she needs more. I wanted to fulfill her wish.

"Alright, go change your clothes, and we'll go out ourselves. On my bike," I said in a calm tone.

"Really…??" Suzy was both surprised and delighted. She had been longing to ride on my bike for a while.

She jumped off and rushed to her room, and I took a moment to stroll around the balcony, enjoying the fresh air.

After a while, I showered and got ready as well, then headed downstairs. Mumma was sitting in the living room, reading the Quran.

"Suzy…?" I called out, but she was nowhere to be seen. I approached Mumma.

"Mumma…?? Where's Suzy?"

I asked. Mumma closed the Quran, touched it gently on her forehead, and set it aside before calling me closer.

When I stepped nearer, she performed a protective prayer over me, as if she were warding off all evil.

"Mumma…?? Where is Suzy?"

I asked again, and she smiled and pointed towards the large glass door in our living room, where my bike was parked.

Suzy had been waiting there for quite some time, looking overjoyed. Just as I was about to leave, Mumma said:

> "By the way, since you're heading out, why don't you drop this off at Uncle Sarem's house? Baba mentioned it."

"Mumma, you know I don't like visiting people's homes, and I especially won't go to theirs. Let Baba drop it off himself. You relax, I'm just taking Suzy out." With that, I headed outside.

"Say 'Fi Amanillah' when you leave, Ilham, and drive carefully," Mumma reminded me. I ignored her words and walked out.

I reached my bike, sat Suzy in front of me, and started it.

Her hair was loose and getting in my eyes, so I put on my goggles and revved the engine, speeding off. Suzy was absolutely thrilled.

Why wouldn't she be? She's my sister, after all.

She shares my passions.

Suzy had a keen interest in paintings, cars, and bikes. Her fascination with bikes and cars matched mine, and one day, I would definitely teach her how to ride.

After a solid twenty-minute ride, we arrived at S-Mart, a supermarket where everything is available.

It was connected to a bookstore and a cinema theatre. I bought Suzy chocolates and ice cream, and she sat on a bench, happily devouring her ice cream, making a mess of her clothes.

"Eat properly, you little troublemaker, and if you mess up my white shirt, I swear I'll throw you in the trash—right where I found you." I pushed her hair back gently.

Suzy, her face covered in ice cream, started teasing me with a mischievous grin.

Just then, I caught sight of someone near the bookstore.

That girl—she looked exactly like Zieba. She wore a black abaya, her face hidden by a niqab, but I recognized her eyes immediately.

Those eyes always had a strange, radiant spark that was unmistakable.

"Miss J3…?? Here…?"

A smile crept onto my face as I watched her browse the books.

فسانوں کی دنیا کافی نہیں تھی...؟

،جو حقیقت بھی اب کہانی سی بننے لگی

،اتفاقاً ملاقاتیں تو فسانوں میں ہوتی ہیں

یہ دنیا کب افسانہ بننے لگی؟

-Was the world of tales not enough,

That reality now feels like a story too?

Chance encounters belong in fables,

Since when did this world turn into a fantasy anew?

"Suzy…? You want books?" I asked her.

"No, I have no interest in becoming a bookworm," Suzy replied, wiping her hands and face with a tissue.

"You should study. Be quite and follow me," I said, dragging her to the bookstore by force.

And as fate would have it, I set out to turn a chance encounter with Zieba from a fantasy into reality, so she could also feel what it's like to meet someone unexpectedly.

We reached the bookstore, and I approached Zieba, calling out to her softly,

"Hello, Miss J3."

Zieba jumped, startled, and dropped all the books in her hands onto the floor, her eyes wide open as if I had caught her doing something wrong.

"Relax, it's me, Miss J3," I said gently. Just then, I noticed someone in a black hoodie, with a cap and mask, walking out of the bookstore. Zieba was watching him leave; he was quite tall.

"Who was that?" I asked, helping her pick up the fallen books.

"Who…? Who was that?" Zieba stammered nervously.

"That one your masked man…," I stated clearly. Zieba stared at me without blinking. ~~Could this be the 'Bade Sahab' she mentioned before?~~

"I… I don't know. I just came to buy books," she said, snatching the books from my hands.

"Then why are you so scared? Is there something wrong, Zieba? Tell me… I'm here for you," I asked, looking at her closely. For a moment, she gazed at me with an unreadable expression.

"Say something…"

"What should I say? You're the kind of person that scares people by sneaking up behind them like that," Zieba replied, heading toward the counter. I glanced at Suzy, who was busy flipping through car magazines.

"I'll pay. Anything else you need? Highlighters? Sticky notes? Tell me, I'll get them for you," I offered gently.

"Why would you pay? I can do it myself. Move aside. And if I asked for the whole bookstore, would you buy it for me?" Zieba snapped, pushing me away. This girl, as frail as she looks, is not as weak as she seems. There's real strength in those delicate bones.

"I would buy it if you asked, but it might take some time. I want to earn enough to give you the whole world," I said quietly. Zieba stared at me, her eyes unwavering—*What are you even saying, Ilham? Shit…!*

"Whatever, I don't need this fake world. Give it to someone else," Zieba replied, diverting her gaze from me. I looked down at her hands resting on the counter, and my eyes lingered there as if mesmerized by the softness and delicate beauty of her skin, glowing in the light. Her hands were smooth and flawless, except for a few scratches, which only added to their charm—some fresh and red, others fading.

Immediately, I knew the culprit—Zieba's cat.

A wave of jealousy surged in my heart, and I silently cursed the cat.

One day, I would get even with it.

Her hands weren't too fragile, nor were they too strong—rather, they were a harmonious blend of grace and beauty.

Her fingers were long, slender, and perfectly proportioned, as if crafted by a master artisan.

Beneath her soft skin, faint veins ran like delicate rivers, giving her hands a true sense of beauty.

As my thoughts wandered, another realization dawned on me—a desire I had never felt before. For the first time in my life, I wanted to hold a girl's hand. And this wasn't just any girl—*this was Zieba.*

In that moment, I couldn't help but think how perfectly those soft hands would fit in mine, as if they were meant to rest in mine not for just once but for eternity. It felt like fate had designed them to come together.

Standing there, I found myself imagining what it would feel like to hold those hands, a connection that could only exist between us.

It wasn't just a fleeting thought—it was becoming a deep, growing need with each passing moment. *I just want to hold her hands.*

"All right, consider it a gift,"

I said, snapping back to reality and insisting gently.

I wanted to give her something, anything, that would make her think of me when she saw it.

"Gifts are given, not something you've already bought for yourself. I came here to replace these books; I've already bought them," Zieba replied, handing her books to the girl at the counter, who wrote the date behind them and scanned them into the system.

"What genre do you like?" I asked her.

"And why do you think, I should tell you?"

"Come on, stop acting so hard to get attention, why are you like this?"

"Good question, actually……." She started saying,

"I didn't get enough food in my childhood, so I learned to survive on attention," Zieba said.

I listened so intently, as if she were saying something profound, but she walked out, leaving me laughing at her words.

And this girl always looks back at me before leaving. I didn't hold back either—I waved goodbye and winked. Zieba made a fist, pretending to punch me, before disappearing into the crowd.

"Come on, troublemaker," I said to Suzy, who grabbed my hand, and we left the bookstore.

I took Suzy home.

She was quite happy today, and so was I…

Of course the reason was her.

* * *

"Bruh, Zieba… we should visit here, what say?" Maryam said, her eyes focused on her phone.

Clearly, these two were plotting to bunk class.

Fateen and I were sitting against the wall in the corridor, leaning on the open lawn area. Across from us were Maryam and Zieba.

"Yeah, absolutely. Wherever you go, I'm with you. Let's go," Zieba replied to Maryam. I had no idea where they were planning to go.

"But Maryam, this seems too low-profile. Look for something else," Zieba added, while Maryam rattled off more options.

"Where do you think they're planning to go, Ilham?"

Fateen asked. Today, both of us were hanging out together in the corridor—*not eavesdropping at all.* They were just talking so loudly that we couldn't help but overhear.

"How should I know? Let's keep listening," I said, and we leaned in to catch more of their conversation.

"Maryam, this still feels pretty low-key. Just imagine, princess, it's us going… You, Maryam Siddiqui, and me, Zieba Ansari. Now, tell me, shouldn't the place match our level?" Zieba said to Maryam, as if they were selecting a destination based on their status.

Fateen and I couldn't help but laugh at their conversation.

"You're right. Wherever we go, it has to live up to our standards," Maryam chimed in. Then, almost immediately, she said, "Look, this place is perfect for us."

"Yeah, absolutely! Maryam, you've hit the mark. This place is ideal. We're definitely going to fit right in there," Zieba agreed, and both of them burst out laughing.

"No doubt about it," Maryam added.

"Where on earth are these two planning to go?" I wondered to myself.

"Alright then, let's go," Maryam said, standing up.

"Yeah, let's,"

Zieba echoed, and the two of them rose to leave. Were they really going somewhere? During school hours? How could they...? I couldn't resist asking.

"Where are you two off to?"

I lowered my head slightly, so they could see me, and Fateen joined in, asking Maryam.

"Yeah, tell us where you're going."

They exchanged a glance and burst out laughing again, though Zieba only offered a faint smile—that adorable dimple forming on her cheek.

"Come on, spill it!" Fateen urged.

My eyes remained locked with Zieba's for a moment longer than I intended. *Look away, Zieba... please.*

"Mental hospital,"

Maryam finally answered, and the two of them walked off, giggling.

I was stunned.

Had they really just been planning to go to a mental hospital?

As Zieba walked away, she glanced back one last time, her soft smile and tender eyes lingering in my mind. I exhaled deeply.

Why do you keep looking at me like that?

"Man, they're really something else... Who plans a trip to a mental hospital like it's some kind of getaway?" Fateen and I shook our heads in disbelief.

"You can never figure out girls,"

We said, laughing as we threw our arms around each other's shoulders, heading back to class.

"Should we follow them?" Fateen asked, grinning.

"Is that even a question?" I responded playfully.

We both laughed and made our way down the corridor.

* * *

"Ilham, turn the music down—it's time for Azaan, and go offer your prayers,"

Mumma said as she walked into my room. I was standing there in just my loose track pants, flexing my biceps and showing off my body to Suzy.

"Suzy... come on, get ready. The Maulvi Sahab is coming to teach you, and you, Ilham, put on some clothes and go pray,"

Mumma insisted, and I let out a frustrated sigh.

"I don't need to—"

"Prayer isn't something you need; it's Fardh for everyone. Everything will be accounted for, Ilham," Mumma said, and I was tired of hearing this same old lecture.

Just then, I got a call from Fateen.

Fateen: "Ilham, let's head to the club."

Ilham: "On my way."

I hung up the phone.

"Where are you going?" Mumma asked.

"I got a call by the club, Mumma," I replied.

"And what about the call to prayer, Ilham? Didn't you hear the Azaan? Go offer your prayers, son," Mumma urged.

"Mumma, don't push me. I don't need any prayers… I need nothing," I said firmly.

"Ya Allah, please guide my child…"

Mumma's face creased with worry. I laughed, kissed her forehead playfully, and said,

"Ameen, Mumma."

I wasn't sure why those words came out of my mouth—it just slipped.

"Ameen. Ameen…"

Mumma echoed softly and left the room, leaving me to my thoughts.

I went to take a shower, got dressed, and headed out to the club.

When we arrived at the club, the atmosphere was mesmerizing. Fateen, as usual, was with the girls, while I, as always, was lost in a haze of drugs and alcohol. Today, I didn't just take the powder through my nose; I tasted it on my tongue as well.

I didn't know why no amount of intoxication seemed to fill the void in my heart.

Why did this emptiness, this agony, never seem to end?

I took one last hit of the powder, inhaling deeply, and leaned back, letting the high wash over me.

"Ilham, why don't you come with us tonight?" Aswad asked, sipping on his drink.

"Where?" I asked, already bored with the conversation.

"To the land of Houris… paradise," Aswad said, laughing loudly.

"I don't have any desire towards Houris," I replied, taking another sip of my beer.

"Why not? I've heard the new stock is really good this time, even some foreign ones…" He tried to persuade me, while the others laughed at his joke.

"It's not about them, Aswad. It's about my desires. I don't have the desire for those girls or any Houris," I said, shutting down the conversation. Aswad didn't push it further and instead offered me another line of powder. I inhaled it deeply, taking another swig of beer.

Just then, a girl with a soft, foreign accent approached me, sitting down next to me.

"Hi, handsome," she said in a sultry voice, reaching for my hand.

"Don't touch me," I said firmly, pulling my hand away.

She had golden hair, cut short, and her eyes were a smoky gray.

Her outfit barely covered her, and most of her body was visible. She wasn't wearing much makeup except for her lipstick and eye shadow.

This girl wasn't Indian—she was a foreigner.

I found myself staring at her to know her, but then I heard a familiar voice.

"Ilham…"

"Ilham…"

Even with the loud music blaring in the background, I could still hear Zieba's voice echoing in my ears.

"Ilham…"

I shook my head, trying to clear it, but her voice grew louder as soon as the girl placed her hand on my thigh, caressing it slowly. I felt an overwhelming sense of suffocation.

It disgusted me so much that I wanted to slap the girl.

"Ilham…"

I suddenly pushed her hand away and stumbled out of the club. The fresh air outside made me feel a little better.

I couldn't believe it—this was the first time I had felt suffocated in a club. How could that even be possible?

"What are you trying to do, Zieba…?

Why are you invading my mind like this?"

I muttered to myself, pacing outside, waiting for Fateen. I guess I'd be staying at his place again tonight.

"Why can't I forget your voice…?"

* * *

Today was the last day of school, and we were all celebrating the "Last Day of School."

There would be no classes today, and no one would stop us. Even if it weren't this occasion not anyone could stop us either…

Everyone was busy taking pictures with each other and writing hidden messages on their shirts.

Fateen's shirt was covered in nothing but girls' phone numbers.

I couldn't bear even a single stain on my white shirt—I always preferred to stay spotless. I called over that bee's nest, Fateen.

"What's up?" Fateen asked.

"I need to take a picture," I said quietly.

"Sure, let's go take one," Fateen replied calmly, pulling out his phone to snap a picture.

"Not with you!" I clarified. "I meant with someone else."

The words weren't quite coming out the way I wanted. I had never taken a picture, and I had certainly never desired to take one with a girl before.

"With who?" Fateen asked, eyeing me.

I didn't answer, instead glancing toward the library.

"Bro, are you out of your mind?" Fateen asked, confused. "If you want to get yourself killed, fine, do with all pleasures. But why drag an innocent one like me into it?"

He grabbed my arm as I began dragging him towards the library.

"What are you talking about?"

"Bro, she doesn't even talk to you, and you want to take a picture with her?" Fateen looked incredulous, trying to free himself from my grip.

"That's why I want to take the picture without her knowing. I'll sit next to her, and you just take the shot at the right moment," I explained, pulling him closer to the library.

"Man, if anything happens, I don't know you, and you don't know me!" Fateen said dramatically but laughed as he followed me reluctantly.

"Nothing will happen, let's go." I dragged him inside the library.

Taking a deep breath, I started looking for Zieba, but she wasn't visible.

"She's not here, let's go," Fateen said, tugging on my sleeve.

Just then, I spotted her, sitting there, smiling while reading a book—*another one of her book boyfriends. Miss J3…? Not fair.*

"There she is," I said, and I grabbed a book, whistling as I casually sat down next to her. I pretended to flip through the pages while Zieba, after a while, bookmarked her page and glanced my way.

"What are you doing here?" Zieba asked, her voice sharp.

I pointed to myself as if to ask, "Me?"

"Yes, you," she emphasized, her tone demanding.

"Nothing, just chilling," I replied, trying to sound casual as I looked at her.

For a moment, I forgot why I was there.

All I saw was the beautiful, rare sight before me. I couldn't help but stare at her.

Zieba waved her hand in front of my face, snapping me out of my daze.

"Get out of here," she ordered like a queen.

"It's the last day, Miss J3, take a good look at me while you can—" I leaned back in my chair, settling into a relaxed position, our gazes locked in an intense moment.

After a brief silence, I finished my words, "Because soon, you'll long to see me again…"

I glanced at her hands. She was wearing a beautiful bracelet on her wrist. Today, she had a black hijab, and her eyes, lined with kohl, looked at me so intensely, it was as if they were wounding me.

"Long to see you? Me?" she mocked with sarcasm. "You're living in dreams, Mr. Attention Seeker." She opened her book again and resumed reading.

"When you do long to see me, that smile of yours will be gone too. But I won't be around to make you laugh. I'll come back, though, to make you smile again," I said, rising to leave. She glanced at me as I turned away, and I winked, waving my hand.

She hid her face behind her book, but after a moment, lowered it slightly to look at me again.

She and her cute tactics —those adorable little gestures—made me smile as I walked away.

I began searching for Fateen, eager to see how the pictures had turned out. Just then, I heard notifications from my phone. Fateen had sent me all the pictures, the candid shots where Zieba and I were smiling softly at each other.

Her smile was mocking, but mine… mine was something else entirely.

"I don't usually like taking pictures, but if the picture is with you, I'd wait forever to take thousands of them. Who says a perfect picture doesn't exist? Whoever says that hasn't seen this one—Miss J3 and Mr. Attention Seeker. Perfect."

I put my phone back into my pocket and turned around, only to find Shameen standing there, watching me.

"Can we… take a picture together?"

Shameen asked hesitantly, her voice trembling slightly.

She hadn't tried to contact me or come near me since that day.

"Alright, just one. Okay? And maintain some distance,"

I said, patting her head lightly. She smiled and began fixing her hair for the picture.

As we were about to take it, Zieba walked out of the library, and my eyes were only on her. Suddenly, Shameen kissed my cheek just as the picture was taken.

Zieba lowered her gaze and walked away.

"What the hell, Shameen?"

I snapped at her, more out of fear of what Zieba might think than anger at her behaviour.

"If I'd asked directly, you would've said no, so I had to do it this way. I apologize for my actions. At least now I have this picture. It's my keepsake—at least in one picture, we're together," she said with a smile and walked off.

I saw a reflection of myself in Shameen—just as I had wanted a picture, she had wanted the same.

But what would Zieba think of me now? That me as well—

Why do I care so much about what she thinks…? Would it even matter to her…?

I ran my hand over my face and took a step back.

From today, her path and mine would diverge. Our journeys were separate now—neither of us would cross the other's path again.

Her destination was different from mine, and our meeting on this journey was impossible.

If our destinations had been the same, things would have been different…!

Zieba is a good girl, but she won't fit in my world.

* * *

While everyone was waiting for the exam results, I, Ilham Osman Khaan, was busy sending an email for admissions to one of Canada's top universities.

I knew that they couldn't possibly overlook my application—my academic record was so impressive that they would read my email and likely offer me a fully-funded scholarship on their own.

And even if that didn't happen, it wouldn't be an issue; I could always go on Baba's money.

In the meantime, I was sitting idly at home, and the more time I spent with nothing to do, the more she, Miss J3, occupied my thoughts.

A pistol lay on the table in front of me, and I absentmindedly spun it with my finger as I contemplated.

"I wonder what she's like. It's been almost four months since I saw or met her."

The thought crossed my mind that maybe I should go near school and meet her.

But then again, the other thought hit me: there's no point getting humiliated for no reason if I went to meet her there.

"Ilham...?"

My classmates called out to me from outside the house. I walked over to the window and replied, "Yeah, what's up?"

"The results are out...," one of them said, and Fateen also showed up at my house—no doubt to tell me about the results as well.

"Is that something he even needs to hear?" Fateen said with a wry smile.

"Yeah, man, just like every time, you're at the top," my classmates informed me about the exam results.

"Come on, let's head out to celebrate...,"

Rehan said, revving his bike's accelerator. I smiled, agreed, and got ready, heading downstairs. My eyes lingered on the pistol as I passed by it.

I was just about to step outside when Baba's voice stopped me.

"What about your results...?? Tell us too." Baba asked about the results as if he didn't already know that his son had topped at his own school.

"What's there to tell...?" I replied.

"What do you mean, 'what's there to tell'...?" Baba asked, frowning and giving me a stern look. Mumma was helping him with his suit and tie.

"Don't look at me like that—you might start liking me..." I said jokingly with a small smile. Suzy chuckled from behind Baba.

"Stop talking nonsense and say clearly," Baba said, his tone serious.

"Clearly...," I responded, laughing, and Susaina burst out laughing even louder from behind Baba.

"Wow, that was a good one, bhai———"

"This boy is becoming more and more insolent! Donkey's child..." Baba slapped his forehead in frustration. Mumma gently held his hand to stop him, and Baba kissed her hand in return.

Mumma lowered her gaze shyly.

Ah, they both and their 55-year-old romance—my Baba is quite the romantic. I couldn't resist teasing them, wondering if I was adding to the atmosphere or spoiling it.

"One minute, Baba, I *am* your son, right...? So, does that make you a ___...?"

Before I could finish my sentence, Baba was already coming after me to hit me, and I dashed outside.

Despite his age, Baba still had the strength and vitality of his youth.

I headed to the open field near our school with my friends. After spending a good while pulling stunts with our bikes, we sat down and started talking.

We were so engrossed in our antics that we didn't even realize when evening crept in.

"Hey, isn't that your Miss J3?" Fateen said, glancing behind me.

Just hearing her name made me whip around, my heart suddenly restless at the mere mention of her, longing to catch a glimpse.

"Shut up. And don't you dare call her Miss J3 again—**that's my right alone**," I said, staring at the hairband I wore around my wrist.

Yet a few moments later, Fateen said again, teasingly,

"Hey, that's Zieba… Ilham…"

"I know… stop messing around with me,"

I started to say, but before I could finish, someone grabbed my shirt from behind, yanked me around, and delivered a sharp slap across my left cheek.

I turned, and there she was—Zieba.

To tell you the truth, I saw stars in broad daylight! She hit me so hard.

Her eyelids were swollen, and her beautiful eyes were red, tears still streaming down her face.

I instinctively reached out to wipe her tears, but she slapped me again, hard.

Before I could say a word, Zieba grabbed my collar, her voice heavy with emotion.

"What do you think of yourself…?" she demanded, her grip tightening as she pulled me closer.

My friends started to move toward us, but I raised my hand, signaling them to stay back. I gave them a nod, and they turned away.

"Who made you cry, Zieba…?"

It was the only question I could ask as I gently wiped away her tears, though she was standing so close to me.

"You…" she said through a sob, and the sound of her soft weeping made my heart stop.

"It's b-because of you. If you hadn't c-come to me that day, none of this would have happened. If you ha-had-hadn't been there, this wouldn't have happened. Why d-d-did you do this to me...? What did I ever do to you?" she said, her voice breaking as she cried. She kept gesturing with her hands, tears spilling down her face as I wiped them away, my fingers barely grazing her skin.

"How could you even think that I could make you cry? I'd rather you slap me again, as many times as you want, with these very hands. Because Ilham Osman Khaan may cry himself, but he will never let Zieba shed a tear...!" I said softly. This conversation was just between the two of us.

Anger and pain twisted inside my chest, both at the same time—anger that someone had made Zieba cry, and I was somehow connected to it, and pain from seeing her precious eyes swollen and red. How long had she been crying? And I wasn't there to wipe away her tears.

"I don't even understand what you're saying. And if you ever show up in front of me again, I'll dig your grave myself. Remember that—I'll kill you," she said, shaking off my hands that had been wiping her relentless tears. She tossed a photograph at my face.

For one last moment, she looked at me through her tear-filled eyes. In that very instant, I felt a strange sensation stir deep in my heart.

Zieba was leaving, and for the first time in my life, someone's tears twisted my soul in a way I had never felt before.

"Maryam...? What's going on? Who made her cry?" I asked, my voice filled with concern.

"Look at this picture and read what's written behind it. Ilham, you have no idea how much she's been crying since morning because of your actions... I really thought you liked her, man. But I was wrong. Someone was right when they said, **'Ilham is loyal to no one.'** You really did her wrong this time," Maryam said, shaking her head in disappointment.

I looked at the picture. It was the one I took with Zieba in the library. Written on the back were the words:

Breaking News: Zieba caught cozying up to the big apple—insiders claim this is how she secures top grades and lives like a princess with her 'Big Catch.'

This was definitely a ploy to harass her, but who would dare pull something like this? Whoever it is, I'll kill that bastard.

"Maryam, I could never do this to Zieba… You know that."

I tried to defend myself, though it stung that Maryam would even consider I was capable of such a thing—yeah, I might do but with her…?? With Zieba…?? I would never…!! **Never Ever!**

"Well then, whoever did it, you better sort them out fast. You have no idea, Ilham, how strict her father is. If this picture reaches him… forget forgiveness; you won't even get a grave of her. She's terrified, Ilham," Maryam said gravely, her voice low with warning.

"I'll fix everything. I'll make sure this gets sorted out. Please, just… just stay with her, okay? Don't let her cry anymore,"

I pleaded with Maryam, hoping she'd stay by Zieba's side.

Maryam nodded and hurried after Zieba. As she left, a wave of guilt and frustration washed over me.

I had never felt this much pain for myself as I did, seeing those tears in Zieba's eyes today.

"Fateen, that picture was only on your phone… How the hell did it get leaked?" I clenched my teeth, anger boiling inside me.

"I took the picture, but I left my phone charging. Besides, I deleted all your pictures with her from my phone,"

Fateen explained, looking genuinely baffled.

"Who else was there?"

I asked, confident that Fateen wouldn't pull off such a low stunt. He may be reckless, but not like this.

"I think Farooq was around," Fateen said, and as soon as his name was mentioned, we exchanged knowing looks.

My fists tightened as I stormed toward my bike, starting it up without a second thought.

"Ilham, wait up!"

Fateen called out. I glared at him, fury in my eyes.

"I mean, I'm coming with you. To save him!" Fateen started his bike and followed behind me as we sped through the streets, leaving the wind in our wake, heading straight for Farooq's house.

Fateen is the one person who stands by my side in every fight, whether it concerns him or not...

Farooq and I have been at odds for years.

The reason? His ex-girlfriends.

Every single one of them was obsessed with me—not that I did anything. I swear. But Farooq thought I seduced them... Now tell me, is being handsome a crime?

That jealousy always festered inside him. He wanted to outdo me academically, but there's no way Ilham Osman Khaan will ever let that happen.

One time, our fight escalated so much that we were both suspended—three months for Farooq, and only one for me.

Perks of being the dean's son. But even that didn't work in my favour because I had to repeat the 10th grade, and Farooq was forced to study with the juniors in 9th. Ever since, neither of us was allowed in each other's classes.

I have no doubt that his latest stunt was seeing my interest in Zieba. He did this just to ruin my image in her eyes.

-Farooq, you have no idea what you've done by making her cry. I swear on God, every tear she shed will be paid for with drops of your blood.

As soon as I reached his house, I began ringing the doorbell incessantly, pressing it without pause until someone came to answer the door.

The neighbours around me had stopped to watch, and after a short while, Farooq's mother opened the door, clearly irritated.

"What's the matter with you? Why are you ringing the bell like this? Has the world come to an end or something?" she snapped.

"Yes, a storm by the name of Ilham has arrived! Where is your failed lab experiment?" I asked through gritted teeth, barely containing my rage.

Just then, Farooq's voice came from inside, "Who is it, Mom?"

The moment I heard his voice, I forcefully shoved the door open and lunged at him like a hungry lion.

I attacked him with such fury that he didn't even have time to comprehend what was happening.

"How dare you bring tears to her eyes?!" I shouted as I landed a solid punch on his nose.

The blow was so strong that his vision blurred, and his labored breathing was a futile attempt to stay conscious.

The storm of my punches continued relentlessly.

Today, I wasn't going to let him walk away alive.

"Stop! Why are you beating my son like this?" Farooq's mother tried to intervene, but neither her pleas nor my own fury could stop my fists.

I hit him so much that I altered the shape of his face, and this wasn't the first time I had done it.

In despair, Farooq's mother cried out to Fateen,

"Are you just here to watch the spectacle?!"

"No, I'm here to save your son's life," Fateen replied as he pulled me back,

"Then save him, For God's sake…!!" his mother shouted,

"Ilham, enough! He must have realized his mistake by now."

Fateen struggled to pull me off Farooq, but I shook his hand away and hissed,

"Tomorrow, you'll go and lower your head in front of her and apologize. You'll tell her that Ilham had nothing to do with this—it was all your doing. And if her name ever crosses your tongue again, I'll cut that tongue of yours." I gripped his jaw tightly, my voice cold and seething with anger.

"If you so much as look at her again, I'll gouge your eyes out. And if you even ever for a moment think about her, I'll fill this skull of yours with bullets," I threatened, pulling out a pistol from my waistband and pressing it to his forehead. I wasn't joking; if he dared repeat his actions, I would kill him without hesitation.

"And when all of this is done, I'll bury you in a place so deep no one will ever find you." With those final words, I let go of his collar and delivered one last punch to his face before stepping away.

His mother was crying uncontrollably.

"One last thing," I said, turning to her.

"Whether you've taught your son to respect women or not is your business. But as far as Zieba Ansari is concerned, you better teach him to respect her, or you'll regret not raising him properly. When your son doesn't even have a grave for his loved ones to read Fatiha at, you'll understand what you've failed to do. And Auntie, remember one thing—Ilham doesn't bluff. I always do what I say."

With that, I wiped the blood from my nose with the back of my hand and walked away.

"What are you all staring at? Get lost!" I barked at the onlookers, brandishing the pistol.

"That's the same Ilham, isn't it? The one who always beats you like a dog?" Farooq's mother asked, turning to him and starting to hit him herself.

Blood was oozing from my knuckles, so I wrapped a handkerchief around them.

I couldn't go home in this condition, so I decided to stay at Fateen's place for the night. We made our way to his house.

"Ilham!"

Razzaq Uncle greeted me with a smile and pulled me into a hug as we entered.

"How are you, son? I heard you topped your exams again this time. Shameen told me."

Shameen rushed over, standing there, looking at me.

"I'm fine, Uncle. And yes, you heard right," I replied, trying to hide my bloodied hands behind my back.

"Well, since you're here, you must stay for dinner," Uncle said as he headed outside.

"I'll be staying here for the night," I responded, and Shameen stepped forward with a smile,

"That's great," Uncle said as he left.

"Shameen, bring dinner up to my room for me and Ilham," Fateen said.

She nodded eagerly and happily headed to the kitchen while we went upstairs to his room. I unwrapped the handkerchief from my hand and placed it on the table.

Just then, my phone rang. It was my father calling.

Mr. Osman: "Where are you? Why haven't you come home yet?"

Ilham: "Oh, I seem to have forgotten the way home. Might take me… the entire night to find it."

Mr. Osman: "Cut the nonsense and tell me where you are. When will you be back?"

Ilham: "Like I said, I forgot the way—so, I will be back by the morning."

Mr. Osman: "You disrespectful donkey! Is that any way to speak to your father?"

Ilham: "You're confusing me again, Baba."

Mr. Osman: "Confusing you? How?"

Ilham: "Yeah, confusing me about whether I'm your son or a donkey's. Or maybe you'd like to clarify if the donkey was—"

Mr. Osman: "Get home, and I'll show you!"

Ilham: "Oh? What will you show me? Something special? Never mind, I'll see it tomorrow. Bye."

Saying this, I hung up the call and collapsed onto Fateen's bed. "You shouldn't have beaten him up so badly, Ilham," Fateen said, resting his hands behind his head.

"All I wanted to do was bury him right there and then," I replied, struggling to control my anger.

"Just pray his family doesn't file a police complaint against us," Fateen said with concern.

I glanced at him, gave a slight smile, and asked, "Why? Are you scared?"

"I lost my fear the day I became friends with a bizarre creature like you," Fateen laughed—Besides, if his sayings become true, even if the police get involved, I'm not worried. My uncle's a lawyer—I can get out of it.

At that moment, there was a gentle knock at the door, and who else could it be but Shameen.

"Come in," Fateen responded, and Shameen entered, carrying our dinner.

Today, she was modestly draped in a dupatta, worn with proper etiquette.

Thank God she finally understood.

Fateen and I sat up, and as I adjusted my shirt, I pulled a chair over and sat down calmly.

Just as we were about to start eating, Fateen got a call. "I'll be back in a bit, you go ahead and eat," he said, stepping out of the room.

"Fateen—" I tried to stop him, but he didn't hear me. I was certain it was a call from some girl—~~most likely Maryam.~~

Shameen's eyes hadn't left me since the moment she walked in.

After her behaviour the other day, I felt an uneasy tension being alone with her, unsure of what she might do next.

I began eating, and Shameen sat down in front of me. Taking my hand, she asked,

"Oh Allah, what happened to your hand? Did you get into a fight, Ilham?"

I pulled my hand away from her grip and said, irritated, "Shameen, don't touch me like that."

"Okay, I won't touch you, but at least let me clean your wound," she said, fetching the medical kit from Fateen's cupboard. Gently, she started to clean my injury.

I could feel the warmth of her tears falling onto my hand, one after the other.

"Why are you crying, kid?" I asked in a softer tone. Despite her stubbornness, Shameen had a good heart and was a virtuous girl.

She had never spoken to another boy the way she did with me, nor had she shared such a bond with anyone else.

"I can't bear to see you in pain, Ilham," she said, placing my hand against her forehead as she continued to cry.

"You're truly crazy, Shameen. These little cuts and bruises happen all the time. Stop crying; I can't stand girls who cry," I said, pulling my hand away from hers. Despite her goodness, being close to her always left me feeling suffocated.

"I can't bear to see even a scratch on you, Ilham. It pains me so much," Shameen said, her tear-filled eyes locked on mine.

"Shameen, listen. You're too young to be having these kinds of conversations," I began, but before I could continue, she cut me off.

"Oh, and Zieba *is* old enough to have these conversations? She's the same age as me, Ilham, so why is there such a difference between us? She only just came into your life, but I've loved you since the first day you became friends with my brother..."

Shameen's voice trembled as she spoke, revealing that she had figured out Zieba was her classmate.

"Never mention Zieba's name again, Shameen. And never speak of this matter again, or you'll face a level of coldness and hatred you're not prepared for. Right now, I'm speaking to you with patience, but that will change. As I said, you will always be a child to me because I have only ever seen you as my sister."

My tone was firm, and she nodded in silent agreement, wiping her tears as she continued to dress my wounds.

She gathered her things and quietly left the room.

I know she'll cry—a lot. Shameen is a good girl, but not in the way I need. In fact, no one really appeals to me… except for Zieba.

After eating a little, I lay down on Fateen's bed, face down, my gaze falling on the hairband wrapped around my wrist—Zieba's hairband. Her tear-streaked face was all I could see. I wanted to see her smile.

I messaged Maryam.

Ilham: Maryam, is she okay now?

It took a while for her to reply, and in the meantime, Fateen returned to the room.

Maryam: Yes, she's fine now. I just got back from her house.

Ilham: You should've stayed over. She would've liked that.

Maryam: Would *she* have liked it, or would *you*? Besides, we don't live the same carefree lives as you boys, Ilham. We can't just do whatever we want.

Ilham: Stop being so dramatic.

Maryam: Wow, so when she's upset, it's pain and suffering, but when it's us, it's just drama? Nice double standard—I'm hurt.

Ilham: Be quiet, I don't care.

Maryam: Ilham, did you tell her?

Ilham: Tell her what?

Maryam: That you love her.

Her message caught me off guard. When did I say I was in love with Zieba? But strangely, reading those words made me feel... something.

Fateen glanced at my phone, and I gave him a shove.

Ilham: Stop talking nonsense. And if you ever bring this up in front of Zieba, I swear I'll rip your tongue out.

Maryam: Dude you really don't know how to talk to girls, do you, Ilham?

Ilham: You're not even a girl to me.

Maryam: Oh? Then what am I?

Ilham: A witch. 😏

Maryam: Is that supposed to be a joke? 😏

Ilham: If it made you laugh, yes. If it made you mad, then consider it a compliment. It's up to you.

Maryam: Huh...

Ilham: Did Zieba say anything?

Maryam: No! And anyway, she's cut off contact with everyone. She's not talking to anyone. You know how she is; she never really talked to people before. And after all these things..., just forget about it... You already know how new students are treated at our school. Even when I try to be nice, she thinks I'm just like the rest of them.

Ilham: Don't leave her alone like that, Maryam. As for the ones who bother her, I'll take care of it. No one will dare mess with her again.

Maryam: She told me she's happiest when she's alone. She doesn't want friends, doesn't want to talk to anyone. She said, "I was fine alone before, and I'm fine alone now."

Ilham: So, she's never going to talk to anyone again?

Maryam: Yep.

Ilham: But don't give up on her, Maryam. Make her realize that not everyone is the same, that you're a good friend, and that I'm not the kind of guy she thinks I am.

Maryam: I can try on my end, but if I mention you, she'll probably kill me! But now I'm sure of one thing—our dear Ilham is finally falling into the trap of **LOVE!**

Ilham: Stop your nonsense, witch.

I tossed my phone aside, but I couldn't help feeling… good. Is this what love feels like?

My thoughts drifted back to Zieba.

Why? ~~Why do I like her so much?~~

Love? ~~What is love?~~

I, who have always been oblivious to the concept of love… could I really fall in love?Is it even possible for me to love someone? Someone why?

~~To love Zieba…? Could it really be possible for Ilham to fall in love with Zieba?~~

* * *

CHAPTER – 10

(Who is She…??? The ONE I Hate or the ONE I Like…??)

The night was pitch dark.

Rain poured like a raging storm, drowning the silence that haunted every street. Soaked to the bone, intoxicated beyond control, I kept walking—alone—on an empty road.

And even in that storm… her face wouldn't leave my mind for a second. She was everywhere.

In every shadow, every breath, every heartbeat—*only her.*

After all that chaos… all those bruises from the fight… I still couldn't clear my head.

The rage boiling in my chest—I had just unleashed it on someone. Probably broke his jaw or his head—*like always.*

You all must be thinking—*this guy's always fighting, always losing it.*

Let me make one thing clear:

'Sometimes it's good to break their skulls and move on proudly.'

That is… if you've got the guts of Ilham Osman Khaan, and Osman Ahmed Khaan standing as your backup.

Otherwise, just back off—like you're already doing.

Still fuming, staggering with every step, I finally reached home. As I pulled out my phone to call Asi Khala, the screen lit up with a message from Baba—flashing bold after several missed calls:

"Ilham, don't come home tonight. Stay where you are—or go to Fateen's."

Great.

My mood is already wrecked, and Baba wants me to *stay away* from my own house?

I ignored it. Obviously. Since when do I *ever* listen to him?

Didn't even bother calling Asi Khala.

I just leaned on the wall and walked right through the lawn, quietly sneaking into the house.

The wet shirt clung to my skin like a curse, irritating the hell out of me—so I ripped it off and walked.

I made my way upstairs.

Something was off. The door to my room—closed. Lights off.

That had *never* happened before. Asi Khala always kept my room open, lights on. Always.

I stood there for a moment, confused.

Then slipped on the floor—the water from my clothes made it slippery. I crashed right into the door with a loud thud. My head hit the wood hard, and for a second, my vision blurred.

Then… the door opened.

And I saw a shadow rise from my bed—scared as hell.

I stood upright, cautiously stepping toward it, tossing my wet shirt near the bed.

The room was too dark to make out who it was, but the silhouette—the long veil trailing down—it was unmistakably a girl.

"Who the hell are you…?!" I snapped.

No answer.

"What the hell are you doing in my room?!"

Still nothing.

"Speak, damn it!" I growled, voice sharp enough to slice through the darkness.

She started sobbing. Trembling.

"Just shut up! STOP crying! If I hear one more sound, I swear I'll strangle you with my own hands! I *hate* it when girls cry."

She moved—tried to leave.

I stepped right in front of her, blocking her path.

"Answer me first. Who. The. Hell. Are. You?"

Still no answer. My fury only escalated.

And then—*lightning* struck somewhere outside. The power went out.

Pitch black.

I couldn't see her, she couldn't see me.

But her presence—so close—I could *feel* her fear, she was shivering.

"Speak, damn you." My voice echoed like an order from hell. She flinched, hands flying to cover her ears.

Scared. Fragile. Probably beautiful—beautiful because I am loving it when she's scared.

I needed to see her face. I *wanted* to see that terror.

She began to sob again—and I… I only made it worse.

"How *dare* you enter my room? Sleep on *my* bed? Huh?!"

I leaned in close, whispering poison.

She covered her face with her dupatta, trying to hide from me… or maybe from the storm outside—or the one *inside* me.

"Who let you in, huh?! Speak up, you—"

I slammed my hand against the cupboard beside us.

She jumped, scared out of her skin.

Tried to say something, but her voice failed her.

"You're Sarem's daughter, aren't you?"

There it was. A flicker of recognition.

"Aha… so *you're* the one."

"Taking over my father wasn't enough for you? Now you've come for my *house*? Tonight, I'll give you a lesson so brutal, you'll never dare even dream of coming back. Not even in your nightmares."

I stepped closer. She stepped back.

Paralyzed in fear.

Didn't I warn—*"I will not spare her. She better not cross my path."*

Well now she wasn't just in my path.

She was in my *house.*

In my *room.*

Alone.

I tried to grab her hand—but instead caught her dupatta. I yanked it—pulling her toward me.

And just then—

She slapped me.

A hard, *real* slap. Like Zieba's.

How DARE she slaps me?

Only Zieba has the right to do that. *Only Zieba.*

But I didn't let go of her dupatta. I pulled her even closer.

"How dare you to slap me, you bloody—"

All I wanted to ask was this but I asked,

"Why are you crying..????" my voice gentle, my right hand gently raised to there where her tears are falling maybe, "Are you scared..?" but before I touch her,

"BABAaaaaaaaaa!!!"

She screamed—put every last drop of energy into that one cry.

I was back in my devilish soul.

"You think he's going to save you?!" I hissed. And I laughed devilishly.

In all that chaos, I hadn't even realized how close we were.

Her hands were on my chest, pushing me back, hitting me with all her delicate strength.

And then—

Two strong arms gripped me from behind and yanked me back.

I fell.

Crashing onto the floor.

"Shameless… disgusting! Get the hell out of here!"

"B-Baba…"

She collapsed into Baba's chest, sobbing uncontrollably.

Her body shook with each breathless cry. Mumma rushed to hold her, to calm her down.

So-called *victim card women.*

I muttered coldly.

"Reshma, take him away right now or I swear I'll forget that he's even Osman's son…"

Baba clenched his teeth in fury, trying to hold himself back. He was burning with rage.

But her tears just wouldn't stop—~~something felt inside me.~~

It was like the more I raised my voice, the more frightened she became. The louder the. crash of things I threw, the tighter she clung to Baba's chest, as if it was the only place she felt safe.

"Do you even remember you have a son?" I snapped, losing all control.

"Ever since *she* arrived, all you care about is making her your daughter."

My voice roared through the room as I smashed everything within my reach.

"Ilham, enough!"

Mumma snapped at me for the *first time in my life*. Her tone struck like thunder.

"When you don't know the about anything! You have no right to speak like that. Get out! Just leave!"

All… because of *her*. This so-called girl.

"Oh please, Mumma," I hissed, sarcasm dripping from every word.

"She's just an attention-seeker. That's all these girls know—cry, weep, turn their tears into sympathy, and manipulate everyone around them. Bloody sympathy gainer."

"Say *one more word* and I'll rip your tongue out myself…"

Baba growled, his voice terrifyingly low.

"Baba… I don't want to stay here anymore," she whispered through her sobs.

"Oh please," I scoffed.

"You don't even *deserve* to stay here. Leave—if you still have any honour left."

"Asiya, take him away," Mumma commanded, her voice trembling in rage.

"My baby, everything is okay, calm down…" he whispered to her,

Baba held the girl close to his chest, gently stroking her back, trying to soothe her pain as she continued to cry.

Asiya Khala grabbed my arm and dragged me out of the room, away from the wreckage I'd caused.

Once outside my room, she took me into her room.

It always happened—whenever it got too late or started raining heavily, Khala never went back home. She stayed here.

I dropped myself on her bed, fuming.

She sat beside me and gently dried my wet hair with her dupatta.

"Why do you hate that poor girl so much, Chhote Khaan Baba?"

She asked softly.

I looked up at her, held her hand, and pulled her close, resting my head in her lap—something she'd taught me as a child, and something I still did whenever my world felt upside down.

"Asi Khala… I hate her. I just hate her…" I whispered.

Her fingers gently moved through my damp hair.

"She's a good girl, Chhote Khaan Baba. May no one ever live the life that poor soul has seen…"

She spoke with such calmness it almost pierced me.

"What do you mean?" I asked, my brows knitting together.

"She looks fragile, yes. But she's braver than most. That tiny little life has seen storms you couldn't even imagine. May Allah ease her fate. Maybe you can't be kind to her… but at least don't hate her."

Khala's voice trembled at the end.

"And how do *you* know so much about her?" I challenged, narrowing my eyes.

"She must have fed you all this crap. Bloody sympathy gainer…"

"No, not her."

Khala said calmly.

"My sister Fauzia works at the place where she lives. She told me everything. That girl barely speaks to anyone. It's like she really is mute…"

That hit me. Hard.

For the first time, I heard more than just her cries. I heard her *story*.

But enough. I didn't want to feel this.

"Whatever. I don't care about her," I muttered.

"Well, that's totally you."

Khala smirked, dropping the line in English.

That pulled a smile from me despite myself.

"You're improving, Khala. Great job."

I teased.

She laughed, and I sat there, beside her, letting the storm inside me settle—for now.

* * *

"Yes, I'm coming. We'll be leaving home in a little while."

Baba was talking to someone on the phone, smiling, and I was sure he was heading to Sarem uncle's house.

The mention of his name only fuelled my growing dislike for his daughter.

Baba maintained a friendship with Sarem uncle that ran deeper than any bond he had ever considered forming with anyone else.

"Reshma, hurry up! They've been waiting for us for a while now," Baba called out to Mumma.

Susaina came running and sat beside me on the couch, while Baba waited for Mumma.

"What is that on your wrist? I've been noticing it for a while now. What's going on?" Baba asked, as I lay on the couch, stomach-down, with Suzy sitting on my back.

"Oh, nothing. Just a little talisman. You know, to ward off the evil eye—too many girls are staring at your son." I replied playfully, and Suzy burst into laughter, playing with my hair. Every time I thought of Zieba, my feelings for her only deepened.

"Alright, Ilham, listen. We're going to Sarem's place, and—" Baba began, but I interrupted him.

"No, I have no interest in visiting your friend's house. You all go ahead. And take this troublemaker with you," I said, pointing to Suzy, who was perched on my back.

"Quiet down. I'm not asking you to come along. You're staying home anyway. I have a parcel coming, and I'll need you to sign for it on my behalf," Baba said, picking Susaina up in his arms as she stuck her tongue out at me, teasing.

"Besides what you have done with my daughter I would never let you go near her, never." He said as if I am dying to go near her.

Mumma had arrived by then, and today she looked exceptionally beautiful, though she always did. But today, she was blooming like a rose in her pink saree.

Mumma's hair reached her knees—I have no idea how she manages such long hair—and she was wearing the diamond necklace Baba had gifted her, adding a touch of elegance to her outfit. Her brown eyes, mysterious and deep, could only be understood by Baba's golden ones.

Mumma was a puzzle that only Osman Ahmed Khaan could solve.

It was no wonder Baba was so obsessed with her.

Both of them were still as beautiful and dashing as they were in their youth.

Baba's tall, commanding presence was always impressive, and his broad shoulders seemed made to embrace Mumma and build a beautiful home together. His smile radiated enough warmth to light up the house, a house that was made even more beautiful by Mumma's presence.

"How do I look?" Mumma asked Baba.

"You look like the wife of Osman Reshma Ateeq Khaan, the queen of beauty,"

Baba said, showering her with compliments as I turned on the music on my phone.

By the way, Ateeq was my maternal grandfather's name, which Baba had proudly added to his own, just as Mumma had added his name to hers. Enough of their admiration now—this was getting boring.

"Guys… please, just go already," I said, watching Baba kiss Mumma's forehead as they headed out the door.

"They say the cheesiest things…" I thought to myself.

I lay back down again, and after a moment, turned on the TV, putting on my favourite movie—Marvel.

"Asi Khala, bring me a glass of apple juice…" I said, while watching TV,

My interest is mostly in action movies. I've never watched a romantic movie in my life, nor do I ever plan to.

Who even likes cheesy romantic stuff? Eww.

"Here, chote khaan baba. Anything else you need..??" Asi Khala asked me softly, I shook my head. She left.

I was watching *Marvel's Endgame* when the doorbell rang just as the best scene was about to start.

I paused the movie and checked the screen. Fateen, Aswad, and Rehan were at the door. I turned on the microphone and told them to come in. "Come on up. Fateen knows the passcode."

The three of them entered.

"What are you all doing here?" I asked, while they calmly made themselves comfortable on the sofa, glancing around.

"Just came to hang out," Fateen replied.

I turned the TV back on, and they all stared at me.

"What?" I asked.

"What are you watching, man? Put something good on," Rehan said.

"What do you mean by 'something good'?" I raised an eyebrow.

"Something that'll set every fibre of being into warmness and which makes the soul crave connection," Aswad and Rehan said in unison, a sly grin spreading across their faces. I knew exactly what they were hinting at.

"I'm not interested in watching that crap. There's nothing in it that's worth all the hype you guys are giving it. Overreaction, I've seen it before,"

I said dismissively while sipping my apple juice.

Fateen reached over and took the last sip from my glass.

"Well, if you don't want to watch, we will,"

Aswad said, laughing along with the others.

I threw the remote at them.

Aswad took the remote and typed in the key panel on the screen, searching for pornographic films.

Within moments, explicit videos were playing on the screen, and they were completely engrossed.

But an unsettling discomfort began to creep up inside me.

My mind wasn't on the screen in front of me but somewhere else, lost in thoughts of Zieba, the picture of her in my mind.

How could I even think about her in this filthy atmosphere?

It felt like a monumental sin.

My heart grew heavy, and my conscience gnawed at me like a termite eating away at my soul.

I couldn't take it anymore.

I shot up from the couch and turned off the TV.

My breaths were labored, my eyes stung with unshed tears, and my chest felt tight.

I touched my face and realized tears were streaming down.

All three of them stared at me in shock.

"What's wrong, Ilham?" Rehan asked softly. "You okay…??"

"Just go. I don't want you guys here,"

I snapped, still feeling the disgust that churned inside me.

I held my head in my hands, trying to understand this strange turmoil.

Aswad, ever the rude one, chuckled and said,

"What's the matter? You weren't thinking about Zieba while watching, were you? I have to admit, she's pretty hot, even with her modesty. If she ever removed the veil…"

He hadn't even finished his sentence when my fist connected with his face. The rage in me flared like wildfire, and I couldn't control myself.

Punch after punch, I didn't stop to count.

Then I grabbed the vase from the nearby table and smashed it over his head.

"What did you say? How dare you, you bastard?"

I snarled, delivering another blow to his already bloodied face.

My voice shook with fury.

Blood dripped from Aswad's mouth, his jaw dislocated, but I didn't stop.

Fateen stood frozen—he knew better than to intervene.

He had seen me in this state before and understood that stepping in would only make things worse.

Rehan had already fled the lounge, running out of fear.

"If you ever dare mention Zieba's name with your filthy mouth again, I swear, I'll kill you," I hissed, my voice barely audible as if even my breath was failing to keep up with my rage.

Aswad collapsed, unconscious, at my feet. I shot Fateen a hard glare and said through gritted teeth,

"Never bring this gutter-born scum to my house again."

My fists were still clenched, my veins pulsing with adrenaline.

Fateen hurriedly dragged Aswad out of my house.

How dare he say something like that about the woman I lo..

The doorbell rang.

"Asi Khala, clean the lounge quickly before Baba arrives," I instructed the woman who worked at our house.

She immediately went to the lounge while I stepped outside to collect Baba's parcel.

After signing for it, I handed it back to the delivery man.

"Are you Osman Ahmed?" the delivery man asked, noticing that I had signed with my father's name—*Baba had instructed me to sign on his behalf, right?*

"Yes—Why? Should I show you my Aadhar card?" I replied. The delivery man laughed and left. I brought the parcel inside and placed it on the tea table.

"Chote Khaan Baba, apply something to your hand, or shall I do it for you?" Asi Khala asked. She always took good care of us at Qasr-e-Shahi Khaan.

"No need, Asi Khala. Your Chote Khaan Baba isn't so weak that these scratches would cause him pain,"

I responded with a light chuckle, just as Baba called me.

Mr. Osman: Ilham, I forgot the chocolates. Bring them to Sarem's house for me…

Ilham: If you don't give their daughter chocolates just once, she won't cause a scene. I'm not heading.

Mr. Osman: Just shut up and bring them, right now. Or tonight, don't even bother staying at home. Actually, I will kick you out for forever!

Ilham: You and your threats of divorce…

Mr. Osman: Shut up and hurry up.

With that, Baba hung up. Frustrated, I exhaled deeply, grabbed the chocolates from the table, and picked up my bike keys.

"Asi Khala, I'm heading out," I called out.

"Yes, Chote Khaan Baba," she replied.

I headed to Sarem Uncle's house, just a few streets away—ours was Street 6, and theirs was Street 7. My plan was simple: drop off the chocolates and return immediately.

"**I hate you**, Sarem's daughter… I'm having to go through this just to fulfil your demands,"

I muttered to myself, still fuming from the events of the day.

There would definitely be some fallout from today's fight, and I knew I would have to face court soon.

Since Aswad's family was involved in politics, it was clear they'd make a big fuss and beg Baba for money.

I reached Sarem Uncle's house in less than five minutes. When I rang the doorbell, I waited impatiently, my anger intensifying with each passing moment. The door opened slowly, and there she stood—a sight that took my breath away.

She was standing there, wrapped in a delicate sky-blue outfit with a modest dupatta gracefully covering her head and figure.

Her black, soft locks framed her face, and on her right cheek was that distinctive mole…

That mole which only enhanced her already captivating beauty.

But it was her eyes—those deep, mysterious black eyes—that seized me entirely.

When her gaze met mine, they widened in surprise, and my own anger began to dissolve. *Zieba—Zieba Ansari*—was standing right in front of me.

"Ilham, you've hated Zieba all these years…?" I thought to myself.

"Sarem Ansari… Sheikh Abdul Sarem Ansari… how did I not realize this before…?"

She stood before me, more beautiful than ever, even in her simple clothes. The hatred I once harboured for her evaporated, replaced with feelings that overwhelmed me—feelings that made me feel elated. High, even.

I couldn't tear my eyes away from her.

My chest tightened, and her beauty left me breathless.

She had always been mesmerizing, but today—today she was something extraordinary.

God—who's she…?? The one I HATE or the one I LIKE…???

Or Both…???

I continued to stare at her, lost in the moment, until she hesitantly approached me, her voice trembling with nervousness,

"What are you… doing… here…?"

Her voice barely registered in my ears as I struggled to regain my composure. I blinked, trying to shake myself back to reality, and after taking a few deep breaths, I finally spoke.

"You…? Here…?"

"Are you some kind of escapee from a mental hospital?"

Zieba asked,

her voice filled with a strange mixture of fear and confusion.

Zieba had always been a bit of a timid girl.

"What do you mean…?" I asked.

"I mean, why are you here…? Don't you feel ashamed, showing up like this at a girl's house in the middle of the night?"

Her eyes kept darting nervously toward the large door, as if she was terrified someone might catch us like this.

I took advantage of the moment and started teasing her more,

"My heart really desired to see a glimpse of yours……"

I said, completing my sentence, "That's why I came here."

"Ya my Allah, help me! If I slap you twice, all your desires will disappear. For Allah's sake, just leave!"

Zieba pleaded, but that's what I liked about her—she always made a request sound like a threat.

"And what if I don't leave…?" I provoked her further, putting emphasis on my last words.

"I'll bury you right here, I'm warning you. I may look innocent, but I'm not. I'm… I'm the bad 'Gundi' type,"

Zieba threatened, pointing her finger at me.

I burst into laughter—there was something about her that made me feel this way every time I saw her or talked to her.

Zieba stood there, unconsciously watching me. When I noticed her gaze, she quickly looked away.

"You don't even seem innocent, Miss J3. I'm good at judging people. And 'bad gundi type'? What is this, your Mumbai? Do you think I'm going to be scared by mere words?"

"Yeah right, such a big Mr. Evaluator of people's character. Now get out of here, or I'll slap you," she warned, but just then, her father appeared at the door.

Zieba's throat went dry, and I could see the fear in her eyes—fear that her father might misunderstand the situation.

"Ilham…? Why are you standing outside, son? Come in,"

Zieba's father said, inviting me in.

I winked at Zieba as I entered the house.

She stood there, frozen in surprise, and after a few moments, she closed the door behind us and then came over to stand near the sofa, just staring at me and her father.

-Miss J3, I know exactly what you're thinking… Me, and him, Osman Uncle's son? I was shocked too. Now it'll be even easier for us to meet… Miss J3.

"How are you, Ilham?"

Uncle asked as he seated me beside him.

My eyes were only on Zieba, who stood behind my father. It's no wonder Baba adored her so much—if life had a soul, it would give itself to her as well.

"I'm well, and you?" I replied with a faint smile.

"Alhamdulillah…"

Uncle responded, glancing at Baba, and they engaged in conversation.

Zieba and I exchanged glances again, and the next moment, she looked away, tucking a strand of hair behind her ear.

"Zieba makes great tea. Zieba, go make some tea," her mother directed her.

Zieba adjusted her dupatta and walked slowly toward the kitchen.

"I'll help Zieba," I offered, looking for an excuse to spend more time with her.

"No, Ilham, sit down. She'll manage on her own," Aunt Sabeera replied softly.

She'll manage, I know that, but all I wanted to talk to her… to spend time with her.

"Yeah, I know she can handle it, but I'll get bored here with all you grown-ups," I said, and without waiting for a response, I began walking toward the kitchen. Baba shot me a confused look, while Suzy and Tauqeer were engrossed in playing video games.

A message from Baba popped up on my phone:

Mr. Osman: Stay away from my daughter… Treat her like your sister.

Ilham: I can make every other girl in the world my sister, but not her. And 'stay away from her…?'—Aah (teasing emojis) Chill, Mr. Osman, nothing will happen the way you're imagining.

Baba probably thought I was going to annoy her, but how could I? I like her!

When I reached the kitchen, she was standing on a small step ladder near the counter, trying to pull something down from the upper cupboard.

"Your dad should've had the cupboards made according to your height…" I teased her,

"You're even shorter than Chutki from Chhota Bheem," I added, trying to provoke her more—she never speaks unless someone pushes her.

"Why are you here? To wash the dishes?" she retorted exactly as I expected, and I gave her a slight smile at her response.

Zieba was taking out a bowl to make tea, and I couldn't help but laugh at her.

"How can someone so tiny talk so—so much?" I asked, leaning against the kitchen counter.

She glanced at me and noticed the bruises on my hand from which blood was trickling out.

"You fought, again?"

She asked without any expression on her face.

"Yes,"

I replied with a smile, and suddenly, the pain from the bruises intensified, as if it was craving for the kind of healing that was standing right in front of me.

"Did you put any medicine on it?" she asked, busy with her task, though her words seemed especially meant for me.

"No."

"Why not?"

"Baba called, so I came here. Anyway, it's hurting a lot…"

I said, pretending to be in pain.

Zieba lowered the flame on the stove and took out a medical kit from the cupboard, placing it in front of me.

"Hmm," she said.

"Hmm? What does that mean?" I asked, hoping she would apply the medicine herself.

"Apply it yourself," she said, looking at me.

"I can't do it with my left hand. Come on, help me out. This poor heart will bless you…"

I said softly, and she smiled as if someone had told her that Ilham needed medicine, but she thought smiling would be a better cure.

She stepped closer, holding my hand through her edge of the veil so that her skin wouldn't touch mine.

My face flushed—*am I blushing…?*

Damn yes you are…!

As I grabbed her wrist through the sleeve with my other hand, she glared at me. She looked so beautiful like that.

"It'll hurt, that's why," I made an excuse.

"I have a better option," she said, handing me a sharp knife—just as I said, she resorts to violence when it comes to me.

I laughed and grabbed the knife as if it were her hand. She looked at me for a moment, then at the knife. The smile remained on my face.

Zieba was applying ointment to my wound, gently rubbing it in and blowing softly over it.

"It will hurt," she asked softly. "It'll sting for a while, but you'll feel better soon, okay?" She said this as she began to release my hand, though my heart whispered for me not to let go of her grip.

"Thank you for being my healer,"

I said, and Zieba stared at me momentarily, unable to control herself, before quickly averting her gaze and turning away.

<u>My cheeks flushed red.</u>

Zieba didn't reply, so I brought up a topic to keep the conversation going.

"I'm sorry… for that night, and for my stupid behavior," I said, voice low, heavy with regret.

"The disgusting behavior," she corrected without missing a beat.

"Yeah… the disgusting behavior," I echoed, swallowing the lump in my throat. "I'm so sorry. I didn't know it was you — that *you* were Zieba. If I had known… I swear, I would've never done that to my —"

"To my…???"

She turned to face me, her eyes sharp, stopping the words dead on my tongue.

"To—to my yeah, to my dad's best friend's daughter… yeah…" I finally said,

"You really didn't know it was me…?" she asked, her voice softer this time, almost fragile.

"I didn't. I promise," I said, desperate for her to believe me.

"So, you would never do that if you knew it was me..??" she asked still looking at me, why she's looking at me with such an intensity?

You are just overreacting Ilham

Oh, Shut up.

"I'd die before ever doing that to you. Ilham was meant to be Zieba's gentleman, not her disgrace. I'm sorry Zieba, I meant it."

She stared at me for a long moment — searching, measuring — and then finally gave a small nod.

And then—

A simple "Hmm.".

Just like that, Zieba slipped back into her silent mode, leaving me standing there, wrestling with all the words I still wanted to say.

"I've resolved the issue. Did he apologize to you?" I asked gently.

Zieba, pouring water into a bowl, glanced my way because the previous water had vanished into the air while she was treating my wound.

Her lips quivered as if she wanted to say something.

I watched her every movement intently.

"Actually, I was going to say…"

Zieba trailed off again, taking a deep breath before continuing.

"Good. Let's hope this never happens again, or else you'll see a side of me you won't like," she threatened me playfully, waving a tea strainer in my direction. I couldn't help but laugh.

This is why she's so special to me. All the sweetness in the world couldn't sway me, but her sharp, blunt words in that harsh tone made me fall for her.

"Hey, what's that supposed to mean? I didn't even do anything, and yet you're always giving me a hard time for no reason. Doesn't it ever cross your mind to speak kindly to me, Zieba?"

I moved closer to her but kept a respectful distance. Zieba gazed at me briefly and then shook her head, responding,

"Kindly? And to you?"

Zieba burst into laughter, but it was a mocking laugh, as if teasing me.

"Why? What's so funny? Don't you ever feel like talking nicely to me?" I asked with curiosity as I watched her busy making tea.

"Answer me," I demanded, grabbing both her arms lightly.

No woman had ever touched me, and I had always guarded myself against such closeness.

But today, this woman had compelled me to reach out and touch her.

~~My eyes searched hers, pleading for her to say just once that she did want to talk to me.~~

"Move aside, I'm making tea," Zieba said, freeing herself from my hold.

"Am I really that bad in your eyes?" I asked, keeping my gaze fixed on her, not understanding why I wanted so badly for her to see me in a good light.

"When did I ever say you're bad? I just don't feel like talking, and when someone doesn't want to, that's reason enough. Simple as that,"

Zieba said it so easily, as if she were swatting away a fly from her tea—only, in this case, the fly was my heart.

"So why is it that your heart doesn't incline towards me the way mine does towards you?" I blurted out, almost involuntarily.

"What did you say? I didn't catch that..." Zieba looked at me confused. Yeah, of course you wouldn't understand.

You read all those cheap romantic novels.

Ugh, she's really getting on my nerves.

"Nothing,"

I said, letting out a deep sigh and leaning back against the kitchen counter.

"Anyway, let's drop it. Imagine if that mistake you made—taking that picture—had reached my father. He would've stopped my education, and a beating would've been a bonus. I don't care about anything or anyone; I love my studies, and—"

She stopped mid-sentence as I stared at her, engrossed in her words.

Zieba couldn't help but look back at me.

"And...?" I smiled as I asked.

"And.......?" She said again, and stopped,

"And............?" I asked again, with a raised brow.

"And..., I have to achieve my goals, no matter what. I can tolerate anything, but I can't bear any interruptions in my studies. Nor can I tolerate any blemishes on my reputation from forbidden relationships. Don't you ever make such a mistake again, or else..." Zieba started threatening me again—for someone who hadn't said much, she has threatened me more times than she has ever spoken to me.

I smiled slightly and replied, "I get that your father is strict, but he wouldn't stop your education over something so small, and who would dare to hurt you? Father's love their daughter's more than a princess."

I answered with a calm tone.

She looked at me with unreadable expressions, which made me think again what I just said, and—

"Hah, like you know everything… Mr. Astrologer," Zieba said, glaring at me as she continued, "What do you even know about a girl's life…?"

Zieba took a deep breath and said, "In our lives, whenever problems arise, there's only one solution: stop her education, beat her, and marry her off to some random idiot. They don't even bother to think whether the girl is actually at fault or not! Like they say—whether the knife falls on the watermelon or the watermelon falls on the knife, the watermelon is the one that gets cut. And here, the watermelon represents our lives as girls—and father's princess are also included."

Zieba spoke soberly, as if she had personally witnessed this happen in her own home. I listened to every word with patience and attention.

"And I don't want any problems in my life. I can't bear the burden of these sinful relationships that would force me to give up my education. And that picture… don't keep it on your phone. Got it?"

She finished her statement with these words, and I grew even more proud of her with every word—she's mature enough—*No doubt why baba likes her more than me.*

I couldn't take my eyes off Zieba.

I was looking at her in a way that made me feel like I wanted to absorb her presence into myself, because I knew that even if I wanted to, I wouldn't be able to meet her once I leave India.

Our destinations are too different, and those with different destinations can never become Mehram on the same journey.

"Mehram," because I didn't want to just make her my girlfriend and diminish her self-respect.

Lost in these thoughts, I kept looking at her, and after a long while, I replied to what she had said,

"From today, no problem will ever touch your life again. That's a promise from Ilham Osman Khaan to Zieba Ansari."

I said to her, but her face remained expressionless, with no visible emotions.

"So, what will you do? Become my bodyguard?" she said with a teasing smile, that cute little dimple of hers appearing on just one cheek was so unique… I took a deep breath and said—*Stop smiling, Zieba…!!*

"If needed, I'll become as strong as the Great Wall of China for you, bodyguard is nothing…!! You are under my protection, Miss Zieba, from now on." I murmured in a voice too low for her to hear.

"What did you say?" she asked.

"Nothing…!!" I said with a light smile, brushing off the question.

-I had never seen a girl so focused and obsessed with her goals before, and at such a young age…? ~~Miss J3, you are totally my type…!!!~~

"Ilham…? What are you thinking…?? She may be your type, but don't forget what Baba said—that you're not even worthy to be the dust on her feet…!!" I said to myself, lost in my thoughts.

"You don't even know if you'll meet her again or not because you're not worthy. Where is she, and where are you…!!"

I kept getting tangled in my thoughts as I continued to look at Zieba, until she broke the silence.

"Isn't this my hairband?"

Zieba came a bit closer and started examining the hairband I was wearing on my wrist. I suddenly tried to hide my hand.

For the first time in my life, I felt so nervous.

"No, no… why… would it…?" I stammered with an awkward smile.

"Why would your hairband be with me?"

I responded, trying to avoid eye contact and clearing my throat while running my fingers through my hair.

"Umm… girlfriend, huh?"

Zieba teased me for the first time with such a soft voice, and my cheeks turned red. I felt embarrassed by her remark.

"No, no girlfriend…!" I kept a smile on my face.

"Then stop blushing, or I'll turn your two red cheeks into ketchup…!!" Zieba threatened with a grin.

"Do you always have to threaten me…? Can't you talk sweetly for once…!!" I said softly, holding the edge of Zieba's dupatta.

For the first time, I had a desire to be close to a girl.

"Do you have a boyfriend?" I asked, just wanting to know what she expected from a partner.

"Why would I have a boyfriend…??"

"Why not…??"

"Shut up…!!"

"Come on, tell me…, not boyfriend maybe a crush—"

"No, and I never will."

"Why…??"

"Good girls don't become someone's girlfriend or see any random guy in the name of crush— I would never risk my eternal Hereafter for fleeting worldly emotions. We girls are 'Malika-e-Islam' and they only look good as wives & as a good muslimah."

Her response raised my respect for her even more and made myself feel even lower in my own eyes.

"So, are you just going to stand there, or are you going to help…? Go over there and bring me the cups and the serving tray. I'll get the snacks ready by then…!!"

Zieba commanded me, and I smiled lightly, nodding my head.

Letting go of her dupatta, I brought her the cups.

"Yes, ma'am." I did exactly as she asked.

She poured the tea into the cups and glanced at me. I gave her a slight smile.

"What are you smiling at? Pick up the tray and follow me,"

Zieba commanded.

She's the only person in this world who can make Ilham dance to her every whim, and Ilham has no problem with that.

"As you say, madam,"

I replied, lifting the tea tray and following her.

When we reached the hall, I placed the tray on the tea table, and Mumma chuckled, saying,

"Well done, Zieba! You've done something remarkable. The boy who never lifted a spoon is now carrying a tea tray for you. I'm impressed."

Mumma said playfully, and everyone burst into laughter.

"Mumma—"

I looked at her, feeling a bit embarrassed, thinking- *This is humiliating.*

"Ilham has been admitted to one of the top universities in Canada!" Baba shared with Uncle Sarem, taking a sip of his tea.

"Oh wow, congratulations!"

Uncle offered his congratulations, and I glanced at Zieba, who was making faces and rolling her eyes— *For God's sake, stop doing that!*

My heart can't take it…! I silently cursed to myself.

"Our kids are really smart! Just look at Zieba. She'll be the next topper in my school, after Ilham. And I'm sure she'll even beat his benchmark,"

Baba said proudly, patting Zieba on the head.

"She has to, there's no choice—" Mr. Sarem said,

"She will Sarem, she's my daughter after all." Baba smiled at Zieba kissing her head, Zieba smiled back at him with a dimple on her cheek.

And to me she rolled her eyes.

And in her usual flair, proudly adjusted her collar.

For the first time in my life, I didn't feel even the slightest twinge of envy.

-The same Ilham who couldn't stand seeing anyone surpass him, the Ilham who had harbored resentment for this girl for years, had today changed one of his core principles—*just for her. Only for her.*

After dinner, just like my father, Zieba's father also needed his nightly tea.

As they sipped their tea, I decided to ask about their personal life.

"So, you're originally from Mumbai?"

I inquired, steering the conversation towards more personal details.

"Yes, my wife and I are from Mumbai. After our wedding, we moved to Hyderabad," Uncle answered, sipping his tea.

"Ah, so you must all speak the local language, Marathi," I said, hoping to learn more about Zieba.

"Yes, we do," he replied.

“And Zieba?” I gave her a teasing smile, eager for more insight.

“No, she doesn’t speak it. We’ve never really spoken to her in that language,” Uncle said, matter-of-factly.

“Oh—what a pity,” I said, dragging the words out dramatically.

“मला मराठी येते, परफेक्ट नाही पण थोडं आहे.....!!”

(Mala Marathi yeti…!!! Perfect nahi pan thoda aahe…)

Zieba suddenly interjected, speaking a sentence in Marathi that left everyone, including me, completely astonished.

I wasn’t entirely sure what she had just said, but I could tell it was Marathi.

“What did you say?”

I asked, still in disbelief, glancing over at her father, who looked even more surprised than I was.

“So, after all Zieba did took after you in some ways,” my father remarked, affectionately patting her on the head. Everyone laughed at his comment.

“Yes, that’s right,” my mother added, smiling.

“Zieba blends in very quickly, doesn’t she?” my mother observed.

“Oh, she blends in so well that she threatens to slap me over the smallest things,” I muttered under my breath.

“Did you say something?” Sarem Uncle asked, glancing in my direction.

“Oh, nothing,” I quickly deflected.

After some time, we all gathered outside to say our goodbyes.

As I stood near the door, my eyes searched for Zieba, but she was nowhere to be seen.

Just then, she appeared with my father’s glasses in hand.

"Uncle, you forgot these… again," she said, playfully pointing out his usual forgetfulness.

"And my sweet girl has brought them back, just like always," my father said fondly.

Zieba reached out to hand him the glasses but then mischievously pulled them back. Holding out her right hand, she asked,

"Where are my chocolates? You get the glasses when I get my chocolates."

I couldn't help but smile at her antics while my father shot me a knowing glance.

"Ilham, where are the chocolates?" he asked, nudging me.

I had hidden the chocolates in the back pocket of my jeans.

"Oh… I think I forgot them," I joked, enjoying the moment.

Zieba narrowed her head, and she lowered her gaze, she's upset.

Agh, she's really trying hard to make me fall for her.

"No worries, Osman. Zieba was just joking around, Zieba give the glasses…," her father said, sternly taking the glasses from her and handing them to my father.

But no one seemed to notice her sudden sadness—except my father.

"I'm sorry, dear. I'll bring the chocolates tomorrow, okay? Now, come on, smile, or I won't leave," my father said, coaxing a small, forced smile from her before kissing her on the head and saying goodbye.

As we headed home, my father looked at me with a serious expression. "You weren't going to stay, so what changed your mind?"

Sometimes Mr. Osman Ahmed Khan proves that he truly is Ilham Osman Khan's father.

"Uncle insisted, so I had to. That's all,"

I replied, shrugging it off.

"Anyway, I've got some work to do. I'll be back in a bit."

"Don't you dare go back to Sarem's house." Baba warned, and I winked at him.

With that, I left the house and headed back to Zieba's.

My eyes searched for her.

"How am I going to give her these chocolates now?"

I asked myself. And as if the universe had conspired to answer my question, I saw her walking on the terrace.

She was gazing up at the sky, where the stars twinkled and the full moon shone brightly.

Zieba looked at the moon as though it were the most precious thing she had ever seen.

And I watched her with the same admiration with which she looked at that moon.

I waved my hand to get her attention, trying to make her look my way.

She responded with a gesture, as if saying, "Why are you here? Go away!"

She was starting to get flustered—*and honestly, she looks even more adorable when she's nervous,* **by God.**

"Come down. I have something to give you," I motioned to her.

I could've texted her, but she didn't have a phone or any other way of communicating.

Maybe there was a landline in her house, but it would likely be in her father's room.

"Get lost! I'm not coming down!" she snapped, turning her back on me in frustration.

Not one to be deterred, I vaulted over the wall of her house and climbed up to the roof.

Seeing me suddenly appear there terrified her, and she immediately stormed over, ready to unleash her anger.

"Oh my Allah! Are you even human? You're like a wild animal! A total Tarzan, you uncivilized… cheapster!" Zieba pointed an accusing finger at me, calling me all kinds of names.

I'd never been given such sweet insults before. Other girls might use different terms, but Zieba's creative ones were far more charming.

"Calm down, calm down, Miss J3," I teased, trying to soothe her.

She was fuming, her face turning red with anger.

I traced my finger lightly over her nose but didn't actually touch her—*if I did, she'd slap me for no reason.*

"Oh my dear Allah, you're going to get me killed one day! What kind of person am I dealing with here?" she groaned, throwing her hands in the air dramatically.

I gently grabbed the cloth of her sleeves and pulled her hands down then placed the chocolates in them.

"I… I brought these for you. I told you to come down, but you didn't. Now calm down,"

I said, leaning against the rooftop wall, crossing my arms casually.

"Why did you bring them?"

She looked at the chocolates, a faint smile playing on her lips, but she quickly regained control, hiding her amusement.

"Because you asked, my lady," I teased her again.

"Don't get too comfortable, okay? And what do you think you are, my personal Zomato delivery guy? Just because I ask for something, you bring it?" Zieba said, accepting the chocolates-*Ah, her heart says yes, but her words say no. Classic Zieba.*

"Well, since you placed the order, I had to deliver it. And for your information, I *am* your personal Zomato delivery guy—available 24/7," I replied, flashing her a playful smile.

I leaned closer to her, bringing my face near hers to get a better look.

-Damn, she's even more beautiful up close…

Today, I realized just how breathtaking an open, blue sky can be. Zieba, standing there in the moonlight, looked absolutely captivating. I couldn't take my eyes off her.

I just kept watching her—her nervous breaths, the way her hair swayed gently in the breeze, how she tucked her loose strands behind her ears with her delicate fingers.

And when she gets flustered, her lips tremble slightly, and her deep, beautiful eyes blink rapidly in anxious little flutters.

She was mesmerizing.

"Did you really bring them just because I asked?" Zieba asked softly, her tone gentler than I'd ever heard before.

It was the first time she had spoken to me like this.

"Say it again," I urged her.

"I said, did you bring them just because I asked?" she repeated, biting down on her lower lip, waiting for my response.

I was starting to fall for her soft voice. As sweet as Zieba's voice was, her gentler tone made it even sweeter.

"Once more," I insisted, teasing her.

"Look, this soft tone doesn't suit you. And you keep asking me to speak gently," she said, her brow furrowing in frustration.

"Get lost already!"

"It doesn't take you long to change your mood, does it, madam?" I said with a laugh.

I had subtly grasped the edge of her dupatta without her noticing—~~I just liked being close to her.~~

"No, it doesn't take long. Now leave before someone comes. Aren't you scared at all?" she snapped, irritated.

"No one's here, and if anyone comes, I'll handle it. Don't worry. I'm Ilham Osman Khan. Even fear itself is afraid when it hears my name," I said confidently.

"You're not fearless, but so shameless," she muttered, glaring at me.

Even her glares were endearing.

"Aaaaa….!! If I get an award for being shameless after fulfilling your requests, then so be it—I'll proudly take it," I replied with a slight smile.

"Oh really? And what if I request blueberry ice cream right now? Will you bring it like a shameless person, just to get your award?"

Zieba asked with a mischievous smile, challenging me.

"I will, madam. I'll bring it and claim my shamelessness award. Do you want ice cream, hmm?" I asked earnestly, ready to fulfil her every request without hesitation.

"No, you're already shameless enough—no need to prove it further," Zieba said, shaking her head.

Just then, I heard Zieba's mother, Sabeera Aunty, calling for her from below. Zieba panicked, her eyes darting around.

"Hurry up and leave! If my mother sees you here, I'll be dead! And if my father sees you, he'll think that we're..." Her voice trailed off as she nervously pushed me toward the edge of the roof.

"If you keep pushing me like this, Zieba, I'll end up crippled," I teased, though her forceful shoves were genuinely concerning.

"Yeah, but at least I'll be safe! Now go, or I'll really push you off this roof! My father will think—just leave!" she paused, she pleaded in a panic.

"What will he think?" I asked, still teasing her. "Say it out loud & clear."

"I'll punch you, I'm warning you!" she threatened, forming a fist and waving it at me.

"If you don't say it, I'm not leaving," I declared stubbornly.

She grabbed my collar in frustration, threatening again.

"If you don't leave—"

I cut her off with a smirk.

"Are you challenging me, Zieba? You know I never lose a challenge. Try me."

"What should I even say?" she grumbled, irritated like a child throwing a tantrum.

I gave her a soft smile.

"Say what you left unfinished. What will your father think....... about us?"

"Ugh... He'll think that there's something going on between us, by God." she finally blurted out, loosening her grip on my collar.

~~I didn't know why, but hearing those words made me feel good.~~

"So..., is there something going on between us?"

I teased her further. Zieba started shoving me again.

"If you don't leave right now, I'll hit you so hard your family won't even recognize you," she threatened, clearly flustered.

"Alright, alright, I'm leaving, Miss J3," I said, giving in at last.

The way I had climbed up was the same way I left.

As I walked away, Zieba stood on the roof, watching me. I waved goodbye with a smile as I started my bike. Zieba, pouting, waved her fist at me as if to punch the air.

It's true what they say: When two people's paths are meant to diverge, the journey together becomes even more beautiful.

Perhaps this is where Zieba's role in my journey ends.

When I leave for Canada, I won't be coming back.

There are many facets to life.

One of the most important lessons I've learned is to keep control over it—hold the reins tightly and live life on your own terms. Because if you let life take the reins, it will imprison you.

And Ilham was never born to live under anyone's control.

I am the ruler of my own life.

* * *

CHAPTER – 11

(Fear, Agony, Torment…!!)

I was preparing to leave for Canada, with my flight in two days.

Fateen had come over to help me with packing, but instead of helping, he was making my job more difficult.

"So, tell me, why do you always have that hairband on your wrist?" Fateen asked.

A smile crept onto my face just at the mention of her name—what's happening to me? I wasn't like this before; smiling wasn't this easy for me.

"It's nothing special," I quickly shut down the conversation.

"Yeah, right, whatever you say, man," Fateen teased.

"Come on, tell me, are you ever going to confess your feelings to her or not?" Fateen asked softly, convinced since that day that ~~I had feelings for Zieba.~~

"Who, and what would I even say?" I pretended, not wanting to involve Zieba in any more trouble because of me.

I didn't want her to face any problems, or for her reputation to be tarnished.

"Don't act, Ilham, we can all see that you're in love with Zieba," Fateen said.

"Don't you ever mention this in front of anyone again, Fateen, or else you won't like what happens," I said seriously.

"Why? Is she not interested in you? Or are you the one who isn't interested? If you're not, then why did you beat Aswad like a dog?" Fateen, as usual, tried to drag the conversation out.

He always needed to know every detail.

"I don't know, and I'm not in love with her or anything. She's just a good girl, and she's my father's close friend's daughter, which is why I treat her well. I absolutely don't want her reputation stained because of me. That's why I'm telling you, don't ever bring this up again. Got it?"

I warned him seriously.

"Yeah, alright, I won't. But I have to say, it was nice to hear that,"

Fateen said, and his words rubbed me the wrong way.

What did he mean by that?

And for some reason, I didn't ask him why he found it nice to hear.

We went out for some tea. I'm not much of a tea drinker, but I usually go with Fateen anyway.

That night, we went to a well-known spot at Charminar for Irani chai.

I don't know what it was—the atmosphere, the gentle breeze, the tea, Fateen's chatter, and this strange animal-like friend of mine—but I couldn't stop thinking about when we'd meet again or when we'd have tea together again.

The most important question: would I ever see Zieba again?

And if I didn't, what would happen?

I wanted to see her as much as I could.

Zieba's thoughts constantly filled my mind. It was as if some magnetic force was pulling me toward her, and I was gladly being drawn in.

"Fateen, I've got something to take care of. I'm heading out," I said, grabbing my bike and heading off.

"Hey man, how am I supposed to get back?!"

Fateen shouted, realizing he hadn't brought his bike.

"Sometimes people need to use their feet not their brains—solutions will come naturally," I called back as I sped away.

My bike came to a stop near Zieba's house.

I stood outside for quite some time.

She wasn't physically there, but it felt like she was everywhere.

Zieba had settled so deeply in my mind that I could feel her presence even without seeing her.

Every movement, every word of hers seemed ingrained in me—although it hadn't been long since we met, it felt like I had known her for years.

Lost in my thoughts, I was absorbed in Zieba's presence. She stepped out onto the rooftop, dressed in black.

Tonight, she hadn't worn a dupatta, and her long, dark hair reached down to her waist, gently swaying in the soft breeze.

She breathed. She breathed—deeply, fully.

She inhaled as if she'd been breathless all day, and only now had found air to breathe—more like the peace she had been longing for.

She tried to tame her silky hair with one hand as they slipped through her fingers, her gaze lost in the sky—not in the vast sea of stars but in the lonely, shining moon.

I noticed she had a small tape recorder in her other hand, which she carefully placed on the rooftop railing.

Moments later, she began to speak.

So, Miss Zieba, you keep your inner thoughts locked in a tape recorder, huh?

Her face was full of emotion, and though I couldn't hear what she was saying, I could almost read the words on her lips if I tried hard enough.

Out of respect for her privacy, I didn't try to decipher her words.

There was a hint of sadness on her face as she finished recording and turned off the tape recorder.

Slowly, with soft steps, she began walking across the rooftop, feeling the cool breeze brush against her.

In the moonlight, Zieba looked stunning, her beauty brighter than the glowing moon itself.

She always managed to stop my heartbeat, her inner and outer beauty surpassing everything in the world.

But tonight, her sadness was unsettling me.

I couldn't bear to see her like this.

To bring back her smile, I began walking toward her.

I silently climbed over the wall and landed in her lawn, making my way toward the roof.

With so many plants in their lawn, no one could easily spot me.

My sudden arrival startled her; she spun around, instinctively trying to cover her head.

Her hands trembled, her fear was obvious.

I closed my eyes and took slow steps toward her.

She was about eight steps away from me, I had gauged the distance. Standing close to her, I gently picked up her black dupatta and draped it over her head, just as she always wore it.

I opened my eyes—*perfect.*

In that moment, she looked even more innocent than before, her beauty left me astonished.

Our eyes met, and for a moment, we both forgot to breathe. Her soft, shallow breaths were faint and slow, her hands shook, and her deep black eyes searched my face for an answer—wondering why I had come.

That small mole on her right cheek, as always, tested my self-control. I leaned in closer, lost in her nearness.

Her lips trembled, as if she were about to say something, and I waited, feeling safe in the moment.

But it seemed like she might take all night just to try, so I broke the silence.

"Hello, Miss J3," I whispered softly.

Zieba, with trembling hands, adjusted her veil.

"Allah—Allah, shameless as always, by God. Don't you have an ounce of decency? Why are you here?" she snapped, stepping back and gritting her teeth.

Her throat was dry; she always seemed so scared.

"Relax, I'm leaving for Canada this weekend. You might miss me, so I just came to see you one last time… so you could get a final look at me," I said.

After my words, a faint smile appeared on my face as I leaned against the wall of the roof and stared at her—she looked beautiful in black—no—the black looked beautiful on her—no, everything looked beautiful on her.

Lost in her beauty, I could only think of that.

"Miss you? I'd be grateful if I never have to see you again,"

Zieba's words stung me.

"Really? It doesn't matter to you if I leave forever?"

I asked, stepping closer to her.

"No,"

"No…??"

"No, I didn't mean it like that, I just said it without thinking!" Zieba had sensed my restlessness.

"Oh, so does that mean you *would* care?" I teased her with a slight smile.

"Look, stop saying things that make me want to hit you!" Zieba snapped, clearly irritated.

"Alright, tell me why you're here then?" she asked.

"There's a lot I want to say, but I don't think you'd really like to hear what's on my mind," I said softly, revealing my heart's truth.

"Go ahead, say it once… then I'll decide whether it's something worth hitting you for, or maybe burying you alive," Zieba said with a hint of gentleness.

Every word from this girl somehow involved violence—the day I saw her, I chose violence. She *is* pure violence.

"What do you want to hear?" I tried to trap her in my words, foolishly thinking she might fall for them.

"You just can't speak plainly, can you? Go away now. If someone sees you here, I'll be in so much trouble," Zieba said while glancing down from the roof. I ignored her concern and called her name.

"Zieba…?"

"Hmm…"

"Can I have a bit of your time? I've heard your time is quite valuable, and Ilham likes valuable things…" I asked her, and together we began looking up at the lonely moon shining in the sky.

"By the way. You've been taking my time this whole while…" Zieba said, glancing at me for a moment.

"Is there something you want to say?"

Zieba asked, curious to know why I had asked for her time.

"No..."

I exhaled deeply and looked back at the moon.

Sometimes, it's better to keep certain things to yourself, especially when you know you're not worthy of talking about them.

The moon looked beautiful, or maybe it was the effect of Zieba's presence.

Her face, in the moonlight, was glowing even brighter than the moon itself.

"The moon looks so beautiful, doesn't it?"

I asked Zieba, my gaze on the moon for a moment, but the rest of my attention was on her. Zieba kept looking at me too.

"Yes, very," Zieba replied.

We stayed there for a long time, just like that, standing under the open sky on the roof, with the soft breeze brushing past us, gazing at the moon.

Even without any conversation, I felt a deep sense of comfort being with Zieba; her presence was enough for me.

~~I couldn't imagine how I'd survive without her there.~~

"Are you really leaving?" Zieba broke the silence.

"Yes..."

"But why? You can finish your studies here too, can't you?" Zieba asked.

"I want to conquer the world, see myself at those high peaks. I can't be confined to just one place," I replied. Zieba looked at me and smiled, then turned her gaze back to the sky.

"Hmm, just don't end up on your knees chasing those high peaks—because the ground won't give you a place to plant your feet," Zieba said, pausing for a moment before continuing,

"Are you leaving forever?" Zieba asked another question.

I didn't know why she was being so nice to me today; I was getting lost in her words.

"Why? Shouldn't I leave?" I asked, teasing her.

"Huh… I don't care, go where you want," Zieba retorted, and I couldn't help but laugh.

Zieba was truly strange.

One moment she was Zieba, the next moment she was Miss J3.

"Wow, madam, you're really something else," I said, laughing.

"And you're no less, sir."

"Aaaa… right."

"Alright, now get out, I've had enough of you," Zieba said, telling me to leave.

"If you say it like that, I won't go," I teased again.

"Then how should I say it?"

"Say it with a little love…"

"How about I give you two slaps with a little love instead?" Zieba said, motioning with her right hand as if she was about to slap me. For some reason, even the idea of getting slapped by her made me feel happy.

"Go ahead—at least then…" I stopped myself and reined in my words. Zieba was glaring at me like a hungry lioness.

"Alright, alright, I'm leaving. Goodbye, Miss J3," I said, giving her a small smile as a farewell.

She gestured with her hand, telling me to leave.

"At least say goodbye one last time…" I asked her.

"I'm not saying it. Just go, or else I'll push you off, and instead of Canada, you'll end up in the hospital," Zieba said as she started pushing me, but her pushes were so gentle, using only two fingers from each hand. Look at how strong this madam is.

"Have some fear of God, at least a little," I teased her further,

"How can you talk about sending such an innocent guy like me to the hospital, you cruel girl?"

"Innocent? And you?" Zieba burst into laughter. It was the first time I had seen her laugh so openly.

She rarely laughed, and I felt like my reason for coming here had been fulfilled. The sadness on her face had vanished.

"You look so beautiful when you laugh. Why don't you laugh more often? I'm sure someone else must also feel happy seeing your smile, Miss J3."

I looked directly into Zieba's eyes as I spoke, and for the first time, it felt like my happiness could be tied to someone else's, just as her pain had started to feel like my own.

When Zieba is happy, Ilham is happy. When Zieba is in pain, Ilham is in pain too.

"You need someone to make you laugh, Mister Attention Seeker. You won't understand. Go to Canada, conquer your world."

With that, she picked up her tape recorder and started heading downstairs.

Today, for the first time, she didn't look back at me.

~~If it were up to me, I would make myself the reason behind each of your radiant smiles, the reason behind every one of your laughs. But I doubt you'd want that or even care…~~

Still, I make this promise: even if it's not me, someone will make sure you're always laughing. From now on, you won't be alone. I won't let you stay lonely, Miss J3. Be ready to have a best friend—*and she will be none other than Maryam.*

With those words, I stepped away, walking back to my bike, casting one last glance at Zieba's house.

As I reached the bike, I noticed a shadow.

The figure was dressed entirely in black. Before I could get a better look, they disappeared.

He had been standing at the corner of the alley, from where Zieba's rooftop was clearly visible.

I didn't think much of it and drove home. Once there, I called Maryam.

Maryam: "Yes, what's up? What happened?"

Ilham: "From now on, you're Zieba's only friend. I don't care how you do it, but you will become her friend again. Do you understand?"

Maryam: "If I don't agree, you won't let me live in peace, will you?"

Ilham: "Good. And not just at school. You'll join her in her course."

Maryam: "What? Have you lost your mind? Me? Study to become a doctor? I feel like dying just hearing the word 'study'."

Ilham: "You can die for all I care, but you *will* study. And it'll be medical."

Maryam: "Oh, Ilham! You have no idea how hard medical school is."

Ilham: "I don't care!"

Maryam: "Oh Allah, what kind of disaster have I brought upon myself?"

Ilham: "Don't you dare say anything to Zieba…"

Maryam: "Who said anything about Zieba? I'm talking about *you*!"

Ilham: "Stop your nonsense and engrave what I've said into your mind. Otherwise..."

Maryam: "Otherwise, what? You'll bury me alive like you've already bought a plot in the cemetery? Fine, I'll do it. Now hang up. I need to talk to Zieba."

Ilham: "Do you even have her number?"

Maryam: "No, just her landline. She talks when her father's watching the news."

Ilham: "Alright. Text me the landline number."

Maryam: "Okay, I will."

I ended the call. Maryam's family was open-minded and quite friendly, and I was sure they wouldn't object to her studying medicine.

Even if she didn't pass the entrance test, her father would pull some strings and get her in under the management quota.

And as for studying, Zieba would help her. She'd manage to pass, for sure.

* * *

Tension gripped the police station, yet I sat there carelessly, perched on a metal chair with my left leg crossed over my right knee, as if this were just another ordinary day.

And for me, it truly was—this was my norm. I took sips of my drink, completely at ease. My gaze was sharp yet calm, indifferent to the chaos surrounding me, because in truth, none of it mattered.

Mr. Osman would soon get me out of here.

The officers stood at a distance, fully aware of who was sitting in front of them: Mr. Osman Ahmed Khaan, the only son of Qasr-e-Shahi Khaan.

My father wasn't just a businessman—he wielded immense power, and everyone knew it.

The respect, or perhaps the fear, in the room was palpable.

One policeman stood nearby, fanning me, while another waited with a tray of refreshments, awaiting my signal.

Despite the oppressive heat, this scene resembled more of a royal gathering than an investigative proceeding.

The cold drink in my hand was not just something to quench my thirst; it was a symbol of my disdain for the system.

I wasn't nervous—just as I'd never been in courtrooms or during confrontations, always coming out on top.

This moment was no different.

An hour had passed since my arrival, and exactly one hour later, my father walked into the station with the kind of confidence that made it seem as though he owned every inch of the ground he stepped on.

His eyes fell on me, brazenly sipping my drink. There was a flicker of anger hidden beneath his calm exterior.

But, as always, an unspoken understanding passed between father and son.

To the world, I could do no wrong in his eyes. He may say things at home, but in public, he would never allow anything to tarnish my reputation.

The officer in charge hesitated, fully aware of the delicate nature of the situation.

This wasn't just any ordinary fight—Aswad, the son of a prominent politician, was in a coma.

I had nearly killed him, yet here I sat, as if it were no big deal.

Had it come to murder, I would have killed him without blinking an eye—*bloody bastard.*

"Why isn't he dead yet? Why is he only in a coma? He should have died when I cracked his skull with that vase. How is he still alive?"

I asked, as I accepted another glass—this wasn't just a drink; it was liquor.

My father's voice sliced through the tension like a knife through rope. "How dare you arrest Ilham Osman Khaan, the son of Osman Ahmed Khaan? What were you thinking when you committed this audacity?"

His voice was cold and controlled, though rage simmered beneath the surface.

The officers, who had already been treating me with undue deference, now fell entirely under the shadow of Mr. Osman's authority.

The two exchanged glances, caught between the politician's threats and the fear of Osman's power.

"Sir, we had no choice. There was pressure from above—orders came from high up…"

"I don't care what kind of pressure you're under. Tear up that FIR right now! On the word of some MLA, you dared to arrest my son? You must value neither your job nor your life. Have you forgotten who I am and who he is?"

My father's voice was calm but carried undeniable weight.

He always proves, in both court and police stations, that he is Ilham's father.

"Sir, please forgive us…"

The officer muttered, his hands trembling as he quickly ripped the papers to shreds.

Mr. Osman turned toward his phone and, with eerie composure, called Aswad's father.

"If you want to win the next election, you'll never dare file another FIR against my son. Don't forget, Rasheed Norein, you survive on my scraps. If I stop feeding you, you'll be left begging. Meet me at my office within an hour. I'll give you a blank check. Fill in your worth, but don't ever associate your son's name with mine again—or else... Osman doesn't give warnings twice."

With that, he ended the call, effectively closing the matter.

The police, now fully under my father's sway, continued to serve me like a VIP—after all, I wasn't just a VIP, I was the son of a kingmaker.

As the situation was diffused, I stood up from my seat, a slight smirk on my face.

I stretched leisurely and ran my hand through my hair, picking up my black sunglasses from where they hung on my collar and slipping them on.

My father, in sync with me, did the same with his own glasses.

But his anger had not cooled.

His eyes were filled with a reproach, though he said nothing.

Once again, I had evaded the consequences of my actions by leaning on my father's power.

As he got into the car that would take me back to Qasr-e-Shahi Khaan, my father finally spoke, his words cutting deep.

"One day, Allah's will strike you down with His staff, and when that day comes, there will be no one to save you—not even your father, not the mother who would weep for you, nor the friends who stand by your side. No one. No matter how much power I have, I cannot protect you from the real consequences, the ones that lie beyond human hands. Because those consequences belong to Allah Himself—so real that your soul, swollen with arrogance and pride, will be changed with fear, agony, and unimaginable torment. And when that time comes, not even Allah will have mercy on you."

He said this as we drove away.

For the first time, I saw a profound disappointment in his eyes—not for me, but for his son.

I was speechless. It wasn't that I lacked words, but that I lacked the courage to speak them. I had nothing to say.

"Fear? Agony? Torment?"

I scoffed inwardly.

Father, you speak nonsense. None of that exists.

Everything in this world is in human hands—it's all about what you choose to feel.

* * *

I was lying face down on the couch in my house, listening to music, when Baba came over and handed me some documents.

"These are important papers, take them. I have some work, and I'm running late," he said.

"I'm not going anywhere, I'm busy," I replied carelessly, as I looked at Zieba's hairband tied around my wrist.

"You don't look busy to me," Baba said seriously.

"I may not look busy, but I definitely am," I responded, turning my head to the other side of the couch.

"What kind of boy are you…?? Now I'll have to go to Sarem's house myself-

Reshma Begum, come here——" Baba called out to Mumma, picked up the documents from the tea table, and started heading outside. -*Wait… Does this mean Zieba's house? Ilham, get up…*

I immediately jumped up and tried to snatch the documents from Baba's hands.

"I'll take them, no need for a lecture…!!"

"Yes, tell me——" Mumma answered. Luckily, Mumma arrived after a while.

I happily skipped outside. Taking a deep breath,

I took my bike and headed toward Zieba's house. I don't know what excuse I can give you all, but I like her. I like her voice, her sharp words, and even her constant threats…!!

It's not just that I like her; the point is that only she is the one I like…!!

I reached Zieba's house, and before ringing the bell, I started fixing my hair and adjusting my shirt.

I was hoping, like the other day, that Zieba would open the door again today. I rang the bell. After a short while, someone opened the door, but it wasn't Zieba; it was her father—~~disappointed.~~

"Baba gave me some files to deliver to you," I said, handing him the documents.

"I'll be on my way," I added and turned to leave.

"No, come inside and have some tea," Sarem uncle invited me in, and I thought that maybe, through this tea, I'd get a chance to meet Zieba. I immediately agreed and walked in.

"Sabeera, Ilham is here…, bring a cup of tea," Sarem uncle told Sabeera aunty.

"Okay, you wait here. She'll bring the tea shortly. I have to go for some work. Good thing you brought the files on time." Uncle patted my back and left.

I sat there, impatiently waiting for tea made by Zieba's hands. Normally, I'm not a fan of tea, but if it's made by her, I'd drink anything.

- - *Where are you, Miss J3…?*

The wait grew longer, and time kept passing, but she was nowhere to be seen. I felt both calm and restless—restless because I couldn't see her———

Then, I heard a soft voice. I recognized it immediately—it was Zieba's voice.

She was reciting the Quran, and her voice soothed me just like it did that day.

For some reason, my eyes closed on their own, and I felt like I was getting lost in her voice…

Zieba's voice grew louder, and though I've read the Quran before, it felt like I was hearing it for the first time…

She was reciting the Holy Quran in her sweet voice, reading Surah Al Mulk…

Every sentence coming from her mouth was pleasing to my ears, until she began reading the translation of the verses…

"Exalted and Supreme is the One in whose hands lies the dominion of the universe, and He has power over everything,"

Zieba's voice began to grow louder—or was it just my perception? I couldn't open my eyes.

"He is the One who created death and life to test which of you is best in deeds, and He is the Mighty, the Forgiving…"

Her translation made me feel uneasy, and I tried, in vain, to open my eyes. I felt a powerful grip on my body, rendering me numb.

"For those who disbelieve in their Lord, there is the punishment of Hell, and what an evil destination it is…"

"Stop reading this… stop it, Zieba…"

I wanted to scream, but her voice started to irritate me for the first time, or maybe it was the meaning of her words that bothered me.

Her voice wasn't fading; instead, it was becoming louder—loud as if someone had placed speakers directly in my ears.

I covered my ears, but it was no use.

The sound was so deafening that even if I were deaf, I would still hear it.

What the hell is going on?

An invisible force gripped my tongue, rendering me completely silent.

"When they are thrown into it, they will hear the terrifying sound of its roaring, as it seethes with fury. It will almost burst with rage. Every time a group is cast into it, its keepers will ask them, 'Did no warner come to you?'"

"They will say, 'Yes, a warner did come to us, but we denied him and said, 'Allah has not sent down anything. You are in great error...'"

Every part of my heart and every vein in my body was screaming in agony.

Behind my closed eyes, the number **67** flashed repeatedly, intensifying my anxiety.

Yes, the same number that is tattooed on my body, the same number that appears in my dreams, the number that compelled me to search the world for answers.

"And they will say, 'If only we had listened or used our intelligence, we would not be among the inhabitants of this blazing fire.' Thus, they will confess their sin. So away with the dwellers of the blaze."

Fear enveloped me like a suffocating sheet, and I could feel cold sweat trickling down my skin.

Drops of sweat fell from my forehead, sliding down my nose, and gathered in my trembling hands.

"***Curse be upon the dwellers of Hell...***"

"***Curse be upon the dwellers of Hell...***"

"***Curse be upon the dwellers of Hell...***"

But I was paralyzed. I couldn't open my eyes, nor could I move an inch.

For the first time, Zieba's voice assaulted my nerves, a voice I suddenly despised.

All I wanted was not to hear her anymore—if only I could become deaf. But she wouldn't stop.

-Just stop... I don't want to hear any of this. I need to get out of here. I need to open my eyes... Stop it... stop reading...!

I was a mere puppet, waiting for the hands that controlled my movement to make me move again.

Although my body was intact, I remained paralyzed in place, without any physical chains or firm grip holding me. *-What is happening to me?*

I had never heard anyone recite the Quran with such intensity, or maybe it was the first time I had truly listened to someone reciting it.

Every part of my body was in pain, I felt restless, suffocated.

-I can't breathe......................

"Ilham...?"

Zieba's voice began to fade as Sabeera Aunty called my name.

I opened my eyes and realized they weren't just moist—I had been crying, and crying hard.

I wiped the blur from my eyes with the back of my hand.

"Ilham, my dear, were you crying?" Aunty asked with concern.

"What...? Me? No, no. I just remembered something urgent," I said hastily, rising abruptly from my seat.

"Ilham, dear, at least have some tea—"

But I was already out the door.

My hands and feet were still trembling, my breath unsteady.

Somehow, I managed to make it home, but an overwhelming sense of suffocation clung to me.

I locked myself in my room, yet no matter how hard I tried, Zieba's voice wouldn't leave my mind.

"Curse be upon the dwellers of Hell..."

"Curse be upon the dwellers of Hell..."

"Curse be upon the dwellers of Hell..."

"What is happening to me? Shut up... just shut up, you bloody hell, shut up!"

I screamed and began to destroy everything in my room. My head felt like it was going to explode, the pressure in my chest unbearable.

"Ilham, my child, what's wrong?"

My mother's voice came from the other side of the door, but I was too far gone.

I yelled like a madman, desperate to silence the voice in my head.

"Just shut up!"

"Tell her to stop, Mumma—tell her to be quiet! Mumma, make her stop!" I screamed, grabbing a flower vase and smashing it against the wall.

"Oh Allah, protect my child..."

My mother sobbed as I collapsed in the corner, curling into myself, covering my ears.

"This can't be Zieba's voice. Zieba's voice soothes me, it doesn't terrify me,"

I muttered, trying to calm myself, but rage consumed me.

In my fury, I destroyed everything in the room.

"Shut up... shut up!"

"Please..., Zieba.........!!"

* * *

CHAPTER – 12

(Freedom....!!)

Three Years Later -

"Good evening, ladies and gentlemen! Tonight, we are in for a mesmerizing treat as we welcome a performer who needs no introduction. With moves that are as smooth as his charisma and an energy that captivates every soul in the room, he is all set to light up the stage.

From his first step to his final bow, his passion and grace leave us all spellbound. So, without further ado, let's give a thunderous round of applause to the one and only ILHAM, as he takes the stage for a performance that promises to be unforgettable!"

The stage lights had gone out as the anchor called my name.

I took my place alongside the girls who were part of my dance performance.

My entrance at the university's welcome party was nothing short of spectacular.

With the soft glow of the auditorium lights and the music beginning to play, the atmosphere was set to perfection.

My confident smile and captivating personality drew everyone's attention in the first heartbeat.

Dressed in black, a colour that emphasized my sharp features, I moved with an unparalleled grace.

Every movement I made was filled with allure and emotion, capturing the audience in a trance.

The girls on stage seemed drawn to me like moths to a flame, lost in the spell of my presence.

As we danced in sync, it became clear who was in command.

My movements were powerful, perfectly in tune with the pulsating beats of the music.

We were dancing to a popular Bollywood remix of 'Aadat Se Majboor' and 'Thug Le,' and with each step, the girls came closer to me, their gazes fixed as if I was the only person on stage.

Occasionally, I would reach out my hand, giving them a subtle signal that sent waves of excitement through the audience.

With every twirl and turn, the girls followed my lead, the performance becoming an intense display of chemistry and synchronization.

As the dance progressed, my confidence soared.

My smile widened into a full grin, and the emotional exchange between me and the girls added a layer of irresistible charm to the performance.

The crowd erupted in joy, captivated by my flawless command and magnetic style on stage.

Both juniors and seniors were entranced by the spectacle, with some even joining the girls on stage, making it clear that I was the shining star of the night.

My dance wasn't just a performance; it was a silent proclamation of my allure and my dominance over others.

As the music came to an end, the stage lights dimmed, and I finished the performance with a dramatic final move alongside the girls.

The auditorium burst into applause.

As usual, I flung my jacket and black t-shirt into the crowd, and the girls in the audience fought over them, desperate to grab hold of them.

A triumphant smile played on my lips.

The girls on stage moved even closer, their hands tracing my body, each touch driving the audience wilder.

"*Just a few more seconds, Ilham,*" I thought to myself, pushing through the intensity of the moment.

Then, as soon as the lights went completely out, I brushed their hands off me—"*Waqar, I won't let you get away with this, you rascal!*"

My performance became the talk of the night, and the memory of it would live on in everyone's minds for years to come.

—Of course, I'm Ilham Osman Khaan, and this was my way of introducing myself to the juniors at the university in Canada.

Waqar had lost a bet the day before, and this was part of the deal. Otherwise, I could've performed solo, just like I do every year without the need for girls.

"Excuse me…?"

A girl approached me backstage after the performance.

She was one of the dancers I had shared the stage with.

"Yes?"

I replied, wiping the sweat from my body with a towel, noticing how her eyes were fixed on me.

I snapped my fingers to get her attention.

"Can we exchange numbers…?"

she asked, though she wasn't the first girl to make this request.

I gave her a playful smile, nodded, and took her phone, locking eyes with her as I began typing on the screen.

Handing the phone back to her, I leaned in close as I put on my shirt, gently blowing near her ear before walking away with a grin.

She stood there, watching me leave, smiling uncontrollably.

But as she looked down at her phone, her smile quickly vanished. I couldn't help but chuckle to myself—*Ilham's number, that easily? And yeah, you're probably wondering what I typed, right?*

—"You are not worthy, baby girl." That's all I wrote.

* * *

I, Ilham Osman Khaan, could feel the freedom all around me in Canada. The environment and the liberty here meant no one could stop me from indulging in the pleasures of the world. I started living exactly how I always wanted to—free.

Yet, even amid these distractions, I never lost sight of my goal. My destination remained the same as it was a few years ago.

I've rented a flat in an apartment complex called 'Grave's Arcade,' conveniently located near clubs and pubs.

It's perfect for whenever I feel like going out—and believe me, I feel like going there every day.

"Ilham, man, your performance last night was something else! It was worth watching… half the juniors are already crazy about you after just one night," Waqar said as the lecture was about to begin.

"Girls going crazy for Ilham? Has that ever *not* happened? And don't involve me in stupid bets like that again, or I'll beat you so bad you'll forget your own name," I replied with a playful smile, glancing at the constant stream of messages on my phone.

Ever since last night, juniors and seniors alike had been texting me—you know they're obsessed with me now.

"Good morning, class," the lecturer greeted us as we started the lesson.

"Ilham, bro, let's do something fun this weekend. It's been a while since we've gone anywhere. Our last trip was to Paris, and that was three months ago. We need to get out,"

Waqar whispered, kissing his girlfriend's hand.

Waqar is a Pakistani guy who's my age and in the same class as me.

Since I arrived in Canada, we've been hanging out together.

But after he got a girlfriend, I kicked him out of my flat.

I can't tolerate his personal activities.

"Yeah, let's go. Now shut up and let me listen to the lecture. We're not getting these notes anywhere else,"

I responded, but Waqar didn't care at all.

"You look beautiful, baby," Waqar said to his girlfriend, Jenny.

"Aww, really?" she replied.

Their lovey-dovey nonsense was getting on my nerves.

Was I destined to be surrounded by all these lovebirds?

"I think you two should find a nice, quiet place to enjoy your privacy," I said to Waqar, who was busy playing with his girlfriend's hair.

"And I think you should focus on your studies, Mr. Ilham," Waqar shot back. I ignored them and continued listening to the lecture.

Since becoming friends with Waqar, I've developed enough patience to stay focused no matter how much distraction is around me.

If I can handle a walking, talking disturbance like him, I can handle anything.

After the lecture ended, we headed to the cafeteria—me, Waqar, and some of our classmates.

While they were chatting away, I had no interest in their conversations.

I was lost in my phone, barely paying attention to what they were saying.

"Hey, why did you and Arfaz end up in the red-light district near the club on Saturday night, and that too, stumbling around?" one of our classmates asked them, his expression clearly showing that both of them wanted to keep this quiet.

I could sense the unease behind their faces that no one else seemed to notice.

Before answering, Arfaz cleared his throat.

"We had a bit too much to drink last night and, well, we ended up there without realizing it. We were just passing through that street,"

Arfaz and Hamza replied, nodding in agreement.

I couldn't help but laugh at their explanation.

Waqar nudged me to keep quiet. After all, they didn't join us after the welcome party last night but instead went separately to the red-light district.

"Alright, alright," our classmate said, buying into their story—something I would never do because I knew they would've gone there even if they were sober.

Their conversation continued, but I shifted my focus to checking news updates on my phone.

Suddenly, I received a message from an unknown number.

I opened it and read:

Unknown: Hi! Do you know who I am?

I replied:

Ilham: Don't you know who you are? Asking me in a message…??

Unknown: Quite the temper you've got there. Didn't you recognize me?

Ilham: Looks like you're bent on making it worse… No, I didn't recognize you. Introduce yourself.

Unknown: Oh, let it go. You don't even know yourself; how will you know me?

Ilham: So, you are telling me you know me?

Unknown: Yes, very well.

Ilham: Go ahead, tell me. I'd love to hear you praise me…

Unknown: If I start praising you, I'm afraid you might fall for yourself… My heart trembles at the thought that you might take away what's mine…!!

Ilham: First of all, here's some advice: if you flirt like that, no one's going to give you the time of day. Secondly, I already have enough self-love; I won't need your praise for that. And lastly, don't you dare text me again.

I sent that reply firmly, and she didn't respond.

"No idea who she was…!!!"

There was a strange feeling in my chest, one I couldn't quite put into words.

Every time I see a message or call from an Indian number, there's always a hope that it might be Zieba, and no one else.

But as luck would have it, my wish never comes true.

Any girl in the world might message or call me, but Zieba…? Never—*stop dreaming, Ilham.*

Before I got lost in thoughts of Zieba again, I decided to keep myself occupied. I started taking interest in their conversation.

When I'm with Waqar, we just talk, but when I'm with our classmates, our discussions turn into debates.

-How? You must be wondering, right? Well, you can see for yourself!

"I don't know, man. What's happening in the world? Have you heard about that virus? A lot of people are dying,"

Hamza mentioned, referring to a new virus recently named COVID.

It's a disease for which no one has found a cure yet. Laboratories worldwide are racing to find a solution.

The number of deaths from this disease is unlike anything we've ever seen—*it's a pandemic.*

People are dying in a way that no one can bury them, let alone see them one last time.

No one knows where their graves are or where their bodies are.

Hearing this, we started following WHO's guidelines to take precautions.

I was growing bored of their conversation, so I went back to browsing my phone, specifically checking the university Zieba had enrolled in.

-Surprised I know that? Well, I didn't make Maryam my friend for nothing. She may be her friend, but she's my informant first.

I learn everything about Zieba through her.

"Yeah, it won't be long before we start starving," Arfaz said gloomily. For some reason, despite not being interested, I decided to jump into the conversation, because I enjoy it. *Simple.*

"Why, don't you have faith in your abilities?" I asked Arfaz, turning off my phone screen, knowing this debate would last a while.

"What do my abilities have to do with any of this?" Arfaz turned towards me, puffing on his cigarette, surrounded by our other friends.

"You just said we'd be starving, didn't you? So, do you not trust your own abilities? Because anyone who reaches their goal never stays hungry or poor," I said, smiling at Arfaz. My smile was clear—it was a taunting smile.

"Ilham, you're forgetting that there's something greater than ability, and that's Allah's will. No matter how rich or capable I become, even if I have all the wealth in the world, without Allah's will, I won't even be able to swallow a bite," Arfaz said, throwing his cigarette on the ground and crushing it under his foot.

"Whatever, I don't believe that. Allah gave you two hands so you could earn and feed yourself. If you sit in front of food and just wait for Allah to feed you, then go ahead—just sit there saying 'Allah, Allah,' and do nothing. I'd like to see who brings you your food or feeds you," I said with a mischievous smile and a soft tone, leaving everyone speechless, but they looked at me as if they were staring at a devil.

"But don't you think, Ilham, that this virus is Allah's punishment? Like He's punishing us for our sins?" A girl named Amina, who is Pakistani, asked. Normally, I don't talk to girls much, but this needed a response.

"Yeah, it does make you think. Look at how everything is falling apart, people are getting sick and dying—it almost feels like the end of the world," said Sarah, who is Indian.

"You seriously believe that? That a virus, which we can see under a microscope, is some kind of divine punishment?" I said sarcastically, finding it hard to believe people could say such foolish things.

"It's not just about the virus, Ilham. How did all of this happen so suddenly? It feels like some kind of warning," Hamza added.

These guys and their ideas.

"I understand where you're coming from, but think logically for a second. COVID-19, like other viruses, has a scientific explanation. It's the result of natural processes—genetic mutations, zoonotic transmission.

These are things we've seen before. There's nothing mysterious about it," I said, and they all stared at me in disbelief.

"But what about the timing? It's almost too perfect, like this was meant to happen," Sarah said, and everyone around started nodding in agreement.

"The timing is just a coincidence. The Spanish flu, SARS, MERS—these pandemics came long before COVID. And what about other disasters? Earthquakes, tsunamis, famines? Are those punishments too? Or are they natural events in a world that operates under physical laws?" I said, and they all started looking at each other. Sarah had gone quiet.

"But if all of this is natural, why does it seem like it's targeting the weakest among us? The elderly, the sick—it almost feels like they're being singled out," Arfaz said, his eyes searching my face for an answer, while Waqar, as always, was busy chatting with Jenny—those two always had their own thing going on.

"A virus doesn't have intent. It simply exploits weakness, like people do. It's Biology, haven't you studied it? The elderly and those already sick are more vulnerable because their immune systems are weaker. It's not targeting them—it's just that their bodies can't fight back," I said with a shrug, and everyone was listening closely, nodding along.

"Isn't there some wisdom in the fact that everything happens for a reason?" Sarah asked thoughtfully.

"Everything has a reason, yes, but those reasons aren't always supernatural. Science explains the causes behind these events. The virus didn't choose its victims based on morality; it spread through biological means—just like any other disease, that's it. Don't exaggerate it by calling it a divine punishment," I replied calmly.

"If it were a punishment then what would you say about Palestine, Ukraine, Syria..??" I asked,

"But if this isn't divine punishment, then why does it feel like the world is being tested?" Amina paused and asked.

"Tested by whom? And why? If this is some divine test or punishment, then why are innocent people affected just as much as the guilty? What about the children? What sin have they committed that your Allah is punishing them? They can't even speak properly, so why are they getting sick and dying? It's beyond reason! Just grow up, guys," I answered her question.

"If this is a punishment, it should only befall the guilty, not the innocent," I completed my thought, and my gaze shifted to Arfaz and Hamza as I said that final sentence.

"You wouldn't understand, Ilham. Let it be. Someone who doesn't even know how to pray can't possibly comprehend these things," Hamza said.

His words didn't anger me, though I admit, I don't pray.

But I do enjoy arguing, especially with people whose secrets I know well, and whose faults make me feel superior.

"Yes, you've achieved a lot by offering your prayers. Don't forget that what I do, you all do as well. The only difference is that you pray and hide your flaws behind the veil of prayer, while I don't. And in my eyes, there's no point in such prayer if a person is doing it just for show," I finished my statement. My words provoked them.

I didn't lie—Hamza and Arfaz have plenty of girlfriends.

They all hook up too.

I'm not saying it's wrong—it's their choice.

And they all use drugs.

I've seen them many times going to the red-light district. So, if they're already doing all this, why pretend to be righteous?

Why the need to act virtuous in front of others?

"Who said we're pretending?"

Arfaz growled, clearly displeased by my words.

And this proves that the truth always stings, but this time it didn't just sting—it hit hard.

"You didn't say it, but you all forced me to point it out," I said, leaning back in my chair with a calm tone.

I was relishing my sense of superiority over them.

Why wouldn't I? I'm Ilham, after all.

"What did we force you to say? And who are you to judge us? What do you even know about us? You don't even have control over your own life, yet you're busy talking about others. You don't even know how to speak respectfully," Hamza said angrily.

They think I don't know anything about them, as if no one else knows either. Well, today I might as well tell them what I do know.

"You are mistaken, Hamza. Firstly, I'm not judging you. I don't care what you are. Because I know everything about you all. Every weekend we all go to the same clubs and get high; you all go too. Maybe not there, but you do go to clubs, you get high, and you visit the red-light district…." As soon as I revealed their secrets in front of everyone, they were left breathless, their eyes wide with shock.

"Secondly, I am aware of myself. I'm one of those who can stay conscious even while intoxicated. At least I don't make excuses like, 'Oh, I lost control and ended up at the red-light district.' I know exactly what I do and what I don't. You guys, on the other hand, are deceiving people with excuses. Or perhaps deceiving yourselves. Or maybe your beloved God, in whose fear you perform your showy prayers. He sees everything, right? And thirdly, Ilham has never been concerned with politeness, isn't now, and never will be!"

I finished my statement and took slow sips from the water bottle on the table, just as they were trying to catch their breath, slowly swallowing their suppressed reactions.

Arfaz, Hamza, and the others were silenced as if they had been struck dumb.

No one was left with the courage to speak because they didn't want their secrets exposed.

That's why I always say—don't mess with Ilham. If you do, I'll bite like a venomous snake, leaving you speechless for life in front of Ilham.

Oh, the self-proclaimed guardians of faith…

Every weekend they hold these gatherings.

I have no issue with it, seriously, I don't give a damn about it.

But guess who the speakers are at these gatherings, where they talk about religion, living by its teachings, and all that? Of course, Arfaz, Hamza, and their many friends.

Now, you tell me, when these people present themselves as righteous in front of others, should they really be at clubs, pubs, and parties with me?

If I'm wrong, then what are they?

Isn't pretending to worship also a form of hypocrisy?

And as for the red-light district, I don't go there, but they do.

What's the point of these people when they act all pious and virtuous in front of the world, but then those same pious and virtuous people become shadows of the devil in the darkness of the night?

Just like they call me the devil!

So, what does that make them?

People say that others fall prey to the devil's temptations.

I don't believe in this devil stuff, but if we're talking about the devil, all he does is plant suggestions; he doesn't have any real power beyond that.

It's humans and their desires that go beyond even the devil.

Because in my view, every person who pretends to be righteous and virtuous in front of others, and then reveals their true, animalistic nature in private, is more dangerous than the devil.

And they still have the audacity to say, 'Allah sees everything.' If they know He sees everything, then why do they do it?

Humans are the only creatures who don't need a mask to hide their inner darkness and bad intentions.

Behind their smiling faces lie countless hidden emotions.

In any case, I'm not even slightly interested in these matters because I'm good the way I am. I'm the master of my own world, and I live my life on my own terms. And I'll continue to live this way because *it's Ilham's personal heaven… a heaven made by Ilham.*

"Guys, seriously, just stop with this conversation. Hamza, Arfaz, I've told you so many times not to get into arguments with Ilham. You're only going to lose. See now? Your secrets are out." Waqar said.

Arfaz and Hamza stood up and left, visibly angry. And again, I couldn't care less.

"Hey, Ilham, why are you wearing a girl's hairband on your wrist?" Waqar asked, touching the hairband on my wrist.

I pulled my hand back, ignoring his question.

I can't tell anyone about this secret.

People hide their sins, but I'm the only one who hides the fact that I'm ~~interested in someone who isn't interested in me.~~

"Come on, tell the truth, are you in love with someone?"

Waqar pressed further, and I could see shades of Fateen in him.

The way Fateen tries to get every secret out of me, Waqar is exactly the same.

Was I destined to meet people like this?

Sarah and Amina started laughing, and so did Jenny.

"Shut up with your nonsense, there's nothing like that…." I said, avoiding his gaze.

'I wonder what she's doing right now…? I wonder who she's slapping now…!!! Does she even remember me…!!'

"I'm going to the library…"

I said as I left the cafeteria.

Yeah, yeah… I was making an excuse for studying, but in reality, I always sit in the library lost in her thoughts.

She may not come, but her words, the moments I spent with her, seem to surround me in that quiet place, as if she's right there with me.

I sat in a quiet corner with my books open, and hidden in my wallet was a picture of Zieba.

I stared at it, lost in her memory—*Yes, she told me not to keep her picture on my phone, but she didn't say anything about the wallet, did she?*

"You must have changed a lot by now, haven't you, Miss J3…? Do you even remember this Mister Attention Seeker…?" I started muttering to myself.

I let out a deep sigh and ran my fingers over her picture, like I was actually touching her, trying to feel her presence in front of me.

Or maybe

I just wanted to get slapped by her again, just so she would claim her right over me by touching me…!!

"Someone was right when they said love and memories have no boundaries, they are free from all constraints and can reach anywhere, anytime————

Just like your memory has reached me across seven seas right now—
———-

"Miss J3, you may look innocent, but you're not…, yes, even being so far away, do you have any idea how you're still making me fall for you…???"

I started complaining to her picture, and as always, after talking to her, my face lit up…!!

Like always, all my time passed in conversations with Miss J3, and then Waqar came looking for me.

"Come on, man, how much are you going to study…? Just by looking at you, I feel like I'll pass too…!!"

Waqar teased as he picked up a random book from the library shelf.

I gave a small smile and was just about to put my wallet back into my jeans pocket when Waqar snatched it from my hand.

"Waqar, stop fooling around—give me back my wallet…" I said through gritted teeth.

"Let me see which lady has turned you into such a melancholic lover….?" Waqar teased as he started running out of the library with my wallet.

"Waqar, I swear, if you even open it, I'll kill you….!"

I shouted at him, my voice loud enough that everyone in the corridor was staring at us.

Waqar suddenly stopped in his tracks and looked at me with uncertainty.

He had sensed my anger; I would have really hit him if he had opened the wallet.

I snatched my wallet back from his hands and shoved it into the left back pocket of my jeans as I started walking away.

"Do you love that girl…?"

Waqar asked, placing his hand on my shoulder and matching his steps with mine.

"Waqar, shut up—"

I looked at him and shrugged his hand off my shoulder.

"You really are a secret lover, aren't you...! Is she from India...?" Waqar teased me further.

A smile spread across my face at Waqar's comment—

Do I really love Zieba...??

Is this what they call love...??

But how can I love her...??

She's up there, and I'm down here...??

We are worlds apart, we don't even match...

I'm not even worthy enough to admit that I love that pure girl.

The very thought of my love would taint her. Ilham would never let that happen...!! She was right; I'm not up to her standards.

"Okay, tomorrow's the weekend, and we've all decided to go paragliding and do some other activities. You're coming with us, right?" Waqar said as he caught up with me, walking in step.

"Yeah, adventures without Ilham? Has that ever happened?" I replied, glancing at him with a playful smile.

"Great, it's settled then! We're going!" Waqar said excitedly, before heading off to meet his girlfriend.

You might be wondering why I don't have a girlfriend...

How could I?

My heart has been imprisoned since **February 24, 2017,** precisely at **9:38 PM,** by *that* girl. I have no freedom to look at anyone else, ~~nor do I even want to. There's no one for me but her.~~

We were heading home, and I was driving Waqar back to his apartment in my car, a black Chevrolet Corvette— a birthday gift from my dad.

Waqar and I sped down the highway, the road stretching out before us, when I turned on some music. And as if fate was playing its own little game, the song "Gulabi Ankhein" began to play.

Gulabi aankhen jo teri dekhi

Sharabi ye dil ho gaya

Sambhalo mujhko o mere yaaron

Sambhalna mushqil ho gaya

Gulabi aankhen jo teri dekhi

Sharabi ye dil ho gaya

The melody was so captivating that both of us started singing along instinctively, as if the words had permanently found their place on our tongues.

Usually, when I drive, I'm a bit careless and tend to overlook caution. But this song… it made me feel something entirely different.

Dil mein mere khwaab tere

Tasveer jaise ho deewar pe

Tujhpe fidaa main kyun hua

Aata hai gussa mujhe pyar pe

Waqar, too, began singing along to every note of the music with me, but that was only until I pushed him to the edge of his nerves with the reckless speed of my car.

I drove so fast that even the wind seemed to be left behind.

Main lut gaya

Maan ke dil ka kaha

Main kahin ka na raha

Kya kahu main dilruba

"Brother—Ilham Bhai—what are you doing?" Waqar said nervously, glancing around in panic as he quickly fastened his seatbelt, even though he never wears one.

Bura ye jaadu

Teri aankhon ka

Ye mera qaatil ho gaya

Gulabi aankhen jo teri dekhi

Sharabi ye dil ho gaya

"Who the hell killed you, that you're so set on killing me now—Ilham, please!" Waqar began shouting.

His words sank deep into my thoughts, and suddenly, Zieba's face flashed before my eyes.

"Ilham, slow down," Waqar pleaded, his throat going dry.

Maine sada chaha yahi

Daaman bacha lu haseeno se main

Teri kasam khwabon mein bhi

Bachta firaa naazneeno se main

I started singing from the depths of my heart, as if every word was dedicated to her, silently blaming her for imprisoning my mind and soul.

"Ilham, slow down, man—I don't want to die just yet," Waqar's voice trembled, restless and scared by my reckless driving.

Tauba magar

Mill gayi tujhse nazar

Mill gaya dard-e-jigar

Sun zara oh bekhabar

"Ilham, listen to me, you son of a lovestruck fool!" Waqar started pushing me, gripping the safety panels tightly for support.

But I was lost in the rhythm of the song, every word dragging me deeper into the melody and Zieba's memories.

I sang along, completely absorbed, and began driving even more recklessly.

On the crowded road, I overtook every car in sight, my excitement and adrenaline taking over.

I was so caught up in the rush that I didn't even notice Waqar's growing panic.

Zara sa hans ke jo dekha tune

Main tera bismil ho gaya

"Man—I haven't even confessed my love to Jenny yet," Waqar muttered fearfully.

He shrank into his seat, too scared to move, pleading with me to slow down.

But his voice was swallowed by the music that had me completely entranced, holding me captive in its spell.

Gulabi aankhen jo teri dekhi

Sharabi ye dil ho gaya

"Allah… Allah… please save me… save me…" Waqar muttered under his breath.

I, on the other hand, kept singing the lyrics, ignoring his desperate prayers, and pressed the pedal even harder instead of slowing down.

His fear skyrocketed, and he pulled out his phone, trembling, tears of terror welling in his eyes as he tried to call Jenny.

"Jenny, if I don't make it home safely, file a case against this idiot Ilham! And Jenny, listen… I love you, Jenny,"

Waqar said, his voice cracking with fear, like a frightened child.

He kept saying that if he stayed in the car with me for even two more minutes, he might not survive.

Sambhalo mujhko o mere yaaron

Sambhalna mushqil ho gaya

"Shut up, man! How am I supposed to handle you? My heart's already in my throat, drive slower Ilham, I haven't even gotten married yet! I haven't proposed to Jenny! I still need to make you an uncle—please, for God's sake—don't take the future kids' father away! Don't make them orphans before they're even born!" Waqar was freaking out, pleading desperately.

I was so lost in the song, driving out of control, that I didn't even notice his panic until I made a sharp drift.

The car skidded, and Waqar's head slammed hard against the window.

"Ya Allah…"

For a moment, everything slowed down.

He clutched his head, trying to regain consciousness.

When he finally looked at me, there were tears in his eyes.

Real fear, mixed with a strange relief, flickered in his gaze. I couldn't help but burst into laughter.

With a trembling voice, he said,

"Ilham, you are never playing romantic or breakup songs again, at least not when I'm around."

I shook my head, still laughing, feeling strangely energized as if I'd let everything out through the song.

"I should do this every day," I thought.

"Thank you for bringing me home in one piece and not killing me," Waqar said, though his words carried an unspoken plea that I should never put him through this again.

He got out of the car, walking slowly toward his apartment.

Before leaving, he looked back at me, and I waved goodbye.

Waqar folded his hands, signaling me to just leave, and I couldn't help but laugh again as I turned my car towards my apartment.

I returned to my apartment, tidied up my room, and freshened up.

I didn't feel like going to any party or club tonight. I was really missing Zieba.

It's not that I hadn't thought about her before, but tonight, for some reason, her absence was hitting me hard.

It felt like her absence was tearing me apart from the inside, and whenever I feel this overwhelming void, I lock myself in this room.

I made dinner, as usual. I'm a bit of a health freak; outside food doesn't appeal to me, and street food even less.

I prepared my own version of Steak Diane and Fettuccine Alfredo and sat down to eat.

Just then, Baba called. I picked up the phone with my other hand and placed it against my ear.

Ilham: "Yes, Mr. Osman."

Mr. Osman: "You could at least greet me properly once in a while…"

Ilham: "Alright, why did you call?"

Mr. Osman: "How are you? It's been a while since you came home. Your mother misses you a lot… come visit just once."

Ilham: "I'm not coming back until I've reached my destination. Tell Mom I'm fine—nothing will happen to her son."

Mr. Osman: "I told you he wouldn't listen to this…," I heard him say to Mom.

Ilham: "Alright, now let me eat in peace. Bye."

Mr. Osman: "Ilh—"

I hung up the call, put my phone down on the table, and continued eating. After finishing my meal, I washed the dishes, cleaned up the kitchen, and headed back to my room.

I took off my t-shirt and lay face down on the bed. Looking at the hairband on my wrist, I began reminiscing about the first time I saw Zieba.

"Why do you always come into my thoughts? What do you want, Miss J3?"

Lost in thoughts of Zieba, I didn't even realize when I drifted off to sleep. And, as always, she appeared again.

There hasn't been a single night where I haven't seen her in that white dress, walking softly among the fragrant flowers by the edge of a clear lake, smiling at me from a distance.

Every time I dream, it's the same shadow of Zieba, and I never want to wake up.

When she calls my name—Ilham…

At least, in my thoughts, she's with me.

But suddenly, my dream began to change.

The fresh water lake transformed into boiling lava, the beautiful flowers started wilting, and flames began spreading around me. Zieba was nowhere to be seen.

"Zieba... Zieba..." I called out, but she was gone.

"This is a dream, Ilham..."

And then I saw a loophole in the dream, where the number **67** was glowing.

I ran toward the loophole, trying to escape the flames that seemed to have been starving for ages, eager to engulf someone.

But the fire consumed me as I struggled to escape..............

"What the bloody hell............."

I woke up, gasping for breath.

Even in the cool air-conditioned room, my body was drenched in sweat.

My throat was parched.

I got up, drank a glass of water, and lay back down.

I felt strange—an unfamiliar sensation I had never experienced before.

Usually, I could understand my dreams and their loopholes, but for the first time, I couldn't reach this one.

And that number—'**67**'—still wouldn't leave me.

I had no idea what it meant.

"These dreams are beautiful one moment and terrifying the next..."

I muttered to myself, running a hand over my face before resting it under my head, staring up at the ceiling of my flat.

I lay there, staring blankly at the ceiling, until my eyes finally started to close on their own.

Just as I was about to fall asleep, my phone rang. I picked it up and saw an unknown number.

I ignored it and tried to sleep again. *Could it be Zieba?*

I quickly grabbed my phone and answered the call before it cut off.

Ilham: "Who's this?"

Unknown: "Ilham? It's Shameen."

Ilham: "What now? How many times have I told you not to call me? Why don't you ever listen?"

Shameen: "I just called to check on you, Ilham."

Ilham: "Don't call me again. I'm not going to die lying here."

Shameen: "For Allah's sake, don't say that, Ilham… May all your troubles fall on me instead."

Ilham: "Oh, please, just stop it, Shameen. I'm hanging up."

I was about to end the call when another unknown number rang.

This time, I ignored it for real.

Would Zieba ever call me? Impossible. It could never happen.

She probably doesn't even think of me, and here I am, waiting for her call?

Ilham… snap out of these impossible thoughts and focus on your goal!

I pushed all thoughts aside and drifted off to sleep again.

"What is 67?"

These two dreams used to come to me separately, but now, how have they merged into one?

And what does Zieba have to do with all of this?

* * *

CHAPTER – 13

(Emptiness…!!!)

"Ilham…?? You should have told us before coming,"

Jenny, Waqar's girlfriend, remarked.

"I already called and texted both of you, Jenny, for your kind information. Now let's get going before I change my mind and leave you both here,"

I said, entering Waqar's flat.

It's 6 a.m., and we need to leave, yet these two are still caught up in their personal activities. *Huh.*

"Ilham, just 10 minutes. We'll be out after a quick shower!" they said before heading to their room.

I couldn't believe Waqar was this interested in a girl. Waqar and I had been friends since the 11th grade.

His father is one of Pakistan's most prominent lawyers, and like him, Waqar came here to pursue law.

But honestly, his focus is less on his studies and more on girls.

Don't even ask me how he manages to pass his exams—I won't disclose that.

As much as Waqar and I have vibed over the years, I haven't connected with anyone else like I have with him.

There are plenty of guys in our class, both Indian and Pakistani, but none like Waqar.

"Waqar, are you coming or not? I'm leaving," I shouted toward him, unable to sit still any longer.

"Yes, yes, Ilham, just a little more time," Waqar called back.

"This guy is never going to change,"

I muttered to myself, putting on my headphones to pass the time.

Waqar had never shown this much interest in any of his past girlfriends.

As usual, his "10 minutes" turned into a full 30 minutes of my time wasted.

"Alright, let's go," Waqar finally said, as he and Jenny walked toward me with their bags. Both of their faces were flushed.

"Seriously, you two…" I sighed deeply, shaking my head in disbelief as we set off for our adventure and weekend activities.

We'd all booked bus tickets to Dawson City, Yukon—an epic place on our bucket list where we were eager to experience thrills and adventure.

Our group consisted of Waqar, Jenny, Arfaz, Shainaaz, Hamza, Alex, Juliana (Alex's girlfriend), Sarah, Amina, and me.

All of them were just like me, eager to dive into every adventure we could find.

The journey was long, and whenever I'm alone, I'm never truly alone, because she stays with me in my thoughts.

Zieba. My heart longs to return to India just to see her once.

But I wonder—would she even be happy to see me?

What reason could I give her for showing up?

Both to myself and to her?

If she doesn't want to see me, how would I handle that situation? The biggest issue is that I've been suppressing my feelings for the past three years because I don't want to be caught up in my emotions.

If I do, I know for certain I'll do whatever it takes to have her—even against her will.

And that's something I don't want to do.

My pride matters most to me.

If my father found out I desired her, it would become an issue of my self-respect.

The journey was 10 hours long, and I spent a good 8 hours thinking about Zieba.

Yes, I told myself not to dwell on her, but can anyone just stop living? Ever since I met her, I've been living in her thoughts.

She's created a new world for herself, but somehow, I started weaving my own story into hers.

In her world, I exist—following behind her with my incomplete story. Only she can complete it.

The thing is…, Zieba is a disease to me, and she's the only cure.

Until I bring her to me, this disease won't end.

And the fact is, though, it's impossible. She'll never come close to someone like me.

Eventually, I fell asleep, my thoughts still lingering on her.

At 5 p.m., we finally arrived in Dawson City, Yukon. I grabbed my bag and stepped off the bus. The atmosphere was fantastic, surrounded by mountains. Paragliding, skydiving, bungee jumping—so many activities awaited us. We headed straight to the hotel to rest, excited to dive into our adventures with full energy the next day.

Amidst the highest peaks of the world, I feel truly alive. The snowy mountains and blue lakes of Dawson City, Yukon, bring peace to my soul.

Soaring through the air while paragliding, free-falling toward the ground in skydiving, and feeling my heart race during bungee jumping—these are the most exhilarating moments of my life.

Seeing the world from a bird's eye view, feeling small amidst the towering mountains, and imprinting nature's magnificent scenes into my heart give me a renewed strength.

I'm constantly trying to fulfil all my desires.

For me, it's not just thrill-seeking but a way to understand life's true essence.

As I landed from paragliding and freed myself from the safety gear, someone crashed into me from behind, knocking me to the ground.

"What the hell? Are you blind?"

I gritted my teeth as I turned around.

It was a girl; I could tell from her voice.

"I'm really, really sorry! I was… um… are you okay?" she asked, taking off her helmet and mask.

My eyes didn't leave her for a second.

Why? It wasn't the girl I was looking at—it was the mole on her cheek.

That mole transported me back to the first time I saw Zieba…

"It's okay," I replied calmly, walking back to my friends.

"Wait… um… it doesn't look okay at all. Can we grab a cup of coffee?" she asked, tucking her hair behind her ears.

There were now dirt stains on my brown shirt.

"I don't prefer having coffee with strangers," I said coldly, about to walk away, when she grabbed my hand to stop me.

I pulled my hand free and glared at her.

"Don't. Ever. Do. That. Again." I growled.

I never let anyone, especially women, touch me without my consent.

I hate it.

"Well, in that case, let's be friends. I'm Rossy, and you are...?" she asked, extending her hand.

"I also don't prefer being friends with strangers," I said, stepping back.

Looking at the hairband around my wrist, a smile crept onto my face. Zieba, I wish you had bumped into me instead.

How wonderful that would have been! I would've been over the moon, Zieba! Here, in Dawson City, Ilham Osman Khaan would've lost his mind. I miss you, Miss J3...

"Ilham, where do you disappear to every time?" Waqar asked, seeing me approaching the group.

"I'm here now, let's go," I replied, and we headed toward the heart of Dawson City to take in the night.

There's something magical about Dawson City at night.

In the moonlit sky, with stars glittering, I feel like a part of a story.

A story no one has ever read.

The colourful streets, the bazaars full of lights, and the inns all tell tales of new beginnings.

The various cafes and gatherings, where people recite poetry and ghazals, show me new paths for my soul.

I feel good when I travel around the world.

Sitting on the cliff above the Yukon River under the stars, I watch the colors of my dreams unfold

The silence of the night and the bustle of the city together create a world that only seems possible here in Dawson City.

The liveliness of the night and the vibrancy of life—they teach my heart a new way of living.

"Ilham, let's hit the club," Waqar suggested, entering with Jenny.

I decided to join them, and we spent the night dancing, drinking, and doing drugs in the club.

-Now, you might wonder, where does Ilham always find drugs?

This world isn't as innocent as it seems. If you want, you can buy anything with money…

Some people's wealth exists to satisfy their desires, and my desires are also fulfilled by my wealth.

We had an amazing weekend in Dawson City, Yukon, experiencing adventure, thrills, and the colourful nightlife.

But as always, in the end, I was left in that same emptiness. And again, the same question echoed in my mind:

-What is the purpose of a heart that yearns, if all desires end in emptiness?

The cold wind bit at my face as I stood outside the club, feeling the chill on my skin.

I took a long drag from my cigarette, letting the smoke fill my lungs before exhaling slowly into the dark night.

The lights of Dawson City shimmered, but there was nothing special about them.

I had come outside, away from the noise, the lights, and the people, just to escape the suffocating feeling that always loomed over me.

This place always pressed down on me.

Maybe this is what happens when you stop pretending there's any grand purpose, any real pleasure, or any true peace in all of it.

Because there isn't.

No purpose, no pleasure, no peace.

I slipped my hand into my pocket and leaned back against the wall, waiting. Suddenly, Jenny stumbled outside and threw up.

She looked awful.

After rinsing her mouth with water, she stared at me.

"Why are you outside?"

She asked, her voice rough as she tried to steady herself.

"Found your voice?" I replied sarcastically, as she started talking in our native language.

"Yeah, Waqar taught me," she said with a faint smile.

I averted my eyes, avoiding her gaze.

Jenny's clothes left little to the imagination, but the truth was, I had no interest in looking.

Not out of shame, but because I simply didn't care.

"Just fed up," I muttered, taking another drag from the cigarette. "Needed a break."

"Me too," she sighed and leaned against the wall next to me.

Without asking, she took the cigarette from my hand, and I let her. She took a long drag, exhaling the smoke slowly.

We stood there in silence, our backs to the world.

Then suddenly, she spoke, quietly this time, as if she'd been thinking about it for a while.

"Ilham… do you ever feel like there's something greater than all of this? Greater than us?" Her voice trembled slightly, as if she was scared to even talk about it. "I mean, have you ever wondered what's the point of it all?"

I frowned, looking at her. "What do you mean?"

"Have you read your religious book?" she asked.

"Yeah," I replied.

"You know, God, life, the world, the afterlife, the purpose?" Her voice shook a little, like she was afraid even to ask. "I think about it sometimes. Like, what's the point of all of us?"

I stared straight ahead, slowly exhaling a puff of cigarette smoke. "I don't know. Never really thought about it," I lied because, deep down, maybe I was searching for the same answer.

"Really...?" She looked at me.

"But you're a Muslim, right? You should believe in something, or at least know something," she said.

I let out a laugh, but it felt more like mockery than amusement.

"Yeah, maybe on paper, just like the law books we have—filled with rules, regulations, and the punishments for breaking them. But that's it. I don't believe in any of it. Allah, fate, the afterlife—they all seem like fairy tales to me. Nothing more than that."

Jenny looked down at the ground, silent for a moment.

"But what if they aren't just stories? What if there's more to it—something we're missing? What if we're the ones who are wrong?"

I took another drag from the cigarette, feeling the warmth of the smoke, and then handed it back to her.

"Look, Jenny, people believe in this stuff because they're afraid. Afraid of death. That's why they create these stories, so they can comfort themselves. That's all religion is—comforting lies. If it were true, then the world wouldn't be so messed up. Everyone would be good, no one would do wrong. Some people have even turned religion into a business. If it were real, why do they live like this? It's all lies, and everyone is a liar."

She hesitated at my words, unsure.

"And what if these are not just stories? I've been reading about other religions. Even Islam. It talks about the purpose of life, the afterlife—it answers questions like these."

I raised an eyebrow, surprised.

Jenny asking questions about Islam? This was something new.

But then again, people often look for meaning when they're searching for a purpose.

"So, what have you learned?" I asked, unable to hide my curiosity.

She took a drag from the cigarette, looking down at her boots, which glimmered in the moonlight.

"I've been bothered by this question for a long time—why is there so much suffering in the world? If God exists, why doesn't He do anything? I've been reading about Islam, and… it actually gives reasons and answers to every question. Like, there's a bigger plan, something beyond this life… the afterlife, our deeds, our destination—everything."

I let out a breath, shaking my head.

"A bigger plan, huh? That just sounds like another way to make sense of this mess. Look, Jenny, people suffer with pain and stress because life is meaningless to them or because they don't know how to live it. There's no bigger plan, no divine intervention. We just live, we die, and that's it. There's no such thing as an afterlife. When there's no life left in the body, how could there be any pain?"

She stared at me in silence for a long time, her eyes clouded with thought.

She couldn't digest my words.

I wasn't interested in having a debate about religion right then.

But then she said, "You just said you've read the Quran…"

"Yeah," I nodded.

"I'm telling you; you actually haven't read it… sadly,"

Jenny gave me a faint smile, like she pitied me, and just then, Waqar appeared.

"What are you two doing out here?" he asked. I didn't respond, and Jenny walked over to him.

"You were with another girl, that's why I came outside…"

"Were you jealous…?" Waqar asked.

"Yes… maybe," she replied.

"I wanted you to be jealous…" Waqar said, and he kissed her.

Their conversation turned into whispered exchanges as I left the two of them alone and headed back toward the hotel.

Jenny's words echoed in my mind:

"I'm telling you; you actually haven't read it… sadly…"

Sadly? Sad about what…?

Huh—I don't care.

* * *

EPISODE – 14

(Do I Love Her….!!!)

We had returned to Toronto, settling back into our regular routine.

The next day, we had organized a grand birthday party for Waqar at a club that was conveniently close to our apartment.

At the Toro-to-Frans club, we celebrated Waqar's birthday.

In the darkness of the night, amidst the lights and the blaring music, we all came together for a unique celebration.

No one even thought about a birthday cake, because we had all grown past that stage.

Instead of cake cutting, we turned to alcohol and drugs, spending the night in a whirlwind of energy and excitement.

The club's dance floor echoed with laughter, shouts, and moments brimming with life, turning everything into a beautiful memory. Waqar's birthday, that night, and the party itself became an unforgettable experience.

As the party reached its conclusion, I felt a deep sense of boredom with the club, the noise, and the celebration.

This always happens to me—at first, I feel full of myself, completely energized, but in the next moment, I get tired of it all, leaving me with a sense of emptiness at the end.

Without telling anyone, I slipped out and headed back to my apartment.

The entire walk home, my mind was consumed with thoughts of Zieba. Zieba, the one people say ~~I might like~~, though I've never admitted it to myself.

Perhaps I don't want to admit that ~~I like her.~~

Her memories, her smile, her presence—all of it brought a strange mix of comfort and pain to my heart.

As I walked in the cool, gentle breeze of the night, my heart was caught in the warmth of her memories.

I had never spoken these words to myself, but tonight, my silence was saying everything…

یہ کیسا جادو ہے، جو تم نے کر دیا؟

تمہارے عکس کو دل کے آئینے میں اتار لیا۔

نہ جانے کیوں تمہارا خیال ہر دم ستاتا ہے

میرے دل کو بس تمہاری یادوں سے سکون آتا ہے۔

کبھی تمہارے خیال سے دل میں بہار آتی ہے

کبھی تمہاری کمی سے روح تڑپ کے رہ جاتی ہے۔

ہر صبح، ہر شام تمہاری پرچھائی نظر آتی ہے

تمہارے بغیر یہ دنیا ادھوری سی نظر آتی ہے۔

تمہیں بھولنے کی کوشش ہر بار بیکار جاتی ہے

تمہاری یادیں ہر لمحہ میری راہیں سجاتی ہیں۔

الہام کے لیے ایک پہیلی سی ہو تم، جو ہر لمحہ ایک نئی داستان سناتی ہے

زیبا کی ہر شکایت میں محبت بھی مسکرا جاتی ہے۔

What is this magic you've woven around me?

Your image has quietly settled in my heart's reflection, you see.

I wonder why your thoughts torment me night and day,

Only your memories can soothe my heart in this way.

At times, your presence brings a springtime bloom,

Yet in your absence, my soul withers in gloom.

Morning to evening, I catch glimpses of your trace,

Without you, this world feels an empty, hollow place.

Every effort to forget you turns to dust,

Your memories pave my path, as if they must.

To Ilham, you're a riddle, a story ever untold,

And in Zieba's every complaint, love's smile unfolds.

* * *

I was lost in thoughts of Zieba as I made my way back to my apartment.

When I arrived, I noticed someone moving their belongings at this late hour, but I didn't pay much attention and entered my apartment.

Just as I was about to climb the stairs, my phone rang. I pulled out my mobile and saw it was Maryam calling.

Maryam: Ilham—we need to talk…………,

Maryam's voice came through the line.

Ilham: Yeah, go ahead. I'm listening.

Maryam: There's trouble, man," she said with a sigh.

Ilham: Is my Zie—" I corrected myself, "I mean, is Zieba involved in any way?"

Maryam: No… but—

Ilham: Then handle it on your own, Maryam. I don't need this.

Maryam: What's with you weirdo and this attitude—?"

I cut her off, ending the call.

As I stared at the stairs, I tried to steady myself and climb them slowly.

I managed to make it up a few steps, but suddenly……….

Something heavy hit the back of my head, and before I could even react, everything went black.

* * *

Last night, I was drowning in alcohol and drugs.

When I opened my eyes, the piercing morning light from the sun stabbed at them.

My head throbbed with a severe hangover, and I groaned in pain.

When I looked around, I realized this wasn't my room.

Hell, it wasn't even my apartment.

My room was never this messy or chaotic. I was in some unfamiliar place.

I got out of bed and walked out of the room, only to see a girl standing there.

She had long, loose black hair cascading down her back and was wearing a casual outfit—a long t-shirt that reached her knees and shorts that revealed her bare legs. She glanced at me with a playful smile.

"Well, hello there, handsome," she greeted me, then turned to make coffee in the kitchen.

"Rossy…? How did I end up here?" I asked, running my fingers through my disheveled hair.

"Wow, impressive. You actually remember my name," she teased, her tone dripping with sarcasm. She let out a deep sigh before continuing.

"You were in a pretty bad state last night, and since I didn't know where you lived, I brought you here. I did the right thing, didn't I?"

She handed me a mug of coffee as she spoke.

She looked Indian but seemed like she had been living here for quite some time.

"I need my jacket and phone," I said curtly, scanning the room for my belongings.

"First, have some coffee, then you can get what you need," she insisted.

"I don't like coffee," I replied, my tone flat.

She grinned, clearly enjoying the interaction. "So, what do you like?"

"I don't like anything," I snapped back, dumping the coffee into the sink and turning to face her. "Now, give me my coat and phone."

Rossy rolled her eyes but went into another room, returning with my coat and phone.

As I reached out to take them, she pulled them back, teasing me.

"I'll be honest because I'm always honest… Can we date?" she asked, her question casual, as if this was the most natural thing to ask someone she'd just met.

"I don't like you,"

I said sharply, grabbing my jacket from her hands, along with my phone.

"But I like tough guys," she responded with a sly smile.

Ignoring her, I quickly made my way out of her apartment.

As I stepped out, I realized Rossy wasn't just a renter in my building—she was my next-door neighbour.

I made a mental note of that as I entered my own flat.

Glancing at the time, I realized I was running late for university.

I rushed through a quick shower and got ready as fast as I could.

My stomach growled, reminding me I hadn't eaten. I hurriedly made myself some breakfast.

Just as I sat down to eat, there was a knock at the door.

It was Waqar.

He walked in casually and threw himself onto the couch in the living room.

"Where'd you disappear to last night, man?"

Waqar asked, lounging comfortably, his eyes half-closed in contentment.

"I get bored easily if I stay in one place for too long, so I just left,"

I replied, focusing on my breakfast.

"Don't give me that nonsense crap. I came to your apartment earlier, and you weren't here. Tell me the truth—where were you all night?"

Waqar walked over to my chair, pressing me for an answer.

"I don't owe you any explanations," I said, locking eyes with him.

"You were with a girl, weren't you?"

Waqar grinned mischievously, his tone playful.

"You know I'm not into that kind of thing. If I were with a girl, I wouldn't hide it. I'd be out in the open about it,"

I said, trying to divert my attention back to my breakfast.

"Your actions are telling me a different story, brother…!" Waqar teased.

"Wait a minute… Did you make some new friends? I will never allow this…, because I'm super possessive about you, Ilham. No new friends without my approval!"

He shot me a serious look, but I could see the humour behind his words.

"I just blacked out, that's all. Some girl took me back to her apartment. She lives next door, apparently," I explained, still feeling disoriented.

Waqar gave me a wide-eyed stare.

"Wait—so you spent the night at some girl's place? Ilham, I didn't know you had it in you!" He laughed out loud.

"Cut the crap. She just didn't know where I lived, so she brought me back to her place. I stayed the night, but it wasn't like that,"

I clarified, finishing my breakfast.

"Fine, I believe you. You're the only guy I know who's never shown interest in a girl. No way you'd actually spend the night with one," Waqar smirked, grabbing his bag as we prepared to leave for university.

As we walked out, Waqar couldn't help checking himself in the mirror one last time, flexing his muscles.

"Let's be real, you will always be going to look like a gorilla, no matter how much you try."

"Shut up. You know every girl's crazy about me,"

he said,

"Yeah, because I don't give them the attention....,"

I said, rolling my eyes as Waqar wrapped his arm around my neck playfully, pulling me into a mock chokehold.

I chuckled.

He wasn't wrong—girls did fall for him all the time.

With his striking complexion, he stood out, and his disheveled black hair only added to his appeal.

His dark eyes were intense and captivating, drawing people in with their depth.

Whenever he smiled, his dimples deepened, giving his face a charming, boyish look.

All of these features combined made him unforgettable, and his magnetic presence left a lasting impact on everyone he met.

Waqar and I got into my car and headed to university. We had become friends because of how much we had in common.

I drove fast, recklessly weaving through traffic, but Waqar, who used to be terrified of my driving, was now completely used to it.

We always played Bollywood songs on our drives, and today was no exception.

We were blasting *Desi Boyz* and enjoying the ride.

Waqar had control of the playlist, carefully avoiding any romantic or heartbreak songs. He wasn't ready to say hello to death again.

We arrived at the university quickly, and as usual, Jenny was waiting for Waqar near the parking lot.

He stepped out of the car and immediately went to greet her with a kiss. Today, Jenny looked different—she was wearing a scarf.

"Why are you wearing that?" Waqar asked.

"I just thought it looked nice," she replied with a shrug.

Waqar, ever the flirt, kissed her neck in appreciation, while I left them and made my way to class.

"Ilham, we have a seminar today, and I haven't prepared at all!" Waqar hurried after me, while saying.

"You should've prepared, Waqar. We're not just presenting case studies today—we have to prove our point of view as well," I reminded him, barely holding back my annoyance.

"I can't do this!" Waqar raised his hands in surrender.

"Who said you had to?" I said, entering the classroom and taking my seat.

There were only five minutes left before the lecture began.

The professor walked in… accompanied by none other than Rossy.

I was stunned to see her.

What is this girl doing here?

Why is she following me?

My thoughts raced.

And that mole on her cheek—damn it, that's Zieba's thing.

That mole should only belong to Zieba, not her…

It's not because I am losing my control but the pain of Zieba's absence is deeply felt, whenever I see that mole.

As the professor introduced the girl, he said, "You may sit wherever you like." Rossy glanced in my direction, gave me a slight smile, and started walking toward me.

"Hell no…"

"If you don't mind, can we switch seats?" Rossy asked Waqar in a soft tone. I signaled Waqar to say no, and that was my mistake because I knew he would do the exact opposite of what I expected.

"Oh, of course, beautiful," Waqar said, standing up and moving to the seat beside hers.

I shot Waqar a serious look, but in return, he burst into laughter. I tried to focus on the professor's lecture, pretending to be engrossed.

"Hello again, handsome," Rossy said to me during the lecture.

"I don't prefer talking during lectures," I replied, using it as an excuse to avoid interacting with her.

"Then tell me what you do prefer, and we can adjust accordingly," Rossy said with a subtle, mysterious smile, though not the kind of mystery I have concern with.

"Just be quiet—or leave the lecture," I snapped, irritated. She didn't bother me again after that, as I had firmly shut her down.

A long while later, the lecture ended, and it was time for our seminar. The room fell completely silent when Professor Dr. Anwar called me to the podium, as I had been the only one to solve the case for this seminar.

As I reached the podium, Dr. Anwar took his seat, and the room's attention shifted to me with a silent curiosity.

Standing at the podium, I quickly surveyed the room before connecting my laptop to the projector screen behind me. My presentation illuminated the whiteboard, displaying the thesis title—**"Legal Strategies in Complex Corporate Disputes: The Case of Vaswani Industries Ltd."**

I began to speak, "Good afternoon, everyone. Today, I'll be presenting a case study on Vaswani Industries Ltd., a case that has sparked much debate and confusion within the legal community. You all are familiar with it, aren't you?" I asked the room, to which everyone nodded in agreement. I rolled up my sleeves to my elbows.

"Good," I continued with my presentation. "This case, involving a complex corporate dispute, remained unsolved for years due to its intricate web of contracts, financial irregularities, and stakeholder conflicts. However, after meticulous research and analysis, I was able to uncover the underlying issues and provide a viable legal strategy for resolution."

I clicked the forward button on the remote, advancing the slide to reveal a flowchart that outlined the key aspects of the case.

The room remained fully engaged, carefully observing and listening to every detail.

Continuing, I explained, "Vaswani Industries Ltd., a major player in the steel manufacturing sector, was entangled in a legal battle with its suppliers and shareholders. At the heart of the dispute was a breach of contract and allegations of financial mismanagement. Previous attempts to resolve the case had failed due to the lack of clear evidence and the complexity of the contractual agreements."

I paused for a moment, allowing everyone to process what I had just said.

They whispered among themselves briefly, then turned their attention back to my explanation.

"However," I resumed, "after reviewing the case files and re-examining the contracts, I discovered several inconsistencies in the financial reports submitted by the company's CFO. By cross-referencing these reports with independent audits, I was able to prove that the CFO had falsified documents to cover up embezzlement. This not only breached the contract with the suppliers but also violated corporate governance laws, strengthening the case against the CFO and allowing the company to negotiate new terms with the suppliers."

Despite my efforts to stay focused, my eyes involuntarily drifted toward Rossy, who was staring at me intently.

I composed myself, determined to ignore her gaze, and advanced the presentation to the next slide.

I began explaining the legal provisions and clauses that supported my conclusions.

"The legal strategy I proposed was twofold: First, to pursue criminal charges against the CFO for financial fraud, which would set a precedent and ensure compliance with corporate governance laws. Second, to renegotiate the contracts with the suppliers under the new management, based on recalibrated financial reports. This approach not only resolved the dispute but also restored the company's reputation in the market."

My voice was steady and confident, every word projected clearly enough for everyone in the room to hear.

I could tell from their expressions that they were fully engaged and following my explanation closely.

"This case demonstrates the importance of attention to detail and the necessity of a thorough understanding of corporate law and financial management in resolving complex disputes."

I took a deep breath and then continued, "It also highlights the critical role that legal professionals play in safeguarding the integrity of the corporate sector."

I glanced at Dr. Anwar, who was watching me with a proud smile.

Finally, I concluded, "In conclusion, this case was a challenging one, but with the right legal strategies and a firm commitment to uncovering the truth, even the most complex cases can be resolved. I look forward to your feedback, Professor Dr. Anwar."

The room fell into an almost eerie silence, as if no one else existed besides me.

Dr. Anwar stood up and began clapping, making his way toward me at the podium.

"Excellent work, Mr. Ilham Osman Khaan," he said, taking the thesis files from my hand. "Your ability to dissect such a complicated case and present a clear, strategic solution is commendable. This is exactly the kind of sharp legal mind we need in the field."

"Does anyone have any questions?" the professor asked, and I glanced at my class.

Three students raised their hands, one of them being Rossy.

"You first, go ahead with your question," I said, pointing to the guy sitting at the very back.

"Ilham, your analysis of the financial irregularities was impressive. But given the complexity of the case, how did you manage to identify the inconsistencies in the CFO's reports when others failed to do so?"

"That's a great question," I began. "The key wasn't just in looking at the numbers but in understanding the story behind them. I approached the financial reports with a critical eye, looking for patterns and cross-referencing them with independent audits. I also paid close attention to the timing of the transactions and how they aligned—or rather, didn't align—with the company's contractual obligations. By digging deeper into the context and not just the content, I was able to spot the discrepancies that others overlooked."

My response seemed to leave him satisfied. He smiled and nodded, sitting back down.

"You, in the second row, the girl with the white t-shirt and red wine-colored hair, go ahead," I said.

"You mentioned renegotiating contracts under new management. How did you ensure that the suppliers would agree to the new terms after such a breach of trust?"

Her question didn't really seem like a tough one, but I still had to answer it. "That's an important aspect of the case," I replied. "Trust had been severely damaged, but the new management played a crucial role in rebuilding it. I advised the company to be transparent about the issues that had occurred and to offer terms that were not only fair but also beneficial to the suppliers in the long run. By demonstrating a genuine commitment to rectifying past mistakes and ensuring future compliance, the company was able to convince the suppliers that this new arrangement would be mutually advantageous."

"Mm, got it," she said, returning to her seat.

"Alright, you, the new girl, go ahead," I said, referring to Rossy without even looking at her. I didn't want to look at her; her mole was bothering me more than I wanted to admit.

"Considering the legal implications, why did you choose to pursue criminal charges against the CFO rather than a civil suit for breach of contract?" she asked, standing still, waiting for my response.

I looked at her and began my explanation.

"Choosing to pursue criminal charges was a strategic decision. While a civil suit would have addressed the breach of contract, it wouldn't have fully captured the gravity of the CFO's actions, which included fraud and embezzlement. Criminal charges not only held the CFO accountable on a more serious level but also served as a deterrent to future misconduct within the company. Moreover, it sent a clear message to all stakeholders that the company was committed to upholding the highest standards of corporate governance. This approach ultimately strengthened the company's position both legally and reputationally."

With that, Rossy sat back down.

"Any more questions?" I asked, scanning the room.

No one seemed to have anything else to ask.

"Good,"

I said, shaking hands with Dr. Anwar before stepping down from the podium, gathering my laptop and other things.

I sat back down, feeling at ease as the room continued to echo with applause for quite some time.

It wasn't the first time that applause filled the room whenever I was around. Wherever Ilham Osman Khaan is, applause is bound to follow.

Rossy gave me a soft smile and congratulated me on the seminar, but I ignored her, or rather, I ignored the mole on her cheek.

The more I thought about Zieba in her absence, the more I found myself thinking about her now—because of this girl. Seeing Rossy only made me miss Zieba even more.

* * *

"Wait..., handsome."

Rossy followed me after the seminar, determined to catch up.

"Stop—-calling—-me—-that," I said sternly, fed up with this girl who wouldn't leave me alone. Why couldn't she just stop pestering me?

"Then tell me your name, I'll call you by that," she insisted, a persistent smile glued to her face.

"Ilham, Ilham Osman Khaan. And yours, beautiful?"

Waqar, overhearing our conversation, chimed in from behind with a teasing grin.

"Oh, Ilham... that's a unique name." Rossy repeated my name, her eyes lingering on me. I tried to ignore her.

"Hello, I'm Rossy, Ilham's new neighbour," she introduced herself, extending a hand towards Waqar.

"What a lovely name, as beautiful as a rose, Miss Rossy," Waqar flirted shamelessly, taking her hand and kissing it lightly.

Jenny, who had been watching all this, was visibly upset. This was the first time tension had surfaced between them. Jenny's anger was palpable, and Waqar, sensing her frustration, quickly grabbed her hand.

"So, as you said, neighbour... you're the one Ilham spent the night with?" Waqar remarked cheekily.

I shoved him, stopping his nonsense.

"Yeah, but your friend here is quite ungrateful. I gave him shelter, and he didn't even bother to say a proper thank you," Rossy retorted, tucking a strand of hair behind her ear.

"What? Ilham, are you serious? You didn't thank such a beautiful girl? That's unacceptable, brother."

Waqar winked at Rossy, clearly enjoying the situation.

"Get lost, Waqar. If you like her so much, you say it." I turned to leave.

"Ilham, how about a coffee? You could at least thank me that way."

She insisted, and I reluctantly agreed. It seemed better to settle this once and for all over a cup of coffee. I figured we could go to the university café, but she had other plans.

"Not here, Ilham. Let's go somewhere else… anyway, the lectures are over."

She said in a soft tone. -*Coffee, and now demands? Fine, she can pay for it.*

"Where do you want to go? Doesn't the coffee here suit your taste?" I asked, a bit annoyed.

"Let's go out, please."

Her persistent tone made me give in.

"Fine, but you're paying the bill," I said.

"Okay, fine, I'll pay."

We ended up at a nearby café, where it was quiet and peaceful. After we ordered our coffee, I decided not to engage in any more conversation and focused on my phone instead.

I noticed a message from Maryam that I had somehow missed the night before. Opening it, I read:

Maryam: Ilham, you're such a big potato. I swear, I won't tell you anything about Zieba anymore. You're the worst! (Crying emojis).

A faint smile tugged at my lips as I read her message.

She was probably dealing with some mess, but Fateen was with her, so he must have handled it.

Ilham: Maryam, you French fries, you're grown up now. You should solve your own problems. This isn't some fairy tale where a hero or hero's friend comes to save you.

Maryam responded almost instantly, probably online late into the night as usual.

Maryam: What kind of person are you? Can't you ever see someone else's pain or suffering?

Ilham: No, unless it's hers.

Maryam: Oh, so if Zieba's in trouble, you'd come immediately?

Ilham: Yes, immediately.

Maryam: But what if she's in trouble and doesn't call for you?

Ilham: Then I'd run even faster.

Maryam: Wow, Zieba is going to love this.

Ilham: If you tell her about these chats, Maryam, you'll be the one in actual trouble.

Maryam: Huh… so back to your true form? You don't like anyone besides her, do you, Ilham?

Ilham: Is there anyone else besides her, Maryam? She's everywhere, in everything.

Maryam: Why don't you just tell her how you feel, man?

Ilham: Do you really think she'd accept me?

Maryam: Have you even tried, Ilham? Girls can take years to accept love. Do you really expect her to just embrace it? She probably has her own dreams and expectations about her boyfriend too. Show some effort, dude.

I started to type: [Maryam, I don't want to be her boyfriend, I want to be her husband—just like she desires.] But instead, I backspaced it and decided to give a different reply.

Ilham: Maryam, I don't want to be her boyfriend—she's just a good girl, and I don't have any feelings of love or anything like that.

At that moment, Rossy cleared her throat, snapping me out of my thoughts. I glanced at her briefly and put my phone aside.

"Look, Ilham, I'll get straight to the point. I like you, okay? And I want to date you." Rossy said bluntly, without a hint of hesitation.

If I had said something this straightforward to Zieba, maybe things would've been different. Maybe I wouldn't be sitting here with Rossy but with Zieba instead.

"Dating's not my thing," I replied.

"How would you know if you don't give it a try?" she challenged.

"And even if I wanted to try, do you really think I'd choose you? Don't you think you're aiming a bit too high?" I made myself perfectly clear.

"Okay, listen. I'm not asking you to marry me. Let's just try and see where we end up."

Rossy must have thought this was all so simple, given the environment she was used to.

If I wanted, I could've easily agreed to her offer, but my heart? My mind? And this Ilham...? Everything was still locked away in that corner of India where a girl named Zieba lived.

"Look, I'm not interested in any of this," I cut her off, making an excuse to end the conversation.

"And if you insist, we can be friends. But nothing more. And even with friends, I have boundaries. Don't forget that."

"Fine, friends it is, then?" she said, extending her hand. I shook it.

"Yeah."

She finished her coffee, and I left her at the café. I headed home, glad it was over… at least for now.

* * *

I, Waqar, Jenny, and now Rossy have added her to our group.

Whenever Waqar and Jenny are engrossed with each other, Rossy comes in handy, and we often spend our nights partying in clubs—dancing, drinking, and indulging in drugs.

Tonight was no different.

We were at a nearby club, losing ourselves in the haze of too many drinks.

The atmosphere around us was filled with people my age, lost in the intoxication of alcohol and drugs.

Bright lights flickered, and the drug-laced air filled the club, while our minds indulged in every possible pleasure.

Our high was reaching new heights, and we were completely lost in the thrill of it.

The drugs were so powerful that my vision started to blur.

As soon as I inhaled the drugged air through my nose, I felt it course through every vein in my body.

But no high in this world could ever connect me with my soul.

As the pleasure from the drugs subsided, I began gulping down sips of alcohol—*sheer bliss.*

After a while, we all moved to the dance floor, and I, being the most interested in dancing, let myself go.

Rossy started getting closer, her proximity making me feel suffocated and irritated.

I don't like girls getting this close to me, especially when I'm high.

Her closeness became unbearable, so I gently pushed her away and headed outside the club.

I escaped the noise and chaos, sitting on the bonnet of my car. The air was cool, and I was still slightly intoxicated from the drinks and drugs.

Not long after, Rossy joined me, sitting beside me on the car's bonnet.

"Why can't you just be my boyfriend…??" she asked, her voice slurred with intoxication as she tucked her hair behind her ear.

If it had been someone else in my place, they might have been instantly charmed by her beauty.

"Don't I look pretty…??" she asked.

I had forced every girl I met to ask this question, searching for flaws in themselves when I wouldn't let anyone get close to me.

"I don't want to be anyone's man, except hers…" I replied,

"Hers…??" Rossy asked, looking at me curiously.

"Zieba—Zieba Ansari—the quiet girl…" I said, smiling as I spoke her name.

There's something about Zieba's name that evokes a feeling no drug has ever given me.

"Was she your girlfriend?" Rossy asked calmly. I couldn't help but laugh at her question.

"Girlfriend…???————————————" I laughed even harder.

“Why are you laughing…??” Rossy smiled, watching me as I laughed. “Was she your ex-girlfriend?” she asked again, but I couldn’t even imagine Zieba in such a relationship, not even in a fantasy.

“No, my Zieba isn’t one of those girls. She is a pure soul…, my Zieba is among the virtuous. She has no interest in things like this. If anyone even comes close to her, it’s as if her life is at stake. How could she be someone’s girlfriend? She isn’t girlfriend material; she is wife material.” I said as I looked at the hairband Zieba’s hairband, which I wore on my wrist, since the Annual day night.

“Then what’s the problem…? Why don’t you just go to her…??” Rossy asked.

“The problem…?? It’s me. If she even looks at someone like me, she’d need Zam Zam water to cleanse her eyes. I can’t go to her, and she would never come near someone like me.” I replied with a hint of despair, feeling my eyes begin to water.

“Then forget her…, there are plenty of other girls in the world…” Rossy said, and she was right—there were plenty of girls. But the problem was that they were all blurry in my eyes.

The only one I saw clearly was Zieba, and my heart was only for her.

“I can forget every face in this world, but not hers. There are many girls, but the one who has become the purpose of my life can never be replaced—and I don’t want to replace her.”

“The right to be close to me is something I’ve given only to Zieba, which, in reality, is impossible. That girl has imprisoned me without even realizing it, and I’m more than happy to spend my life in her captivity. I don’t need anyone else’s love or fleeting moments of happiness. That one glimpse of her, that feeling, is enough for me. I can live my entire life in those memories.”

As I said this, I got off the car bonnet, and when Rossy tried to help me, I pulled my hand away from her grasp and started walking toward my apartment.

I've indulged in so much intoxication, yet there's still this emptiness eating me up inside, a strange longing in my heart, though I can't quite understand what it wants...

Rossy followed behind me, and after walking for a while, we reached the apartment. She went to her flat,

"Good night, Ilham."

I gave a faint smile and entered my flat, heading straight to my room. I collapsed face down on my bed.

"I miss you, Zieba...

I miss you....

I miss you a lot————

As always, Zieba's shadow appeared behind my closed eyes, like a shining light in the darkness. Her white dress, her radiant face, her sweet smile, the way she softly said my name,

'Ilham...??'

It had become as natural as the sun setting and the moon rising. Her appearing in my thoughts felt like a law of nature, and who can change the laws of nature...??

Her voice brought a sense of peace to my ears in the noisy life I led.

There isn't a single day or night when you haven't crossed my mind, Zieba.

Tell me, what did you do to me that I'm always lost in thoughts of you...??

What kind of prison is this where you've trapped me without any chains...?

Do you even know...??

That I'm here, across seven seas, being only loyal for you...?

Only yours…!!!

People say when a person is intoxicated, they're no longer themselves.

But if that's true, then why do I hear your voice everywhere when I'm high…?

Why do I feel your presence around me…?

Why do I search for you in every girl…?

Do I really ~~love Zieba…?~~

And if I do, then why doesn't she feel the same…??

Why….??

Why…??

Why…??"

* * *

EPISODE – 15

(The Lockdown—Or—The Coffin.)

I was lying in bed, my body aching, and my head felt heavy from the remnants of the alcohol and drugs from last night.

This was the first time I felt such intense pain; I had felt pain before, but never like this.

As I blinked my eyes, trying to adjust my vision, the sunlight pierced through, making it hard to see.

I dragged myself out of bed and went to the bathroom to freshen up. After getting ready, I returned to my room, drying my hair, when Waqar called.

Waqar: "Ilham, are you okay…? Rossy said you were pretty high and seemed upset."

Ilham: "It's nothing, I'm fine."

Waqar: "Alright, I just called to tell you that a lockdown has been imposed globally. Grocery stores will remain open for a while, so go and get whatever essentials you need."

Ilham: "What did you say…?? Lockdown…??"

Waqar: "Yes, lockdown. The disease has spread widely, so they've enforced a temporary lockdown to prevent further spread."

Ilham: "Okay."

Waqar: "Yeah, I'll let you go. Jenny and I have moved in together, so if I don't answer your call, just know that I'm busy and don't call me again."

Ilham: "Don't worry, you're of no use to me anyway."

With that, I hung up the call.

So, does this mean we'll be stuck within these four walls all the time now…? What a bizarre situation… ugh! If only these walls could speak…!!

I grabbed my car keys and wallet and headed to the grocery store. It was just a 10-minute drive from my apartment, and I got there quickly.

I gathered the essentials—food, daily-use items—and, of course, included my daily necessities: drinks and beer.

After finishing my grocery shopping, I headed back.

I cleaned my flat, changed the bedsheets, and worked out, as we were in lockdown and obviously, the gyms would be closed.

After a long workout session, I showered and had oatmeal with lemon tea for breakfast.

Just as I was about to dive into my case study, I got a call from my father.

Ilham: "Yes, Mr. Osman…?"

Mr. Osman: "At least say Salam, Ilham."

Ilham: "Okay, why did you call?"

Mr. Osman: "How are things over there…? Why don't you come back…?"

Ilham: "Absolutely not! If I come back now, the government will put me in quarantine. It's better that I stay here."

Mr. Osman: "Yes, that makes sense… Just take care of yourself, Ilham."

Ilham: "I'm home, so why are you worried, now…?"

Mr. Osman: "Anything can happen, even at home, Ilham. May Allah protect you."

Ilham: "Alright, alright. I'm hanging up now."

I ended the call, thinking about my father and his constant worrying—something bad could happen, things could go wrong anywhere.

I laughed to myself,

"What could these lifeless walls possibly do to me?"

His words made me chuckle.

I then returned to my studies, finished my thesis work, and completed the case project I needed to submit to my professor.

* * *

The lockdown was still in place, with no end in sight.

A year had already passed, and it was now 2021.

My studies were continuing online, and even the exams were being conducted online.

Although we were required to present our case thesis as well to substantiate our argument.

The law I was studying was criminal law, which was quite interesting, but it would have been even more enjoyable if we could attend university in person.

I had fully completed my thesis when I received a call from an unknown number.

I don't know why all the unknown numbers in the world seem to call only on my phone—Sure, I know I could ignore it, but I won't because I'm still hoping that one day, I'll get a call from Zieba.

Now, don't laugh at my condition—I know she won't call.

Ilham: "Yes?"

Unknown: "Ilham, it's Shameen. How are you?"

Ilham: "Tell me something, Shameen, how do you keep getting so many numbers? I've gotten tired of blocking you."

Shameen: "If someone really wants to talk, they find a way, Ilham. And I'm not bothering you; I'm just asking about your well-being."

Ilham: "Shameen, stop saying things like that to me. I honestly don't like having to treat you like this every time, kid, and—"

Shameen: "Yes, yes, I know. Good girls don't chase after love like this, and I'm not chasing after you. I just want to talk to you a little, and that's enough for me. It would make me happy."

Ilham: "I don't make anyone happy, and I won't make you happy either. Now hang up, I have work to do."

Shameen: "I called because I wanted to tell you something. Today, I saw Zieba with some strange guy at a bookstore—they were together for quite a while and—"

Ilham: "Shameen, shut up—okay? Just shut up. Don't give me wrong information about her."

Shameen: "Ilham, why would I lie? I'm telling you this because I care about Zieba and you. You're misunderstanding me; that guy seemed strange."

Ilham: "I know everything—I'm not misunderstanding anything. Just because I'm not there doesn't mean I don't know about Zieba. And don't go around accusing her like this."

Shameen: "Will you ever trust me? Are people who love one-sidedly always subjected to suspicion? Are those who love one-sidedly always wrong?"

Ilham: "Yes, they are wrong because they need to clear their own path, and they're willing to go to any extent to do that. It would be better if you stopped bringing Zieba into this and stopped calling me."

Shameen: "One day, this misunderstanding of yours will make you regret, Ilham. And I will be waiting for the day when you admit that not all people who love one-sidedly are selfish. You'll shed tears that day."

"Goodbye, take care of yourself. Fi Amanillah."

This time, Shameen hung up on her own. I set my phone aside and leaned back on the couch, my head tilted downward.

"Why…? Why does Shameen love me…?" I asked myself.

~~"Why…? Why doesn't Zieba love me…?"~~

I was losing myself in my thoughts.

The anger I felt wasn't because Shameen loved me, but because Zieba didn't.

I wanted Zieba to love me, to be drawn to me, just like Shameen was. Zieba… Zieba… Zieba…

I don't know what's happening, why these thoughts are coming to me.

Why is my body, my mind, my heart sinking deeper and deeper into you? I can't even stop myself.

Everywhere else, I have the power to control things, but when it comes to this, all my strength fails me.

~~Or maybe, deep down, I want to be pulled toward her…~~

It was evening, and someone knocked on my door, forcing me out of my thoughts.

When I opened the door, I saw it wasn't anyone else but Rossy standing there, smiling. I was without a shirt, only wearing loose track pants.

Rossy was looking at me intently, and her gaze landed on the tattoo on my chest. I cleared my throat to bring her back to reality.

"I'm bored staying with those non-talkative walls. Can we share tonight… and yes as friends, of course?" Rossy asked, fidgeting with her shirt.

Honestly, I was pretty bored myself. It had been a while since we had drinks, so I agreed, thinking her company might be a good distraction.

Rossy stepped into my flat.

"Wow, your flat is way neater than mine!" she said, breathing in the atmosphere with satisfaction. I always kept my place clean and fresh.

I headed to my room to put my thesis files in a safe place because I didn't want them getting ruined when we started drinking and doing drugs. I also put on my t-shirt.

When I came back into the hall, Rossy had already set the table, soft music was playing, and she had taken out some beer from my fridge and even set up some snacks.

I took out the powdered drugs, and we both began our little party, lost in dancing, drinks, and the high of the music.

It's always more fun with someone else. It felt like after such a long time, I was finally enjoying myself again.

When we inhaled the drugs, it was like we were both lifted to the seventh heaven.

The high was strong—I liked it.

It felt like paradise.

Every vein in my body could feel it, and it was so soothing.

I relaxed on the sofa.

Rossy sat very close to me, which made me feel suffocated, so I shifted forward a bit.

The room was dimly lit, filled with the smoke of cigarettes and the smell of alcohol.

We were both slumped on the couch, surrounded by empty bottles and the remnants of the night's chaos.

My mind was lost in my thoughts, while Rossy, even in her intoxicated state, was watching me with a strange desire and sadness in her eyes.

Soft music was playing in the background, adding to the serene, hazy atmosphere.

"What does this tattoo mean?" she asked.

"I don't know... I'm still searching for it," I replied, taking a sip from my beer can. Rossy kept looking at me without blinking.

She moved closer.

"Ilham," she said softly, leaning toward me. She placed my hand on her face and whispered, "Lose control..."

I smiled at her and said, "I will never do that." I gently touched the mole on her face with my thumb and said,

"I won't." This was the first time I had touched her mole, but it didn't have the same effect on me as the one on Zieba's face.

I immediately pulled my hand away.

In my intoxicated state, Rossy seemed less like herself and more like Zieba to me, so I looked away from her.

In a soft tone, Rossy said, "I can make you forget her, just give it a shot, Ilham." She leaned in to kiss me, but I pulled back and smiled.

"You think you can make me forget the girl who lives inside me?" I laughed,

"How can you even say that? You really think this high... this moment... can erase everything that's inside me? Tell me... how can you make me forget her when I'm not even ready to forget her, Rossy?" I said quietly.

"She's not here, Ilham. That's what I'm trying to say," Rossy's words made sense to her, but for me, Zieba was here.

-Where is she?

-She's inside me, in every part of me.

"You think she's not here, Rossy? She's everywhere. I see her every time I close my eyes. She's in every breath I take, in every heartbeat. If she's not in me, then I'm just a lifeless body," I expressed my feelings. For some reason, today my words flowed on their own.

"She's not just a memory stuck in my mind. She's in my soul. She's the fire running through my veins, a fire that maybe even she can't extinguish now. She's the only peace in the storm inside me. She's in my every thought, every heartbeat. She's in every particle of my existence. She's not someone who can be forgotten, Rossy… she's the reason I'm alive… she's become the reason I live." I ran my hands through my hair in helplessness.

"But practically, I'm here, Ilham. At least for tonight, let me share your pain. Just for tonight, forget about her and focus on me…" Rossy said softly, constantly trying to touch my hands.

"No, Rossy—you won't understand. If I forget her even for a moment, my heart would stop beating, and you're talking about tonight…" I replied.

"What is so special about Zieba?" Rossy asked, her irritation clear.

"She's not a wound that needs to be healed; she's the pulse in my veins. Even in her absence, she is more real to me than anyone else could ever be. Ilham no longer has control over his heart, mind, or body—Zieba does." I placed my hands on my head, feeling an unexpected headache.

For some reason, even looking at Rossy felt burdensome, and my lips kept moving.

"She's not someone who can be forgotten for a moment, Rossy. She's someone to be remembered moment by moment, like how a person doesn't need to remind themselves to breathe or signal their heart to beat. Now tell me—can anyone stop living, even for a second? Because Zieba is the nourishment for my soul, and I take her in with every breath I draw." I finished speaking, my eyes wet, though the dim light in the room wouldn't let her see that.

Rossy, growing furious, stood abruptly. I told her, "Just go, Rossy."

She stormed out, slamming the door of my flat behind her.

My heart grew heavy, and tears filled my eyes.

I pulled out my wallet and gazed at Zieba's picture, smiling softly as I touched it.

"Am I really not worthy of you, Zieba? If I wanted to be worthy of you, what would I have to do? Tell me… I'm willing to do anything… anything at all…"

"I want to be with you, Zieba, but I don't think I deserve you… How could a pure woman like you ever love a sinner like me?"

"Why are you so far away, yet feel so close?"

Tears streamed down my face uncontrollably.

I don't know why, but tonight I just wanted to cry.

Was I crying for Zieba's memory, for her absence… or for the unknown acceptance of my sins…?

For the first time, I called myself a **sinner…**

Why was I crying so much…? What was softening my heart so suddenly…?

I began to sob uncontrollably. My breathing grew shallow.

I was down on my knees, clutching my chest, as the pain inside me intensified—like someone was driving nails into it!

I struggled to breathe, and the stabbing pain in my chest kept growing—*I can't breathe*……………..

I couldn't make a sound no matter how hard I tried.

The pain was unbearable, and I felt like I would die from it right there.

I fought against it for as long as I could, but my endurance broke, and I collapsed onto the floor.

Darkness descended over me…

And this darkness was no ordinary one…

* * *

The darkness was so suffocating that it felt as though I wasn't breathing, yet I couldn't be sure if my breath had really stopped.

But I could hear faint whispers from afar, like the static of an old radio stuck between stations.

Sometimes I heard my name, sometimes broken sentences—someone was crying.

Was it my friend…? Waqar…?

But why…? *"I'm right here, Waqar…"*

"Why are you crying…?"

I tried to scream, to move my body, but I was lifeless, as if my being had abandoned me.

The weight of silence pressed down on me, as if some unseen force was crushing me.

I writhed in helplessness and despair, feeling the world around me but unable to reach it.

Every whisper reminded me that I was still here, but no one could hear the screams of my silence!

"Why can't I move…?"

"Mumma… Baba…

Waqar… why are you crying…?"

"Don't cry, Waqar…"

"Get me out of this darkness, maybe I'm tied down…"

"Someone, untie me… why have I been wrapped in this soft fabric…?"

Why was Waqar clinging to my chest, crying so much…?

I lay there, trapped, motionless and helpless, but nothing changed. The whispers continued to unsettle me.

What were they saying? Why couldn't I understand anything?

"Can't anyone hear me…?"

* * *

When I opened my eyes, it felt like I hadn't opened them at all—such darkness surrounded me, a strange and oppressive gloom that clung to me like a shadow, blurring all the boundaries of my reality.

There was no light, neither from outside nor within.

It felt as though even the sun had been extinguished, and I was trapped in an eternal sea of darkness.

"Where am I…?"

"Why is it so dark…?"

I was lying motionless, feeling as though someone had imprisoned my body in the suffocating grip of my own mind.

This realization grew gradually, like something cold and slimy brushing against my skin.

At first, it felt like a gentle, eerie movement from some unearthly force, but as my heart started racing, panic sank its claws into me.

This creature wasn't soft. In fact, they were countless worms, slithering across my body, their slimy forms spreading over every inch of my skin.

I wanted to scream, to shake them off, but I couldn't move—I was paralyzed.

What the hell…?

Frustration shot through me as I felt them crawling over me.

I tried to get up, hoping to find a switch, a window, or any way to break through the darkness—but my hands waved helplessly in the void. It was as if my very existence had been erased, where touch, sound, and light had no presence.

Even my own body felt distant, numb, and weightless, like a wandering, purposeless soul.

I tried to call out, but my voice barely echoed, drowned by the silence that hung over me like a heavy curtain. I could feel the worms crawling under my clothes now, their tiny bodies slithering into my ears, creeping up my legs, and spreading across my neck.

The sensation was unbearable, and every movement amplified my panic.

What is this…?

Where did these strange worms come from…?

I was feeling both unease and confused.

I couldn't understand anything.

I was stuck in one place, unable to lift myself no matter how hard I tried.

Some strange force had rendered me completely paralyzed, and I laid there for what seemed like an eternity.

The more I tried to push the worms away, the closer they came.

I tried to move my hands and feet, but nothing happened.

My chest was tight with panic, feeling the worms on me, yet I was paralyzed and unable to shake them off.

"What's happening to me…??

Where am I…??

And why is it so dark…??

Why these worms…??"

I asked myself, but the questions rose within me only to die in silence.

The voice boomed through the darkness, strong and thunderous, echoing three times around him.

"من ربك؟"

I'm motionless, lips sealed, heart pounding.

I didn't understand—I didn't know what was happening to me.

Whose voice was this? Why was it so loud, so overpowering?

Confusion clouded my mind.

"ما دينك؟"

I'm remained frozen, clueless, lost in a terrifying haze.

The questions meant nothing to me now; I was unaware, detached, helpless.

A third time, the voice shook the very ground:

"من نبيك؟"

"Who are you…???" I wanted to ask but my lips sealed.

I could not answer.

I was drowning in a silence that screamed louder than the voice itself.

The silence was torturous.

It wasn't a peaceful silence, but one that pressed down on my chest like a weight, suffocating me more with each passing moment.

I was trapped in a place where time had no meaning, where day and night had merged into an unending moment.

I couldn't tell how long I had been there—hours…? Days…? There was no escape, no sign of a way out.

And it wasn't just the sensation of the worms crawling on me; it was the oppressive weight of their existence, as if the ground had swallowed me whole and plunged my being into a state of living decay.

FEAR—TERROR.

For the first time, I understood these words.

Fear gripped my spine when I realized I was completely alone, severed from everything and everyone, utterly abandoned.

~~"I'm scared of being alone…"~~

I tried to say, but my tongue wouldn't move, nor would my body.

I couldn't feel the structure of my body, my breaths, or the beating of my heart.

The walls were closing in on me, shifting, warping, twisting, trapping me in an infinite loop.

The worms burrowed deeper into my skin, as though they knew they were devouring a soul unworthy of rest—*Please, save me, get rid of these worms… they're going to consume me… please.*

I whimpered, and every time I tried to move, I found myself in the same place, in that empty corner, trapped within my own mind—a prisoner shackled by my own consciousness.

What the hell is happening to me?

Despair tightened its grip around me, tears welled up in my eyes, but even they didn't feel real.

Why can't I feel my tears…?

I couldn't cry, I couldn't scream, I couldn't move.

"Is anyone out there…?

Somebody, open the door—I'm trapped here…!"

"Open the damn door!"

The words were locked inside me, never making it to my lips.

What the hell… what kind of joke is this? Am I dreaming?

Yes, I must be dreaming.

Ilham—find the loophole, find it—find—find—find…

I closed my eyes, hoping when I opened them again, everything would be different.

But when I opened them, the same scene awaited me.

Panic gripped me harder.

Whatever was happening to me, my skin felt like it was rotting, layer by layer, as those tiny mouths gnawed at my flesh.

What is happening? Why am I trapped here like this?

With every question, the pain in my chest felt like nails being hammered into it.

Every time I tried to breathe, the pain only grew worse.

Why this pain…?

I couldn't feel anything but pain. It consumed me.

For the first time in my life, I was truly terrified.

The darkness made me even more restless.

This wasn't just any darkness; it was the kind where I couldn't even see myself. It felt like I had lost myself within it, and there was no light, no hope to pull me out.

Trapped in that dark room, I tried to crawl toward the door, but seeing it closed made me break down like a child.

I, a 22-year-old man, suddenly found myself in this nightmare, and it made my soul tremble.

Anyone else in my place would have been equally shaken.

My stomach twisted in hunger, and my throat felt parched, desperate for water.

I broke down in sobs, lying on the cold floor, and I don't remember when I lost consciousness.

When I woke up, it was the same scene. The same lifeless body. The same darkness. Everything was the same.

"I… I'm so hungry…" I muttered to myself.

The hunger tore at my insides, and my throat burned with thirst, but no matter how hard I tried, it was all in vain.

Though the kitchen was only a few steps away, it felt like miles, as if an impossible distance separated me from it.

Water bottles and food—all just out of reach, close yet far.

My stomach twisted in agony, but there was no relief, only the relentless emptiness—the darkness—and my soulless body, wracked with pain.

And those worms—they were devouring me.

Please, someone get these worms off me, please! They're biting me, get them off!

It hurts!

Fear gripped me............

Yes, fear—this was the first time I truly understood the meaning of fear. When the life has drained from your body, when pain is so overwhelming that it consumes you, when cold sweat drips down your skin, when your body trembles uncontrollably, when the pain seeps into your very soul—and yet, no sound escapes your lips.

No cry, no scream, no breath of relief.

Yes, this is fear—this is what they call **Terror**.

I convulsed helplessly, crying out, but there was nothing more I could do.

I passed out again, weeping on the cold ground, and when I woke up, it was the same scene all over again—like my life had become stuck in an endless time loop. I was trapped inside it forever.

No loophole to escape, no path to another place, not even a glimmer of light to offer me relief from the suffocating darkness.

Is this my room? It didn't feel like it anymore.

Maybe a month had passed.

Or perhaps many months.

Or was it years?

I had no idea how long I'd been stuck here.

Dark circles had formed under my eyes, my lips cracked and parched from the unbearable thirst. My body felt like it was decaying, rotting from the inside, as hunger gnawed at me relentlessly.

Blood began seeping from the cracks in my dry lips. My hair was matted and wild, like someone who'd been living in the wilderness for years.

I had become so thin that I couldn't bear the sight of myself—disgust welled up inside me ~~fear welled up inside me.~~

I lay there, sobbing helplessly at my own wretched state. My misery seemed to mock me, laughing at my helplessness, and I could do nothing.

Nothing except feel the sharp, unrelenting pain in my chest.

Suddenly, I started vomiting blood, the pain in my chest intensifying. I collapsed where I was, motionless.

What's happening to me?

Why is this happening to me?

What did I do to deserve this?

Am I going to die here?

Is this how my life ends?

Is this taking me closer to death, or have I already died?

What kind of torment is this…?

What kind of test is this? ~~A test I was never prepared for.~~

Suddenly, my entire life flashed before my eyes, as though someone had played the film reel of my existence.

But as I watched, there wasn't a single moment that made me feel like I had truly lived.

My life had been steeped in darkness, like I had only ever existed for fleeting moments.

It was as if my sins were parading before me, showing me every instance of my pride and arrogance, reminding me of everything that had brought me to this point.

Time moved forward, yet I remained trapped here, stuck in the endless night with no sense of morning or evening—just a **Never-Ending Time Loop**.

Fear became my constant companion, but it wasn't an ordinary fear like the kind I had known before.

This was a suffocating restlessness, a haunting sensation that took root deep in my soul, without reason or explanation.

It felt as though a massive weight had been placed on my chest, making it hard to breathe.

My heart pounded violently, and with each beat, my emptiness deepened.

This darkness… it wasn't just around me. It was inside me—the very darkness that had taken over my thoughts.

Silence reigned everywhere, yet even in that silence, I could hear something—a strange whisper, an eerie murmur that echoed in my mind, ~~reminding me of my mistakes.~~

I was alone, yet the void was so overwhelming that even my own presence terrified me. That fear… it was rising from the depths of my heart. I had never felt so weak, so powerless.

Everything frightened me—my thoughts, my solitude, and that consuming darkness ready to swallow me whole.

That **fear** wasn't just about the darkness—it was a reflection of my hatred. My hatred for myself, for my actions, for the life I had lived.

Why this fear…?

What's happening to me?

I asked myself, ~~but the answer… the answer was hidden somewhere in the darkness.~~

This fear didn't just come from the blackness around me—it came from the emptiness within me, that hollow space in my heart.

It was forcing me to confront the truth of who I had become.

I recalled a voice I had heard long ago—the same three questions echoing now in the darkness:

من ربک؟

ما دینک؟

من نبیک؟

Am I dead…?

Am I in my grave…?

Is this the punishment of the grave…?

For the first time, I realized that this wasn't just the torment of the grave.

It was the punishment of a grave I had created for myself—a prison of darkness I had chosen with my own actions.

This darkness was my grave.

Its punishment was the reflection of the empty space inside me. There was no escape, and I couldn't move—just like a lifeless corpse, unable to stir.

It was an endless void of suffering, a never-ending cycle of anguish, and I finally understood with a soul-shaking horror that I was truly alone—completely alone. "Everyone is alone in the grave, aren't they…?"

The realization made my very soul tremble, and I broke down, sobbing uncontrollably at my helplessness.

* * *

AUTHOR's Point of View-

Ilham lay motionless, his mind pleading for mercy, but no sound escaped his lips.

His eyes, wide open in that horrifying scene, stared blankly into the boundless darkness.

There was no escape, no salvation. After all, who has ever found deliverance from the torment of the grave throughout the history of mankind…?

The silence around him mocked his helplessness, laughing at him just as he once used to laugh.

It dawned on him that this was the punishment he had heard of—a punishment far worse than physical pain.

It was a consequence of the arrogance and denial that had consumed his life, just as the tiny worms were now consuming his flesh, tearing at his decaying skin.

Each crawling insect reminded him of how invincible he once believed himself to be, untouchable by anyone or anything.

But now, stripped of power, wealth, and pride, he was nothing.

The one who had always escaped trouble by leaning on his father's support was now recalling his father.

But relationships, no matter how strong, exist only outside the grave. In the grave, there is only you and your deeds.

And it is your deeds that you come to despise, because they refuse to leave your side.

They cling to you, reminding you of everything you had once ignored.

In the grave, you are nothing but a body—just a body—motionless, rotting, and utterly alone with your fear.

His breath caught in his throat as the worms began to crawl into his mouth, suffocating him with the bitter taste of his own sins. He remembered the words he had once spoken with such pride, declaring himself the creator of his own destiny.

But now, he wondered, if he was the creator of his life, why couldn't he escape this fate?

إِنَّ رَبَّكُمُ اللَّهُ الَّذِي خَلَقَ السَّمَاوَاتِ وَالْأَرْضَ فِي سِتَّةِ أَيَّامٍ ثُمَّ اسْتَوَىٰ عَلَى الْعَرْشِ يُغْشِي اللَّيْلَ النَّهَارَ يَطْلُبُهُ حَثِيثًا وَالشَّمْسَ
وَالْقَمَرَ وَالنُّجُومَ مُسَخَّرَاتٍ بِأَمْرِهِ أَلَا لَهُ الْخَلْقُ وَالْأَمْرُ تَبَارَكَ اللَّهُ رَبُّ الْعَالَمِينَ

Indeed, your Lord is Allah, who created the heavens and earth in six days and then established Himself above the Throne. He covers the night with the day, [another night] chasing it rapidly; and [He created] the sun, the moon, and the stars, subjected by His command. Unquestionably, His is the creation and the command; blessed is Allah, Lord of the worlds. **(Surah Al-A'raf – 7:54)**

Ilham had read the Quran, but he had read it without truly understanding it. Had he read and comprehended its meaning, he might not have ended up in this state.

And then, the terror intensified. He could feel his limbs dissolving under the touch of those creeping creatures, a cold, damp sensation seeping into his very bones.

Yet, through it all, he endured—fully aware of every crawling, slimy movement across his decaying body.

His physical form was betraying him, rotting away, while his soul desperately cried out for mercy—a mercy that would never be granted.

This was the horrifying reality of his punishment in the grave—a nightmare from which he could not wake, a terrifying ordeal that, deep down, he knew he deserved.

"Was I aware of this torment…?" he wept, though his tongue refused to move.

"Or was I oblivious to it all…?" He was trapped in the unbearable realization that he had chosen this fate for himself in the afterlife.

لَقَدْ أَرْسَلْنَا نُوحًا إِلَىٰ قَوْمِهِ فَقَالَ يَا قَوْمِ اعْبُدُوا اللَّهَ مَا لَكُم مِّنْ إِلَٰهٍ غَيْرُهُ إِنِّي أَخَافُ عَلَيْكُمْ عَذَابَ يَوْمٍ عَظِيمٍ

-We had certainly sent Noah to his people, and he said, "O my people, worship Allah; you have no deity other than Him. Indeed, I fear for you the punishment of a tremendous Day. **(Surah Al-A'raf – 7:59)**

This is the torment that begins in the grave, when a person's body returns to the earth.

A truth is revealed—a truth that we often ignore in the comforts of our worldly lives.

As soon as the soul departs from the body, your mouth will be silenced, your voice will be gone, and that once beautiful body will start to decay and decompose.

The pain will be indescribable, just as Ilham was now experiencing.

Worms will come, tearing at your flesh, gnawing at your skin, and reaching your very bones. With every moment, your soul will feel a torment beyond anything that can be understood in life.

But after death, you won't be able to scream; your mouth will be shut, your body motionless, while your soul writhes in agony. This is the punishment—an unspeakable suffering where you will be utterly helpless, and your internal screams will go unheard by the world.

Then, you will realize that in the grave, you are truly alone. No family will stand beside you, no friends will offer a comforting hand, and no one will share in your pain.

The wealth you accumulated, the titles you earned, the fame you chased—all of it will vanish, scattered like dust.

Only your deeds will remain, faithfully clinging to your soul like a shadow from which you cannot escape. And those deeds will testify on your behalf—whether good or bad, they will speak for you.

On that day, everything will give testimony, even the lifeless things we once ignored, they too will become witnesses to your life.

اليوم نختم على أفواههم وتكلمنا أيديهم وتشهد أرجلهم بما كانوا يكسبون

-That Day, we will seal over their mouths, and their hands will speak to Us, and their feet will testify about what they used to earn. **(Surah Al-Yasin- 36:65)**

The weight of this reality rests solely on your shoulders. No one else can accompany you on this journey, and when you find yourself in that dark, narrow space, no one will be able to help you.

It will just be you and your deeds—the very deeds you chose yourself.

It was you who decided whether they would be good or bad, whether you followed the right path or ignored it.

Deep down, every human harbours the desire to be counted among the righteous, to find peace in both worlds.

But very few are willing to walk the straight path that leads them to that goal. Yet, this path is not as difficult as we often believe, as our inner desires make it seem.

Out of His boundless mercy, Allah has already shown us this path—through the blessed Sunnah of His beloved Prophet Muhammad ﷺ and through the Quran. These are the companions that will stay with you, from this world to the grave, and from the grave to the Hereafter.

If you live according to their guidance, your life will be filled with peace, and your soul will be nourished by your good deeds. These are the keys to unlocking comfort in the grave and the eternal reward that follows.

Understand this—your soul is your responsibility. In both this world and the Hereafter, it is up to you how you nurture, guide, and protect it.

No one else can carry this burden but you.

When the time of death arrives, when you are lowered into the earth, all relationships, friendships, love, and attachments will cease to exist. All that will remain are your deeds, standing between you and your final destiny.

Therefore, strive to make your deeds righteous.

Do those things that bring peace to your soul, not torment, because in the end, it will be just you and your deeds when the Day of Judgment comes.

When you stand before Allah, ensure that your actions are worthy of His pleasure, so that you may enter Paradise and not be cast into Hell.

Stay committed to the path that leads to Jannah, and gather good deeds that will remain loyal to you, in this world and the Hereafter.

* * *

EPISODE – 16

(The Message from Messenger….!!!)

I don't know how many months I had been trapped in this horrifying nightmare, but for the first time today, for reasons beyond me, Allah's name escaped my lips along with a painful sigh.

"Ya Allah…

Ya Allah, what is happening to me?

I need… I need to get out of here.

I don't want to die like this, helpless, writhing in pain. I'm terrified of this place, terrified of these tiny crawling creatures."

Like a scared child, I cried, sobbed, and called out to the One who says He loves His creation more than seventy mothers.

He wouldn't want to see His servant suffering like this, would He? I am His creature, too, right?

"Ya Allah… Ya Allah!"

I placed both hands on my chest and screamed in pain as I looked up at the ceiling.

My tongue could only utter Allah's name, and my hands instinctively rose, trembling, as if to beg for mercy.

I could hear my voice; I could feel my own cries echoing through the emptiness. And I could feel my endless stream of tears, flowing without pause.

"You respond when we call out to You, don't You? I need You now, Ya Allah, I need You to save me from here. I'm terrified of this place. Please, please get me out… save me…"

I broke down, sobbing uncontrollably. Never in my life had I shed so many tears as I did now.

"Baba used to say that everything is in Your power, that if You willed, you could move mountains. I just need to escape this darkness. I don't want to die like this. Ya Allah, please hear my plea… I need You, I only need You."

Tears kept pouring from my eyes, beyond my control. And then, I heard Zieba's voice in my ears.

But her voice unsettled me…

And when she started reciting those verses again—No, not again, Zieba! I'm already terrified enough.

"For those who disbelieved in their Lord, there is the punishment of Hell, and what a terrible fate it is."

Zieba's voice kept reverberating in my ears, every word slicing through my soul.

My breathing felt like it was stopping, like I couldn't catch my breath.

"When they are thrown into it, they will hear its terrifying roar as it blazes fiercely."

Each word Zieba spoke felt like knives stabbing my body, like every inch of my flesh was being nailed down, the pain unbearable.

I wept in agony, choking on my sobs, covering my tear-streaked face with my hands.

I tried to block out her voice by covering my ears, but Zieba's voice only grew louder, just like it had three years ago.

Her recitation haunted me, and the whispers of regret swirled around me, suffocating me.

My selfishness, my mistakes—they all weighed down on me, crushing my soul.

"It will almost burst with rage. Every time a group is cast into it, its keepers will ask them, 'Did no warner come to you?'"

I screamed through my tears,

"Yes! Yes, a warner did come! He did come!" I yelled out in agony, crying louder.

"One day, Allah will strike you down with His rod, and no one will save you—not your father, not your mother who sheds tears for you, not a single friend. No one. No matter how much strength I have, I won't be able to protect you from the real consequences that are not in human hands, because those consequences belong to Him—the One whose decrees are so real, so true, that your soul, bloated with pride and arrogance, will be engulfed in **fear, agony**, and **torment.** And on that day, even Allah Himself will not have mercy on you..."

"The warner was my Baba, the one who tried to guide me.

I didn't listen to him.

Forgive me, forgive me for not listening him.

I know now the weight of my wrongs, please forgive me. Show me mercy... please show me mercy."

I covered my face with my hands and sobbed in despair.

These lifeless walls seemed to speak, their silence louder than ever, terrifying me to my core.

"And they will say, 'If only we had listened or understood, we would not be among the people of this blazing fire.'

In this way, they will confess their guilt themselves; cursed are the dwellers of Hell."

Zieba's voice grew louder and louder. For the second time in my life, her voice was suffocating me.

The more I tried to stop her voice, the louder it became.

"Oh Allah...

Why don't You understand?

Can't You see my suffering?

Can't You hear the cries of my pain?

Get me out of here! Is my voice not reaching You? Have I gone so far from You?" I began to sob, screaming out loud.

"Whether you speak secretly or loudly (it is all the same to Allah), He knows even what is hidden in the hearts. Does He not know, He who created them? Yet He is the Subtle, the All-Aware."

Zieba's voice kept rising, and it felt like someone had breathed life into these lifeless walls, and they were now speaking as her voice echoed from every direction.

The walls of my room were speaking...! These lifeless walls were speaking...!!

"Someone please, save me... Someone please save me! Someone come, and get me out of here...!! I feel suffocated here," I cried out, trembling.

'Tell me, what army do you have that can help you against the Most Merciful? The truth is that these deniers are deluded.

Or tell me, who can provide for you if the Most Merciful withholds His provision? In reality, these people are persistent in arrogance and avoidance of the truth."

Hearing this, I fell to the ground in prostration, and I began to weep uncontrollably.

'There is no one to help but You. I understand now…

I understand everything…!!

No one can receive provision without Your will.

I… I am hungry…

I am desperately thirsty… My… my throat has dried up completely… it's parched… my stomach has shrunk from hunger…

Please take me out of here, my Allah—"

I uttered every word through sobs.

Zieba's voice echoed even louder…

"Stop it, Zieba, stop it…!!!

What are you? Who are you? Why are you scaring me like this? Just stop it…!!! I'm starting to hate your voice, Zieba. Stop reading this… please…!!!" I screamed with trembling hands, covering my ears, trying to block out her voice, but it was impossible.

"The knowledge of this is with Allah alone; I am merely a clear warner,"

Zieba's words unsettled me even more.

Her voice wouldn't stop. It echoed in my ears as if someone had placed her voice on high-volume speakers permanently in my ears. If this continued, I would go deaf…!!!

I felt blood dripping from my ears, and at the same time, a stream of blood began flowing from my nose. I started vomiting blood.

The pain in my chest was so severe that I could barely form words, but this girl's voice wouldn't stop…!!

"I'm going to die! Stop speaking…!! I'm terrified, Zieba, please be quiet. Stop reading the translations of these verses. Please, stop…!!!" I screamed as I grabbed the vase from the tea table and smashed it hard against the wall.

Crying, I collapsed onto the floor, but I couldn't even feel the tears in my eyes. Every drop of tear felt like blood-filled tears. The pain in my chest had no cure, nor did the torment of this ***'Azaab of the Grave.'***

Yes, this is indeed the torment of the grave, where people cannot escape from that closed grave. They cannot speak, and even if their souls cry out, no one can hear them.

They suffer alone in torment because it is their own deeds that have earned them this fate. In that darkness, in that closed grave, without food or drink, our bodies begin to decay and rot, just as mine is. There is no one with us in that grave to hear our cries, to understand our pain, or to witness our suffering.

I am in the grave, and the terrifying torment of that grave has been unleashed upon me………………..

"I will die lying here. I will keep crying out from hunger, and there will be no one to see me…!!!" I began sobbing uncontrollably…!!

"I don't understand anything, O Allah, but if You take me out of here just once, I promise I will keep myself away from all forbidden things. I won't drink alcohol, I won't touch any intoxicants, I will stop every wrongdoing… just get me out of here…!!! I won't consider myself the master of my world anymore, I won't ever think of myself as better than You—

Greater than You," I curled up in a corner, sobbing helplessly. The sound of my own sobs made me pity myself.

After crying for a long time, like always, I lost myself in the darkness. My eyes started closing on their own.

"Will I never be able to get out of here…????

Will I have to stay like this until the Day of Judgment…???"

* * *

When I opened my eyes, I found myself lying by the edge of a clear lake…

It was the same scene where I always saw Zieba, but as I looked around, I realized no one was there—not even Zieba.

I tried to drink the crystal-clear water from the lake, but neither could my hands get wet nor could I drink the water…

Frustrated, I plunged into the water, but I emerged just as dry as if I had never entered. I sat by the lake's edge, crying.

"O Allah, what kind of test is this? There's water right in front of me, but I can't drink it!"

I was weeping, my sobs echoing in the stillness.

Suddenly, I felt the warmth of someone's touch on my shoulder.

I turned around to see the figure behind me, and in his eyes was a light brighter and more mysterious than any other. This person radiated an aura of majesty and compassion, each movement bringing a strange sense of peace and serenity.

His face was clear, radiant, and luminous, like the gentle glow of the moon with a calming softness.

His skin shimmered with a delicate pinkish hue, and his eyes held a depth that reached the heart, dissolving all fear and sorrow—just as mine were vanishing.

Their long, dark hair, flowing in waves not of hatred but of love, framed their face gracefully.

Clad in pure white fabric, from which an aura of light emanated—a symbol of purity and divine favor. The garments were impeccably clean, exuding an air of dignity and reverence that filled the observer's heart with awe.

He wore a white robe, and his head was adorned with a white cap, wrapped with a cloth like a turban.

He sat beside me and said,

"You seem to be in a lot of pain, what's troubling you?"

His voice was so calming that tears streamed down my face, and though I didn't want to speak, the words came out on their own,

"I've been trapped in a dark void for what feels like months. I don't know what's happening… I keep hearing verses from the Holy Quran, translated, but they only speak of hell and punishment…! And I feel the torment…!" I began to sob.

He placed their hand on my shoulder, gently stroking my back, and said,

"And…?"

The warmth of his hand brought me such comfort that I looked up at his face in amazement and, with tears in my eyes, said,

"The verses scare me. I'm afraid of the Quran. I'm terrified of the thought of death, of what comes after. I can't find a way out, and no one is coming to help me…! Everywhere I look, I used to find a loophole, but now I see none." I told them.

He asked me a question, "Do you know the purpose of your existence in this world? Are you aware of your destination…?"

Wiping the tears from my eyes, I replied, "No…"

His question felt eerily similar to Jenny's question…!!

He gave a soft smile and said,

"It is essential that you understand the purpose for which you were brought into this world and choose the right path to reach your true destination. Once you comprehend the nature of this life and what the Hereafter holds, when you realize where your true destination lies, you will grasp the reason you were sent to this world. You have only strayed from the path, and Allah, the Most Merciful and Compassionate, is guiding you toward the straight path. It is your duty to return to your Lord, the One to whom you truly belong."

In utter confusion, I asked, "How will I know what my purpose is? What my destination is?"

He smiled gently and replied, "I answered all those questions a long ages ago…"

"Where?" I asked, bewildered.

"The very verses that frighten you—they hold the solution to all your troubles."

With that, he lovingly placed his hand on my head, his mere presence lending significance to everything around me.

It was as though he wasn't just a man but a divine message in human form. He gave a final, serene smile before standing to leave.

As he walked away, his departing words tore my heart apart, **"Ya Allah… My Ummah… My Ummah…"**

I watched him walk into the distance, every step he took exuding such grace and dignity that even the ground beneath his feet seemed to bow in reverence.

His posture was noble, his chest lifted high, his every movement speaking of majesty far greater than mere royalty.

Overcome with emotion, I started to cry uncontrollably, calling out to him,

"Please, take me with you! Don't leave me here! Please…!"

I wanted to run to him, but my body was bound, as though invisible chains had locked my hands and feet in place.

I sobbed, reaching out my hand toward him in despair… when suddenly, a calm voice spoke behind me,

"Ilham……….."

I turned around, and there she stood.

Dressed in white from head to toe, veiled in purity and modesty, it was Zieba.

When my eyes met hers, I saw a light shining brighter than I had ever seen before.

Her beauty, which I had witnessed in life, was now magnified tenfold.

Zieba was standing among fragrant flowers, yet she looked more beautiful than all of them.

The mere sight of her soothed the pain in my chest. As she approached me, my heartbeat quickened—it felt as if I was coming back to life, feeling…, everything I had been numb to for so long.

With a tender smile, she spoke,

"You must be hungry… aren't you? Come, let me feed you with my own hands." Zieba sat down next to me, offering her comfort.

I tried to hold back my tears, but I couldn't. Zieba gently wiped my face with the edge of her veil, "You look so weak…"

She held out a piece of bread toward me and said softly,

"Here, have a bite."

I grabbed her hands and, breaking into uncontrollable sobs, cried, "Zieba… Zieba… You… you're here… you'll save me, won't you? You'll get me out of here, won't you?" I pleaded through my sobs.

"First, eat. Have faith on Allah. Everything will be fine, In sha Allah…."

"Bismillah…" she whispered as she placed the first bite in my mouth. In that moment, I truly understood the meaning of 'Bismillah.'

Without His consent, not even sustenance could pass through my throat.

It had been months since I had taken a bite of food, and in that moment, I realized the true value of sustenance—something I had always taken for granted, something I had wasted or never appreciated.

Every bite I took now was a reminder of Allah's mercy, and I thanked Him endlessly for the gift of food He had granted me.

Zieba fed me small pieces of bread one by one—even that dry bread tasted delicious, as though it contained flavours I had never noticed before.

My tears were a witness to how much I wanted to express my gratitude to the Almighty. Zieba continued feeding me each bite with her own hands, gently wiping away the tears that streamed down my face with her veil.

When she brought the last morsel to my mouth, her eyes lingered on me. In that moment, I took the bite from her hand and gently offered it back to her.

Zieba smiled as she accepted it and ate from my hand. With tender care, she wiped my face once more and softly said, "Alhamdulillah."

I repeated after her, "Alhamdulillah…"

Zieba stood up and, with a serene smile, asked me to join her by the nearby lake.

I rose and walked alongside her. Every step I took towards the lake with Zieba felt as though she was guiding me out of an endless time loop of loneliness.

She offered me water from the lake with her hands. I closed my eyes and drank, feeling a sense of peace wash over me.

When I opened my eyes again, I found myself lying in a hospital bed.

Transparent plastic curtains surrounded me, and tubes were attached to my arms. There were various medical devices connected to my chest, and I was wearing an oxygen mask.

"Z…Zzeeba…"

I tried to rise, but my body felt weak in a way I had never experienced before. Just then, the doctor approached me.

"So, how are you feeling?" the doctor asked while checking my pulse.

I nodded weakly, acknowledging her question.

"No need to worry, you've had a drug overdose," she explained, while reviewing my medical reports.

"You really pushed it during this lockdown, Ilham. If you look at your blood reports, you'd be shocked. I made a false report that you've been diagnosed with COVID, so we've kept you here in quarantine."

It started to make sense.

This doctor was no stranger—she was a close friend of my father, always saving me from one crisis or another.

But how could I tell her that my condition wasn't just because of a drug overdose?

There was something deeper, something far more complex that had brought me to this point.

Yes, I indulged in substances, but not to the extent that my body couldn't handle. I'd never taken so much that it would bring me to this state.

I removed my mask slightly and asked in a faint voice, "How long have I been here? How many days?"

The doctor examined me carefully. "You've been in a coma for 2 months and 16 days, including today," she said with calm precision.

She then checked my eyes with a small flashlight. "All set. Nurse, keep him under observation for the next 24 hours, change his diet, and remove the nutrition supply drips," she instructed while scribbling down some prescriptions.

"And you, Ilham," she said, handing me her phone, "Call your Baba. It'll bring him peace of mind to know you're awake."

I was filled with shame.

How could I face my Baba?

How could I speak to him after everything?

No, I couldn't do it. I shook my head in refusal, avoiding eye contact.

"No. I don't want to talk to anyone," I replied, my gaze cast downward in guilt.

"Don't say foolish things, Ilham. Do you have any idea what state your father and mother are in because of your actions? It's only because of your father that you were saved from being sent to a rehabilitation centre. And it's at his request that I've kept you here, safe and sound, even risking my own job. If not for anyone else, at least think about your parents. How ungrateful you've become..." Dr. Sakeena said sternly, her words striking me for the first time—not as an attack, but as a harsh truth.

"Here, talk to him..." she handed me her phone. With trembling, weak hands, I took it from her.

Baba: "Sakeena, is my son okay? Has he regained consciousness? He must have shown some sign, right? He's my brave boy, he never takes this long to wake up. Sakeena, you're checking on him, right?"

Ilham: "B...Ba...Baba...! It's me... It's Ilham!"

Baba: "Ya Allah! A thousand thanks to You, my boy is safe. Reshma, look, Ilham... Ilham is awake! My boy, how are you?"

Ilham: "Baba... I... I'm so ashamed... I—"

Baba: "Nothing happened, Ilham, nothing happened. Baba is here—I won't let anything happen to you. Don't cry... Talk to your mother." (He must be crying).

Mumma: "My child, how are you?"

Ilham: "I'm fine, Mumma. Don't worry, I won't do anything like this again."

Mumma: "Don't even think about it, Ilham. If anything happens to you, we'll die even while living. Have mercy on us, son. Please, stop doing this, don't put us through this anymore."

Mumma began to cry, and I sank deeper into my guilt, drowning in the weight of her tears. My own tears began to flow uncontrollably.

Ilham: "Mumma, I promise, I won't do this again."

Mumma: "Your father and I will come see you as soon as this lockdown is over. For Allah's sake, take care of yourself, Ilham."

Ilham: "Yes, Mumma. Fi Amaanillah."

Mumma: "Fi Amaanillah, my child."

I put the phone aside and broke down, unable to stop myself from crying.

"You'd better behave while you're here, and if you ever pull something like this again, I swear I'll kill you with my own hands. Don't forget, I'm a doctor—I know how to save lives, but I also know how to end them," Dr. Sakeena scolded me harshly.

This wasn't the first time she had treated me. She'd handled all my injuries from the bike accidents I'd had in India.

She's grown tired of saving me. She took her phone and left the room.

It's clear that someone like me shouldn't expect comfort from anyone. But—

"How can I explain to them that, even if I wanted to, I won't be able to do it again? I might be the first person to return from the grave...! And there is no other being that would dare to go back there willingly..."

اے اولادآدم

چل اس راہ پہ، جہاں ہے رحمتِ رب کا نور

اس فانی جہاں فریب سے مت کر دل مجبور۔

توبہ کا در اب تک ہے کھلا، لوٹ آ بے حجاب

نفس کے دھندلکوں سے نکل، ابھی ہے وقت کا حساب۔

یہ دنیا ایک جال ہے، فریب ہے یہ رقص

ہر شے فانی ہے یہاں، نہ کر تُو اس پہ کوئی وقف۔

سنبھل ابھی، کہ وقت ہے مسلسل ایک آزمائش

رحمتِ حق سے پا سکتا ہے تُو ہر خطا کی گزارش۔

زندگی کی حقیقت کو پہچان، یہ چھلاوا ہے بس

دریائے مغفرت میں ڈوب کے پالے روح کی اصل قسط

O Children of Adam…

Walk the path where God's mercy shines bright,

Do not let your heart be swayed by this fleeting world's deceitful light.

The door of repentance is still open wide, return unveiled,

Escape the shadows of your desires, before time is curtailed.

This world is but a trap, a dance of illusion,

Everything here will perish, don't make it your life's conclusion.

Awaken now, for life is a constant test,

With God's mercy, every sin can find rest.

Recognize the truth of life, it's merely a disguise,

Dive into the ocean of forgiveness, and find your soul's true prize!

* * *

EPISODE – 17

(Back to Life…!!)

"Ilham, look at yourself, what have you done to your health?"

Waqar said softly. I didn't respond, just remained silent.

A week later, I was discharged from the hospital, and Waqar had come to take me home.

This was the 20th time during the ride he tried to start a conversation.

"Ilham…?"

"Tell me, what's going on? You haven't spoken to me in a week. This isn't like you." Waqar said while placing my bag in my flat.

We both sat down on the couch, and I took a deep breath before saying,

"I don't know, Waqar… I've been feeling strange for the past few days. My heart feels heavy all the time, like there's a constant pricking sensation…" I mustered up the courage to admit.

I wasn't someone who usually shared my feelings, but what had happened was eating me alive.

I couldn't keep it bottled up any longer.

"What do you mean, strange?" Waqar asked. I stayed silent again.

"You probably just need a party, nothing more. You're just craving it," Waqar broke the silence, taking my hand and pulling me towards the door.

"Where are you taking me?" I asked.

Waqar didn't reply, staying quiet as he guided me to his car. He got in and started driving fast, his silence heavy.

"Waqar, where are we going?" I asked again.

"To paradise," he said with a small smile.

"The lockdown's over, so why not take a trip to paradise?" Waqar said as he stopped the car after driving for a while.

He got out, and as I looked ahead, I saw a club and the red-light district right next to it. My breath caught in my throat.

"No, I don't want to go," I said, refusing him.

"Come on, Ilham, you'll have fun." Waqar dragged me towards the club despite my protests.

Cold sweat broke out on my forehead. This was the first time in my life I'd ever felt like this.

I—Ilham—who used to get excited at the mere mention of clubs and pubs, was now trembling at the thought of entering one.

"Waqar, let me go. I don't want to go in," I said, but it was as if Waqar couldn't hear me, or maybe I just couldn't speak loud enough.

He pulled me inside, and as soon as I stepped in, I felt an overwhelming suffocation in my chest.

The scene inside didn't look like paradise—it looked like hell, just as described in the verses I had heard before.

The people drinking, taking drugs, raising their hands to celebrate with the girls—all of it now looked like they were being thrown into the fires of hell by the command of Allah.

Their raised hands no longer seemed like they were celebrating but instead like they were screaming for someone to save them. But no one could save them—because this was hell.

And no one can escape hell. No one, not you, not me.

I quickly turned and walked back towards the exit, but I accidentally bumped into a girl.

"Hello," she said.

The girl was dressed in skimpy clothes, her face caked with makeup, presenting herself like an object on display for every passing man.

I avoided her gaze and hurried away from there.

"Ilham...? What's wrong? Why did you come back?" Waqar asked, placing a concerned hand on my shoulder as I struggled to catch my breath.

"I need to rest. I don't want to go to the club," I said, starting to walk back towards my apartment.

"Wait, let me drop you off," Waqar offered.

"No, I'll go by myself."

"I want to stay with you, Ilham."

"I want to be alone, Waqar..." I replied, quickening my pace to get away from that atmosphere as fast as possible.

I walked alone down the snow-covered streets, my mind clouded. The snow was falling lightly, and I shoved my hands into my pockets, wandering aimlessly with small, unsure steps.

After walking for a while, I found myself in a deserted alley, and suddenly, the power went out.

All I could see was darkness on the road. I stood frozen in place, my hands and feet trembling.

Cold sweat began dripping from my forehead and body, and the faint sound of insects only heightened my fear.

I collapsed to my knees, and tears started flowing.

"Is anyone there? Someone, please… turn the lights on! I'm scared…, I'm scared…..," I kept calling out in a trembling voice.

"No—no, I didn't go there—I didn't go there on my own—I didn't want to go there… I had turned back… Ya Allah, don't make me go through that agony, that pain again… don't put me back in that place…"

I wept into my hands, covering my wet face.

Just then, a light shone in my eyes.

I wiped my tear-filled eyes and saw, through blurry vision, that someone was standing in front of me, holding a torch. The person extended a hand towards me.

"Are you okay, brother?" The person bent down to help me up.

I didn't say anything in reply—I couldn't.

My tongue was tied, and I was gripped with fear. But when I saw this person, I felt relief, knowing I wasn't alone.

It was then that I realized—I had become autophobic.

"Whenever there's even a little rain or snowfall, the power goes out here. Are you alright? You didn't get hurt, did you?" The person spoke as he helped guide me to the corner of the alley.

"Take care, Fi Amanillah," he said before leading me to the next lane, where there was electricity, and then disappeared back into the darkness. He wore a white shirt, and by the way he said "Fi Amanillah," I knew he was Muslim.

He came like an angel and vanished just as suddenly. I couldn't even ask who he was or where he lived. I didn't even try to talk to him.

I reached near my apartment and glanced at the building—Grave's Arcade—it really did look like a grave. I was too terrified to even enter my own flat. I gathered my courage and walked up to the door, but that was where my courage ended. I couldn't bring myself to go inside.

I was scared that once again, I might end up in that room...

I sat outside my flat for a long time, unable to calm myself down enough to even think about sleeping. The weather was freezing, and my body was turning to ice in the cold.

My lips were cracking, and my hands were going numb. I made a futile attempt to warm myself by rubbing my hands together.

"I can survive out here in the cold, but alone in that room? No..."

My empty room was terrifying me...

I spent the entire night sitting there, thinking that I couldn't keep staying outside like this every day. I needed to move to a new apartment.

With my frozen, numb hands, I opened a rental app on my phone and contacted all the ready-to-move-in flats. Luckily, I found one that was available.

By the next morning, I would move all my stuff.

* * *

"Why did you suddenly decide to move here?"

Waqar asked while helping me shift my things.

"I just didn't want to stay there anymore," I replied.

"Ilham, you seem really different lately. What's going on? Rossy was telling me that you spent the whole night outside yesterday. What's happening to you, man? We can sort it out." Waqar asked, concerned.

"Nothing, I'm fine," I answered, though we both knew I was lying.

After a brief silence, Waqar spoke again,

"I'm going back to Pakistan, Ilham." He leaned back against the sofa, speaking calmly.

"Why? So suddenly? We still have to finish our internship."

I sat down beside him, noticing how troubled he looked.

"Yeah, you already know I'm not really interested in these studies," Waqar said, rubbing his hands together, clearly showing his unease.

"Tell me what's going on!" I placed a hand on his shoulder, urging him to talk. He seemed really upset.

"Jenny…"

When he mentioned Jenny, he looked at me with tear-filled eyes. It was the first time I had ever seen Waqar cry, and it was because of Jenny.

"What happened to Jenny?" I asked.

"We agreed it would just be fun, you know, friends-with-benefits. But now that she's left me, I feel like something's missing, Ilham. I tried to forget her, but I've fallen in love with her, man. I'm in love with Jenny."

Waqar poured his heart out, sharing everything.

"Then talk to her. I think Jenny loves you too," I said, but he interrupted me.

"I did talk to her. I asked her to marry me. She refused," Waqar said, nervously intertwining his fingers.

"Why did she refuse?" I asked, shocked.

"I asked her to accept Islam, and she turned it around on me, asking, 'So will you accept Islam too, then?' I was stunned by her question."

I was just as shocked.

What did she mean—Waqar would accept his own religion?

"I told her I'm a born Muslim. She laughed and said, 'Then what difference will it make if I accept Islam? What's the difference between you and me? You do the same things as people from my religion or any other religion. If you're going to live the same way, then what's the point of bringing religion into this? If you were any different, I might have considered your request. Instead of trying to bring others to Islam, you should focus on your own faith. The lack of faith is greatest among your own people.' And then she left."

As Waqar explained in detail, tears streamed down his face.

"Her words really struck a chord with me. I don't know what to do, Ilham," Waqar said quietly.

"Me either…"

I was left speechless.

Jenny was right—we have no right to invite others to Islam when we ourselves are so distant from our own religion and faith.

What right do we have to ask someone to join us in our faith when we are so far from it ourselves?

Jenny's words made me realize that just being a Muslim isn't enough. We have to truly become Muslims, embrace Islam, and live by it. Only then can we truly call ourselves Muslims, followers of our beloved Prophet Muhammad (ﷺ).

"My flight is tonight," Waqar said, wiping his eyes with the back of his hand.

"So soon? You could stay a few more days, maybe…" I began, but he cut me off.

"No, if I stay here, I'll become obsessed with her love. Besides, my father needs me; he's not been feeling well." Waqar gave a faint smile as he said this. I placed my hand on his shoulder.

"Will you come back or not?" I asked calmly.

"I'll think about it,"

He replied, standing up to help me finish moving my stuff.

We shifted everything and after a long while, we sat down to have a peaceful meal together. Later, I dropped Waqar off at the airport.

Throughout the journey, Jenny's words kept echoing in my mind, whispering to me…

"I'm telling you, you haven't read it… Sadly…"

* * *

Chapter unknown ☒

Zieba's Point of view- understand her silence.

By God, talking is such a boring art............!!!

EPISODE – 18

(Redemption.....!!!)

I dropped Waqar off at the airport and returned to my flat. I realized it was already night, and there were only three hours left until dawn. I lay down on my bed.

After a long time, when I closed my eyes, Zieba's face appeared behind my eyelids, and her voice echoed in my mind—every word she spoke now was filled with nothing but verses from the Quran.

She no longer said my name; instead, she recited Quranic verses.

"Stop it..."

I got up from my bed and walked toward the terrace. Once I reached the rooftop, I took a deep, calming breath. It felt good to be in the open air.

"So, you're the new neighbour?"

Someone approached me, saying.

The man was a few inches taller than me, with a neatly trimmed light beard and fair skin.

"Yes, and you are...?" I asked.

"I'm Mohammad Abu Bakr, but people just call me Mohammad," he introduced himself, and as soon as he mentioned his name, I was taken back to that terrifying memory.

The words of the man with the radiant face flashed in my mind again.

"I'm... Ilh—" I started to introduce myself, but Mohammad interrupted me.

"Ilham, I know," Mohammad said with a smile. His smile didn't match the surprised expression on my face. I've heard this voice before somewhere...

"How do you know?" I asked, puzzled.

"Mohammad knows everything, Ilham Sahab," he said, smiling. If I were still my old self, I probably would've smiled back at his remark, but I neither felt like laughing nor had any interest in it.

"What's the matter? You seem troubled..." Mohammad suddenly asked. I was even more surprised by his question—were my emotions that obvious?

"No," I brushed off his concern.

"Liar," he said, stepping closer to me. I stared at him in disbelief, unable to react.

"You're lying. The signs of your worries are clearly visible on your face," Mohammad said as he wiped the sweat beads from my forehead with his handkerchief.

I lowered my gaze, unable to respond, and at that moment, the call to prayer (Azaan) began.

The sound was so loud, it felt like the mosque was just a few steps away from my apartment.

"Let's go, let's offer our prayers," Mohammad calmly invited me to join him for prayer. I looked at him with uncertainty.

"What's the matter? Did I say something wrong?" Mohammad asked, glancing around.

Until now, I had only ever been invited to clubs, pubs, and parties. This was the first time someone had invited me to prayer.

And what surprised me even more was that, unlike my usual quick acceptance of invitations to clubs, I found myself hesitating.

Why was I feeling this unease?

"No, I can't pray," I responded, turning away from Mohammad.

"What do you mean you can't pray?" he asked. I remained silent.

'What should I say… What could I possibly answer?'

He turned me back toward him and asked again, "Tell me—why can't you pray?"

"I'm… I'm scared of the Quranic verses, and prayers are filled with verses from the Quran. I can't do it, not for Allah," I said, wiping the sweat from my forehead as Zieba's voice continued to echo in whispers in my ears.

"You're scared of the Quranic verses…???" he asked, shocked.

He took a deep breathe.

"And who told you that Allah needs your prayers…?? Ilham, that Lord neither needs you—nor ever did—nor ever will. But you need Him, and always will. These prayers are a blessing for us, a way to connect with our Lord, the only path to gain His guidance. Those who are chosen by Allah to bow before Him are truly fortunate; otherwise, no one receives the ability to perform prostration in a state of Allah's displeasure. I want you to be among those fortunate ones. Now come—one should never refuse an invitation to prayer, especially not to Mohammad, or else I get upset…"

Mohammad smiled softly, took my hand, and started leading me. I was trapped in his grasp in such a way that, despite not wanting to, I walked with him.

Within a few steps, we reached the mosque. My heart started racing, my breaths became deep. Mohammad smiled and urged me to go inside.

"Come on…"

For the first time in my life, I stepped inside a mosque. Since my Nanu and Nano passed away, I had stopped going.

I used to go with Nanu to pray when I was five years old, and even though I didn't want to, tears involuntarily started falling from my eyes. I wanted to fall into prostration and cry uncontrollably…!!

Mohammad led me to the place for ablution, and I watched him as I began to make wudu myself.

Every drop of water felt warm to me, even in the cold. My heart felt a strange sense of peace, but at the same time, a restlessness, a fear—why this unease…? Why this fear…??

After making wudu, we stood with the congregation. As surprised as I was to find myself in the mosque, I was even more astonished to see that the congregation consisted of only about ten to twelve people and one Imam.

Gathering the courage, I stood in line with Mohammad. As soon as the Imam began to lead the prayer, each of his words felt like a burden weighing on my soul.

His recitation made me restless—why didn't I understand any of this…??

I didn't know what was causing my fear, whether it was the prayer or the verses. Watching the congregation, I bowed in ruku, and then similarly in sujood. Somehow, I managed to complete two units of prayer with great difficulty, but I couldn't continue any longer.

Just as I was about to leave, Mohammad grabbed my hand. "Since you've started, finish the prayer properly before you go." He held my hand gently but firmly, keeping his grip until I stood back in line with the congregation.

Relenting to Mohammad's insistence, I completed the prayer.

My hands and feet had started to feel cold—whether it was due to the weather or fear, I didn't know. I was terrified even of closing my eyes, and I suddenly stretched out both hands and started crying uncontrollably.

I don't know why I was crying like this; I don't know what pain I was feeling, I don't know why these tears were falling. All I knew was that I wanted to cry my heart out...!!!

"Cry as much as you need to, but remember one thing: Allah never ignores the pleas of His servant, no matter how long it takes for them to be answered. And I can help you if you allow me... Tell me, what is it that's eating you up inside... Ilham?"

Mohammad placed his hand on my shoulder with a compassionate expression, looking at me with concern.

Wiping my wet face with my sleeve, I said, "I don't understand what's happening to me. I've started feeling scared of the dark. I'm terrified to even close my eyes. I'm afraid of the verses of the Quran. Every breath I take feels like a stab in my chest...!!! One thing I do understand is that you have a lot of knowledge about religion and Islam...!!! Will you help me overcome this fear inside me?" I asked with tearful eyes, trembling lips, and a faltering voice.

Mohammad took a deep breath and sat down peacefully. "Hmm..., I don't know the reason for your fear or what you've been through..." Before Mohammad could finish, I interrupted him.

"In my life, I've done every forbidden act imaginable, and now I feel disgusted with myself. Why did I do it...? I don't even know the answer. Maybe I wanted to see the world from every perspective, or perhaps I was searching for something in the pleasures of this world to fill the emptiness inside me—a void that was never filled. But those worldly pleasures led me into such a darkness that I've forgotten who I am. My soul has been shaken to its core by that darkness..."

For some reason, I wanted to tell Mohammad everything that was in my heart, and I confessed to him everything that had happened to me—the terrifying scenes that made my soul tremble at the mere thought of them.

"All the time, I hear Quranic verses in the voice of a girl… I don't know how long—maybe for two months or more—I was trapped in an empty, dark room, and I've gone mad. Even when food was placed in front of me, I couldn't eat it. I couldn't even touch water. Everything turned to dust and vanished into the air…!! I don't know what was happening to me…!!! I became a prisoner in my own mind…, and now that image of captivity haunts me."

Tears started to flow from my eyes. Mohammad listened to every word of mine with calm patience.

"A man met me by the lakeside. He was much older than me…, and he said that the solution to my problem lies in the very verses I'm afraid of…!! I couldn't understand what he meant…!!! Then, he left me there alone…!!! I felt so alone…, and suddenly, the girl whose voice I hear reciting the verses, the girl who is so distant from my real life, she appeared before me in a white parda, surrounded by blooming flowers. There was a strange light and peace in her eyes. She came to me, spoke comforting words, and fed me with her own hands. Only then was I able to swallow the food…!!!"

Sitting in the mosque, I poured my heart out to Mohammad, telling him everything. I had so much inside me that I needed to say, and I had found someone I could trust as a friend—Mohammad.

"All of this is driving me crazy. I don't understand what's happening or why it's happening. Those verses are stuck in my mind, they're not leaving me, I can't get them out…!!!" Tears streamed uncontrollably from my eyes as I grabbed my head with both hands and kept speaking.

I, who had never cried before anyone, was now crying and sharing my deepest pain with someone.

Even I didn't understand why I was telling all of this to Mohammad when my closest friend was Waqar. I hadn't mentioned any of this to Waqar.

"Hmm…, your situation is quite serious, Ilham," Mohammad said calmly.

"But I'll tell you the solution to your problem. Let's go home..." Mohammad said confidently, and we both got up and started walking towards our apartment.

We arrived at home, and Mohammad invited me inside. He went towards the bookshelves in his living room and took out a thick book, placing it in front of me.

"If only people understood that the solution to every problem they face is right there in their own homes, placed in a shelf. But they never bother to look at it. If only they realized that it's not just a showpiece to be put away and forgotten..."

I looked at Mohammad in surprise, and he gave a gentle smile before saying,

"Yes, I'm talking about the Holy Quran. Have you ever read its translation carefully?" Mohammad asked, sitting down in the chair opposite me.

"No, I just memorized all the Surahs..." I replied in a quiet voice, feeling somewhat ashamed.

"Memorization isn't just about reciting and remembering the Surahs; you need to know the meaning of every letter. Here, take this Quran with translation and keep reading. Every Surah is here with its translation." Mohammad said with assurance, sitting beside me.

I hesitated and said, "I can't do it..., I'm afraid to read the translation..." I handed the Quran back to Mohammad.

With a slight smile, Mohammad responded, "You're not afraid of the verses; you're afraid of admitting your own sins." His words left me stunned, as if he had spoken the undeniable truth.

"I can help you, but only to the extent that I can show you the right path and encourage you to discover it for yourself. It's up to you to walk that path—only you can uncover your own destination. A thirsty person goes to the well; the well doesn't come to the thirsty person," Mohammad's words were full of wisdom, his firm faith and trust in his Lord, which I felt I lacked.

"Ilham, Allah Ta'ala has chosen to guide you. He has selected you and bestowed His mercy and guidance upon you. Don't be foolish and waste this opportunity. I also want you to not just read this but to become a Hafiz-e-Quran. I wouldn't suggest this if you hadn't already told me that you've memorized all the Surahs. That's why I'm advising you."

Mohammad gently placed the Quran in my hands, and at that moment, I saw in him the reflection of that enlightened man who had spoken to me with the same softness.

"Who knows, this might be your last chance? And last chances don't come again and again. Make use of this opportunity…" Mohammad said calmly, explaining everything while looking at me.

I stood there with mixed feelings of fear and hope, holding the Quran in my hands.

"I could give you answers to everything if I wanted to, but no scholar, no Imam, no person can give you better answers than the Quran-e-Pak. That's why you should uncover everything for yourself—find the answers to all your questions. There is no question in it that doesn't have an answer…," Mohammad's words were filled with truth, and despite the doubts in my eyes, his sincerity touched my heart.

"I'll think about it," I said softly, and taking the Quran in my hands, I started walking toward my flat.

Once in my room, I placed the Quran on my study table and glanced around the room. I sat on the sofa, restlessly shaking my left leg and rubbing my palms together in nervousness.

A deep sense of unease was building inside me. I stood up, picked up the Quran, and sat down at my study table. Gathering my courage, I opened the Quran.

My breath caught, my hands began to tremble, and I immediately closed it when I heard Zieba's voice echoing in my ears, loudly and clearly. Then, suddenly, Mohammad's voice resonated in my mind: **"You're not afraid of the verses; you're afraid of admitting the sins you've committed!"**

Taking a deep breath, I reopened the Quran and began reading the first chapter: **Surah Al-Fatiha**.

My heart was filled with fear and shame. The trembling in my hands reflected the inner turmoil I was going through. As I read the verses of the Quran, tears filled my eyes, reflecting the state of my heart.

Every word left a deep impact on my soul, as though these words were cleansing my spirit.

I was in a fragile state, but Mohammad's words gave me the strength to continue reading the Quran, with hope and faith in my heart, that perhaps this journey would lead me towards truth and guidance—towards the path that leads to Paradise (Jannath Ki Raahguzar.)

الحمد لله رب العلمين

[All] praise is [due] to Allah, Lord of the worlds –

الرحمن الرحيم

The Entirely Merciful, the Especially Merciful,

ملك يوم الدين

Sovereign of the Day of Recompense.

إياك نعبد وإياك نستعين

It is You we worship and You we ask for help.

اهدنا الصرط المستقيم

Guide us to the straight path –

صرط الذين أنعمت عليهم غير المغضوب عليهم ولا الضالين

The path of those upon whom You have bestowed favor, not of those who have evoked [Your] anger or of those who are astray.

My eyes had turned red from crying so much, and my sobs were evidence of my anguish. I had realized that my fear stemmed not from the verses of the Quran, but from confronting my own sins. Before I could truly understand the verses, I needed to grasp the significance of the Quran itself.

—Why was the Quran revealed? What is the Quran?

This is a profound question. The Quran is a divine guide for humanity. It is not just a book, but a complete code of life that teaches how to live in accordance with the will of Allah. Its revelation began in the 7th century CE and was sent down over 23 years to the Prophet Muhammad ﷺ.

—What is written in the Quran? What does it talk about?

The Quran discusses a variety of topics.

Its primary purpose is to emphasize the oneness of Allah and the importance of worshiping Him alone.

It guides believers on matters of faith, morality, and human conduct. It sheds light on both personal and societal aspects of life, teaching justice, compassion, and wisdom in how to live.

I had finally understood the importance of the Quran—the very Quran that Allah sent down to guide us, to show us the right path.

And I? I was so foolish that even after having it, I never truly read it. The disgust I felt toward myself grew. How far I had been from Allah… so far, and yet, with just one call from me, He had drawn me so close. Truly, He is the Most Merciful and Compassionate!

I locked myself in my room the entire day, reading the meaning of every verse of the Quran…

And I realized that the Quran contains several important themes that help us understand everything and guide us in life.

Tawheed (The Oneness of Allah): This theme emphasizes that there is only one Allah, the Creator and Sustainer of the entire universe.

Prophethood (Risalat): It speaks of the prophets who conveyed Allah's message to humanity.

The Hereafter (Aakhirah): It mentions Heaven and Hell, teaching that one must adopt righteous behaviour with the awareness of the Hereafter, not act with the careless attitude I had.

Morality and Ethics (Akhlaaq): It lays out principles for living a life based on truthfulness, kindness, and justice.

Guidance for Personal Conduct: The Quran provides teachings on personal behaviour, family relations, and social justice.

Historical Accounts: It recounts stories of past nations and prophets, serving as lessons and warnings for humanity.

Spiritual Reflection: The Quran encourages contemplation on creation and existence, inviting people to reflect on the signs of Allah's presence in the world.

These themes provided me with a deeper understanding of what I had been missing.

I sat in silence, the weight of my past arrogance crushing my heart. Once, I had chased the fleeting pleasures of this world, believing myself to be superior, invincible, and untouchable.

How foolish I had been, blinded by the illusions of false happiness and empty dreams spun by this deceitful world.

But now, as the truth unfolded before me, I was overwhelmed by a deep sense of shame and regret.

"How had I drifted so far from my Creator…? How could I have been so ignorant, failing to realize that everything I had, everything I was, belonged solely to Allah…?"

Tears streamed down my face as I confessed my wrongdoings, my heart breaking under the weight of remorse. I realized I had been lost, wandering aimlessly in the darkness of my pride.

Now, with a humbled spirit, I acknowledged my sins before Allah, knowing that I needed to return to Him, to bow in submission to His will.

The realization of my mistakes pierced me deeply, and I wept for the time I had wasted—the 22 years I had squandered chasing this fleeting world, the sins I had committed, and the distance I had kept between myself and my Lord. I cried for the One who is my Creator, for the closeness I had forsaken.

As I delved deeper into the meanings of the Quran's verses, I experienced something profound—something I could only describe as a miracle.

Number **67.**

The number that had been etched onto my skin as a tattoo, haunting me in my dreams for so long, suddenly took on a meaningful form. I had always seen that number floating, glowing in my dreams, but I had never understood its true significance.

Now, overwhelmed with emotion, I realized that Allah had been sending me signs all along, guiding me toward the right path, and I had ignored them…

How could I have been so blind?

That number, 67, was the chapter number of Surah Al-Mulk—the very Surah that Zieba had recited with translation a few years ago.

And my Nano used to recite this and blow on me with all her prayers before sleeping.

The revelation shook me to my core, and I broke down, unable to contain my tears.

I collapsed to my knees, completely shattered, realizing that Allah had always been watching over me, yet I had failed to see myself under His protection.

The light and peace I had been desperately searching for had always been right in front of me. How could I have believed that the fleeting pleasures of this world could ever satisfy the depths of my soul?

A lie so temporary could never bring true peace. True peace only comes through the love of Allah and the realization of His presence.

In that moment, I found my answer. The light I had been seeking for years, the tranquility that had always eluded me, was now clear and visible.

I wept uncontrollably, my sobs revealing the reality of my foolishness. I had strayed so far, but my Lord had found me lost and brought me back to His guidance.

—Yes, *He found me lost, and He guided me.* [93:7]

زندگی کی اندھیروں میں، میں اکیلا بھٹک گیا

وہ جو ملا، تو ہر راستہ روشن ہو گیا۔

-In the darkness of life, I wandered alone,

But when I found Him, every path was illuminated.

* * *

"Wait, let's walk together…"

Mohammad called out from behind, stepping closer. There was a peculiar tranquility on his face, and he looked at me with a smile.

I had spent all my time reciting the Holy Quran, and when I glanced at the clock, I realized it was time for Isha.

Just as I was heading for prayer, Mohammad appeared on my path.

Now, both Mohammad and I walked together toward the mosque. Unlike the restlessness I felt in the morning, a sense of calm replaced it in my heart, easing the ache in my chest.

After performing wudu, I joined the congregation as Imam Sahib began the prayer. Tears started to stream down my cheeks. Throughout the entire Isha prayer, I wept and sobbed, as each word from Imam Sahib reminded me of my sins.

I understood the meanings of the verses Imam Sahib was reciting. After completing my prayer, I bowed down for a long prostration, and while weeping, I confessed my wrongdoings to Allah:

"If You have decided to guide me, then never let me stray from this path again. I fear losing myself once more, and I am terrified of the inner devil within me. I have come to realize my sins, and I wish to change, but I don't know if I can… I just need Your presence, Your guidance."

I spoke, my voice trembling with sobs.

"I have read that You are filled with love for Your creation; surely, it is true, for I have returned safely from that torment. Will You hold me close, my Lord? Will You keep me near to You? Will You bless me with Your love and guidance?

It is Your decision whether to forgive me, or not, but I ask for Your love. Will You love me as much as You love Your dear servants?"

"I am Ilham, yearning for Your guidance and love—my Creator. Include me among those whom You cherish… Ameen…"

After lingering in prostration for a while, I finally rose and began wiping my wet face with my trembling hands. As I set out to return home, I saw Mohammad waiting for me.

"Thank you…" Mohammad said with a reassuring smile.

"For what?" I asked, surprised.

"You didn't give up on your prayers after hearing my words. It's nice to see you here. I was worried you wouldn't come, like the others…" Mohammad replied, and we began walking toward our homes.

"I have decided to change myself. I need to conquer my desires, and I don't want to be unworthy of facing Allah…" I said, watching my steps on the empty street where Mohammad and I were walking.

"Masha Allah… That's good to hear. If everyone thought like you, our mosques wouldn't be so empty today!" Mohammad said with a hint of disappointment.

"I was just about to ask you… Are there really so few Muslims here that the congregation is this small? Besides, the lockdown has already ended." I inquired, trying to understand.

Mohammad chuckled softly. "If clubs, pubs, parties, and concerts are always packed, then obviously, the mosques will remain empty. The mosques aren't empty because there are fewer Muslims; they're empty because of the lack of faith in people's hearts!"

Mohammad's words resonated with reality.

I had noticed that many Muslim friends used to join me in parties and clubs.

My eyes filled with tears, and I said, "I am one of these hypocrites…"

Mohammad interrupted, "You're not; you were… but you're not anymore! Allah has guided you. Just don't let yourself stray from this right path! Ilham, Allah has placed guidance in your heart; Subhan Allah— you are among those whom Allah has blessed with guidance. I believe Allah doesn't grant guidance to just anyone!"

"Allah has showered His love upon you through guidance. Be grateful, let go of the past, and always remember Mohammad's words."

Before we knew it, Mohammad and I had reached my home while chatting.

Mohammad invited me to dinner, saying, "Ilham, let's eat together today; come over to my house. It's nice talking to you."

I nodded in agreement and replied, "Sure, sounds good!"

The more a person considers themselves unfortunate, the less they actually are. I used to see myself as very unfortunate and perceived myself as a sinner, but Allah doesn't allow us to feel how deprived we are due to our distance from Him.

He makes us fortunate at the moment He guides us, and He never judges us based on our past actions. Allah's mercy pulls us out of the darkness of our sins and leads us to the path of light, where all mistakes are forgiven, and we find ourselves close to His will.

After a while, I arrived at Mohammad's house! As I stood at the door, I was surprised to see that Mohammad had a 6-year-old daughter!

Baba, help me with this homework… you know I'm weak in math," she said, approaching Mohammad. Baba? I was astonished.

I smiled at the little girl; in her, I saw a glimpse of someone familiar.

Mohammad said, "Say greetings, Asfi."

The girl said, "Assalamualaikum… I'm Asfiya, and you are…? Wait a minute, I know! You must be my Baba's friend, right? I recognized you, didn't I?"

Asfiya was asking questions and answering them herself, and I could see Zieba reflected in her words.

I replied to her greeting and said, "I'm Ilham… yes, I'm your Baba's friend. And you…?" I leaned down to ask her.

"Wow, you're so big, yet you can't figure out that I'm your friend Mister Mohammad's one and only daughter!"

I was taken aback upon hearing this and asked, "Daughter? You're not old enough to have a daughter. Have you gotten married? Are you married?"

I found myself astonished, realizing that I had just guessed she would be Mohammad's daughter, but she was indeed his daughter!

Mohammad smiled and replied,

"Yes, Ilham, Allah has blessed me with a daughter, and I am married. I couldn't tell you before."

"Maybe you're not fully settled yet, but you're married and have a daughter? Where is your wife?"

I was firing off questions because Mohammad's age didn't seem to match his appearance; I was surprised that he had gotten married at such a young age, or perhaps I was misjudging his age!

"Why do you think I'm not settled? Are you complimenting me by mentioning my age?" Mohammad said with a slight smile.

I listened attentively to his words. Seeing the crease on my face,

Mohammad said,

"Okay, let me explain. Sit down here."

We sat by the table, and Mohammad leaned back comfortably in his chair to tell me about himself.

"We have been granted permission to marry if we find a girl we like, and as for being settled, sustenance will come to you by itself. If you take on the responsibility of a girl with Allah's trust… I followed Allah's guidance, got married, and Alhamdulillah, I have everything because of His grace."

Mohammad said this with a smile on his face, while I could only express my astonishment.

"And where is your wife?" I asked. Mohammad smiled and said,

"She must be waiting for me! My wife passed away when Asfiya was three years old!"

While there was a smile on Mohammad's face, his eyes revealed deep pain. I could sense the loss he had endured in his life.

I said, "Didn't you get angry?" I spoke in a complaining tone because I had felt immense anger at the passing of my Nanu and Nano, who left me. Mohammad should have reacted the way, I was reacting.

"Angry at whom?" Mohammad asked, surprised, looking at me with raised shoulders.

"Maybe—at Allah! He took your wife away from you and left you alone!"

I wasn't even sure what I was saying, but I expressed what was in my heart without thinking.

"No, Allah does whatever He does for our benefit. And who am I to complain to Him? He has promised that we will be together in Paradise with those we love.

And am I really alone? My Lord is with me, and I have my daughter as well—I have to be with her to take care of her. I have responsibilities as a father."

Mohammad answered my questions with confidence.

I looked at Asfiya and asked quietly so she wouldn't hear, "Haven't you ever been interested in another girl?"

Mohammad began to laugh and said, "No!"

"Why not?" I was astonished!

"The love my wife had for me was something I can't find in anyone else, and I won't be able to give that much love to anyone else either. Allah created her for me, and I will remain faithful to her, even in her absence. Perhaps I won't be able to love anyone else as much."

Mohammad expressed his love while reminiscing about his wife, and a smile appeared on his face.

I remained silent for a while, and then Mohammad set the dining table and began to place the plates. Breaking the silence, Mohammad asked,

"So, when are you planning to marry her?" Mohammad made a comment that was so subtle it would have gone unnoticed by most, like finding a needle in a haystack.

"What do you mean? Who should I marry?" I feigned ignorance, avoiding his gaze.

"Ilham—don't hide it," Mohammad said, and we took our seats at the dining table.

"What am I hiding?" I replied, gulping down a glass of water in one go.

Without hesitation, Mohammad said,

"That you are in love with that girl."

I was taken aback by Mohammad's assertion. My voice caught in my throat, and my heartbeat quickened. I shook my head in denial, thinking, *We've only spent a few hours together, and he has read me so thoroughly...!*

"It's not love; I just think she's nice—that's all!"

As Mohammad served rice onto my plate, he asked, "Is she the same girl you saw by the lake, dressed in white among those beautiful flowers?"

I stared at his face in astonishment, nodded, and felt my cheeks turn crimson.

"If I tell you something, will you believe me?" Mohammad asked, his tone gentle as Asfiya thumped her head against her homework book.

"Go ahead; if it's believable, I'll definitely believe you," I replied, looking at Mohammad.

"Perhaps Allah has written your fate with her, and the two months you spent locked away were just a glimpse of hell—or as you said, the torment of the grave. And even in that torment, seeing her proves that Allah wants you to marry her. She has come into your life as a means. Make her your mehram—simple. It's better to love her by keeping her close than to love her secretly in your heart."

With that, Mohammad said *Bismillah* and began to eat.

Could Mohammad really be speaking the truth? Could Allah guide us in such a way?

After a while, I said, "But she won't even bother to look at me, so how can I…?" I lowered my head, feeling embarrassed about my character.

"Allah—are all girls like this?" Mohammad chuckled, perhaps thinking of his wife, Aiza.

"You said she is a good and pious woman, so you should also be a righteous man—extra simple."

Mohammad spoke as if he could resolve my issue with a snap of his fingers. His smile was genuinely beautiful.

Yet, I looked at him in disbelief because I recalled something I had said to Fateen.

Mohammad said, "Don't look at it that way; I'm telling you the truth. In the Quran, Allah Himself says that righteous men are for righteous women and wicked men are for wicked women. Purify yourself, be righteous, and become worthy of her. Allah Himself will be with you, insha'Allah."

One by one, Mohammad addressed each of my concerns.

As I put a spoonful of rice in my mouth, I thought for a moment before saying,

"If I become a righteous man, will she accept me? Will Allah forgive my sins? And will He include me among the righteous?"

I asked in astonishment—*It's hard to imagine someone like me receiving forgiveness and with that burden how can I ask Allah to give Zieba to me as my wife…?? Even if I ask and what if he couldn't make it up then how would I———*

Mohammad replied calmly,

"Absolutely. Sometimes, overthinking is what drags a person down, just like how you are doing right now." He said, I was shocked how did he know? He continued,

"Allah has mentioned forgiveness and mercy far more often than He has mentioned hellfire and punishment in the Quran. Allah is Raheem-o-Kareem, capable of forgiving even the gravest sins. You just need to ask for forgiveness sincerely and never return to that quagmire of sin."

Mohammad spoke with such depth and assurance that I fell into thought. Could it be that my Lord is so merciful that He would forgive every sin?

Indeed, how foolish we all are, unable to comprehend our Lord's love…!

I was torn between feeling fortunate and unfortunate.

Fortunate because I have received my Lord's guidance and discovered the right path, and unfortunate because I had spent 22 years of my life distant from Him, living in His displeasure, thinking I was in paradise while I was actually in hell.

"O Allah, never let me stray from You again. Now the very thought of being away from You terrifies me."

My eyes were welling up. I finished my meal and helped Mohammad clean up.

After helping Asfiya with her math homework, I returned home.

I sat on the couch and took Zieba's picture out of my wallet, gazing at it for a long time.

Tears flowed from my eyes like a river.

"You are one of the reasons Allah has inspired Ilham's heart."

"If I hadn't come to your house that day, Zieba, and hadn't heard the recitation of the Quran in your voice, I might never have realized that I was burning my life in the fires of hell—where the mere thought of going sends shivers down people's spines."

"I was so oblivious that I thought the goal of my life was to achieve success in my career. Because of you, I've come to understand that we all share the same destination... and that is 'Paradise.' We must return to our Lord one day. He has sent us here to reach our destination with our faith and righteous deeds. It is up to us to choose our destination, which is Paradise."

Holding Zieba's picture, I struggled to express my feelings, but the words wouldn't come—

"I am not worthy of that pious woman—I'll never be worthy of her...!"

I am not worthy of her—she deserves someone better, not me...!

* * *

Author's Note

Dear Readers,

What you have just experienced so far in *Safar e Mehram – Jannat ki Raahguzar* is only the beginning — the raw, unapologetic glimpse into Ilham's world, seen entirely through **his own eyes**.

This part captures the era when he was consumed by arrogance, drowning in his own pride, and blinded by the world's illusions. His attitude, his outlook — everything you read — was real.

Yes, this is **a true story**, penned with full consent of the character it was inspired from.

Of course, a few fictional elements were added here and there — just enough to weave the reality into a more gripping narrative — but know this:

His fall, his agony, his burning pain, and his desperate redemption remain untouched, unfiltered.

Not a single ounce of his real journey was altered.

But if you feel that something was left unsaid…

If you find yourself yearning for the emotions you sensed but couldn't fully touch…

Then prepare yourself.

Because *Safar e Mehram – Ek Unkahi Dastan* is where **the untold begins.**

The part you missed.

The words he never said aloud.

The ache he buried.

The love, the regrets, the silent prayers — all waiting for you.

I will share a special glimpse — the **Epilogue of Safar e Mehram – Ek Unkahi Dastan**.

Read it. Feel it. Lose yourself in it.

This journey is far from over.

With heart and soul,

Safiya Abdul.

Epilouge

2 – Years Later

"Here we see Ilham Osman Khan, a junior attorney under the renowned attorney Mr. Hamza. He has decided to fight his first case, one based entirely on lies. Who knows how many innocent girls' dignity will be at risk because of such lawyers? The hearing will begin shortly. Stay tuned with us for every moment, I'm Rabia Quresh, with cameraman Naushair Asaad. Khuda Hafiz."

The live stream played on Ilham's phone, the media frenzy buzzing with energy as the anchors reported on the latest controversy. A man had defaced Ilham's photograph with black ink, fueling the spectacle further.

Ilham let out a low chuckle, unbothered, as he switched off the screen. Sliding his phone into his coat pocket, he was interrupted by yet another call.

He glanced at the screen, recognizing his father's name—*Mr. Osman.* With a sigh that carried the weight of his reluctance, he finally answered what must have been the twentieth call.

"Ilham?" Mr. Osman's voice came through, tense and sharp.

"I warned you to stay out of trouble. Why don't you ever listen? Does our family's honor mean nothing to you?"

Ilham leaned back in his seat, his voice steady, almost playful. "Relax, Baba. I'm Ilham, remember? And Ilham only listens to himself."

A pause on the other end.

Then, Mr. Osman's tone grew graver. "Do you have no fear of Allah? This isn't just about you—it's about a girl's life, Ilham."

Ilham straightened, his expression hardening, though his tone retained its cool edge.

"Baba, I'm a defence lawyer. My job isn't to take sides—it's to defend the law. In court, there's no man or woman, no emotions—only the guilty and the innocent. Equality, Baba. Don't forget that."

"Ilham, listen—"

"Assalamualaikum, Fi Ammanillah!" Ilham cut him off, hanging up before his father could protest further.

It wasn't the first time he'd done so. Mr. Osman got used to it.

Mr. Osman knew this pattern well—his son's defiance was as familiar as the ache it caused.

Still, this time, he silently prayed that Ilham would heed his words. But then again, Ilham was Ilham—unyielding to anyone but himself.

Ilham slid his phone into his pocket and turned to the man seated beside him, his client—a middle-aged man who fidgeted nervously, glancing out at the commotion in front of the courthouse. Protesters had gathered, their chants of justice and defiance growing louder as the car approached.

"Calm your nerves," Ilham said with a faint smile, his voice cool and commanding. "Control over emotions is key. No matter what you feel inside, your face must betray nothing. Otherwise, your opponent will seize on your weakness. Courtroom rule number one."

His client gave a tight nod, his fear evident despite the advice.

"Shall we?" Ilham's smile widened, exuding unshakable confidence.

The client hesitated but nodded again. Ilham stepped out of the car first, his polished shoe hitting the pavement with deliberate poise. As he stood, adjusting his glasses, a voice boomed through a megaphone.

"If you take another step, we'll make sure you never practice law again!"

The speaker belonged to a woman among the protesters, her eyes blazing with determination. A small crowd rallied behind her, their signs and slogans demanding justice.

Ilham paused, glancing in her direction with a smirk that was both infuriating and disarming. He adjusted his cuffs with a calculated nonchalance, his words cutting through the uproar like a blade.

"Let's see what fate has in store for Ilham Osman Khaan," he said, his tone as smooth as it was daring.

With that, he turned to his client, nodding toward the courthouse.

Together, they moved forward, unshaken by the storm waiting for them beyond the doors. For Ilham, this was just another day in the arena.

For the past two years, Ilham Osman Khaan had been a name everyone knew—his face splashed across every news channel and newspaper headline.

He wasn't just a lawyer; he was a force in the courtroom, a man who knew how to turn any case into a spectacle of skill and strategy. Winning wasn't just his goal—it was his certainty.

But Ilham didn't take just any case. He was deliberate in his choices, selecting clients whose stories matched his unyielding principles. As he often said, *"Proving the truth to be a lie is easy, but proving the truth to be the truth—that's the real adventure."*

And Ilham thrived on adventure.

He lived by his principles, never bending, no matter how high the stakes. His reputation was built on a simple but powerful foundation: his actions always aligned with his words, and his words carried the weight of conviction.

"Because that's Ilham," people would say. *"What he says, he does. And what he does, everyone sees."*

Ilham's confidence wasn't arrogance—it was a reflection of his absolute mastery of his craft. In the courtroom, he was a storm in a tailored suit, and anyone who faced him understood one thing:

Ilham Osman Khaan didn't just win cases; he owned them.

The cool breeze swept across the university lawn as two of them sat there, enjoying their snacks—Maryam and Zieba.

Maryam's hair long, thick, straight, and a deep shade of brown. Her fair skin complements her naturally Indian eyes—eyes that shift in the light, appearing brown under the sun but turning almost black in the shadows. It's hard to describe the exact hue, but one thing to know: anyone who looks into her eyes will get lost, with no way back.

That's Maryam for you—effortlessly captivating, capable of driving someone mad without lifting a finger, if they're the right person.

As she remained absorbed in her novel, Zieba gently ran her fingers through her hair, savouring the quiet moment.

Maryam rested her head on Zieba's lap, lost in the pages of her novel, while Zieba took a moment to appreciate the serenity around us, Zieba is a kind of person who always looks for peace around her as she is doing now.

The gentle flutter of butterflies, the vibrant bloom of fresh flowers, and the lush greenery surrounding us created a perfect frame of peace. Students' laughter echoed softly in the distance, adding to the tranquility.

Everything felt right for her—she was enjoying this moment as if she would never get peace again after this.

Suddenly, Maryam jolted upright.

"Damn, he's dead…??" she gasped, wide-eyed.

Zieba smirked, knowing full well that this was coming.

Maryam had a habit of reacting dramatically to book twists, especially when it came to character deaths.

Zieba gently chuckled. "You really didn't see it coming?"

"Dude, you should've warned me," she grumbled, clearly upset, though Zieba knew she secretly liked these moments.

Neither of them was a fan of overly happy endings.

Why is everyone so obsessed with happy endings when real life has a way of bringing us tragedy?

That's the truth of it—every story has a tragic turn, but in the end, we make peace with it. Acceptance is life's quiet reward.

Maryam shifted the conversation, her voice suddenly softer. "Zieba, Mumma's been asking me to marry Amer… my cousin." She lowered her gaze, avoiding Zieba's eyes.

"Do you want to marry him?" She asked to Maryam, gently squeezing her hand.

She shook her head, her face troubled.

"No… but I don't want them to think I'm being disobedient."

'Because a simple *yes* to our parents speaks volumes of our loyalty and respect as daughters—*yes, we are daughters….!!'* Zieba murmured under her breath.

Zieba understood her hesitation all too well, having been in a similar situation herself. "Then talk to Maliha Aunty. She'll listen, or better yet, speak to your Baba. He'll understand you."

"I don't know what they'll think…" she mumbled. Her words hung heavy, filled with doubt.

Then, almost as if unsure herself, she looked at Zieba and asked, "W-Would you… talk to them for me…., please?"

Zieba smiled warmly and nodded. "Of course.., but…, tell me one thing….!"

“Why isn’t he good enough? He is your cousin right..?” Zieba asked gently.

Maryam hesitated, her expression uncertain.

“I think he’s a good man—obedient to his parents and everything. But something doesn’t feel right. I’m getting… strange vibes, you know?” Maryam tried to explain, and though she was usually one to keep things brief, with Zieba, she could open up completely.

“Mmmm…, I get it,” Zieba replied. “But listen, if he seems good but feels wrong, then trust your heart. Just say no—you have the privilege of being able to talk openly in your family, unlike me. I know you’re worried about how they’ll view you, afraid they might think you’re disobedient, but on the Day of Judgment, how will they answer for pushing aside your true feelings out of fear? Islam gives daughters and sons the full right to say ‘yes’ or ‘no’ to marriage proposals. No one, not even parents, can force or pressure you to marry someone against your will.”

Maryam nodded slowly, taking in Zieba’s words.

“But, Zieba, why didn’t you say no when it was your turn? They did bad to you it was a child marriage!” Maryam asked, unknowingly touching a wound that had never fully healed. Zieba offered a gentle, reassuring smile.

“My situation was different,” she said softly. “Allah heard my prayers and, I believe, kept me from ending up with the wrong person.”

Maryam smiled back and hugged Zieba tightly, sensing the sadness in her friend that went beyond words. She could read Zieba’s heart like no one else.

“Alright, I’ll talk to Mom and Dad. And if they don’t listen, you’ll have to step in,” Maryam said, grinning as they shared a supportive look, their smiles full of understanding and resolve.

Maryam hugged her tightly, relief washing over her. Then she pulled back slightly, her teasing tone back in play.

"You know why I asked you, right?"

"Why?" Zieba asked her, with her raised eye-brow…,

"Because my parents will only listen to a *married* woman!" she teased, emphasizing the word "married."

Zieba playfully shoved her, and they both burst out laughing.

Moments like these with Maryam made Zieba feel so grateful—like she had found a true friend who understood her completely.

After finishing their snacks, they went back to their classes, sharing a few more light-hearted moments before getting back to the grind of academic life.

Safar e Mehram – Ek Unkahi Dastan

www.ingramcontent.com/pod-product-compliance
Lightning Source LLC
LaVergne TN
LVHW091524200926
848483LV00002B/297

* 9 7 9 8 8 9 5 8 8 8 1 0 0 *